Knights of the Night

They Call Him El Cabby

Jé Dé Gordeau

All rights reserved. No part of this book shall be reproduced or transmitted in any form or by any means, electronic, mechanical, magnetic, photographic including photocopying, recording or by any information storage and retrieval system, without prior written permission of the publisher. No patent liability is assumed with respect to the use of the information contained herein. Although every precaution has been taken in the preparation of this book, the publisher and author assume no responsibility for errors or omissions. Neither is any liability assumed for damages resulting from the use of the information contained herein.

Copyright © 2009 by Jé Dé Gordeau

ISBN 0-7414-6048-3

Printed in the United States of America

This is a work of fiction. Names, characters, places, and incidents either are the product of the author's imagination or are used fictitiously. Any resemblance to actual events or locales or persons, living or dead, is entirely coincidental.

Published December 2010

INFINITY PUBLISHING
1094 New DeHaven Street, Suite 100
West Conshohocken, PA 19428-2713
Toll-free (877) BUY BOOK
Local Phone (610) 941-9999
Fax (610) 941-9959
Info@buybooksontheweb.com
www.buybooksontheweb.com

For Don and Barbara Ramsey

Family and Friends Forever

Also

For Ruthie

For Your Dedicated Help and Assistance

Prologue

A knight is supposed to follow a strict set of rules for his/her conduct.

These are the knightly virtues:

- Mercy (towards the poor and oppressed)
- Humility
- Honor
- Sacrifice
- Fear of God
- Faithfulness
- Courage
- Utmost graciousness and courtesy to ladies.

There are two evil organizations working together in the world, and they are planning to establish a New World Order. These two organizations created an economic crisis of global proportion in an attempt to force the countries of the world to form unions like the European Union and the North American Union. After seven unions have been formed, they will join together to create the New World Order. The New World Order will bring with it the injection of two microchips into every person on the Earth. The microchips will effectively control every person's activities to the point of denying them the one thing God gave every man, woman, and child, and that is their free will. God-given free will separates mankind from the animal kingdom and allows us to make a personal choice between good and evil. There is another secret organization in the world which is known as The Knights of the Night, which is not evil. The Knights of the Night aren't powerful either, except for their faith in

God. They are the only group in the world who stands between the New World Order and the domination of mankind. The Knights of the Night have decided to take on the Illuminati. Because of the two evil organizations forming the New World Order, they are the group with all the real power. The Genebra Group, the other half of the evil organization, is a very small group with extreme wealth and financial influence which gives them the ability to finance many evil deeds around the world.

The Illuminati plan to control where you go, what you do, what education you receive, and how much you earn, and they could even control whether you live or die. They will literally talk to you inside your head, placing their thoughts in your mind, and you will not know the difference between your thoughts and theirs. Don't even question whether anyone can place their thoughts in your mind without you knowing it, because it's a science that has already been tried and verified, and just because you didn't know it, doesn't mean it hasn't happened.

I invite you to read this story based on many realities. Then check these keywords with your favorite search engine: Mind Control, CIA Project MKULTRA, Brice Taylor, MK ULTRA Victim Testimony, H.A.A.R.P., CBC Broadcast on HAARP, SVALI, Illuminati, Bilderberg Group, and Microwave Weapons. These keywords, plus the references in the addendum, will give you some idea of what motivated me to write this fictional novel. Reading this novel may prepare you for what could be coming to remove your free will. It has been said that truth is stranger than fiction, but in this case, fiction may get your attention, and the truth may scare you into action.

Can The Knights of the Night stop the Illuminati? Do they have the willpower, the money, and enough warriors to win this war, threatening the free will of every man, woman, and child on the Earth? They are outnumbered twenty to one, and they don't have an army, navy, air force, or any organized trained fighting force, so it seems impossible for them to win this war of epic proportions. Without a secret weapon, there doesn't seem to be any hope for The Knights of the Night. If you read this novel, you may renew your faith in the ability of good to fight evil. But, if you never read this novel, you may never understand what's happening in your world in time to take a stand against the evil which may control the world you live in.

Let the story begin………

Chapter 1

March 4

I was sitting quietly in the patio area of La Pirinola Restaurant in Guanajuato, Mexico, having a cold beer and an order of fries. From a distance, I looked like any American or European man who might be a tourist in the city of Guanajuato in central Mexico.

Jose walked up to Martin, the waiter who was a friend of his, and asked, "Who is he? I've never seen him in the restaurant before."

Martin answered, "I don't know; he's been here every day at this time for almost a week now. He always orders a beer and fries, and when he's through eating, he walks across the plaza and into the night. Sometimes he writes notes on small white cards he carries in his shirt pocket, and the rest of the time he just stares into the plaza as he eats. I haven't noticed him speaking to anyone else, but he seems like a nice person. I like him."

Jose said, "Can you get me a hamburger, fries, and an iced tea, and I'll sit here and watch him finish eating. You never know what you might learn about somebody just by watching them eat a meal."

I looked around the plaza and watched the people, as they walked here and there checking out the small stores, as I was finishing my fries and beer. I thought to myself, *I'm an old fool, and I'm too old to be doing this sort of thing anymore. I should be retired and enjoying my senior years before it's too late. My eyes are failing; my hearing is bad, and it probably won't be long until I'm blind, and then what am I going to do? There are some benefits to being retired though. I could start using my real name again, but I wouldn't enjoy being called Tommy. It's been too many years since I went by that name, besides I really enjoy being called El Cabby, and it's the name everyone knows me by. I could never tell anyone that El Cabby is an abbreviation for El Caballero Guerrero (The Warrior Knight) because I know I don't look like a Warrior Knight. I look like an old man.*

It was time to get going, so I gave Martin money for the bill and a tip. Then I stood up and strolled away from the restaurant, crossing the plaza and heading for the main street a few hundred feet away. Sitting down, I probably looked like any other old man. However, when I stood up and walked, I held my shoulders back, my stomach in, and my head up so I could observe everything going on around me. I like to walk as if I have a purpose in my life and a reason for everything I do.

I am only five-feet, eight-inches tall, but when I'm wearing my boots I look much taller. I have gray hair with a small black streak from front to back that's just a little off center on the left. I have always been quiet, never saying much to anyone about what I was thinking. The biggest problem I had was the feminine side of the social world; I couldn't understand women, so I have been a bachelor forever.

Martin returned from inside the restaurant and walked over to Jose who was watching me, as I disappeared into the night, and Martin said, "He's an interesting old man, isn't he?"

Jose replied, "Yes, I think so, and I think I'll have someone keep an eye on him." Jose took out his cell phone and punched in the number for the police station, as Martin went to wait on a few young ladies who had just arrived.

As I walked down the main street, I was thinking to myself, *Let's hope tonight isn't as quiet as the last six nights have been. I'm starting to get bored, and I wouldn't mind flexing my muscles and seeing some action while I help someone tonight. Anyway, if I see some action, it'll be easier* to sleep knowing I made a difference in the world and helped someone in need. I may be getting old, but I'm still a dedicated Knight who can take care of himself if I have to.

I'm a member of "The Knights of the Night," and we're a large, secret organization with some very unusual and dangerous goals as part of our creed. The Knights of the Night are from every country around the world, come from all occupations, and have a passion to bring justice to all people. We decided many years ago the best way to bring justice back to the world was at the local level. Every Knight of the Night would have a week every six months when he, or she, would walk the streets every night in their hometown. The Knight's sole objective each of those nights would be to prevent crime in any way he or she could. It was a simple task of going to the assistance of those being beaten or robbed, and helping them to defend themselves against their attackers. Even though it was a simple task, it was also a dangerous task. If it happened to be a woman Knight performing her duty, then a male Knight would always accompany her. It wasn't because the women needed help physically, but because of the perverts who enjoy finding a woman alone at night.

If we witnessed a robbery taking place, then we tried to prevent the robbery by taking action against the culprits. If we lost our lives in the process, then so be it, because we were willing to give our lives for the sake of justice. If we had a confrontation with evil and won the battle, then we weren't supposed to reveal our identity. We always remain anonymous and humble for what we have done since we are members of a secret organization, and we cannot admit that we're members of The Knights of the Night.

Nor are we allowed to take anything for our service in any way, shape, or form. If someone does give us a gratuity, we give it to our Seneschal, and he will make a donation to one of several organizations that deal with medical research.

Over the years, we have kept our original tradition of protecting the people of the world in an attempt to bring justice to everyone. In the last few years, we have had an even more important task to do, because we are now fighting for the free will of all mankind.

About ten years ago one of our Knights saved a man's life. The man asked the Knight for special help, because the three men trying to kill him were Illuminati. The man didn't realize he was talking to a member of The Knights of the Night. He just believed he was talking to a good person who had come to his rescue. The Knight wasn't sure what to do so he called his Seneschal and explained the situation. The Seneschal told the Knight to take the man to a secure room, and stay with him until someone talked to them the following morning.

The next day the Seneschal showed up and talked with the Knight and the man he had helped. It was an eye-opening session for the Seneschal because what he heard was unbelievable. The man explained he was Illuminati, and was trying to flee the organization. He had come to realize the Illuminati destroyed many innocent lives, and it was bothering his conscience. He also told the Seneschal about another secret organization that had an affiliation with the Illuminati. One of those organizations was the Genebra Group. The Seneschal had heard of the Genebra Group, but he thought they were a philanthropic organization. Now this person was telling the Seneschal the members of the Genebra Group were not as benevolent as everyone had always believed.

The Seneschal knew it would take a full-scale investigation by a committee of The Knights of the Night to verify the facts concerning what he had been told. The Seneschal also knew it could take a long time to do the investigation, and meanwhile the Knights would have to protect this man. In fact, if this man was telling the truth, The Knights of the Night might have to protect him for the rest of his life.

The Seneschal contacted the Grand Seneschal, and they appointed a committee to investigate the information the man had given them about the Illuminati and the Genebra Group. Months later after confirming as much information as they could, a local organization of the Knights had a special meeting and accepted the ex-Illuminati into their organization. They gave him a new name as a Knight that he would use for the rest of his life, and the new name was Nomolos T. Jones. This was just the beginning of The Knights of the Night understanding the Illuminati.

When we comprehended everything the Illuminati was doing, and all the criminal activities they were involved in, we realized we had to take action to counter their plans, and end their evil scheme of establishing a New World Order. Destroying the Illuminati would not be an easy task, but we had to accomplish it in order to save the human rights, dignity, and free will of every man, woman, and child in the world.

We had come to the realization that these two organizations were working together for a common goal in which their plan was to eventually control the world. If the Illuminati and the Genebra Group's plan worked, they would take over the world with the blessing of the world's population. As impossible as it might seem, the Illuminati's plan had been in place for hundreds of years and slowly, but surely, was coming to fruition. In fact, the way things were going in the world today, it wouldn't be much longer until the New World Order was a reality under Illuminati control.

I walked through the streets of Guanajuato thinking about all these things, wondering if we could really stop the Illuminati. I realized in my heart and mind that we're too small to stop the Illuminati. In reality though, there isn't any other organization capable of such an enormous task. So in essence we didn't have a choice, and if we couldn't stop and defeat the Illuminati, the world was lost.

The one major thing we have working for us is the fact that we're a religious organization which trusts in God to accomplish our goals. We believe that one of the biggest mistakes ever made by man throughout the history of the world was underestimating God's power.

I came back to my senses when I heard an unusual sound half a block in front of me. I stopped thinking about the Illuminati, and watched someone slide into the shadows between two buildings up ahead. The sound made me look, but the way the person, or persons, stealthily moved between the buildings raised my concern. Their action made me anticipate trouble because I was the only other person in the area at the time. I slowed down and walked slower while I watched for anything unusual.

Since the beginning of the Global Economic Crisis, the crime rate around the world had more than doubled. Here in Mexico, the number of kidnappings increased at least three times. Americans had become prime targets for two reasons: One, because we were being blamed for the greed of the banking system in the United States which had started the global crisis. Two, because we're Americans and many people in other countries believe we're all wealthy. So even though I'm not wealthy by American standards, by Mexican standards I would be considered very wealthy.

I stopped walking and removed the cell phone from my pocket as if it were ringing. I held the phone to my ear while starting a conversation with an imaginary someone who wasn't there. My eyes scanned the area where I had seen the figure, or figures, disappear. I couldn't see anyone, and I couldn't hear anyone either, but this incident was making me acutely aware of my diminished vision.

Damn, I thought, *I'm sure I saw someone and now...* I didn't finish the thought, because two people stepped out of the dark at the location where I had seen them a minute ago. It was a young man and his girlfriend, holding hands and laughing. *Life is good*, I thought, as I let out a sigh of relief, and resumed my walk at a leisurely stroll.

In three days I will be on a flight to London, England, to meet with the other leaders of The Knights of the Night. I knew something of circumstance was happening in the world, or we wouldn't be having an emergency session called on such short notice.

Then it happened! The young couple I had observed between the two buildings was running at me with knives in their hands. An instant later I felt an arm circling my throat and trying to pull me back. I realized I had been observed and selected as a kidnap or robbery victim, and I only had seconds to defend myself against these three assailants.

I threw my arms over my head and my feet forward in order to slide through the person's arms behind me. The Earth's gravity had control as I fell to the ground landing painfully on my buttocks. I threw my left elbow up, and to my back inflicting a lot of pain to someone's groin, and I was now free of the person behind me. The two running at me were just a few feet away. I threw out my left leg and kicked the knife out of the man's hand. Then I raised my right leg and kicked the woman's knee, causing her to fall towards me. I grabbed the woman's hand holding the knife and twisted it, causing her to release it, and I picked it up as it fell to the street. Then I swung my hand with the knife and stabbed the man in the leg who was standing on my left. He let out a loud moan as he fell to the pavement while he held his leg. Then I heard a loud police whistle as I grabbed the young woman's hand, and held tight, so she couldn't escape. I heard the footsteps of whoever had been behind me running as he tried to escape the police. A few seconds later I heard him stop as the police arrested him.

Within forty-five minutes I was out of the police station where I had given my side of the story, and I was on my way home. The police had arrested the three assailants and locked them up for attempted murder. Perhaps in two or three years, they will make it to a court system that still depends on legal cases by the written word, instead of verbal testimony.

I was tired and headed home earlier than usual for an official duty night for the Knights. The only person I had assisted this evening was me, but by helping myself, and eliminating those three thugs, I had helped bring justice to the world.

I had hurt my back when I hit the pavement, and I needed to give my body some rest. After a taxi ride to my residence in the Rosa Primera colony in Guanajuato, I walked into my home. I prepared an Irish coffee, then ran a bath where I soaked my sore body. A little while later I was in bed for a good night's rest.

Chapter 2

March 7–8

I was now Jonathan Joiner – alias El Cabby, and I was sitting in my first-class seat on British Airways flight 1016 on my way to London, England. We had only been in the air for a few hours, and I had already managed to drink a Scotch on the Rocks. The tranquilizing drink was starting to take effect as I was beginning to feel tired.

We have another eight hours before we get there, I thought. *So I'd better try to get some rest. I will arrive three hours before the meeting begins, and then we'll be sequestered for at least six hours, and I want to be rested and alert. So I had better be rested when we land in London, because it's going to be crazy when I get there.* I closed my eyes, and within a few minutes I was sound asleep.

I opened my eyes, and it was surreal because I was fighting on a medieval battlefield. I was wearing heavy armor and trying to swing my broad sword with all the strength I could muster. I was getting tired, and the enemy was still coming from every direction like ants after a piece of candy, and I had no choice, but to keep fighting or die.

Just as I swung the broad sword around to fend off an enemy warrior I felt the pain. "Oh God!" I cried. It was a sharp, searing pain, and I couldn't help but scream. I dropped my sword and looked around to see where the pain was coming from. There was an arrow in my back just below the left shoulder blade. The arrow had gone through my chest cavity, and the tip was protruding through the skin just below my heart. I felt dizzy, and the world was spinning as I fell to my knees, and then to my face. The weight of one hundred and thirty pounds of armor was dragging me down because I didn't have the strength to wear it anymore. As I lay face down, I heard the sound of the arrow crack as it broke off under the weight of my body and armor. The pain was intense, and I could hear the battle raging around me, but I wasn't part of it anymore. Everything around me was turning black as I drifted into another world in a faraway land.

In the distance I heard a familiar voice softly saying, "Tommy..., Tommy..., I'm so sorry, Tommy. I love you."

Then in an instant of time the voice changed, "Mr. Joiner..., Mr. Joiner...."

As I sat up, I opened my eyes, and I could see someone standing in front of me, and in a confused state, I said, "Yes, what is it?"

"I'm sorry to wake you, Mr. Joiner," the flight attendant said, "but we received a special message for you. It doesn't make any sense to us, but nonetheless we were assured you would know what it meant."

I reached out and took the message, as I said to the flight attendant, "Thank you very much. I wonder, is it possible for me to have a cup of coffee?"

"Of course," the flight attendant replied with a smile, and she headed to the front of the aircraft to make my coffee.

I turned on my private reading light and looked around the first-class cabin to make sure no one was watching as I opened the message. I sat back in my chair and relaxed as I read it; the message read:

To Jonathan Joiner: British Airways flight 1016:

This is an official message to a passenger in flight.

Status: Change in plans. New lock in place.

Imperial 16, line 49, tempo is rock 29.

I took out my Blueberry Personal Organizer and typed in File Imperial 16, line 49. A file opened up and listed a hotel and address in London. I knew the hotel, and it was a surprise there was a change in plans when the meeting was to start in less than six hours from now. I typed in rock 29. The message appeared: time is I29 = II-1. This news was upsetting. Instead of the original meeting time that gave me three hours to relax, I would have to attend the meeting at a different location and time altogether. The II-1 meant immediately after arrival in London I was in an intense meet and greet – which meant that two people would meet me. One person would take my luggage to the original hotel to fake a registration, and then later to the new hotel. The other person would take me from the airport to the new hotel. When I arrived I would immediately go to the conference room, and the meeting would begin soon thereafter.

The flight attendant returned with my coffee, and I asked her, "How much longer will it be until we land in London?"

The flight attendant looked at her watch, smiled, and said, "It's going to be another four hours and fifteen minutes, if we're on time."

I looked at the coffee she had brought me, and I needed my rest more than I needed the coffee. With a pleasant smile on my face, I asked the attendant, "Could you please make the coffee Irish?"

The attendant smiled, and replied, "Of course I can, Mr. Joiner." She left with the cup of coffee in her hand, and returned to the kitchen where she proceeded to add a little whiskey, stirring it with a swizzle stick.

She brought me the cup of coffee, and gave it to me with a smile as she said, "This coffee is Irish, Mr. Joiner. I hope you enjoy it." She then left to return to her duties.

I sat back in my chair, and I sipped on the coffee, enjoying every sip, along with the soothing aroma which was slowly drifting into the air. I drank the Irish coffee and closed my eyes, attempting to get more sleep. I couldn't help but remember the dream I had earlier which was more of a nightmare. It was haunting, and it gave me a chill to remember in the dream I was dying on the battlefield. It was also haunting me because I had dreamt of a voice saying "Tommy." Tommy was my given name, and the voice I heard in the dream was Sarah's, the woman who had fostered me until I was grown. She was now dead, but I couldn't mistake her voice; she was the one person from my past who I knew had really loved me. I would like to see her just one more time to tell her I still loved her.

I didn't know how I ended up in Sarah's care. I just knew I didn't have any family other than Sarah, and her love had been sufficient. I had never been comfortable with the idea I didn't have a family, but there were some benefits at times like these, because it did make my life simpler. Then it happened, slowly, but surely, the Irish coffee was relaxing me as I drifted off to sleep.

A little over four hours later the plane landed in London, and everything happened like clockwork. Within an hour I was sequestered in the conference room with thirty other men, ready to begin the meeting. The Grand Seneschal, whose name is not allowed to be spoken, or written, at any official meeting, entered the room. The silence was deafening, as he strolled across the room and sat down at the head table with the other seven Seneschals who were present. I had been a Grand Seneschal myself, and I had a seat beside the current Grand Seneschal at all high level meetings. Since I was the only ex-Grand Seneschal who was alive, I would always have this seat until I died. If the Knights had a vote, and it ended up in a tie, then I would cast the deciding vote; otherwise I didn't have a vote. The charter of The Knights of the Night would not allow for anyone to be Grand Seneschal more than once. The only exception would be if we were engaged in a serious situation during which the Grand Seneschal died, or was incapable of handling his duties. Then the most senior ex-Grand Seneschal would automatically become the Grand Seneschal until a special meeting was called, and we elected a new leader.

Everyone was attired in their official robes for the meeting, and when the Grand Seneschal stood, and sang in his deep voice, "Oyeeeee..., Oyeeeee..., Oyeeeee...," it sounded like the beginning of a great musical masterpiece. The other members responded with a chantlike reply, "Masterrrrrrr..., Padre..., Son...," then a three-second pause followed by "Espiritu..., forever, and ever." Then another three-second pause followed by, "Strengthen..., Guide..., Educate..., and Lead... Us..." Then everything became calm for fifteen seconds of silence.

The Knights of the Night is a secret organization; however, we're also a religious organization that believes, trusts, and has faith in God. One of our most humbling moments in life is when we have to confess our faults, sins, and errors in front of the whole local Knights of the Night organization. We know God has already forgiven us when we sincerely asked, and it almost seems like a cruel and an unusual punishment to have to do it again. The reason for this requirement is to humble every Knight in front of the other Knights, because we believe no person is greater than another in the eyes of God.

We have over two million members in the United States, and several million more throughout the rest of the world. We are powerful, but the Illuminati have us outnumbered by more than twenty to one. If we have an advantage over the Illuminati it is that we have an organization that believes in God, is benevolent, and runs as smooth as a fine clock most of the time. The Illuminati and the Genebra Group are organizations which are always changing. The Illuminati are always in turmoil and chaos. They believe the turmoil and chaos allows their strongest leaders to rise to the top of the organization quickly. The stronger the leaders are, the stronger the organization will be, and of course the fact they worship Satan feeds this belief. It also encourages the cutthroat attitude of those who are power hungry to destroy those at the top. In my way of thinking, this attitude would reward the radical and possibly create unstable leadership. I certainly hope I'm right because it might give us an edge in the most important war in the history of mankind.

The Grand Seneschal cleared his throat and said, "My friends, we're gathered here to prepare to go to war with the greatest enemy which has ever confronted mankind.

"The world is now divided into seven unions, and they are uniting to bring the New World Order into existence much quicker than we ever thought possible. The European Union has been around for many years, and it has added many countries since its conception. It's a lot stronger than all the other Unions in the world because it's had many years to nurture and grow. Also the North American Union consisting of the United States, Canada, and Mexico is now established and strong enough to stand on its own. The South American Union that used to be called the Rio Group is now ready for the people to start microchip insertion.

"The African Union will complete their new organization in the next three months and plans to do chip insertion within the next nine months. This is a remarkable change of events considering the drought and famine in central Africa. The civil wars which have been threatening three unstable governments in east Africa have all been resolved. The Asian Union with China and India leading the way is stronger than ever, and ready to make ties with the rest of their neighboring countries. A real surprise came last week when they announced that microchip insertion will begin in China and India in the next few months. The Russian Union is ready to forge their new Union with the return of all the former countries of their Federation. Within three months of the Russian Federation being completed, they will start microchip insertion in the countries being returned.

"The Island Union nations with Australia leading the way will be the last Union to join the New World Order. They will be the easiest to receive compliance, especially if they want food, supplies, or communication with the rest of the world. Any island government which is reluctant to join the

Island Union will face a severe crisis of terrible proportions. Their money will not be accepted anywhere in the world, and they will not be able to purchase any commodity. The New World Order will force them to their knees almost instantly if they give them any trouble at all. Chip insertion will be done on the islands last, and should be accomplished quickly. Our best calculation is that the New World Order should have control of the total population of the Earth within eight months."

The Grand Seneschal hesitated a minute, and then he said, "I want all of us to form ten groups of three people, and then discuss what we can do to prevent this takeover of the world by the Illuminati. We will all take a number from the box on the table and form ten groups of three people each. The numbers are marked appropriately with the number of the group. The leader of each group will be the most senior member in the group. We have ten secure rooms set up here at the hotel, and each group will be taken to a room as soon as they are ready. You will have four hours to discuss, or argue, viewpoints on a solution, and then you will have two hours to write your final plan. We will all present our plans at our next meeting at nine a.m. tomorrow morning.

"Food and drinks will be delivered in thirty minutes to your rooms, and you will be able to eat and drink while you work. Every secure room has two double beds for your overnight sleeping, and weapons have been placed in each room for your personal protection. We will be practicing total vigilance tonight which means two people sleep while one person stands guard, and everyone will guard the room for three hours.

"We have Knights from the local Knights of the Night group here in London for security purposes, so if you have an emergency, call seven-seven-seven on your room telephone. The call will activate their alarm, and they should be at your door within thirty seconds.

"Now, have a good planning session, and a good night's sleep, my Knights. You have the fate of free will for the people of the Earth on your shoulders, so plan well."

I ended up being a part of group number three, and it wasn't surprising that I would be the senior person in the group. In taking charge, I also took the opportunity to make a suggestion to the other Knights almost immediately when I said, "We all think differently, have different experiences in life, and analyze things differently. So I recommend we all analyze what happened when the New World Order took over the United States. Let's see if we could have stopped that takeover, and if we could have, then let's figure out if we could use it effectively now.

"Please remember, we need a plan which is better and stronger than outright war because we don't have the strength in numbers, or weapons, to fight a real war with the Illuminati and win. After all, they will soon have control of every legal military force in the world.

"We also know we don't want to fight our own families, friends, and neighbors to the death if we can prevent it. In your planning you might consider whether we can free the people in the concentration camps who have refused the microchips so far. They had to have faith, courage, and strength in order to refuse the microchips, knowing they would lose even more freedom and have to live in those concentration camps. These are the kind of people we need to have fighting on our side during these days of turmoil. If you agree with this approach for working out our individual plans, then we'll get started." A vote was taken and everyone agreed to follow my recommendation.

Each Knight made a list of actions they thought had been taken by the Genebra Group and the Illuminati in order to accomplish the takeover of the United States. Then they scoured the information to see if they could find a weak point where The Knights of the Night could have intervened and prevented the takeover. We were to list anything extra that we thought we could do to strengthen our forces or benefit our cause.

I wrote down everything I could remember that the Illuminati and Genebra Group did during their takeover of the United States. When I compiled the information, it looked like this: The banks and financial institutions encouraged the development of a new type of mortgage for purchasing homes in the United States. Loans would be made at a very low rate, using Adjustable Rate Mortgages with the credit requirements eased for acquiring these types of mortgage. Many of the banks and financial institutions went even further by making mortgages for amounts which were excessive for the applicants financial situations. In some cases the employees in the financial institutions changed the applicant's information so they qualified for the loans.

The bankers and financial institutions made a lot of money during a relatively short period of time while they made these loans. Then the financial organizations around the world knowing what was going on in the United States began making the same kind of, or similar, corrupt loans to practically everyone who applied. Globally the bankers and financial system executives were operating on greed, and the more they made, the more they wanted.

Unfortunately, the middle class and the poor people who purchased the homes around the world didn't know they were being set up for failure by some of the greediest, most power-hungry people in the world. The people borrowing the money were being deceived, and financially raped, while those who were taking advantage of them would never be punished for what they were doing. They would only get wealthier, and actually receive aid to the tune of billions of dollars from the government. The government blamed the people borrowing the money instead of the bankers and financial types who had lied to the borrowers. It was another classic case of the wealthy banks and financial institutions getting wealthier while the poor got poorer.

After all, when the people who are going to loan you the money to purchase your new home tell you everything's okay and you can afford the loan, you tend to believe them. Many of us don't have the financial background to read and comprehend the paperwork given to us to sign at a mortgage closing. It makes it pretty easy to sucker us in, and clean our pockets, as well as ruin our family's lives with paperwork we don't comprehend. Let's face it, we have to trust those who are trained and educated in the financial fields to discern our information and approve our home loans appropriately. Mortgage borrowers don't want loans they will default on, and it's irresponsible to make the borrowers suffer, and reward the bad guys, but that's exactly what happened. To this day the only ones I've seen punished were the middle class and the poor who were taken advantage of by the wealthy.

During those hard times you would see stories on the Internet with titles like "The Rich are Hurting Too." Whenever I read one of those articles, I wondered how many of those wealthy people had to go without food, or were sleeping in tents, while their hungry children were doing without the necessities of life. Perhaps I sound bitter, but I am, because the world has enough suffering without adding more for the sake of making the wealthy wealthier, as they feed their greed.

At the same time the banks and financial institutions were making their corrupt mortgages, they also started to mail out credit cards to qualified and unqualified people. They even offered 0% interest for a short period of time before increasing it to a moderate rate. On the paperwork sent with some of the credit cards in fine print were rules stating if you were one day late on a payment, the interest rate could go as high as 29% or more. The poor American people and the people of the world who received these credit cards accepted and started using them, putting themselves deeper and deeper in debt.

Then someone through their power and influence with OPEC ran a test on the price of oil to see if they could actually control oil commodities. I believe by purchasing the petroleum futures in the stock market they were able to drive the price of oil up to one hundred and forty dollars a barrel over a short period of time. This increase in the price of oil also drove up the price of gasoline and all other oil-based products, to the point it was crippling many people's ability to drive to work and back. The test proved successful in their attempt to control the price of oil, and it seemed impossible to prove who was actually causing the price of the oil to go up. Gasoline throughout the United States was now between three dollars and fifty cents and five dollars a gallon, and even higher throughout most of the world. People living on a tight budget were starting to feel the crisis, and they resorted to using those credit cards they had received in the mail to pay for the gasoline. It was a double boon for those who controlled everything, since they made money from all the credit cards being used to purchase gasoline, as well as from the profit which came from buying the oil futures.

Since everything in the United States, and throughout most of the world, is moved by trucks, the prices for all commodities and food started to increase in order to pay for the expense of gas and diesel fuel to move product from manufacturer to consumer or farm to market. People weren't buying anything new except for the basic necessities needed to survive, and the economy was starting to suffer even more.

Who was benefiting from this round of corruption? Well, it appears that it was a case of the wealthy getting wealthier at the sake of the poor and middle class again. If the people weren't so naïve and if they hadn't trusted their government, they may have stopped this. The problem is the people had come to a point in their history where everything that made them great was being thrown out. Their personal rights and liberties were being thrown out, and their right to privacy had all of a sudden become a thing of the past in the name of the war. The American government had become a government of the wealthy, for the wealthy, and nothing else. Only the corrupt, or the corruptible, were able to be elected to office, and anyone else didn't have a chance.

As the economy continued to slip, many of the people with Adjustable Rate Mortgages couldn't make the higher mortgage payments, and still have money left over for food and gas. They had no choice but to default on some of their mortgage payments, and it started to cause another problem. When people can't make their mortgage payments, the banks start to suffer, because they need the payments for operating capital, as well as for money to make new loans. Consequently, the banks stopped making loans to their customers, as well as other banks, in order to have cash to cover their customers' savings in case there happened to be a run on their bank.

Of course the banks had already made a lot of money with the original mortgage loans, and they knew the government was going to bail them out, so they could make a second windfall profit. It was a blessing for them to be bailed out with the money of those they had financially raped.

The economy was failing, and the middle class and the poor were starting to suffer more and more with each passing week. Interest rates kept rising, and so did the payments on the Adjustable Rate Mortgages. More and more people were being foreclosed on and losing their homes. Complete families were without homes and living in the streets; tent cities were growing around the larger cities; children were homeless, as well as their parents, and it was happening around the world.

The government was going to have to intervene, and finally they did. In the United States the Secretary of the Treasury and the Chairman of the Federal Reserve System asked Congress for billions of dollars to help stabilize the banks that were in trouble. They said it would ultimately help the mortgage holders who were now losing their homes.

The banks and financial systems were stabilized with billions of dollars, but the mortgage holders were forgotten. It didn't seem fair to reward the banks that had caused the problem in the first place, but this is what happened.

To make matters worse, several members of the Genebra Group were actually in the President's cabinet, and they were advising the government and affecting the people of the United States. Following their advice the government and the people continued to make detrimental decisions for the welfare of the middle class and the poor. The big banks and financial institutions were making money without working for it, because the government was giving it to them. Of course, the United States government, unfortunately, sets the example for the other governments of the world to make the same detrimental decisions in the stabilization of their banks. The whole intent was to break the individual countries and to make the banks wealthier. It is said those who control the money also control the world. It was all part of a master plan by the Genebra Group to break the governments of the world and have them fail. *(Open your eyes, listen carefully, discern with caution, and research!)

While Congress debated what to do about the financial crisis, it only worsened. It was apparent the United States Congress didn't know what they were doing, because the financial crisis made them look like sixth graders trying to learn quantum physics. They didn't understand the economic crisis then, and they still don't, because most of the members of Congress don't have the financial knowledge to comprehend what is happening in the financial world. To make matters worse, they were taking advice from members of the Genebra Group who had helped to engineer this crisis. *(Open your eyes, listen carefully, discern with caution, and research!)

The President of the United States because he had the power to do so authorized a handout of one hundred and forty billion dollars over what Congress had given to the banks! Unfortunately, the billions didn't go to those who really needed it, but it did come out of their pockets. The middle class and the poor people were going to be paying for this bailout money for years, and guess who wouldn't have to pay for it? You're absolutely correct if you said the wealthy; after all, the wealthy have loopholes to keep from paying taxes, and we, the people, didn't have a vote on that either. If the poor or middle class don't pay their taxes, guess how many years of misery the government through the IRS will give them? When Congress finally authorized billions of dollars more for the banks to help them start lending, it was after many of the banks had already received billions of dollars through the authority of the President of the United States.

It was so sad to see the United States Government as it floundered in this financial crisis. When one percent of the people have ninety-five percent of the money, you can guess who is controlling the government, and you do know how much the one percent of the people are paying in taxes, don't you? If you don't, perhaps you should be doing a little research into the matter and realize how sad this country you live in has become. *(Open your eyes, listen carefully, discern with caution, and research!)

The situation was getting worse around the world, and the people of the world were suffering more and more, as the banks and financiers were getting richer at the expense of the poor and middle class people of the world. When Congress and the news media of the world asked where the money was going that had been given to the banks, the banks refused to answer and said they weren't required to. *(Open your eyes, listen carefully, discern with caution, and research!)

Meanwhile, millions of people around the world were being laid off from their jobs, and many companies were now closing their doors because of going bankrupt. At the same time millions of people around the world were being foreclosed on and losing their homes. The governments of the world provided lip service to the poor and middle class, but never did anything to help the people who had been led astray by the deceiving banks and financial institutions. The people were like sheep being led to the slaughter.

This was a terrible global catastrophe, and it wasn't just a mistake in banking judgment – it was a financial plan that had been set in place to bankrupt the poor and middle class of the world. It was all done in order to bring them under the control of the Illuminati, so they could form the New World Order. *(Open your eyes, listen carefully, discern with caution, and research!)

Many of the people who were Illuminati knew what was going on and wanted it to happen. They didn't mind watching millions of men, women, and children suffer, and it didn't bother them if they starved to death or died fighting for food in order to feed their children. The Illuminati believed it was a matter of survival of the fittest, and those who suffered, or died, along the way deserved what happened to them. It's even worse when you consider the Genebra Group may have had a part in this great financial catastrophe, and at the same time also influenced the government to bail out the banks and financial institutions.

While this financial crisis was happening, the United States was getting ready to elect a new president. One of the candidates had most of the people believing he was going to change the way the government functioned. It wasn't the first time a candidate promised to change the government, and it won't be the last. The American people seldom pay attention to what a candidate does during election year; instead they pay attention to what the candidate says. Then they choose a candidate because they want to believe that someone really cares about them. I also voted for this candidate because I felt he was the best man for the job. In reality, it didn't matter who was elected president because things were so far out of control that one good president wasn't going to put it back together again, especially without the help of a good cabinet and a knowledgeable Congress.

The Illuminati and Genebra Group were working together to set up the New World Order. Everything was in place except for breaking the governments of the world financially, and that was happening very quickly, because the economic crisis was now global. The countries of the world that depended on selling their products to the people of the United States in order to keep their economies strong were now hurting. The people in the United States weren't buying anything they couldn't afford, because they needed the money to survive and take care of their families. So most every nation was in the same fix as the United States Government.

The plan was to keep everyone so busy in trying to survive that they didn't have time to realize what was happening to them. After all, if you don't have a home anymore, or you don't have food to feed your children, or you don't have a job, you are dependent on your government to take care of you. This was the situation around the world, and every day it was getting a little worse.

A good analogy of what was happening would be a man in the middle of a river who could not swim. While he was so busy trying to keep from drowning, he didn't understand his own government was dumping thousands of gallons of water upriver hoping to keep him busy, so he wouldn't figure out what was actually happening. It gives a whole new meaning to keeping your head above water.

Even at the government level there wasn't a single person who noticed that the Secretary of the Treasury and the Chairman of the Federal Reserve were also members of the Genebra Group. With a little research it was also easy to verify the head of the World Bank was a member of the Genebra Group. The fact is the Genebra Group only had two secret meetings each year, worked in the political and financial background, and was never in the news. It's no wonder why no one could comprehend the effect they were having on the Global Economic Crisis. *(Open your eyes, listen carefully, discern with caution, and research!)

The plan for the takeover of the United States was working just as the Genebra Group had planned. In the end, even with the infusion of trillions of dollars to the banks, the government hadn't changed one policy that could help the poor and middle class people of the United States. Oh they changed the wording on a few things here and there, but that's like putting a band-aid on a bullet hole in the chest. The government had a plan for helping the banks who had created the problem with their poor lending practices. Everyone talked about helping the home owners, but no one really did anything. Congress called the bankers in, and they called in members of the President's Cabinet, and wanted to know why nothing was being done for the American citizens, but there weren't any good answers.

One financial problem leads to another financial problem, and that was all part of the plan too. There were new problems starting to surface because Social Security and Medicare were going broke. The money that had come in for Social Security and Medicare was spent on other items by the government instead of being invested in order to cover the future expenses and other costs of the programs. Now it was evident with hundreds of thousands of people unemployed, or under employed, in the United States, there would not be enough money coming in to finance Medicare through the year 2011. The government had deserted the people on Social Security by telling them they wouldn't get a cost of living raise for the next two years before 2009 was over or 2010 had begun. With inflation looming on the horizon the government abandoned the senior citizens, and why not, after all, they were abandoning the poor and the middle class. The wealthy didn't need Social Security or Medicare and neither did the members of Congress because they had their own plan, and they were only watching out for themselves. The Congress just kept on giving lip service to the people, and the people didn't know what to do other than believe it. It was bad enough having an economic crisis, but now it was touching the aged and vulnerable citizens who had paid their dues but wouldn't get enough benefits to survive.

While Congress was demanding answers from the Secretary of the Treasury and the Chairman of the Federal Reserve, things were rapidly taking a turn for the worse. The big three automobile dealers in the United States were failing because they were also in a financial crisis. The automobile dealers weren't selling cars or trucks because of the credit crunch and the financial crisis. Besides, all the vehicles they had been producing were either poor quality or had poor fuel efficiency compared to foreign vehicles. The automobile manufacturers needed billions of dollars to survive, and if they failed, then millions of workers would be added to the list of the unemployed.

I believe it was at this time the United States Congress started to realize they didn't run the United States at all, but the Treasury and Federal Reserve were now running the country. It was disheartening to see the taxpayers being financially raped over and over again as the government was very quickly running out of cash. The National Debt was growing at an enormous rate as the feds took more and more money and dumped it on the ones who had created the crisis.

There was a meeting of twenty of the most powerful countries in the world, and several of the countries suggested that they establish one currency for the whole world. The United States voted against it along with some of the other countries, and consequently, it wasn't approved. Perhaps it was planned, and the United States would approve the change of currency after the United States government was bankrupt, and then they could say one world currency would help the world situation. Come on, folks! It was just another part of the plan to create the New World Order! *(Open your eyes, listen carefully, discern with caution, and research!)

It was time for the final blows from the Genebra Group's bag of tricks. Things continued to get worse, and millions of people were out of work, while the finances of all the countries of the world were in deep turmoil.

The situation continued to get worse, and it was now starting to affect the local governments. When people aren't working, they aren't paying income tax; when people aren't buying extras in the stores, they aren't paying as much sales tax; when enough people aren't paying taxes, the governments start to fail. When city governments don't have enough money to operate the city, then they look to the county and state governments for help. When county governments begin to fail, the state government needs to step in to maintain the infrastructure of the counties because the county is also part of the infrastructure of the state. The state governments will eventually end up needing the federal government to help them, and without help, the state governments start to deteriorate, and they have to cut services for their residents.

The financial crisis had become a mad vicious cycle which was draining everyone's ability to survive throughout the world. The United States government had a plan to see them through part of their problems, and that plan meant printing more money. Oh, oh! This idea leads to even more problems. You can print more money, but when the money is not backed by anything, it eventually leads to a situation where a loaf of bread might cost hundreds of dollars. This is known as inflation, and if inflation is too bad, it can lead to a government collapsing financially.

If a national government is failing because it doesn't have enough income to see to the needs of the infrastructure, or the people, or the national debt, it is essentially bankrupt, and this is where the United States government was heading. It's also where most of the governments in the world were heading, and again it's what the Genebra Group wanted to happen.

What could anyone do? You will see that eventually the governments will end up bankrupt and forced into joining the

New World Order in order to survive. With one world government, one financial system, and the microchip to eliminate most of the world's crime, the people would be easily led to believe things would get better fast.

The United States contacted the countries that had desired to have one global currency and agreed to vote for it if they called another emergency meeting of the G20. After the meeting was called and held, the new Global Currency was put into effect and was installed on the microchips as credits. The countries who didn't have the chip installed in every person would continue with their own currency until the chip was installed. The new currency was known as the Earth Dollar and was handled like credits because there was no real currency you would physically handle anymore. It only took a few weeks to make the change because the system was already set for the new currency before it had even been approved. It just proved to us this was planned before the financial crisis ever happened. The Genebra Group's new plan was ingenious and would certainly change the world, giving the Illuminati control of the world's population. In fact the people of the world wanted it to happen because they wanted stability in their lives again.

The money of the world was going to be accounted for by personal microchips, scanners, computers, and satellites. The scanners would be installed in every legitimate business in the world. If you needed to purchase groceries, you would go to the grocery stores, select your food, and when you checked out the cost would be taken from your microchip and your financial account automatically. It was just like using any credit card, only better, because this credit card was a microchip and couldn't be stolen or lost.

The microchip furnished a universal service for all countries that automatically received their people's paychecks and gave them credits. If you were retired, then it also received your retirement checks and credited your account. If you purchased anything in any country, you would utilize this same system. It was wonderful in so many ways.

For instance it would eliminate many crimes since there wasn't any real cash needed anymore. Stealing something from someone wouldn't benefit a thief because the thief couldn't sell the stolen item for money. You couldn't steal anything and keep it because everything that was sold had a microchip in it, and the item was identified through a number that was assigned to the owner's account.

If someone owned something such as a television or computer they wanted to sell, they would take it to a government-run swap meet and sell it there on the weekend. When someone purchased the item, the seller and buyer would sign paperwork that listed the selling price, their names, and the item identification number of what was sold. They would then take the items to a government table at the swap meet where the credits were transferred from the buyer's to the seller's account. The identification information on the item was then electronically changed identifying the new owner.

There would also be a universal health care system in place, and all your medical information, medications, and medical history would be on the microchip, eliminating the need for paperwork in the hospitals and doctors' offices. This would save millions of dollars each year as well as furnish all the information to any doctor in a medical emergency.

When the people of the world learned all the things which would happen with the change to the New World Order, they were overjoyed. The microchip and the promises which came with it gave everyone a new hope for the future, and a reason to persevere through the crisis a little longer as everything was put into place.

The leaders of each country realized that everyone would not like the microchip or want it placed in their bodies. The governments also knew that if the people fought against the system the turmoil and chaos could hurt the implementation of the New World Order. So in true benevolence each country had prepared locations where these dissenters could live in peace without the microchip. The locations where the dissenters lived were like concentration camps that were surrounded by fences topped with barbed wire and guards to protect as well as keep the people in who lived there. You see, the people who lived in these camps couldn't survive outside of the camps without the microchip, so it was for their own safety. If the people who lived in these camps changed their minds about accepting the microchip, they could accept the chip, move out of these camps, and return to their homes.

The people loved the microchip, and it was implemented in the North American Union in the United States and Canada at about the same time most of the countries in the European Union and other major countries in the world accepted it. It was to be installed later in Mexico.

There were a few potential problems with the microchip system because it was based on the honesty of the people who controlled the information. The people who controlled the microchip system were the masters, and the rest of us became like slaves, or sheep, that were controlled electronically. This new system was bringing peace and at the same time denying the individuals the right of free will.

God had created man and woman to be equal, and to have free will to decide between good and bad in their lives. God wanted the people to have the ability to choose the right way of life, and to live within His will as a matter of choice. Now men, women, and children were being electronically controlled, and the happiness of choosing how you lived had been removed. This really wasn't an inner peace the people were experiencing. This was indeed a new form of slavery where good and evil were being forced on the people against their will.

It was possible as time passed the people who controlled the system would become reckless with their power, and when that happened they could bring atrocities to the people. For instance: if you were a beautiful young lady who was twelve years old, and happened to be appealing to a member of the Illuminati, you could be kidnapped and used sexually and no one could stop it. In fact no one could even prove who had taken the girl, let alone abused or killed her.

The Presidential election was over, and the new President of the United States was at the helm. People around the world were thrilled he had been elected because everyone loved and trusted him. They believed he was going to return some stability to the United States Government and the complete world. Everyone was watching and wondering whether there was really going to be change or would the world return to politics as usual?

One thing that upset me terribly was the new President replaced the Secretary of the Treasury with another member of the Genebra Group. The Chairman of the Federal Reserve Board stayed in his position and was already a member of the Genebra Group. I had voted for the new President because I wanted to believe he would be honest, and his campaign was real. I felt betrayed as the financial crisis continued. Now the Genebra Group and the Illuminati had reached a point where they were ready to finish the takeover of the world.

I looked at my notes and studied them over and over, trying to find a weak point in the system that had been utilized by the Illuminati and Genebra Group in the takeover of the United States, but I couldn't find one.

Later that afternoon we got together to discuss our options, and the three of us sat there with emotionless faces as if we had just been put through an emotional wringer.

I started the meeting and said, "Well gentlemen, your facial expressions tell me we might be in a terrible situation.

"If I'm wrong in my assumptions, then please forgive me. I will give you my thoughts first because they are short and not very sweet. I could not find one weakness in the Illuminati and Genebra Group's system that we can take advantage of. The best thing I could come up with is to keep our faith in God, and do what we can do. Perhaps we will have a victory because we're on the side of God, and He takes a stand with us against the Illuminati. If that happens, it will be God's strength and not ours that wins this war."

I looked at Carlos, who is from Spain and the next Knight to present his view. Carlos spoke in a soft voice and with dignity as if he were the King of Spain instead of a member of The Knights of the Night. "I believe there is nothing we can do on our own to win the battle for our beloved planet," Carlos began. "I believe if it is up to us, then we will have to surrender, before we begin, to prevent the loss of life which is so precious to God, and ourselves. In the same token I believe with our faith in God all things can, and will, happen if they are within God's will. We know in the Old Testament there are many battles which were won because of God's will, and would otherwise have been defeats. We have all read the story of Jericho where the Jews walked around the walls of the city, and blew their horns, and shouted until the walls fell down. Who are we to deny God's ability to destroy any enemy of The Knights of the Night? God is the architect of the Universe, and we can't believe we will lose in the greatest battle of mankind as long as we have faith in Him. I believe we need to plan as carefully as possible, seeking God's will in our actions, and approach this as Knights of the Night who believe in a God who is all powerful. I suggest we prepare for war and trust in God for our strength and guidance." He stood there in silence for a few moments and then sat down.

I contemplated what Carlos had just said and I replied, "Carlos, you're certainly a great leader, a great man, and a great Knight. You have humbled me in my inability to remember God and His strength during times like these. Thank you."

Then I looked at Roman, who was from Canada, and nodded for him to begin his dissertation.

Roman cleared his throat and wiped a few tears from his eyes because Carlos' speech had also moved him emotionally. He said, "Gentlemen, I have nothing to say except I couldn't find a weakness in the Illuminati and Genebra Group's system either. I did decide, like both of you, it would take a miracle from God for us to win the battle that awaits us. But like El Cabby, I didn't even stop to think that through God we really had a chance. Forgive me for my lack of foresight. I think Carlos rules the day with his eloquent speech. It would be good if we reserved our presentation at the meeting tomorrow, so we are the last to present our views if we can. I also think Carlos should give our presentation for us." Then he looked at me and continued speaking, "I realize, El Cabby, being the most senior member of our group, and a past Grand Seneschal, it would be your honor. However, if you would humbly step aside, so everyone can hear Carlos give his speech, it might motivate others to have faith. This is a time in our history when we have to remember our roots and trust God as we did years ago."

I smiled and said, "Roman, I think you're absolutely correct, and I will ask the Grand Seneschal in the morning before the meeting begins if we can do that. Carlos, we won't ask you if you mind representing our group, and speaking last, because I believe God was responsible for what you said, and how you said it.

"Now gentlemen, I recommend we go to bed and get some rest. It's been a long day, and tomorrow may be even longer. Shall we pray before we retire for the evening and then maintain silence until morning?" I was the senior member of our group, and I had the responsibility of leading the prayer, so I began, "Our Father, we come unto thee and we give thanks for your presence in our meeting, and in our lives. Help us to be the people you would have us be, and help us to do the things you would have us do, so we might accomplish your will on Earth. Finally, Father, give us the strength to live our lives so others will see You through our actions, words, and deeds. Amen."

It took a long time for me to go to sleep, and when I did, it seemed my five hours were up immediately, and I went on watch while my roommates slept. In a few hours we would submit our plan, which was no plan, but to simply have faith and trust in God!

Chapter 3

March 9–11

The night passed too quickly while I was sleeping, and too slowly when I was awake. It seemed like a forty-hour night, and then my roommates and I were dressed and ready for breakfast. An hour later we were back in the meeting, and the first thing that I did was talk to the Grand Seneschal requesting the privilege to speak last with Carlos making our presentation.

One of the groups suggested we break into oil well exploration companies, like Dresser Atlas, to steal their Cesium 137 which was used in logging oil wells. After we stole the Cesium 137 we would use it to make dirty nuclear bombs to be used in battles we couldn't win otherwise. At first it seemed like a good idea until we discussed how much contamination we would spread around the countryside. The effect would be devastating on the environment and the people who lived there. We realized if we did win the war we would want the people to return to their homes instead of the nuclear hell we had created.

We decided to leave the dirty tricks to the Illuminati, because we knew they didn't have a conscience – the Illuminati had a record of using Mind Control techniques to educate and to enslave their own people. Plus the fact they committed murders which were made to look like suicides to eliminate their own members, and the fact they prostitute their own members including children all proved their lack of conscience. The Illuminati were involved in many other crimes also, and every evil thing they were involved in was evidence they didn't have a conscience.

One of the other groups had no idea what to do; however, they reminded us we were going to be fighting a real war, with real weapons, and with all the pain and suffering which comes with a war. We never thought we'd have to fight a war because it wasn't our way of doing things. We had planned to infiltrate and destroy each organization in the Illuminati one at a time. Our way of fighting by infiltrating and destroying would have been so much better than a real war.

There was one thing we had that the Illuminati didn't have, and it was God, and our faith in God. This made us invincible in our own minds, and it also made us positive Knights of the Night who didn't have the same fears as the average person in this world. We would win, or die, based on our willingness to have faith and trust in God. It's one thing to say, "I trust in God," and it's very different to put your life on the line and say, "I trust in God so take your best shot." We were putting our lives in jeopardy because we didn't have a choice. We would be fighting more like guerillas, by being here one minute and somewhere else the next. We would be trying to win the hearts of the people of the world, and by getting them involved we might have a fighting chance. We would still be like the David of biblical times; however, we would be fighting dozens of Goliaths at the same time. If we could maintain the faith David had in his fight with Goliath, we believed we could possibly win this war.

One of the groups came up with the idea of using technology to give our troops a fighting edge. One of the Knights in the group owned a plant which manufactured microwave ovens for name-brand manufacturers. His company also furnished magnetrons used in manufacturing microwave weapons for several government programs and experiments involving crowd control. He had heard through the grapevine that these weapons were modified and tested in the initial invasion of Iraq. The power had been boosted from the magnetrons to unbelievable outputs, and they had been used with a focused beam so they could be utilized against specific targets with unbelievable deadly results. They were only used in a few instances because they violated the code of war and were illegal to use as military weapons. The United States government had signed a treaty to ban any research in the use of microwaves for military purposes, but they didn't honor the treaty they signed and did test microwave-type weapons in a limited capacity.

Consequently, they also developed them as nonlethal weapons for the local police forces, the FBI, and several other law enforcement organizations. He informed us in doing his research on the Internet concerning microwave weapons he discovered a video where Iraqi doctors were being interviewed about some casualties they could not explain. Iraqi soldiers were found in a vehicle with the skin on their faces completely burned off, no eyes in the sockets, and the total body height of the remains was about one meter tall. It sounded ghastly and unbelievable. The Iraqi doctors also reported the victims didn't have any bullet wounds, and the vehicle they were in did not have any sign of explosion or bullet holes. The doctors had never seen anything like this in all their years of experience.

He had also found videos of the army testing the microwave weapons on army personnel who were simulating a crowd. The video showed its reaction first on a number of soldiers simulating a riot situation or a typical crowd control situation. When the weapon was used there was no sound and nothing visual to let you know that any weapon was even being used. The crowd dispersed because they were feeling a burning sensation in their bodies, and they had no choice but to flee in order to escape the intense heat that was making their skin burn. Since they didn't know where the source of the heat was coming from, they dispersed in several directions to get away from the heat that was causing so much pain. In another instance in the video they were using three military people who were spaced about two feet apart to demonstrate their ability in focusing the weapon to a narrow beam in order to be selective about who they beamed. This time you could tell which person they had selected to hit with the microwave beam because only one individual out of three reacted to the weapon. All of us thought what we were seeing was unbelievable, but it was an official U.S. army video.

The Knight stated he was so interested in what he had seen that he and a friend took a magnetron and placed it in a simple box with a handle and a trigger, so they could hold it like a gun. They connected a 115 volt source of power to the magnetron and placed a metal lens from a camera in front of the magnetron to focus the beam. The handle on the box had a trigger device which would turn the power on and off to the magnetron gun, and then they took the weapon to the country to test it. The power source for the magnetron came from a converter that plugged into a car power outlet and converted the power to 115 volts. You can buy these converters in any auto supply store for use on picnics or family outings to watch TV, cook, or to do anything else which requires 115 volts. Although they did not build in any power control system they could use to control the amount of power output from the magnetron, they turned it on and attempted to use it. Although the microwave gun didn't make any noise indicating it was working, it evidently was. When one of them walked 100 feet away and then walked into the beam, they experienced extreme heat that made them uncomfortable, and they had to move away. When they tried to block the microwave beam by hiding behind several items, they still felt the burning sensation. The heating sensation wasn't nearly as bad though when they used an eight-inch mattress in front of them.

With a little research he said he had discovered that wire mesh which was attached to a ground probe protruding from his boot and into the ground did seem to make a shield which appeared to work. They didn't have enough of the metal screen from an old screen door to provide cover for the complete body, and didn't have the time to continue their research into shielding from microwave beams. However, their simple little gun did work and appeared to be nonlethal when they tested it. They placed a piece of raw hamburger several yards away where the beam hit it, and after a few minutes they turned the beam off and checked the meat to see that it was indeed slowly cooking.

The owner of the microwave manufacturing plant decided they could probably produce a limited number of these weapons on weekends, if they had volunteers with a little technical knowledge who were willing to assemble them. It could certainly prove interesting to utilize a weapon that no one else had ever used in combat other than the U.S. Military. We were determined to not amplify the output to vaporize anyone, but instead to keep the weapons at the crowd control levels, and create havoc through the use of the heat they could generate. We voted to see what we could do to procure the parts needed for one hundred microwave guns, and to see if we could find five Knights with the technical knowledge to assemble them.

One of the other groups had an idea to bring members from the South American Countries north to the United States to protest the microchip and create a small conflict in order to attract attention to what was really going on with the New World Order. It was like staging a battle to get media attention which would travel around the world with the evening news. This could take a lot of time and might work if we could get enough South American Knights to the United States in time to make it effective.

First, we would have to create a military diversion with our members in the United States. The diversion would hopefully draw attention away from what was going on in South America and Mexico. If we achieved this, it would be the largest operation we had ever performed. We would actually start minor protests outside of six military bases around the United States at different times.

We would have a short demonstration at Fort Rucker, Alabama. Within six hours of that demonstration, we would create another short demonstration outside the Great Lakes

Naval Training Center at Waukegan, Illinois. The next morning we would start protesting at the main gate of Wright Patterson Air Force Base near Dayton, Ohio. These demonstrations against the New World Order would last less than one day, and then it would end, hopefully turning very peaceful as if they had never happened. Demonstration number four would begin at the Marine Air Field at Yuma, Arizona, and this one would be more intense and we would utilize real weapons if needed. Even though we knew demonstrating against a U.S. Marine base could start a real conflict with the military, we decided to do it anyway. Within six hours of demonstration number four, demonstration number five would begin at El Central Naval Air Station. We would leave a shoulder-fired anti-aircraft missile launcher behind to let them know we had the capability to shoot down military aircraft. Finally demonstration number six would take place when we had our people stage a huge demonstration at the front gate of Fort Riley in Kansas. This demonstration would start near two a.m. in the morning, and would include a group of demonstrators cutting the fence near the main gate to show how seriously we were protesting against the New World Order. The entire occurrence for this demonstration would last less than a half hour from start to finish.

We planned to use at least ten of our new microwave guns at each disturbance if we had to. They would only be used in crowd control mode if troops started to push us back from where we were demonstrating. The microwave guns wouldn't hurt anyone, but it would certainly give the people they were used against a cause for concern. They wouldn't be happy we were capable of causing more problems by using state-of-the-art technology. If we didn't need the microwave guns, we wouldn't use them. They would be even more effective in a conflict with an enemy who didn't know we had them. Besides, we were Knights of the Night, and we didn't want to harm innocent troops who were only following orders. We would use force when it was needed, but we didn't want to use it now, if it wasn't necessary.

The intent of these demonstrations would be to put all these bases on alert and tie up their troops for their own defensive purposes. At the same time as demonstration number six was happening, demonstrations one, two, and three would be reenacted for a very short period of time in order to create a national nightmare for the military.

The news and the government officials would be trying to figure out what we were doing and what our goals were. We would send the radio and television stations fliers saying we were called The Knights of the Night and were patriots from around the world protesting the suppression of personal freedom and free will. We hoped and prayed they would share those fliers on the news. We also wanted to keep the focus of the news, the government, and the military on The Knights of the Night in Eastern and Central United States. We didn't want to get into any actual conflicts with the American military at this time. We did intend to cause major diversions which would allow us to get thousands of our Knights from the South American countries to the border of the United States.

We also thought if we created enough disturbances in the United States then we might get the attention of people around the world. People who would be willing to help in curtailing the Illuminati's planned takeover of the world. We would have fliers printed in every language explaining we were The Knights of the Night. The new posters would also reveal what the Genebra Group and the Illuminati were doing. During the demonstrations we would distribute the handouts throughout the world. We also had aspirations of adding new members around the world to The Knights of the Night in every country. We also hoped we might have people from other countries creating problems for the Illuminati by protesting what was happening in their countries. If we were effective, we might be able to prevent the New World Order from ever being completely established. We knew this would be a huge mission for our organization, but with God's help we might be able to accomplish our goal. The greatest concern we had was we would start a conflict at the Marine Air Base in Yuma, Arizona. We didn't want a real war if we could prevent it. Life is precious, and if we could save the world without a war, we would be very happy.

It was a plan in the rough, but in the next three days we would get it completely worked out and ready to implement in the near future. We would make plans and layout strategy so that when the time came everything would be implemented on time and as planned. When we had everything devised we would disperse back to our home bases. We would spend two weeks preparing handouts in every country, producing microwave guns, and making the final preparations for the demonstrations. This meant calling up thousands of Knights of the Night around the world to protest in their own countries.

The next day we started the strategic planning for the demonstrations and what The Knights of the Night would do in their respective countries to prepare for a worldwide conflict if it happened. By that evening we were tired and I turned in early.

I awoke because my neck was hurting, and I'd fallen asleep while riding my black horse called "Guerrier Minuit," which means "Midnight Warrior" in French. He was a wonderful stallion who was usually full of energy and had seen me through many a conflict. He was loping slowly as if he had just been through a great battle, and was very tired. My neck was hurting because I had fallen asleep as we slowly moved along with another thousand crusaders who were battle weary and worn out from the fight. We were in a small valley with rolling green hills surrounding us.

I had dried blood on my face and hands, and my arms ached. My sword hand was tired from holding my sword during the long battle we had evidently fought. We were in the South of France, trying to make it to safety and a chance to regroup our forces. I grabbed my sword and held it up for inspection. It had dried blood here and there, but otherwise it looked okay. I would clean the dried blood off the next time we passed a stream.

I was so fatigued from the battle we had just fought I couldn't remember who we were fighting. I hit my head with the palm of my hand as if it would jar the neurons loose and reconnect the synapses in my brain allowing me to think clearly. *Oh Lord,* I thought, *I'm fighting for You, and I don't even know who I'm fighting.* Then I realized what must have happened. I had evidently been killed on the battlefield, and now I was riding with a thousand other soldiers who had been killed in the same battle. They were also covered in blood; they were battle weary, and they were also retreating from an enemy that we could not see. Being Crusaders they were also promised a free trip to heaven by the Pope if they fought in the Crusades. I decided we had to be going to heaven, but no one had bothered to tell us we had been killed in battle. Even though the explanation didn't make a lot of sense I had to consider that no one but God really knows what happens after death. If we were really dead, I'm sure we would have a moment of revelation to that fact very soon. After all, what would be accomplished by letting us continue to wander the Earth going nowhere if we were dead?

Then one of the warriors on foot near me moaned and fell to the ground. He kicked one foot on the ground as if to force himself back to his feet, but all it did was roll him over onto his back, where he instantly died with a gasp as his weight forced the broken arrow in his back through his heart.

Now I knew we weren't dead. I should have known anyway because I was in pain, and I don't believe that the dead feel physical pain. They might suffer mental anguish that is far worse than pain, but then I don't know anything about what they experience. All I knew for sure was that I was alive, mentally depleted, physically exhausted, and fleeing an enemy that I couldn't remember. Of course, it's possible I was out of my mind and ready to run screaming into the distance too.

I looked around at the other Crusaders to see if I could recognize any of them. But as far as I could see I was the only real Templar Knight in sight. The others were all Crusaders who carried a different shield and banner than we did. The Templar shield and banners all had the same motif on them. They were painted black for the top one-third of the shield or banner, and the other two-thirds were plain white. The black represented our sins before we had joined the Templar Knights. The white represented the forgiveness of our sins that we received from the Pope for joining the Templar Knights. We had paid a hefty price for becoming Templar Knights even though it meant forgiveness and a guaranteed ticket to heaven when we died. We had to give up all our belongings, our freedom, and our associations with women, not to mention many other things. We had to become monks under Saint Bernard of Clairveaux. We had to sleep in the light if we could, and we had to pray several times every day. When we were not going to, or coming from, assignments we also had to participate in all the same activities a monk would. It was said that in order to be a Templar Knight you had to be a warrior monk, and it was true.

Then I heard the horns blowing, and I felt chills go up and down my spine. It was the horn of the Saracens blowing loudly from the hills around us. I looked around to see thousands of Saracens on horseback on the top of the hills surrounding the valley we were in. They had been searching for us as we retreated, so they could kill us and never have to fight us again. As fast as they had arrived at the top of the hills, they attacked coming full force. We didn't have a chance. Everywhere I looked I saw my comrades in arms being slaughtered. Then I saw a warrior riding towards me from my left, and I knew that he would kill me if I didn't defend myself. I lifted my broad sword over my head with all the strength I could muster, and when I was ready to swing the sword, it wouldn't move. "I'll take your sword," a voice said from behind me. "You are my prisoner, and you should be worth a great ransom." He grabbed my sword and removed it from my battle-weary hands and then he threw it to the ground.

The warrior who had been attacking from my left arrived and reached over to tie my hands together, making me defenseless. He then led me away, and we headed towards the Mediterranean. Meanwhile the warrior who had disarmed me went about his business of making sure everyone else, other than Knights, had been killed or captured. I looked around as I was being led from the battlefield, and it appeared that all the Crusaders had been killed. Because I was a Knight, the Saracens wanted me alive in the hope of receiving a ransom from the King of France or from the Vatican for my safe return. I knew the King of France wouldn't pay anything for me as he was having financial problems caused by the fact he owed a large sum of money to the Templar Knights. My only hope was that the Vatican would be willing to ransom me because I was a Templar Knight and a warrior monk. If the Vatican wouldn't ransom me, then you might guess what would happen to me because the Saracens didn't have much use for Christians that no one else wanted. The Saracens were famous for the games they played with captives who they ended up killing. I had a cold chill run down my spine, as we headed to the south and the Mediterranean Sea.

When we reached the crest of the hill I could see the Mediterranean Sea off in the distance. I could also see the Saracen tents and ships near the beach. When we approached the camp I could see where they were holding the other Knights they had captured earlier. It looked like there were at least ten or twelve Knights, but I didn't recognize any of them. None of them were Templar Knights as far as I could see, but that wasn't unusual, because we had a reputation for dying in battle. We were not trained to give up, and there were many stories of two Templar Knights fighting back-to-back and killing many enemy soldiers before they were killed.

The Saracen took me past the Knights and to the main tent where he kicked me off of my horse. He dismounted and gave orders to someone to take the horse. Then he grabbed the lash which was around my wrists and yanked me to my feet. Oh God that hurt! He almost dragged me into the tent where he took me to his leader and kicked me in the small of my back, so I went to my knees and then fell on my face. He grabbed my hair and pulled me up until I was on my knees. I looked at his leader who was at least twenty years younger than I was, and he looked mean and dangerous. He pulled out his scimitar and raised it as if he were going to cut off my head. Then he said, "Give me one good reason why I shouldn't cut off your head."

I grimaced at the thought. *After all I was worth more for ransom than I was dead. Wasn't I?* Then I said, "Since I'm a Knight we both know I'm worth more alive than dead. I'm sure you can get a ransom for me from someone."

He smiled with a gleam in his eye and he said, "I have captured too many of your Knights already. We know the King of France can't afford to ransom all of you. He has been squandering his wealth for years, and you Templar Knights have most of it in your coffers." He laughed. "Am I correct?"

I looked at him with dismay and said, "I suppose that's true, but I'm sure the King of France or the Pope will pay more for me than for some of the other knights you have out there."

He replied, "Perhaps, perhaps not. What's your name?"

I said, "El Caballero Guerrero."

"The Warrior Knight." He smiled as he walked to one of his men and whispered something into his ear. The man immediately left the tent as the leader said, "We'll make a decision about you in a minute." He ordered a servant to bring me a drink of water, as he slowly walked over to his chair and sat down. He sat there staring out at the sea, and a few seconds later I had a drink of water in my hand. I brought the cup to my lips and drank the cool, refreshing liquid, swallowing it slowly and savoring every drop. *God is this good!* I thought. Then I sat back on the ground awaiting my fate.

A few minutes later the man returned and mumbled something to the leader who then turned to me and said, "Well, my friend, we will have some fun with you in a few hours. We asked the other knights about your name, and who you are, and every one of them denies knowing you. So I would surmise you aren't as important as you think." Then he said to one of his guards, "Set him aside for this evening, and see he is well fed and watered until then."

They led me out of the tent and put me in a small tent closer to the beach where they placed two guards at the entrance. Within minutes I had cooked meat, fruit, and vegetables to eat. *What does this mean?* I thought to myself as I ate and drank, trying to get my strength back. In the back of my mind I knew the food and drink were probably going to be my last meal.

Two hours later two warriors came and tied my arms to my waist, and took me to the beach where they had dug a hole just deep enough for me to stand in and still have my head above the sand. Without a word they kicked me into the hole, and I stood there helplessly as they shoved the sand in around me. The only thing above the sand was my head and neck. The fear I was feeling was causing me to pray silently to God. I looked around, and off to the left was a tent where the leader and a number of his men were sitting, drinking, laughing, and watching me. To the right of me there was another tent, and in it were the other Knights they had captured, and they were watching me too. The captured Knights looked at me with sad eyes and downturned lips because this could have been their fate. I'm sure they didn't know if they were next or not, but for the moment I was the only show in town.

The leader arose and everyone became very quiet as he walked out to where I was. He looked at me rather seriously for a second and then he said, "Well, El Caballero Guerrero, we will see what kind of Knight you are. This is a game we are about to play with your head. I have five archers, and I have five men with spears. One archer will shoot to hit your head from fifty meters. If he misses, then a warrior with a spear gets his chance from thirty meters. Whichever one hits your head and kills you will win the game. If no one hits you, then the second set of contestants gets to try. If the second set of warriors doesn't hit you, then the third set and then the fourth and the fifth. If no one has killed you after they have all tried, we will dig you up and set you free. I really mean free! You will ride out of this camp on your own horse and with your armor and weapons. You will be a free man. However, if you as much as look back, we will kill you instantly. Allah says that if you look death in the face once in a day and survive, then be happy, and don't tempt the Gods. You will have looked death in the face ten times today, and if you survive, and are set free, don't take another chance by looking back. Don't look back!

"If you are set free, then those who tried to take your life will be buried in the same way you are, and the prisoner Knights will have a chance to kill them. The warriors who are dead after your Knights have taken their turn will be buried, and the others set free, but unlike you, the Knights will still be held for ransom. I am going to leave you now, and when I sit down, the games will begin. No one will think you're a coward if you move your head to one side or the other. But, if you cry out at any time, we will know you have no courage. Those without courage have been known to die even if every one of my warriors misses them." Then silently he turned around and walked back to his seat and sat down.

The drums started to roll, and the first archer took his place. When the drums stopped, he had to shoot instantly, because it is considered a moment of truth when the drums stop. The archer was not allowed to wait; he had to use his weapon when the drum stopped, and then hope it hit its target which was my head. The drums rolled as the archer took aim.

I had a thousand things going through my mind as I stood there helplessly waiting. *Oh God*, I prayed silently in my mind, *let me live another day.*

Then the drumroll stopped, and I opened my eyes to watch the arrow arching through the sky as it flew towards me. I could tell it was going to miss me, but not by much. I felt like my heart had stopped when the drumroll stopped, and now it began to beat again. A few minutes ago I wasn't hot, but now I was burning up, and the sweat was rolling off my face and falling on the hot, dry sand.

Then the archer, with a sad expression on his face, stepped aside as another warrior with his spear stepped into position. I didn't like the looks of the warrior with his spear, because he was built for speed and for strength. He was thin, but not skinny, his legs were strong, and his upper body was like a giant ripple of pure muscle. The way he held his spear was as if it were an extension of his body. I was worried because I felt when he threw the spear it would be the end of the contest, and the end of my life.

The drumroll started, and I resigned myself to my fate. After all, there was nothing I could do but move my head an inch or two to the right or left. I didn't think it was going to help me much against this warrior and his spear. However, it seemed as quickly as the drum had started, it stopped, and the warrior let his spear fly towards me. As I watched the spear it seemed like it was taking forever to get to me, but there wasn't any doubt in anyone's mind, including mine, it was going to end the game. The spear was flying straight and true and was going to split my skull in half for sure. Then at the last moment a puff of wind came out of nowhere, and the spear dropped just slightly. The tip of the spear landed where the sand was soft just in front of my throat, and the tip stopped about a tenth of an inch from my jugular vein. When I was watching the spear, I thought I was going to die, yet I had lived. There was a sound of laughter as everyone stared in disbelief because they were also sure I was going to die, and it probably disappointed them I didn't.

I could do the math in my head. Twenty percent of the warriors who were trying to kill me had had their chance and missed. *Thank You, Lord,* I thought. I realized if I lived through this ordeal I would probably be more of a monk than I had ever been. My heart would certainly be more into my prayers and giving thanks than it had ever been before.

After every two warriors had attempted to kill me, a servant would come out and pick up the weapons they had used and take them back to the tent. He also brought a small cup of water and would slowly pour it into my mouth to quench my thirst. It was appreciated very much as I was getting hotter, and hotter, standing there in the sand awaiting my fate. The servant returned to the tent laughing and holding his hands to show how close the spear had come to my throat. I grimaced as the drums started again, and the second archer took aim.

Then they stopped, and the arrow was on its way, and again it looked like my life was going to end for sure. At the last instant when the arrow was just a foot away, I moved my head violently to the right. The arrow found my flesh anyway, but it was the flesh of my left ear, and it split the ear as it cut a small streak into my head before it went into the Earth behind me. This time there was a loud roar of joy, but it was coming from the tent where the other captive Knights were watching. They may not have known who I was, but it was evident they wanted me to live, and they wanted me to know it.

As I was standing there I thought to myself, *God, let's not take me one piece at a time. I'd just as soon get it over with if I am going to die today or is it your idea of a short and fast purgatory.* I almost broke out laughing as I thought about how stupid I must look. I was buried here in the sand talking to a God I believed in, but also a God who could stop this turmoil and end the whole thing right now if He wanted to. A God who chose to let his Son suffer the misery of a slow and painful death on the Cross. I wondered why in the world God would allow His Son to suffer, and then keep me alive. A second later I thought I was losing my mind because I heard a voice inside my head say, *Didn't my Son die and rise again? Have faith! You might be a Templar Knight, but you're not much of a monk, and you are supposed to be both!*

I looked around expecting to see God Himself standing nearby, but there was nothing. Then the drumroll I had forgotten about, and hadn't heard start, stopped. Another spear was flying through the air and headed my way, and it missed its mark by inches to the left of my head. I thought to myself, *Forty percent down, and sixty percent to go.* There had been too many close calls, and I realized sooner or later that either an arrow or a spear would find its mark, and I would be dead. I also thought I had lost my senses because one minute I was hearing God's voice, and the next minute I didn't have faith, because I knew I was going to die. I thought to myself, *I will die like the man God would have me be. Because it would be God's will for me.* I felt my composure and my feelings change as I resolved to die like a good Christian facing death. Without fear! The servant brought my water again and gave it to me to drink. Then he picked up the weapons as they prepared for round three.

The drumroll started again, and the third archer took aim. Only now the archer had something new to worry about because the wind was rising. As the sun was going down the trade winds from the Mediterranean Sea were starting to blow stronger and more erratic, and because of that, the arrow missed its mark by at least six inches. The Knights who had denied knowing me cheered again as though it would make a difference. The winds were blowing stronger by the minute, and when the third spear landed, it also fell short as a gust of wind drove it into the ground about fifteen inches in front of my head.

I thought, *There really is a God, and He did talk with me. He told me to have faith and then He created the winds to protect me. I don't know if I will live to see tomorrow, but if I do, I will know there is a God of faith and He will even save a man like me.* "Oh God, Thank You!" I said out loud. "Two more arrows and two more spears and I'll be free and riding out of here."

The next arrow also missed its mark, and so did the spear. The wind was almost violent, and the sea was getting choppy. The Saracens were moving their boats away from the shore, so they weren't damaged by the wind and the waves. The sky had turned black, and there was lightning and thunder, and it was starting to sprinkle. I expected them to come and set me free, because I was sure it would be impossible for anyone to hit me now.

The drum had started again as the last archer took aim, and then as quickly as it started the drum stopped. Also the wind stopped as the arrow flew a course straight and true. Luckily for me the archer had allowed for the wind, and the arrow flew towards a target at least a foot away from my head. I laughed and said again, "Thank You, Lord!"

The drums started again, and the last warrior prepared to throw his spear; only now things had really changed. As fast as the storm had started, it had stopped. The rain had stopped; the wind had stopped, and so had my heart as the spear found its mark in the center of my head.

"El Cabby, wake up," a voice said. "It's time for us to change. I've never seen anyone sleep so poorly. You slept as if you were fighting with someone. You've been sweating profusely for the last hour, and I believe I heard you talking to God. What in the world were you dreaming?"

It would take me too long to explain, but I feel like I'm a better man because I had that nightmare, or dream, or whatever it was. I headed for the shower because I needed to clean up and get ready to stand my watch while my roommates slept. I also had a lot to think about as I sat there for the rest of the night, pondering the fate of The Knights of the Night. The next day we laid out the plans for the demonstrations which had to take place while we brought our South American Knights across the Mexican border and into the United States.

Within two weeks we could be at war with the United States, and hopefully around the world if it happened, because the people would become aware of what was really happening. It would be a war like no other war had ever been fought. After all, we only had a few weapons ourselves. We didn't have an army, air force, or a navy, and our enemy had more technology and weapons at their disposal than any military in the world had ever had. When the New World Order was complete, they would be the only military force in the world. Our only hope was God would help us in one way or another to win this war.

We closed our last meeting in London that day with a prayer, and the next morning we headed home. We had a lot of work ahead of us in preparation for what was coming.

I boarded my British Airways flight to Mexico City, and as soon as we were in the air, I ordered an Irish coffee. It wasn't long after I drank my Irish coffee that I was asleep.

Chapter 4

March 13

I was back in Guanajuato sitting outside at La Pirinola Restaurant in San Fernando Plaza, drinking a beer, and trying to relax when I heard an infectious female laugh a few feet away. I looked to see who laughed, but I couldn't see her, because there was a large bougainvillea between us. It was evident by her voice she was young, very young, compared to me, and probably in her mid-twenties. I knew I wanted to meet this young lady, because her boisterous laughter reminded me of someone out of my past. Somehow, I would have to find an excuse to meet her before the day was over.

Her voice reminded me of happier times I had enjoyed with Sarah, the lady who had reared me until I was seventeen. I'd left home for the Navy shortly after I graduated from high school, and she was killed in an auto accident a few weeks later. Sarah had been a waitress at an outdoor restaurant in California, and quite often when I was young I'd go there and wait for her to finish work. It was during those times, while I was sitting waiting for her, I would hear her laugh the same kind of boisterous, infectious laugh I was hearing today. It was one of the reasons everyone, including me, loved Sarah so much. The majority of the time, she was happy, even during difficult times. On rare occasions when she felt depressed, she would break out laughing, and then end her laughter with a statement such as, "Look at me, I'm so stupid! I know there are people who are in worse situations than I am. There are people who are paralyzed, people who have just lost their families in a war, or a tragic accident, and here I am with a few minor problems and I break out crying."

I came back to reality when I heard the woman laughing again because her laugh stirred many emotions and feelings I didn't know I had anymore. To my surprise, I found myself yearning for a home and a family of my own, and I hadn't done that for many years. I thought I was beyond feeling anything associated with love in any way, shape, or form. In this moment in time I wanted to break down and cry because of a woman's laugh, and I didn't even know who she was. I know what it is I thought, *It must be the threat of war, and I need someone to fight and die for on a personal basis. I wouldn't be the first person to want something like that in their lives. During the Second World War thousands of young men got married on a whim only knowing someone a week or less. When they faced the enemy in combat, they needed someone other than themselves to fight and die for.*

It was impossible for me to know what was going to happen in the weeks ahead. I decided if the opportunity presented itself, I was going to get to know the young lady with the infectious laugh, and somehow stay close to her as a friend. She would be my family even though she wouldn't know it, and she would be my reason for living. She would be my reason to go on fighting if all hope was lost. And she would be that someone to take care of after the war, even though she wasn't really family. All of a sudden I came back to reality as I heard her laugh again, and I felt like I was just an old man dreaming an impossible dream.

Then a man came out of the restaurant and walked over to the table where she was sitting with her friend, and talked with them. I didn't know who he was, but I would have guessed he was a man of authority, except for the fact he was dressed casually, had a big smile on his face, and acted as though he could possibly be her brother. He was rather portly, but not fat, and his most prominent feature, I'd have to say, was his smile and pleasant attitude. As the man walked back into the restaurant, he strolled by my table, and I couldn't refrain from asking him who the young lady was he had been talking to. I said, "Sir, could I bother you a second?"

"Of course," he said with a smile.

I asked him, "I was wondering, who is the young lady you were just talking to?"

"Sir," he replied with a smile, "I don't give out information about my customers, especially to old men when they're asking about young ladies." Then he broke out laughing and said, "I'm just teasing; she's a good friend and customer, and if you would like to meet her I will bring her over and introduce you. Then she can tell you whatever she wants you to know."

I said, "Hey, I appreciate that, but before you introduce me to her, let me introduce myself to you. My friends call me El Cabby, and I've lived in Guanajuato for a number of years now, but I had never eaten in your restaurant until this month."

The man smiled and said, "I think that explains why you're so thin, and don't smile very much. If you ate here daily you'd be a lot happier, and a little more on the plump side. My customers are happy customers, because of the good food, and the atmosphere we have at La Pirinola Restaurant."

I smiled and said, "I really believe you, and I intend to be back as often as I can in the next six days. What is your name, my friend?"

He smiled and said, "Well, I don't know if I want to tell you my name, if you're not coming back for more than six days; it seems like a waste of time. But, I'll tell you anyway: my name is Cesar and I own this restaurant. Now will you tell me why you will only visit my restaurant six more days if you've lived here for years?"

I looked at Cesar, and smiled, as I contemplated how I would answer his question. I hated being in this situation, but

I hate being untruthful, and yet there are times... I said, "Well, I can't tell you everything, but I have some business to take care of in the United States. My work can be very dangerous, and there's a possibility I could be gone for a long time. I'm a man of my word, and I don't want you to believe I will be here for longer than six days. So I'm going to say this – if everything goes well, and I return in a reasonable time, you'll have the pleasure of seeing my smiling face at least twice a week whenever I'm in town. If I retire before I come back, then it's possible you could see a lot more of me."

Cesar smiled and said, "I like your answer, so let me get my friend, and I'll introduce you to her." Cesar walked over to the young lady, and as he leaned over her table speaking very softly, she glanced my way. She stood up and said something to her friend, and then followed Cesar over to my table. Beauty is in the eyes of the beholder, and I found myself looking into the eyes of a beautiful young woman who was at least forty years younger than I am.

As they approached the table where I was seated, Cesar said, "Berenice, I want you to meet El Cabby. El Cabby, I want you to meet Berenice." He looked at Berenice and continued, "El Cabby asked me about you, and said he would like to meet you. So I told him I would introduce you, and you could tell him whatever you wanted him to know. Now I have to get busy; I have a catering service to prepare." With that statement, Cesar turned and walked back into the restaurant.

I looked at Berenice standing there, and it was apparent she was studying me with a questioning expression on her face as she said, "Can I sit down?"

"Of course," I said, "I don't know what I was thinking, but I thought you would go back to your table to sit with your friend. I didn't believe you would actually sit down and visit with me."

She said as she sat down, "Even if my friend was still here, I would have talked with you for a few minutes. My friend had to leave, and I won't see her again today, so is there any particular reason you wanted to meet me?"

I answered her with a smile, "Well, you're going to think I'm crazy, but I wanted to meet you because your laugh reminds me of a dear friend by the name of Sarah; she's the woman who reared me as a child. You sound very much like she did when she laughed, and the sound of your laughter made me a little melancholy, because she's been dead for many years now." I think I had a tear in my eye as I stopped talking, and after a few seconds I continued, "Look, I'm just a silly old man. I have no family, and I've never had a family except for Sarah, and your laugh reminded me of her. I wanted to meet you, and now I have, and I should be happy. In six days I'm leaving for the United States, and I may not return for a long time, but I wanted to meet you before I left. It would be nice to see you again, and hear your wonderful laugh a few more times before I leave for the United States, and when I return I hope to see you again if it's God's will."

Berenice smiled and said, "Don't worry. I come here almost every day for one thing or another, so if you're here, it's likely our paths will cross again. Would you mind answering a question for me?"

"Of course," I said, "I'll try to answer any question you ask me."

"Well, El Cabby, what's your real name?" She said, "There isn't a person I know of who has a name as unusual as El Cabby. It makes me think you've driven a taxi for thirty years, but I don't believe that's true. So what's your real name?"

After thinking a few seconds I said, "Berenice, you're right; El Cabby isn't my given name. El Cabby is a Spanish nickname which is a little hard to explain right now. Perhaps when I get to know you better we can discuss my nickname, but my given name is Thomas Anthony Rodriguez. If you don't mind I would appreciate it if you called me El Cabby; otherwise, I think Tommy would do. However, I wouldn't be as comfortable being called Tommy."

Berenice smiled and said, "I will call you El Cabby, and I think we'll be friends for a long time. Tell me, is El Cabby for El Caballero, or is there more to it than that?"

I replied, "There is a lot more to my name than El Caballero, but that's a nice try, and perhaps some day I'll tell you the whole meaning behind my name. Besides, if I keep a few things from you it might create some intrigue between us."

Berenice said, "Intrigue it is for sure, my friend. May I ask you another question?"

"Of course, you can ask me as many questions as you would like," I replied.

"In Mexico we still use the peso for money, while the United States and Canada have switched to the microchip. They're now inserting the microchip in people here in Mexico; however, it will not be activated until everyone in the country has one, and they haven't even started in Guanajuato yet. I hate the idea of having a microchip in my body, as it makes me feel invaded to know that other people who I don't know can communicate with something in my body. I will accept the microchip though, because I don't want to live in one of the camps they set up for those who refuse it. So can you tell me what it's like to have a microchip in your arm? I've heard too many horror stories about the microchip, infections, and people's bodies rejecting it a month after receiving it. Knowing you're American I assume you have the microchip and will use it on your trip next week."

I replied, "Berenice, you really have a way of asking me hard questions I don't like to answer. I have the chip; however, I don't have a mark where it was inserted. I hate the microchip just like you do, and I didn't want to accept it, because I have allergic reactions to certain metals. My doctor gave me a temporary waiver until the series-two chip is released. When I return to the States they'll insert the series-two microchip whenever they have one for me. I'm a special case, and if you want to see the microchip I carry now, I can show it to you." I reached into my pocket and pulled out a small plastic card with the chip on it, and showed it to her.

"Geez," Berenice said, "I didn't know they had a chip like this for special cases. I have a friend who works with the Health Department who works with chip insertion, and she has never mentioned it to me, so I'm surprised I haven't heard of this before."

"Berenice, please don't tell your friend about my microchip," I replied. "I have no idea what your country's procedures are for microchip insertion. In the States, they don't want anyone to know about the series-two microchip until it's been tested and approved. You see, the series-two microchip is one hundredth the size of the one inserted in everyone's arm today. The series-two is so small that it will be injected through your eyelid into the skin near the brain. If it works like they think it will, it should be much easier to install, and much harder to remove. If I have anything to say about it, I may never receive the series-two microchip either, but I probably won't have a choice. By the way, I will get the series-two microchip in the arm and in the head because of my allergic reaction to certain metals."

"El Cabby," Berenice said, "would it be possible for me to come and visit with you later this evening in your home? I would like to discuss a few things with you in private."

"I think we can arrange that, Berenice," I said. "Will you be coming alone, or is someone coming with you?"

Berenice said, "I would like to bring a friend with me, if that's okay?"

"Can you give me their name?" I asked. "I would really like to know what their name is, and where they live, before I say yes."

"His name is Juan Pablo, and he's from a little border town up north near Mexicali called Los Algodones," she replied.

El Cabby looked around and said, "Is there a number where I can call you? When I arrive at home and check my schedule I'll call you and tell you what time you, and your friend, can come and visit with me."

"Sure," Berenice said. "My cell number is 473-122-4207, and I leave it on all the time except for when the phone is charging."

"Thanks Berenice," I said. "I will be in touch with you later, and I look forward to this evening when we can discuss everything you want to talk about."

Berenice stood up and said, "Well, my friend, I'll see you later." Then she left.

I immediately sent an encoded message from my Blueberry making an inquiry about Berenice and her friend, Juan Pablo. Depending on the answer I received, I might have to evade, or kill, two people tonight. I couldn't stand the thought of killing either one, especially someone as nice as Berenice appeared to be. Nonetheless, if it's what it came down to, I was capable of murder. The Knights of the Night couldn't take a chance on someone infiltrating our organization, or getting their hands on me for the wrong reasons, so I'd do whatever I had to do.

An hour later I had all the information I needed. In fact, I had a pleasant surprise, because I learned that Berenice was already a person of interest who might possibly want to join The Knights of the Night. She's definitely not an enemy I have to worry about. I also found out that Juan Pablo is a leader in The Knights of the Night already, and very highly regarded in the North Mexican Region. The home office also sent an encrypted picture of Juan Pablo, so I could be sure no one was using a stand-in to get to me for the wrong reasons.

I let out a sigh of relief, and immediately called Berenice and invited both of them to visit me at my home at eight that evening.

Guanajuato is not like any other city in Mexico, and it's like some small cities in Europe. Guanajuato is a very old city built on the sides and tops of mountains, with many small alleys and narrow streets. Most of the people live in small houses that are connected.

It was by pure luck that I found a completely furnished house to rent on top of one of the mountains. It had four bedrooms and three baths, as well as a living room, family room, and kitchen. It was more than I needed, but it gave me a place to hang my swords and plenty of bedrooms in case I had to put someone up for a few days.

Berenice and Juan Pablo arrived on time at my home, and when I cordially invited them inside, Berenice said, "It's really nice to see you again, El Cabby. This is my friend, Juan Pablo, and we went to the same secondary school, but he now lives on the border of the United States."

I interrupted her when I said, "I know, Berenice. Juan Pablo is from Los Algodones. I know who he is, and I know most everything there is to know about him. I also know he's here to help you join The Knights of the Night."

I wasn't trying to be rude, but I wasn't a person for a lot of small talk. Being outspoken was a weakness of mine that many times created problems for me. Berenice looked at me in disbelief and said, "You know everything about Juan Pablo, then I suppose you know everything about me, too. So, what in the hell am I doing here? I don't understand you, except you are the most frustrating person I've ever met."

"Berenice, I'm sorry!" I said. "I didn't mean to upset you, but my work is sensitive and I need to know who I'm talking to. You said you wanted to visit me, and bring a friend, and then you tell me he's a man. I had to be damn sure this wasn't some kind of a setup. After all, I just met you this afternoon, and the bad guys still kidnap people in this country. They hold them for ransom, and kill them if they don't get it, so I'm sorry if you're upset, but that's your problem, not mine."

Berenice was still infuriated and tried to compose herself; however, her anger still showed. She said, "So you thought I was a prostitute and was bringing my pimp so he could kidnap you after we had sex. Oh, that's just great! Then maybe we could have made money twice in the same day by putting you up for ransom. They would have found your body along the road somewhere and then...and they..." and she started to laugh as she continued, "brought you back to Guanajuato in a taxi and it would have given your name, El Cabby, a whole new meaning. Ha, ha, ha!" Then she started laughing uncontrollably as she sat on the couch, and put her head in her hands.

I walked over to Juan Pablo and said, "I'm sorry, Juan Pablo. I hope this doesn't destroy our chance to be friends. It seems you and I have a lot in common, and I would like to start all over from the beginning if we can."

Juan Pablo smiled and said, "Well, El Cabby, I checked you out too, but I couldn't tell Berenice anything, because she doesn't know about our organization. I will only say I'm honored to meet you, and I hope we can be friends for a long time."

Berenice looked at Juan Pablo in disbelief and said, "Not you too! How in the hell did you check El Cabby out? Why did you check him out? You had no reason to worry about anything, and I told you he was a nice man who has experience using the microchip. All I wanted to do was to talk to him this evening, and learn how the microchip has changed things in the United States.

"You had nothing to worry about, and no reason to check him out. I wish I knew what was going on here, because this was supposed to be a quiet evening for me to learn about the U.S." She was quiet for a few seconds and then she said, "Will someone please tell me what the hell is going on here?"

I said, "Berenice, I want you to understand it's important I maintain my anonymity. You also need to know I don't know everything about you. I do know, at this point in time, you are okay in every way as far as I'm concerned to become a member of The Knights of the Night. I also understand you have an interest in joining the Knights, and I can help you if it's true. If you're interested, then we have some serious issues to take care of before we can discuss anything about The Knights of the Night. The first thing you'll have to do is to take your clothes off for a minute, so I can check you for wires and tattoos. If it makes you uncomfortable to have Juan Pablo here he can leave the room."

"You dirty old son of a bitch!" Berenice said. "You haven't got a decent bone in your body! You're just a dirty old man!" Berenice turned and headed for the door to leave, and she would have made it, except for Juan Pablo stepping in front of her, and blocking her exit.

"Berenice," he said, "don't go off the deep end. I understand why El Cabby needs to have you take your clothes off, and it's not because he's a dirty old man. I'm sorry, but if you really want to join The Knights of the Night, then you'll have to do what he says."

You could see Berenice was furious. She looked at Juan Pablo with an angry face and said, "You mean to tell me you also know who El Cabby is, what he does, why he lives here, and what he's up to? Do you? Do you?" She was screaming and almost out of control. "Is there any chance I can find out anything about what's going on here?"

I held up my hand hoping it would distract her and calm her down. "Berenice, if you allow us to do this visual inspection then either Juan Pablo, or I, will tell you a lot of things you'd like to know about The Knights of the Night. It's also possible we'll tell you many things you won't want to know." I reached over to one of my Chinese swords hanging on the wall and grabbed a piece of paper from the printer sitting nearby. I held the paper up as high as my head and then dropped it, and as it fell to the floor, I cut it in three pieces with the sword. "Did you see how sharp the sword is, Berenice? You can have this sword while you take your clothes off, and if I get too close, take the sword and slice me into little pieces."

Berenice looked at me in disbelief and said, "I'll take the sword, but let's hope I don't have to use it, because you won't like it if I do. The first thing I'll cut off will be your manhood."

"Okay," I said as I laughed, "let's keep everything under control."

Berenice reached for the wall switch and was going to turn off the lights in the room, but Juan Pablo's hand stopped her as he said, "Come on, Berenice; just do what El Cabby says. If you don't, you may never become a Knight, and I might have to watch El Cabby as he puts you out of your misery. Believe me, I wouldn't enjoy watching him end your life."

Berenice looked at Juan Pablo in disbelief, but Juan's face had an expression of dead seriousness. Berenice said, "Juan Pablo, you can leave the room, and I should be out in a few minutes. If I'm not, you come in and use this sword on El Cabby."

She started taking her clothes off and I said, "You can place them on the bed if you like. I'm going to sit over here on this chair, and when you're naked just make a slow turn around, and we'll be through in a few seconds. I realize this is very hard on you, and I apologize, but later you'll understand why this procedure is necessary before we can even talk about The Knights of the Night."

It took Berenice a minute to get her clothes off, and slowly turn full circle. Then I said, "You're okay, Berenice; you can put your clothes on, and join us in the other room."

I left Berenice, then joined Juan Pablo in the other room and told him, "Berenice is fine and she'll be out in a minute. My understanding is Berenice has been cleared for membership if she wants to join, and of course she doesn't even know she has already been cleared for membership. I also understand you were sent to Guanajuato to talk to her, and bring her into The Knights of the Night if she wanted to join."

Juan Pablo replied, "El Cabby, you're correct on both counts, but with a temper like Berenice's, do you think she'll make a good Knight?"

"Of course I believe she'll be a good Knight," I replied. "She was shocked by what we knew about each other, and then we tell her she has to take her clothes off. I'm surprised she didn't storm out of here, and tell us both to get lost. When she returns to the room, I think you should take her aside, and explain who I am. I presume you've been given all the information about the demonstrations and possible conflict next week, and I assume you're involved in making it happen, just like I am."

Juan Pablo replied, "Yes, I'll be taking part in the demonstration at the Marine Air Base in Yuma, and when the conflict has actually started, I will be part of the team to neutralize the base. We have made studies of the base and we believe we can capture it without a great loss of life on either side. We're planning on utilizing some of the new microwave guns in the conflict, and I hope it will lead to many of the Marines surrendering to us."

Just as Juan Pablo stopped speaking, Berenice closed the door and entered the room. I looked at her and said, "Berenice, Juan Pablo is going to tell you about The Knights of the Night. It's going to take him at least an hour to tell you everything you need to know, and then he'll answer your questions. When you're through discussing what he has told you, he will ask if you still want to join the Knights. If your answer is yes, then you'll both come to the family room upstairs where I will swear you in. After I swear you in, Juan Pablo will tell you what is happening next week, and he will order you a microchip like I carry in my pocket, and hopefully, you'll never need to have one in your body."

Berenice laughed and said, "What if I decide I don't want to join the Knights, will you kill me?"

"Not tonight," I said with a smile. "Perhaps next week, if you don't keep your mouth shut about everything you're told tonight. Now I'm going to go upstairs and watch TV, and you both come to see me when you're ready, okay?"

Juan Pablo nodded his head and said, "Okay, El Cabby."

Berenice asked me as I was going up the stairs, "El Cabby, you won't tell anyone about my tattoos, will you?"

I looked at her and said, "There's no way I'll tell anyone about those tattoos." At the same time I was thinking, *What in the world is she talking about? She didn't have any tattoos on her body.*

It was over an hour later when they came upstairs and told me Berenice definitely wanted to join the Knights. I asked her, "Are you sure you want to do this? It's going to be very dangerous after next week, and you could be killed just for being a Knight."

Berenice said, "I understand; however, life without freedom of choice isn't really life at all."

Then I swore her in and gave her a copy of our creed which Berenice proceeded to read…

(See Back Cover of Book)

One sword is the sword of redemption and is used to defend the freedom of all people whether rich or poor. The second sword is the sword of justice that is used to cut down the enemies of true freedom and to set the captives of injustice free at last.

The shield within the shield acknowledges that each True Knight recognizes a higher power that is symbolized by the cross of crucifixion that destroyed the lives of thousands during the Dark Ages, and symbolizes a new life free of persecution for those who accept the way of the True Knights.

The hanging scale has a double meaning and one of those meanings is to be kept secret for a period of time.

The other meaning of the hanging scale is for justice for all people regardless of nationality, race, color, gender, wealth, or creed.

The many colored stripes on the background of the broader shield stand for all the colors, languages, and nationalities of the people of this world who were born to be free from injustice and persecution.

The white background of the inner shield represents the purity of heart and mind that is forever being sought by the True Knights of this organization. White is the opposite of darkness and thus fights the darkness of this world brought on by those who believe that wealth and prosperity are the only measures of success for mankind.

The swords are fastened to the back of the shield temporarily, but will soon be released in the struggle for freedom and justice for all.

When Berenice finished reading our creed, we went back downstairs to finish our visit. We sat down and I whispered in Berenice's ear, "What tattoos? I didn't see any tattoos on your body, and I have to report any tattoos you have to the home office so they can use them for identification if necessary."

Berenice smiled and then whispered in my ear, "You're such a nice old man. You were more self-conscious about seeing me nude than I was about letting you see me. You were so busy looking for a microphone, or a wire on my body, you didn't even notice I have a tattoo of a bee on the left cheek of my buttocks, and a bee just above my right nipple. If you would have come closer, you could have been stung." She giggled.

I looked at Berenice and whispered in her ear, "Perhaps I'd better take another look just to be sure those bees haven't moved." Then we both laughed.

Juan Pablo didn't know what was going on, and he was waiting to tell Berenice everything else she needed to know about the Knights. He said, "Hey folks, either you let me in on your secret or I'm going home."

Berenice replied, "Juan Pablo, I guess I'd better sit down with you so we can finish my indoctrination." Then she looked at me with a gleam in her eye and said, "I guarantee you my tattoos haven't moved, and I also guarantee you any decent man my age has a better chance of seeing those tattoos than you do."

When they finally came upstairs, it was during a bombing run in a war movie and I was sound asleep on the couch. Then I jumped to my feet immediately as I heard the sound of air-raid sirens, because Berenice and Juan Pablo had turned up the sound on the TV. Berenice was laughing at me so loudly she could have raised the dead.

I just shook my head and smiled and then said as I sat down, "Okay, Berenice, your first assignment will be with me as my secretary and right-hand man as well as my bodyguard. I will also be your mentor until I retire, or die. I had previously requested a secretary who could also be a bodyguard, and the home office told me if I found the right person for the job to go ahead and fill the position. The only requirement was I could only have one person to fill both positions. Now you know your assignment, Berenice, because you have more responsibility than you ever dreamt was possible, and this could be one of the most difficult things you've ever done in your life."

Berenice just stared at me in disbelief, and said, "Hold on a second, I've just joined The Knights of the Night, and I don't know anything, so how can I possibly be able to do all those things for you?"

I smiled and said, "Look Berenice, I've been with this organization since the very beginning. I've been a Knight, and I've been the Grand Seneschal: I've done it all. Our organization is short of, or lacking, enough men or women to get the regular work done let alone furnish me the help I need. My eyesight is failing, but my brain is still functioning, and I can handle all the tasks that I just gave you to do. However, in the heat of this conflict, I may need all the help I can get. Therefore, if we're in a meeting, you'll take my notes, and that's as much as I need for a secretary other than taking calls when I'm busy with other things. Being the bodyguard is easy after a little training with your new Uzi. If we hire another person who I'm comfortable with, I'll utilize them as a bodyguard and driver. Therefore, you'll be less burdened with doing everything yourself. How does that sound?"

Berenice replied, "I hope you can find someone to help us soon, because I feel overwhelmed right now."

I said, "Juan Pablo, before you return home tomorrow take Berenice to the regional office under the Mercado, and get her a Blueberry, and give her a quick lesson on how to use it. Then go through the manuals with her on sending and receiving encrypted messages. While you're there, I want you to arrange for her to have a course in defensive driving skills the day after tomorrow. I also want you to order her a new Uzi and a thousand rounds of ammunition and then arrange a training schedule for her to learn how to use it. Set up the Uzi school for the day after her driving school is completed if it's possible. With everything happening right now I need her to be online as soon as she can be ready.

"Berenice, I want you to be here every night at eight for the rest of the week for indoctrination class with me on the history of the Knights. You can also brief me every night about how your training is coming along. I will also tell you at the briefings of any changes in our plans for next week. If you want to, you can have dinner with me at La Pirinola Restaurant at six before we come to the house, but I'll leave it up to you. Okay you two, it's time to head home and I hope everything goes fine. If you need my assistance give me a call and I'll see what I can do to help you.

"Juan Pablo, see that Berenice gets home safely. I also hope you have a safe journey home tomorrow after you've arranged for Berenice's training schedule."

Berenice turned and asked, "Can I ask one more question before we go?"

"Just one," I said with a smile.

"Good," she said. "Then what do I do about my job? I'm supposed to go to work tomorrow."

"Oh, I'm sorry," I replied. "You need to quit your job tomorrow morning, before going with Juan Pablo to the office. Since you're starting here on such short notice, you'll receive a stipend from the Knights to help with your expenses.

"Now both of you get out of here, because I want to go to bed and get some rest after I finish my Irish coffee."

They left, and I sat there wondering if I'd done the right thing by hiring Berenice to be my bodyguard. After all, I didn't really know if Berenice could handle the job I had given her. I also knew I was putting her in a lot more danger than most Knights cared for immediately after joining. I was an ex Grand Seneschal, and if we were captured, she would probably be executed as my assistant.

A little while later I went to bed, but it wasn't easy to go to sleep, and I got up again and had a third Irish coffee to help me relax. I finally went to sleep on the couch watching television.

Chapter 5

March 15–19

The next day was a busy day for me because I had several high level meetings in order to organize everything concerning the pending demonstrations in the U.S. Around six in the evening I went to La Pirinola Restaurant, and I wasn't there very long before I heard wonderful laughter in the distance. I didn't have to think twice about who was coming: I knew who it was. It was my new friend and bodyguard, Berenice, and she arrived just as I was ready to order my meal. She had another young lady walking with her who I had never seen before.

I stood up as they approached the table and greeted them both with a kiss on the cheek since it's the normal way to greet a lady in Mexico. Then I said, "Berenice, it's good to see you, and you're just in time to order your meal."

"El Cabby, this is Evangelina," Berenice said with a smile. "She's been a friend of mine for a long time, and when I quit my job today she wouldn't let me out the door until I promised to meet her for dinner this evening. So I hope you don't mind since you're paying the bill," Berenice laughed.

I smiled and said, "Evangelina, it's nice to meet you and I'll gladly buy your dinner tonight." Then with a quick wink I added, "Berenice will buy our dinner tomorrow night."

Evangelina smiled and said, "It's nice to meet you too, El Cabby. I've heard a lot of crazy things about you on my way over here. I'm intrigued because so many things have happened very quickly with Berenice and getting her new job. Berenice happens to be my best friend, and I'm wondering if you could use someone else to add to your team. I'm also asking with the condition I like the job whatever it may be. Berenice won't tell me anything she does for you, so I'm approaching this with caution."

I replied, "Berenice isn't permitted to divulge any information pertaining to her new job because this is a new venture for our company. We're trying to keep what our company does very secret at this point in time, but if you're interested and have an adventurous heart, perhaps I can put you to work doing something. The pay isn't good, and the work is hard, but after next week there shouldn't be a dull moment for a while. Here's a three by five card and you can write down your name, address, phone number, and age on the first three lines, and on the remainder of the card, write down where you work, what kind of work you do, and your education after high school."

When Evangelina had finished filling out the card and returned it to me, I excused myself and went into the restaurant and sat down at an empty table. I took out my Blueberry and submitted the information to the home office asking for her clearance and permission to hire her. I explained that I might want to make her a Knight and use her with Berenice as part of my staff. Then I stipulated that as close as we were to starting the new operation, I would vouch for her based on Berenice's knowledge of her family and background, which I would verify within the next hour.

I returned to the table and said, "Evangelina, will you please excuse us; I need to speak to Berenice privately in the restaurant for a minute. We'll be right back."

I asked, "Berenice, how long have you actually known Evangelina, and be accurate, because it's very important."

Berenice didn't hesitate a second; she answered immediately. "I've known her for six years. I met her when we went to the university together and we've been best friends ever since."

I asked, "Have you ever met her family?"

She replied, "I've met her family several times; they're indigenous Indians from Michoacán and wonderful people."

I said, "Do you think she could work with us, keeping her mouth shut and her ears open, and could she do it for low pay?"

Berenice replied, "Knowing her family, and her background, I'd have to say, she would do anything to keep from being a slave, or losing her freedom."

I said, "Okay, you go back to the table, and enjoy your margarita with Evangelina. If I receive an approval from the home office, I can hire her tonight, and then send her to class with you tomorrow. Now go and visit with Evangelina and I will send a message saying everything checks out."

Berenice left, and I sent the message to the home office requesting a response as soon as possible. Then I returned to the table where the laughter stopped only when Berenice took a drink of her margarita. I sat down and said, "Let's order our meal so we can eat and get out of here since we may have a lot to do tonight." The girls laughed and I knew I was in trouble. I said, "Okay, what's so funny?"

Berenice laughed and said, "We've already ordered our meals and yours, and we hope you like what we ordered for you."

Evangelina sat there staring into space like she was completely innocent of everything and perhaps she was. I said with a concerned look on my face and a voice that was serious, "What did you order for me?"

Berenice said, "I ordered you a hamburger and fries."

I laughed and said, "It's my favorite meal, and it's exactly what I would have ordered. I'm a hamburger lover, and in my opinion, it's God's most perfect meal. You have meat for strength; you have veggies that include lettuce, tomatoes, and onions for most of your vitamins, and you have grains in the bun for fiber. What more could a man, or woman, ask for in a meal?"

The reply came from Berenice as she said, "Good Mexican food with lots of hot peppers, grease, and beans. Whether it's healthy or not doesn't matter, because if you're Mexican, you'll live forever in heart, as well as mind." She broke into one of her hilarious laughs as she sat back in her chair waiting for her meal to be served.

I laughed and sat back in my chair while I studied the two of them as they talked to each other. Berenice was cute, and a little on the thin side, about five-foot six-inches tall, and so fair skinned she almost looked Caucasian instead of Mexican. She had beautiful bright eyes, a quick mind, and a laugh that can knock you off your feet! She was a pleasure to be around, but perhaps too much fun for an old man like me. Evangelina was quite different: she was almost exactly the same height as Berenice, but she was what I call pleasantly plump, but definitely not fat. Her eyes were bright, and if you looked into them, you could see all the way to her heart. She had braids in her hair, and her skin was darker than Berenice's. I anticipated her becoming a great Knight, and I also knew I wanted her on my team as much as I had wanted Berenice working with me.

Our food was served and we started to eat. I'd only finished half my meal when my Blueberry beeped, and when I checked it the message read, "Evangelina is verified; however, this is based on your word and your willingness to take responsibility for her actions."

I smiled and said, "Well Evangelina, we're now beyond step one. After dinner if you come with us to my house, we'll see what we can do about hiring you for a position similar to the one that Berenice has. Of course, that depends on whether you're still serious about having a job with us."

"Yeaaaa! Caramba! Ooooeeee!" They screamed in unison. Everyone in San Fernando Plaza heard them screaming with joy, and even Cesar came running from inside the restaurant.

I said to the girls, "Hey cool it! You're attracting a lot of attention, and we need to stay low profile." The girls became quiet, but they were still grinning from ear to ear.

Everyone in the plaza was looking at us like we were crazy! After the girls calmed down, I said, "Don't get too excited. I didn't say Evangelina was hired yet; we have a lot more to talk about when we get to the house. You know, Berenice, she may not even want this job once she knows everything about it, so let's eat and head for the house as soon as we can."

We finished eating and left for my home. We all walked quietly which seemed unusual, especially since Berenice was with us, so I thought I would mention it. I asked, "Why's everyone so quiet all of a sudden?"

Berenice answered, speaking with a soft voice for a change, "It's something I learned from Evangelina a number of years ago. We were walking near her home in Michoacán, and while I was talking to her, she turned to me and told me to keep quiet and listen. When I stopped talking I heard the birds, the insects, even a wisp of wind as it passed through the trees. It's probably the first time I ever heard the voice of God as He speaks to us through His creation, and I just wanted to cry."

We sat down for a while in the forest, and then Evangelina told me to listen to the sound of impending terror and death. I strained my ears, and listening intensely, using every sense I had, I still couldn't hear anything more than the sound of an animal or a bird in a tree. She whispered for me to stay very quiet and follow her. Very quietly, we got up and tiptoed about thirty feet where she studied the trees. Then she pointed to a spot in one of the trees where we saw a cat crouched on a branch ready to pounce on a bird. A few seconds later, there was a loud noise as the cat killed the bird and then proceeded to eat its lunch. I told Evangelina the cat had just ruined my afternoon, and she couldn't comprehend why. She explained to me all things live, and die, and regardless of who we are, someday we will also die. It was an epiphany to me, and I understood Evangelina and her people knew more about life than I could ever comprehend. I was just her friend when we took that walk in the woods, but I've loved her as a sister from then on.

I looked at Berenice and could see a tear welling up in her eye and I said, "Thanks for sharing your story, Berenice, and thank you for being who you are, Evangelina." They just nodded their heads, and we continued on our way in silence.

I was proud of both these girls for different reasons, and I knew at this moment in time, I would be very blessed if I could make Evangelina a member of The Knights of the Night. When we arrived home, we knew we had to get serious about the task of bringing Evangelina into the Knights. It was much easier to get Evangelina to take her clothes off for inspection because Berenice was there and holding the sword. She taunted me, "Come on, big guy, just one false move, and you've had it!" I just laughed at her as she laughed back.

When Evangelina was naked, I asked her if she had tattoos and she answered, "No."

I said, "Well Berenice says she has tattoos of two bees on her body, but I didn't see the damn things from all the way over here."

Berenice said, "Do I need to undress again?"

I replied, "I am just teasing, Berenice. I believe you."

The rest of the night went quickly and we finished earlier than I thought we would. I asked Berenice to show Evangelina how to use the Blueberry for sending and receiving encoded messages. I also asked her to take Evangelina with her to the Defensive Driving course the next day, and I sent a note with her authorizing the training. I told them I would call and authorize an Uzi for Evangelina, and they could take the Uzi course together. I hoped everything would be okay; however, I told them to call me if they had any problems. It was about midnight when we completed everything and made Evangelina a Knight, and then I sent the girls home.

The next day was unusual because I didn't have any meetings scheduled so I got up early and took a walk around the Panoramica, which is a scenic route around Guanajuato. It was a long two-hour walk, which encompassed a distance of several miles up and down the mountains.

In the afternoon I went back over the logistics for the operation next week. One of the problems I face is a matter of logistics, and for me logistics means seeing to the needs of our Knights who are going into battle.

Even though we're preparing to fight the greatest army the world has ever known, we have some things in our favor. One of our advantages is that the United States is fighting a war in Afghanistan. With the conflict in Afghanistan to deal with, the Army and the Marines in the United States have their hands full. No one even knows for sure whether the U.S. military is capable of defending the United States against an invasion from a major adversary. Second, no one in their right mind expects a ragtag army of Knights without tanks, trucks, support, Navy, or Air Force to attack a military giant like the United States has.

We don't even have basic support for our Knights; for instance, if our troops need to eat, they have military surplus C-rations or whatever they can obtain from local stores or markets. We don't have trucks to carry supplies in large quantities to the troops, nor do we have any artillery, or air cover, like the U.S. military has. If the enemy knows where we are, they can easily wipe us out by sending in a few tanks and Apache helicopters. The final analysis is that it doesn't look good for us if we don't stay elusive by constantly changing location.

It will be to our advantage if we can disrupt the daily operations of their military and detain their forces by using our microwave guns effectively. We know we will suffer some casualties, and we also know we can only fight for two days at the most. If we last two days, we may accomplish our goal of getting the media's attention around the world, but the hardest part of the whole operation is in knowing we will lose the lives of good men and women in a battle we cannot win.

There are also some things in our favor: one is we will only be attacking military bases which are not highly defended because of their function and location. In our case, we only want to demonstrate at those bases long enough to get the media involved in order to get our own message out to the world. If we are on the news around the world for every disturbance we create, we will catch the attention of the people around the world six times or more.

We don't have any elaborate or unrealistic goals, except for one, and it's to get the people to read the handouts we will be giving out. Most people don't read handouts; they just glance at them and then throw them away. We're hoping people will read the handouts we're passing out in every country explaining the true purpose of the Illuminati and the Genebra Group. We also anticipate many people will be enraged by the information concerning our enemy, and then rally to our aid in any way they can. If enough people join the Knights, we could generate a situation which might set the enemy back for years. If we gain enough time to educate the masses where they are angered and concerned as to what is happening, we might achieve our goals and stop the New World Order. If we fail, we are lost forever, and there won't be another chance to fight this battle again in the future. The world will be lost to slavery through mind control of the human race forever.

Our plans are to only bring troops north to the border that can speak some English, and in this way, they can infiltrate the countryside easier because in the Desert Southwest there are thousands of Mexican Americans who don't speak much English. They live in Spanish communities and have Spanish-speaking employers and friends, so they don't really have a need to speak English.

The news in Mexico and the other South American countries is starting to report that thousands of people are moving to the north for the first mass pilgrimage of its kind. The Knights under the name of Latino Brotherhood for Christianity and Freedom had organized a pilgrimage to Guanajuato, Mexico, in order to climb the mountain to Christo Rey, and pray for an end to the insertion of the microchip in all the people of the Earth.

At Christo Rey there is a giant statue of Christ that can be seen for miles, and millions of people visit it every year for spiritual renewal and healing. Hopefully, the press will report that the people coming north to the city of Guanajuato in Mexico are coming for a pilgrimage, because that's what we planned.

When the Knights arrive here they are going to Christo Rey and pray at the statue of Christ. Then they will move by bus to the U.S. border at one of three locations. When they reach the border, they will also have a prayer vigil for those Mexicans who have already received the microchip. They will also protest the future insertion of the series-two chip that will be inserted through the eyelid and near the brain. The microchip that has been used in the arm is fairly easy to remove, but the new series-two will almost be impossible to remove because it is so small you can't even find it on an x-ray after it's installed.

Everything we have planned to do is taking place on schedule; for instance we ordered hundreds of buses to be at Christo Rey to pick up those on their pilgrimage and take them north to one of three locations for prayer and demonstrations. One of the groups of demonstrators, which are estimated at one thousand, will be bussed to Nogales about one hundred and nineteen miles south of Tucson, Arizona. They will protest the microchip for three days while they have Christian meetings and prayer. Meanwhile the second group of roughly eight hundred demonstrators will be bussed to Algodones which is seven miles from Yuma, Arizona, and the Marine air base. The third and largest group of demonstrators will be sent to Mexicali where a very large demonstration will take place near the border. In fact, we decided to have such a large demonstration at the border with people charging the gates, and creating turmoil that we are hoping the Border patrol will have to bring in reinforcements from the east to help control the crowds. We plan to explode some explosives, and destroy part of the fence along the border to make sure the border patrol and the U.S. Government take us seriously. Meanwhile, our troops at Algodones will make their way across the border, and take action at the Marine air base at Yuma.

After studying the situations we have to address dealing with the demonstrations in Arizona, it was evident we had more to deal with than I had realized before. Now, there wasn't any doubt in anyone's mind that we would be in full conflict with the Marines at their air base in Yuma. We weren't sure if we would last for two hours, or two days.

*   *   *

Four days later near Los Algodones, and in the heat of battle, the girls and I had become separated, and I hadn't seen them for over an hour when I was called to a meeting. We were about a mile and a half from the front lines, and we could hear the guns and mortar fire in the distance, and they sounded like they were getting dangerously close. I was tired and fearful for the girls because I didn't know if they were dead or alive. They had taken one of the Seneschals to the front lines in a Jeep to see how things were going. Since we'd gotten separated, and I hadn't heard anything, I was worried that something terrible had happened to them.

When the Grand Seneschal entered the room, his presence distracted my thoughts as he said, "Okay, we need to keep this meeting short and get out of here. From all indications every one should realize things aren't going in our favor. We've lost over a thousand Knights in two hours at the Marine base in Yuma, and we've lost four of our medics and we only had seven when we started. We aren't even close to taking the base, or even surviving the remainder of the day against the Marines. If we can't turn this battle around in the next two hours, we need to pack up and head back to Mexico. Let's face it: we're better off to have Knights who are alive, and ready to fight another day, than to have dead Knights who will never fight again."

The door opened, and a hand grenade flew across the room. "Hit the deck!" someone shouted.

In the same instant of time someone grabbed the hand grenade which was rolling around on the floor and shouted, "Open the door, quick!"

Someone opened the door, and just before he threw the grenade, I saw Berenice and Evangelina standing in the other room. In horror, I screamed, "Berenice and Evangelina, get out of there!"

By then, the hand grenade was on its way towards the door; however, it hit the doorframe causing it to bounce back into the room where we were. I immediately hit the floor; however, the grenade was now rolling towards me when suddenly it came to a stop approximately ten feet from where I was laying. Fearful for my life all I could do was pray that most of the shrapnel would go up instead of sideways.

The grenade exploded and so did I! I felt searing, burning pain down my right side, and it was the worst thing I had ever felt in my life. Everything around me was growing dim, and then black, and in the darkness, I could hear people shouting, but I couldn't comprehend what was being said. I was losing consciousness as I lost blood, and in the back of my mind, I knew I was slowly dying.

I woke up groggy and half blind, and didn't know where I was, but I could hear explosions in the distance. I could see two doctors and a nurse in the room with me, and they were talking to each other discussing a procedure they needed to perform.

One of the doctors was speaking, "He's in bad shape, and he could die even if we stay here. It's better if we load him in the truck and take him to Monterrey as soon as possible."

The other doctor said, "I personally know of miracles which occurred in MASH units during the war, and patients as bad as this one survived longer moves than from here to Monterrey, so let's get him ready to move. We'll load our equipment, and we'll all get out of here while we can."

"I think it's a great idea," one of the nurses said. "If he needs special medical attention on the way, we will be in the same truck where we can help him."

The doctor said, "I agree, prepare the patient for the move to Monterrey. We have been officially closed down for over an hour now, and we have to get out of here as fast as we can. We'll be back as soon as we are through with the patient in the other room. Meanwhile, give El Cabby a shot of morphine for the pain, and keep him calm while we finish up."

I could hear voices like they were somewhere off in the distance, and I was in total darkness feeling incapable of moving some parts of my body. It was a weird feeling like being frozen in time and space, but there wasn't anything I could do to change it even if I wanted to.

The nurse gave me a shot and I sank deeper into the darkness, and my pain disappeared as I entered into a different world where there was no pain, no worries, just peace and rest.

Later I woke up and I had no idea how long I had been unconscious. It could have been hours, days, months, or even years, as I had nothing to gauge time by. I decided I hadn't been out long though, because I still had pain from my head to my feet with most of it down my right side. I quickly discovered I had limited vision and I could also hear sounds of the conflict, and it sounded closer. Most of all, I was relieved to be back in the world again, even though it meant suffering some discomfort. I looked around the room, and didn't see anyone, and I realized my vision was worse than it had ever been. It was as if I could only see out of one eye, and I wanted to know why, so I lifted my right hand causing an excruciating pain in my shoulder and arm. I was determined to find out what had happened to my vision so I moved my arm in spite of the pain. After a few painful seconds of moving my arm, my right hand touched my head, and I realized why I couldn't see very well. My head was wrapped on the right side of my head and face, and the bandage covered my right eye causing some loss of vision. My right side, my right arm, my head, and my lower back were all very sore. I tried putting my arm back down at my side; however, the pain was so intense it caused me to black out again.

I woke up later and this time there was a nurse in the room, and I asked her, "Can you help me?"

"Only for a second," she said. "We have to get out of here and head for Monterrey, so make it quick and tell me what you need."

"What's going on?" I asked. "Where are my friends? You know, the two ladies who are part of my staff?"

She replied. "We're trying to get ready to move, because it's too dangerous to stay here any longer. You're in San Luis, Mexico, across the border from Yuma, Arizona, and in a little while we're moving you south to Monterrey. The good thing is you're still alive, and with all the blood you lost, I'd say you received a minor miracle; however, you have a long way to go before you're completely out of danger. We're getting ready to put you in the back of a pickup truck, and it won't be very comfortable, but we'll be with you. We'll stop every now and then, and give you pain medicine to try and keep you comfortable."

I asked, "Please, just one more question. Where are the girls who are part of my staff?"

She replied, "When we were cleaning up, and closing your wounds in Winterhaven, California, the girls were in a different building next door, and we believe a mortar round hit the building killing them both instantly."

When she finished her answer, I screamed, "Oh my God! Why didn't you take my life and let them live?" Then I blacked out again because the physical pain, along with the emotional pain, was too much for me to endure.

The nurse looked at me as I lay there unconscious, and she said, "It'll be a miracle if you survive the move to Monterrey, but I'll pray for God's blessing on your poor soul."

I was in a world of darkness looking for a light that wasn't coming, yet I could hear the nurse's voice. I was able to understand what she was saying, and I wanted to thank her for her concern for my soul, but I couldn't move, talk, or respond in any way. I was completely helpless, and it was okay, because I was at peace. The morphine was beginning to take effect again.

Chapter 6

March 20–April 11

I woke up in dread fear of losing my life. I was in the back of a pickup truck flying down a highway in total darkness. An explosion had just missed us causing both the truck and I to fly into the air. We both made a loud, sickening sound as the truck hit the pavement, and I hit the bed of the truck. The pillow which had been under my head was now on my feet, and my feet were moving with my body as I rapidly slid forward. I was sliding towards the front wall of the truck, "Oh God," I yelled as I hit my head. The pain was unbelievable from my head to feet and it was evident that the morphine had worn off, because I felt like a raw nerve in a broken tooth exposed to cold air. I thought I was dying right here and now, and as I finished the thought, another explosion hit next to the truck. Once again I was flying through the air as the truck, which was now on fire, continued on down the highway. After what seemed like a lifetime I landed in a mud puddle along the side of the road with such force I could feel my blood flowing from all my wounds at the same time. I felt like I was dying for sure, and there wasn't anyone around to save me this time.

My doctors and nurse died when the truck I had been riding in exploded. The explosion lit the night sky with a brilliant light, and made a sickening noise which muffled the cry of those in the truck who died almost instantly. Then everything was silent as if nothing had happened, and I knew it was only a matter of time until I would die as the others had. *Oh well,* I thought, *it doesn't matter because we all have to die some time anyway.*

It felt like blood was running from all my wounds again, and I wanted to get out of the mud puddle and on dry ground. I didn't want to be in a mud puddle. I slowly worked myself to my knees, and tried to stand up, but the pain from my back was too great, and I passed out as I fell on my face.

*   *   *

I could hear birds singing, and I could smell good Mexican food as I opened my eyes to survey my surroundings. I was in a bed in a small room which was maybe six-feet wide by nine-feet long with room enough for a bed, an armoire, and a bookcase. There were several blankets covering my body as it became slowly evident I was warm and alive. There was a soft breeze blowing through the open door, and a curtain moved back and forth, as the wind made it dance across the opening,

I listened quietly because I could hear a few people talking in Spanish outside my room, and I tried to figure out what they were saying, but I couldn't comprehend their words. Although I had lived in Mexico for several years, I had never learned enough Spanish to do me any good, so I wasn't sure what they were saying. I didn't know whether to get out of bed and go see what was going on, or just wait until someone came in. After a few minutes I decided the best thing I could do was walk to where the people were and try to communicate with them.

I started to slide out from under the covers, and I had only moved a few inches when I realized I wasn't going to get out of this bed at all. I was completely nude under the blankets, and I looked around the room, and there weren't any clothes laying around for me to put on. I certainly wasn't going to walk outside naked for the whole world to see. It gave me no other choice than to lie back in bed, and wait to see if someone had heard me moving around. When no one came in after a few minutes, I yelled, "Hey, can anyone help me?"

There was a lot of noise as people scurried around outside my room. "Cristina," someone yelled, then another person's voice about twenty feet away yelled Cristina's name again. The people were speaking in Spanish so quickly I couldn't understand what they were saying. Then I heard someone say, "El hombre, el hombre está despertando." (The man is awake.)

Less than a minute later a young lady came into the room and said, "Hello, my name is Cristina. I thought we would never see you wake up, but here you are, and I believe it's a miracle as well as an answer to prayer. What's your name, and what in the world happened to you?"

I looked at Cristina and didn't know what to say for a minute, and Cristina must have read my mind because she managed to get a smile on her face as she said, "It's okay. I won't tell anyone your name if you don't want me to."

I replied, "My name is El Cabby, and I'm a member of The Knights of the Night who were fighting the Americans on the border. I have been hurt in a blast from a hand grenade, and they were transferring me to Monterrey to a hospital when the truck I was in was blown up by artillery or something."

Cristina smiled and said, "We were hoping you're a member of the Knights, and we were right. Now take it easy and rest because you've been unconscious for over three weeks now. We weren't sure whether you were going to live or die, but everyone in our family camp prayed for you, and thank God you survived. You're in our family camp, and there are ten of us who live here, but I'm the only one who speaks much English. After the doctor looks at you and checks you out you'll get to meet the rest of my family. One of my sisters went to get the doctor, and hopefully, they will be here soon."

I said, "Cristina, I could use some clothes to wear after the doctor examines me because I don't want to run around naked for your whole family to see."

Cristina smiled and said, "You don't have to worry about being naked, because we've all seen you naked anyway. You see, we've all taken care of you since you've been here. Even my younger sisters needed to see your body when they bathed you, or changed the sheets, so El Cabby, I'd have to say everyone here already knows what you look like naked.

"I imagine you would like some clothes though, and I'll get you some to put on after Dr. Escobedo has examined you." She left the room, and I could hear her talking to someone in the adjacent room. When she returned, she had a small pile of clothes with underwear folded neatly on top. She smiled and said, "These clothes are my brother-in-law's, and he's a big man for a Mexican. I'm almost certain they'll fit you. I hope they're not too big, because you've lost a lot of weight in the last few weeks while you were fighting for your life."

I said, "Cristina, it's better if the clothes are too big, instead of too small, but looking at them I think they will fit me just fine. Can you tell me where I am, and how I got here?"

Cristina answered, "It was one night after the border war had started and we were at the central base in Algodones where we had been issued an Uzi submachine gun and some ammunition. Five Marine helicopters attacked us, and it was terrible with everyone running in different directions as the helicopters fired rockets to destroy everything in sight. We jumped in a hole, and there was a Knight who was bleeding from several wounds in it. He told us to take what we could and to return home as quickly as possible because they were about to lose the base. He said he was also leaving as soon as his driver returned to pick him up. He also told us we shouldn't return, until we heard the Knights were reorganizing.

"At any rate, we were coming down the road from Algodones as fast as we could with our headlights off and as we came around a corner we saw a burning truck a few hundred yards ahead of us. We stopped immediately, because we didn't know whether there were enemy ground troops around the burning truck or not. We wanted to wait and watch for a few minutes to make sure it was safe before we drove any closer. It was very quiet except for the occasional noise of artillery in the distance, and we just stood there in the darkness watching the truck burn. After we had been standing there for a minute, or so, we heard someone moaning, and we looked around and saw you lying in a mud puddle about fifteen feet in front of us. We didn't know if you were Mexican, or American, because it was too dark, and we didn't want to turn any lights on to see. We knew we couldn't leave you there to die whether you were a Knight, or an American, or a Mexican, because we're better people than that. We picked you up and laid you in the back of our pickup, and when we thought it was safe to travel we brought you with us. When we arrived here we carried you into our family camp, and when we saw you in the light we thought you would surely die. We felt perhaps we had risked our own lives in vain by trying to save a man who was dying anyway."

"Cristina," someone yelled, "the doctor's here."

A few moments later a young lady came in with a young man who was evidently the doctor. Cristina said, "This is one of my younger sisters, Veronica, and this is Doctor Escobedo."

I shook hands with the doctor, and he said, "Mucho gusto!" (It is my pleasure!) Then he turned to Cristina and said something in Spanish and waited for her to respond.

Cristina turned to me and said, "He only speaks Spanish; therefore, he will speak to me, and I will translate for you, okay?"

The doctor took his stethoscope out of his bag and listened to my chest. I studied his face as he listened. He was a young doctor maybe thirty-five years old, approximately five feet, six inches tall, well built, and looked like he worked out on a regular basis. He didn't smile, and you could tell he was serious about what he was doing as he checked me out.

He said something to Cristina, and she said to me, "Roll over on your left side and be still." I felt his cold stethoscope touch my bare back, and I jerked involuntarily as he listened to one lung and then the other. When he moved to get something else out of his bag, he made a comment to Cristina. "You can roll onto your back again," Cristina said, then the doctor said something else to Cristina, and she said, "Put the thermometer in your mouth and he is going to check your eyes as he takes your temperature." He checked my eyes and my ears very slowly as if he expected to find something wrong, and after a few minutes he removed the thermometer from my mouth and read it. Then he said something else to Cristina.

Cristina said, "Okay, now he wants you to sit up, very slowly, and hang your feet over the side of the bed."

I moved slowly because I was experiencing some pain in my back as I sat up, but I finally accomplished it as I lowered my feet towards the floor. The doctor had a sharp tool of some kind and was running it down my feet as he watched for a reaction. He said something else to Cristina who said, "Do you feel anything as the doctor runs the tool over your feet?"

"Of course I do," I replied.

The doctor smiled and spoke to Cristina, and I could tell he was happy with all the tests he had run. Cristina said to me with a smile, "The doctor says you look pretty good, considering what you've been through. He wants you to get dressed tomorrow, and you can start walking to the bathroom with our assistance. He also said you can have soft foods and fruits as well as drinking lots of fluids. He will come by again and see you tomorrow afternoon when he returns from Celaya.

"We will have to be careful, and make sure no one in the pueblo knows you're here, because the Mexican soldiers are searching for anyone who may have been in the fighting at Algodones three weeks ago. If anyone discovers you, they may turn you over to the soldiers, and then prosecute us for aiding the enemy."

I frowned and said, "I'm sorry I've put you and your family at risk, Cristina. I will leave as soon as I'm able to get around."

The doctor left and I looked at Cristina and her sister Veronica and said, "Is there any word regarding what The Knights of the Night are doing?"

Cristina replied, "We don't receive much news here, although every now and then they report on the news about the demonstrations going on around the world. It's also common knowledge many people around the world are joining the Knights because of what has happened."

I said, "Worldwide – did you say worldwide?"

Cristina smiled, and said, "You may have lost the battle, but you've temporarily won the war. The battles you fought, and lost, drew a lot of attention worldwide, and the fliers The Knights of the Night distributed have been very effective. Millions of people around the world became outraged concerning what the fliers said was happening, and they demanded to know if the fliers were correct. After a few days without receiving any logical answers about what was going on, some of the people decided to join the Knights. I don't know how many people actually joined, but I would guess millions of new people around the world have joined The Knights of the Night since the battle at Algodones. Here in Mexico, they stopped implanting the chip and they're having a hard time explaining what's happened. The

Mexican people are also upset because the Americans are demanding any Knights of the Night living in Mexico turn themselves in whether they were involved in the border fight or not. They're also pressuring the Mexican Army to find any Americans who fought in those battles and turn them in so they can be tried for treason. So far, the Mexican Army has been doing a halfhearted search for people like you. The people of Mexico think you're doing the right thing, and they've waited a long time for a hero to set them free from political oppression.

"However, the Mexican Army may get more involved in looking for The Knights of the Night in this country. We have many Mexican people living in the United States, and our government doesn't want to create problems for them by not being cooperative. I also think there will be thousands more Mexicans joining in the fight as Knights of the Night over the next few months."

I sat back in the bed and thought a few seconds about what Cristina had just said, and then I said, "If you two will leave me alone, I'll put on some underclothes, and then you can help me to the bathroom."

Cristina looked at Veronica, and said something in Spanish, then looked at me and said, "Hey, Doctor Escobedo said you could put your clothes on and go to the bathroom tomorrow. He's counting on you getting some nutrition and liquids into your body before we start taking you around our family camp, and that's the way it's going to be!"

I looked at Cristina and said, "Who put you in charge here? Where are your parents?"

Cristina frowned, and said, "All I need is a grown man to take care of who can't follow doctor's orders. Look, El Cabby, my father works in the United States, and when he's there I'm in charge here, and I am to take care of everything he would do if he were still here. Since you don't know enough Spanish to communicate, you fall under the same category as one of my sisters whether you like it or not."

I said, "Okay! You win, but I'm not one of your sisters. You said everyone helped take care of me, and everyone saw me nude; therefore, you must know I'm a man, right? I'm not, nor will I ever be, one of your sisters!"

Cristina said, "El Cabby, if there is something on your body which points to the fact you're a man... Well, I didn't notice it." Then she broke out laughing as she said, "I'm sorry, I shouldn't have said that."

Struggling to suppress a laugh I said, "It's okay – when you quit laughing, let's have a truce. I have to go to the bathroom, but I only have to pee, so what do we do?"

Cristina smiled and said, "Now you're being more cooperative." Then she reached under the bed, pulled out a bedpan, and handed it to me. "Someone will be here in a few minutes to pick it up, and empty it, meanwhile, I'll see if I can find something for you to eat and drink."

A few minutes later one of Cristina's other sisters came in, and smiled as she said, "My name is Socorro."

I pointed a finger at myself as I said, "My name is El Cabby."

Then she smiled, as she picked up the bedpan, and left the room. A few minutes later she returned and placed it back under the bed before leaving again.

I thought to myself, *Oh, this is going to be great fun.*

Ten minutes later Cristina brought me some purple water to drink, and some mashed fruit to eat. Cristina explained, "The purple water is made from a local flower called Jamaica, and is full of vitamins which are good for all of us." Then after I had eaten some of the fruit she brought, she left the room and returned with more of her family members.

There was her mother Luz, her younger sister Socorro, a sister Maria, another sister Rocio, and another sister Veronica. After she introduced them to me, I asked her to tell them thanks for their assistance in helping me. When Cristina told them what I had said, they all stood there smiling, as if to tell me it's okay. As they left the room, they shook my hand one at a time and gave me a kiss on the cheek, and I was completely overwhelmed with all the attention.

Then Cristina left again only to return with more family. There was her grandfather Salvador, his wife Antonia, along with a friend of the family whose name is Jorge. Cristina also gave them my message, and they all shook my hand and gave me a kiss on the cheek as most of them left. Jorge and Cristina stayed behind.

Cristina said, "Now you have met all the people in our family camp, and every one of them helped take care of you in one way or another. Even Jorge came to help us in moving you around when we needed extra muscle."

I said, "Cristina, please tell Jorge I appreciate his help too."

Cristina smiled and said, "You can tell him; he's standing in front of you, and he knows some English too. He's studying English at the University of Guanajuato, as well as tourism, which he hopes to make his career."

I smiled and said, "Thanks Jorge, I really appreciate your help, and I'm sure Cristina's family does too."

Jorge smiled and said, "It's okay. I was glad to help, and I will be just as happy when you're gone."

I sat up, and said, "Is there something wrong I don't know about?"

Jorge said, "You may not know it, El Cabby, but Cañada de Caracheo is a small pueblo, and there aren't many men here because most of them work in the States. If the military discovers you are here, it could be dangerous for all of us, and I don't want that to happen. Imagine the harassment the women and children would have to endure if the army found you here. So, I'll feel better when you're long gone, and we return to normal."

I could tell by his facial expression it wasn't easy for Jorge to say what he'd just said, and I wasn't sure what to say to him. I looked directly at Jorge hoping he would realize I was serious as I said, "I understand, Jorge, and I plan to leave just as soon as I can."

He looked down so I couldn't see his eyes, and said in a very low voice, "I'm sorry, El Cabby. I probably shouldn't have said those things to you."

I responded, "It's okay, Jorge. I'm not upset with you, and I appreciate the fact you're outspoken. Let's see how quickly I can recover and get out of here."

Cristina spoke up and said, "Well El Cabby, one of the things you need to do now is to get your rest, and build up your strength, so why don't you get some sleep, and we'll see you in the morning. I'll tell everyone they don't have to do anything for you tonight so they can also get some rest. If you need anything, just ring the bell by the bed, and I'll be here within a minute." Then Cristina and Jorge left the room.

I turned out the light and sat in the dark contemplating what I would do next. First, I would have to get my health back, and become strong enough to travel. Then I'd have to move out of here and back to Guanajuato as soon as possible, so I didn't put anyone here in jeopardy. They've already put themselves in enough danger, and I don't want to jeopardize them any more than I already have. I lay back in bed, and after a few minutes, I slid under the covers and fell asleep.

I woke up early the next morning when I heard someone moving around outside my room. I didn't know who it was, but they were making too much noise to be an intruder.

Whoever it was must have been in the kitchen, because after a few minutes I could smell coffee brewing and bacon cooking. Oh God, I wanted some bacon; my mouth was watering from the smell, and I hoped I would be eating my share of the bacon soon. A half an hour later, Cristina came into the room with a plate of watermelon, some natural grain cereal, and juice.

I said, "Cristina, you can't expect me to eat this after lying here and smelling bacon cook all morning – I love bacon!"

Cristina smiled, and said, "El Cabby, the doctor said to give you soft foods and liquids today, but I'll tell you what I'll do if you promise to quit complaining. I'll bring you a cup of coffee, and one piece of bacon after you've finished all the food I just brought you."

"Okay Cristina, I'll shut up right now, and you can get my coffee and bacon, meanwhile I'll get busy and eat this breakfast."

Cristina smiled and said, "I'll bring your coffee and bacon after I eat my breakfast, and by then, you should have finished yours." Then Cristina left to go eat her breakfast.

While I was eating breakfast I thought about Cristina: she's a very thin woman about five feet, six inches tall with black hair and beautiful olive-colored skin, which helps give her a youthful look. Most of the time, she has a very serious expression on her face, but then I suppose it comes from having to be the man of the family and trying to take care of her sisters. She isn't serious all the time because I had seen her smile a few times in the last day since I regained consciousness: once, when Jorge told me he would be glad to see me go, and the other, when she told me everyone had seen me naked. When she told me about everyone seeing me naked, I got the impression she was enjoying the moment because she possibly has a taunting side which makes her want to tease me. She appears to be very young and probably in her mid 20s, highly educated, and a good athlete. She will make some man a good wife someday if she can settle down and stop being the father in this family camp, and live her own life. Within five minutes Cristina came back with my coffee and half a piece of bacon.

I whined, "Cristina, I said a piece of bacon, not half a piece of bacon."

She smiled and said, "This is a piece of bacon, but I agree it's not a strip of bacon like you probably wanted." She shoved the bacon into her mouth and ate it, and then said with a smile, "You promised not to complain all day, and look what's happened already."

I just frowned and tried to look melancholy as I finished my breakfast. When I finished eating Cristina reached into her shirt pocket, and pulled out a full strip of bacon wrapped in a napkin. She handed it to me with the cup of coffee, and said, "I hope this makes you happy. How do you feel this morning?"

"Thank you, I feel pretty good now," I replied, as I shoved the bacon into my mouth and then chewed it slowly savoring the flavor before I continued, "I'm anxious to start getting around and building up my strength."

"Good," she said. "Here are your clothes. I'll give you thirty minutes to put them on, and then I'll return, and we'll take a walk to the bathroom and back. We'll see how that goes before we plan any other activities for today." She started to leave the room, and then she stopped to ask me, "If you need help with getting dressed just ring the bell, and someone will come to assist you." She then left the room taking my dirty dishes with her.

Thirty minutes later Cristina and her grandfather Salvador were in the room and ready to take me for my first walk to the bathroom. Salvador is a small man compared to me, and Cristina isn't very big either, so holding me upright could be a challenge if we had any problems. I said, "Do you really think the two of you can support me if I start to fall?"

"I don't know," Cristina said. "Let me get my mother to walk behind us just in case we need some help."

A minute later the four of us started through the family camp to the bathroom, and when we got there after walking thirty-five feet we headed back, and instead of going back to my room, we decided to sit outside in the fresh air. Someone had set up chairs from the kitchen in an open space, and it was ready for us to sit down as soon as we got there.

Cristina's mother Luz, her grandmother Antonia, her sisters Maria and Veronica, Cristina, and her grandfather Salvador were all there. It was a beautiful day with amazing blue skies, a few wispy clouds, and a slight breeze. Looming behind the family camp was a mountain shaped like an upside-down cone with communication towers on the top. The Ortiz's family camp and Cañada de Caracheo sat right at the base of the mountain.

I said, "This is really nice, but you didn't tell me we were sitting at the base of a mountain."

"Culiacan," her grandfather Salvador said with a smile.

I looked at Cristina, and said, "I didn't think anyone else spoke English in the camp?"

Cristina smiled and said, "Everyone speaks a little English because they teach some English in the elementary schools. My grandfather Salvador worked in the United States many years ago, not only in the state of Florida, but also in several other states. He still remembers some of the English words he used at that time. I also have a brother who lives and works on a farm in Wisconsin. My father lives in the Los Angeles area and works in construction, and my father and brother both speak some English.

"There's no one other than myself in the family camp who speaks enough English to carry on a conversation with you. The longer you're here, the more you'll find everyone will be learning more English and trying to communicate."

Everyone just sat there quietly contemplating me, or the weather, or something, but no one said anything. Finally, I said, "Tell me about Cañada de Caracheo: How big is it? Where is it located other than at the base of Culiacan? How many people live here?"

Cristina smiled and said, "Cañada de Caracheo is near the city of Cortazar and the nearest big city is Celaya. Celaya is one of the largest cities in the state of Guanajuato, and it's about ninety miles from the city of Guanajuato, which is the capital of the state. We have close to a thousand people in Cañada de Caracheo when everyone is home from the United States. This time of year, we might have seven hundred people and seventy to eighty percent of those people are women and children. We sit at the base of the mountain since it's a favorite place for all of us because it represents home. The mountain has everything a person could possibly want, including the ruins of pyramids, huge caves, wild animals, water, and places to sit and appreciate God and nature. Jorge and I love to camp on the mountain."

"Wow!" I said. "Maybe when I get stronger we can climb up the mountain and see the caves and pyramids."

Cristina replied, "Perhaps, and only if it's safe for you to move around outside. I don't think it'd be safe for you now, because the army has a checkpoint a kilometer down the road. They are constantly checking to see if anyone has seen any Americans."

"I know," I said, "but sometime I hope we will get to do more than walk around the family camp."

"You don't expect much of yourself, do you?" Cristina said. "You've just had your first walk in over three weeks, and you're ready to climb Culiacan and walk the streets of Cañada de Caracheo. I think perhaps you can wait a few days before you try doing those things, don't you?"

"Okay Cristina," I said, "I know you're right, and I am getting tired, so if you'll forgive me, I will go lie down for a while. In a few hours I would like to take a walk to the bathroom again. In fact, I would like to do it four times today and maybe six times tomorrow, if someone's willing to help me. Possibly, in a few days we'll add a walk around the family camp, and then see where we can go from there."

Cristina and her mother came over to help me get up and back to my bed because I was really tired. We did take a walk to the bathroom three more times before the day was over, and I was exhausted when I went to bed that night.

I grew stronger by the day, and within a few weeks I felt like I was ready to do even more to get my strength back. I decided it was time to take a walk through the streets of Cañada de Caracheo and maybe even climb a little on Culiacan.

Chapter 7

April 25–May 4

It was two weeks later around two a.m. and I was getting dressed as quietly as possible, so I could sneak out of the family camp and take a look around Cañada de Caracheo in the dark. I have to admit, I was excited at the thought of exploring the pueblo because I had been in the family camp too long. I wasn't going alone though: Cristina was coming with me to show me around, and keep me out of trouble. We both wore dark clothing since it made it easier to hide in the shadows if we needed to. There were only a few people who knew I was here, and we wanted to keep it that way as long as possible. I stepped out of the bedroom to find Cristina standing there waiting for me.

I whispered, "Good morning, Cristina."

She replied with a whisper, "Good morning, El Cabby; are you ready to go?"

I answered, "Of course, I'm looking forward to getting out of the family camp for a change."

Cristina smiled at me and said, "This is a sleepy little place in the middle of nowhere, and you don't hear or see much this late at night. We don't have any police because it's such a safe place to live and we don't need any. The speed bumps keep the traffic moving slowly, and we don't have many visitors here in the middle of the night. The most noise you'll hear is when we have the religious festivals a few times a year, and the rest of the time it's the dogs barking. Dogs are the Mexican burglar alarm, and they're very effective. So El Cabby, if you stay with me, and stay quiet, we'll probably be okay. If we talk out loud instead of whispering, or if we make too much noise, we'll wake one of the dogs. If one dog starts to bark for a few minutes, they'll all bark and everyone in Cañada de Caracheo will be checking to see why they're barking. You can guess who they're going to see stalking outside in the middle of the night, can't you?"

"I understand," I said. "I'll stay quiet and very close to you, then everything is going to be fine."

Cristina said, "Okay, here we go," as she started toward the door. When she got there she unlocked and opened it very quietly. Then she looked up and down the road making sure everything was clear. She motioned for me to follow her, and I moved through the doorway very quietly, then Cristina locked the door.

We had two steps to go down and then we started towards downtown and the middle of the pueblo. All the family camps, or houses, along the way were attached to each other, and this gave them a special kind of security. Since they had common outer walls which were six- to eight-inch concrete along with steel doors, a thief would have a difficult time breaking into any of them without getting caught.

I hadn't realized Cristina's family camp was on one of the outer borders of Cañada de Caracheo, and I'm certain this probably attributed to its peacefulness. Only a sliver of the moon was showing in the night sky, giving off very little reflective light. It was very quiet except for the sound of a few snap bugs and locust in the distance. Even in the dark I knew I was seeing one of the most beautiful places I had ever been to. The only problem was that the streets became narrow and more like small lanes, compared to the road we'd been on. The road had transitioned from a two-way street to a one-way lane the closer we got to the center of town.

After walking another hundred yards or so, we arrived at the church, and it looked like a beautiful place to come to on Sunday to worship God. They were building an addition on the church, and even in the dark, you could tell it was a project of significant size, and would take a long time to complete. I couldn't help thinking that God should be in the heart of every man, and a good church should be the center and the heartbeat of every community. My prayer was that this church would continue making an impact in the lives of the people here for many years to come.

Then Cristina motioned for us to turn to the left and walk down another street where there were very few houses with lights on. We continued to walk about three hundred yards down the street, and then we were near the last streetlight on the west side of Cañada de Caracheo.

You could see the elevation of the ground was rapidly starting to change as we progressively got closer to the mountain. Cristina stopped me again, and whispered, "This is the base of Culiacan, and if we went forward another hundred feet past the house in front of us we would find a trail that goes all the way to the top. We can't get too near the house because they have several dogs and they could start barking, giving away our presence."

We then retraced our steps back towards the church, and when we came to the first street, we turned to our right, taking a different way back towards Cristina's family camp. A few minutes later, we were in an open area, which resembled a park. There was a wall in front of us which was approximately seven or eight feet high, encompassing an orchard, house, or garden, I didn't know which. On the north side, about ten feet away from the wall, was a small stream with rapidly flowing water, which was about eighteen inches across and two or three inches deep.

On this side of the wall there were park benches every ten or twelve feet with small trees between them so you could sit and enjoy the park. Cristina and I went over and sat down on one of the benches to rest for a few minutes. It had been a long time since I'd had this much exercise, and I was feeling a little tired, so being able to sit down and relax was refreshing. We sat there in silence for a few minutes, and enjoyed the peace and quiet of the night. The ripple of the stream, the trees here and there, and the sliver of the moon furnishing the light – all gave the park an ethereal feeling.

You could hear a rustling sound like a squirrel makes as it searches for food, and there were a few dogs barking in the distance. Then all of a sudden I jumped as the sound of a hoot owl pierced the night from somewhere nearby. These were the sounds that Evangelina could explain, so you would understand God's plan for the world as seen through the eyes of the Mexican indigenous people. For a second, a tear welled up in my eye, because I missed Evangelina and Berenice, and I hated myself for getting them involved in the Knights, and then having them lose their lives just a few days later.

Cristina leaned towards me, and whispered, "On the other side of the wall behind us is an orchard, and it's privately owned. Someday when we have a chance I will show it to you. This park is a wonderful place to come and be with God because it doesn't matter what time of day you come here; it's always peaceful and relaxing."

Cristina stood up and motioned for me to follow her as she whispered, "It's time for us to go, but we've covered a lot of territory for your first night out." We stood up and started walking out of the park, and when we reached the edge of the park I looked back to the spot where we had been sitting and noticed something moving in the shadows. I reached out tapping Cristina on her arm and then brought my fingers to my mouth as a symbol to stay quiet. I pointed to where I noticed the movement, and we both stood silently, straining our eyes to see what it was. Now, I didn't see anything, and evidently neither could Cristina. I motioned for her to follow me a few feet so we were standing in the shadow of a tree where we stood in hidden silence. Then I saw a shadow or something moving, and it wasn't a small animal, but it was very human in size and shape. It was moving slowly and quietly as though it were planning to catch something, or someone, in the dark. Chills ran up my spine because I knew I didn't have the strength yet to defend us. However, I had no choice now since the person had come within fifteen yards of where we were standing.

I whispered to Cristina to stay still while I carefully snuck up behind the intruder. Cristina looked at me in disbelief and she whispered in my ear, "Are you out of your mind? What if it's a soldier? You don't have a weapon; you're not in good physical shape, and all you can do is to get yourself caught, and I don't think it's very smart, is it? You don't even know he knows we're here. We should stay here, and grab whoever it is if they come after us, because it's the only time there's any real danger."

I knew Cristina was right, and it irritated me, because I hate to admit some young woman I was hell-bent on protecting had ten times more sense than I did. I had an excuse because of my age, I suppose, but I should have been more mature, and I should have used good sense. "Okay Cristina, you're right," I whispered reluctantly, and then I motioned for us to crouch under the tree so we would be closer to the ground and harder to see in the shade.

We stayed there for a few minutes as we watched the person moving around. Whoever it was evidently hadn't seen us yet, although it was obvious they were looking for something or someone. All of a sudden, the person moved towards us as if they had observed us crouching under the tree, and I was getting nervous as I whispered to Cristina to stay down and let me handle this.

I realized after a few seconds that whoever was coming evidently hadn't seen us, because he was going to be a few feet away as he passed by where we were hiding. I slowly stood up, and was prepared to take action; however, as the person passed by he stopped to put a cigarette in his mouth, and when he lit it I knew who was standing there.

I whispered very softly in the man's ear, "Stay quiet if you want to live, or I'll have to kill you." Then I said, "Martin, what in the world brought you here in the middle of the night?"

Martin smiled, and whispered, "El Cabby, is that you?" He walked over and gave me a big hug, and whispered, "I was told you might be here in Cañada de Caracheo, and I came here to investigate for myself and see if I could find you."

I whispered, "Why in the world would anyone think I was here?"

"Evidently, you have a friend named Juan Pablo and he was wounded during the battle at Algodones just like you were. He said he had been in a foxhole with some Mexicans who had come from Cañada de Caracheo to join the Knights. He remembered sending them home about the same time you were being moved to Monterrey, and he never saw them again. They also knew you had never arrived at the hospital, and then they searched the highways and found the ruins of the truck you were traveling in, but you weren't there either. It wasn't until that time Juan Pablo remembered the Mexicans from Cañada de Caracheo. He realized they might have taken the same roads to return home as your truck took to Monterrey. So he thought there was a possibility they may have picked you up, and you might still be with them. I volunteered to come and look for you – and look what I found. If you don't mind, we need to go someplace more private where we can talk."

Cristina nudged me to remind me she was there, because I hadn't introduced her yet. I whispered, "Martin, this is Cristina; she and her family have taken me in and nursed me back to health."

Martin said, "It's good to meet you, Cristina; we appreciate what you and your family have done for El Cabby. He's a great guy, and a good friend."

Cristina smiled and whispered, "We think highly of him too, Martin."

I looked at Cristina and whispered, "Can we take Martin to the family camp?"

Cristina nodded her head affirmatively and motioned for us to follow her, and in five minutes we were safe sitting in the kitchen talking. I said, "Martin, the last thing I remember about you is you were working as a waiter in La Pirinola Restaurant. I thought you were quite happy so why did you take it upon yourself to find me?"

Martin looked down and thought for a second, and then he said, "El Cabby, when I heard what happened on the border, and I hadn't seen you, or Berenice, or Evangelina, I put two and two together. I decided that possibly all three of you had something to do with what happened in the conflict at Algodones. Then one day Jose, one of Berenice's brothers, stopped at the restaurant with his girlfriend. They told me Berenice was home recovering from shrapnel wounds, and she was in bad shape when she came home, but was doing a lot better."

"You're kidding!" I said almost gleefully, "Berenice is alive, and what about Evangelina – did she survive too?"

"El Cabby," Martin said, "they are both fine, but please let me finish my story."

"I'm sorry," I said. "Go ahead, Martin, and tell us the rest of your story."

"While Berenice was recovering at her parents' home in Leon, she told her family about the Illuminati, and the Genebra Group, and how they were planning to take free will from the people of the world. She had a profound influence on her family, her friends, and many other people she and her family knew in Leon resulting in many people, other than her family, joining the Knights. Her brother Jose was so proud of her; he and several other members of the family joined the Knights also. Several days after talking to Jose I decided it was time for me to quit wavering, and join the Knights too.

"A few days ago word got out you might not have died in the battle at Algodones, so I came here yesterday to look for you. I ran into the Mexican Army at the checkpoint down the road and decided to sneak around them last night. I was in the park looking for a place to rest, and if it wouldn't have been for the other person sneaking around I would have slept there on the bench. All I wanted to do was to wait for daylight so I could search for you."

"What other person? We didn't see anyone else in the park."

Cristina looked at me with a puzzled expression on her face, and said, "Martin, I'm sure we were the only people in the park, unless the other person arrived at the same time you did."

"I only know there was another man in the park. He was about my size and weight and was wearing dark clothing. He moved very quickly up the mountain when I approached him, and he disappeared into the darkness. I thought if I could find him he might be able to tell me where you were."

I said, "I don't know what to say, Martin; tonight was the first time I've been out of the family camp. My wounds had to heal before I could do anything else."

"Well Berenice, Evangelina, and the other Knights will be overjoyed when I return and tell them you're safe and healing. We will have new strength and vitality because you're like a legend to us, and we need all the experience an ex Grand Seneschal can bring, El Caballero Guerrero." (The Warrior Knight)

Cristina looked up with a smile, and said, "So that's what El Cabby stands for. I would have never guessed. You never told us what El Cabby really meant; however, you can be assured I'm going to tell everyone when they get up in the morning."

"No Cristina!" I said. "You can't tell anyone in the camp or in Cañada de Caracheo who I really am. You can tell them when the war's over, if we've won, but not beforehand. If the enemy knows I'm alive it would be dangerous for all of you. Let them believe I'm dead, and maybe they'll remain content, but if they think I'm living they'll be like a thousand bees in a forest fire."

I looked at Martin and said, "I need you to return to Guanajuato later today, and when you get there, go to the Mercado and our office. Tell them you need to talk to the Grand Seneschal, and no one else. If they won't put you in touch with him, tell them you have word of what happened to El Cabby. You can take a digital picture of Cristina and me to take with you, and I think Juan Pablo will remember her. I want you to tell the Grand Seneschal I'm alive and well, although I'm still recuperating from my wounds. Ask him to approve a transmitter receiver and a decoder for the latest communication system so I can communicate with the home office. If he authorizes the equipment, I want you to return the day after tomorrow, or as soon as you have everything you need."

Martin looked at me and said, "El Cabby, I don't have a pickup truck or any way to bring the equipment back. Without a vehicle I'd never get it past the army checkpoint, and I've never owned or driven a car, or truck, in my life."

Cristina looked at us and said, "I have an idea that might work. My brother-in-law Ivan has a pickup truck, and he also has a field he farms near here on the other side of the checkpoint. They are used to seeing him drive through the checkpoint all the time and they usually just wave him through. Ivan could take you with him in his truck to Guanajuato. When you return, he could hide the equipment in the back of the truck and they would probably wave him right through."

I smiled at Cristina and said, "Do you think Ivan would mind being shot if they checked his truck and found the equipment? I think he needs to know the possible danger he's getting into, and the fact he's risking his life. Don't you, Cristina?"

"Well, he was with me when I went to join the Knights at Los Algodones. He picked up your wounded body and placed it in the back of the truck. He helped make the decision to bring you home and save your life. Yes, I think he'll be willing to take the chance, even if he doesn't know how important you are to The Knights of the Night. If he accompanies Martin to the Mercado, he can officially join the Knights and return home even more willing to give his life for the cause. Is it possible for him to join the Knights while he's there?"

"Normally it would take more time to join the Knights than he'll have. I'll send a letter with Ivan explaining he helped save my life, and I'll vouch for him."

"It sounds like a good plan to me."

I said, "Look, Martin, you can use my bed and get a few hours' sleep, then this afternoon you and Ivan can go to Guanajuato if he's able to help us out."

Cristina laughed and said, "You have a lot of nerve, El Cabby; it's my bed you've been sleeping in, and it's not up to you to tell Martin he can use it." Then she laughed and said, "Martin, you can sleep in my bed and get some rest before you go to Guanajuato this afternoon."

I looked at Cristina and said, "I'm sorry, I didn't realize I've been sleeping in your bed. I should have known I was sleeping in someone's bed, but I didn't think about it."

Cristina said, "Don't worry about it; when we win this war and everything's been recorded in the history books, I'll sell the bed for ten thousand dollars as the bed the famous El Caballero Guerrero slept in. I will put a sign on the bed saying, 'El Caballero Guerrero (The Warrior Knight) and Cristina slept here.' I won't tell them we used the bed at different times so it'll bring more money. I'll be a wealthy lady when someone buys it," she laughed.

Martin went to lie down, and I sat there sipping my coffee as I contemplated everything happening around me. Would we, or could we, actually survive and win this war? It seemed impossible at times, but I knew, with the help of God, anything could happen. I also knew we had to try and find the man in the park Martin had seen. If he had a loose tongue and told someone he had seen an American in Cañada de Caracheo, it could prove very dangerous for me, for Cristina's family, and everyone else who lived in this pueblo.

Several hours later, Martin and Ivan left with some equipment, fertilizer, and burlap bags in the back of the truck so it looked like they were going to work in the field. After dinner, I told Cristina we had to try and find the man Martin had seen in the park. She just laughed and said, "You Americans have a saying about finding a needle in a haystack, and I think this is what we will be doing if we try to find him. There are many caves on the mountain and sometimes transients use them as a temporary home, or a place to hide from the law. It can be dangerous to even look for him if he's hiding from the police."

"If he goes to the army and tells them he saw an American in the park, it might bring soldiers into Cañada de Caracheo to do a house by house search. I think it's worth the effort to try and find him to see if we can prevent the house by house search from happening, don't you?"

"Of course, we'll go back at three in the morning to look for him, and we'll take an Uzi, and a machete, just in case we need them. We'll also see if Jorge can go with us because the man may not be alone; sometimes there are two or three men together."

"That sounds good to me," I said. "Let's go to bed early tonight, so we'll be alert when we leave in the morning. I also recommend we leave at two, instead of three, so we'll have more time if we need it."

*   *   *

We stepped outside the door to the family camp at ten minutes after two the next morning, and Jorge was sitting on the steps waiting for us. Jorge said, "I thought I'd wait another five minutes, and if you weren't here, I was going to go home and go back to bed."

I replied, "Jorge, I know you don't like me being here, because of the danger I bring to Cañada de Caracheo, and I don't blame you. If you're uncomfortable going with us, then go back home, and I will certainly understand."

"Can the two of you sit down here for a minute and listen to me?"

We nodded yes and Jorge began, "Look, at first I wasn't pleased you were here, El Cabby. But, the more I hear, and read, about The Knights of the Night, the happier I am with who you are and what you're doing. When we get a chance, I would like to talk to you about joining The Knights of the Night. I realize now that every patriotic Mexican should be fighting this war if they value their freedom. It's very hard to find heroes in Mexico, but it's the right time for some Mexicans to make a difference and return their country to its former glory."

Cristina spoke first, "Oh Jorge, I'm so proud of you, you've always been my best friend. I never dreamed I could love you more than I do already, but I do now."

I thought she was going to cry as I said, "Jorge, I will be honored to bring you into The Knights of the Night. We will take some time later today, or tonight, and discuss everything involved in becoming a member, and if you agree, I will make you a member of The Knights of the Night this evening." I looked at Cristina and said, "Cristina, if you would like, I will also initiate you at the same time, and anyone else in your family who would like to join."

Cristina replied, "I think it's great, El Cabby, and what an honor to become a Knight at the same time as my best friend. Now, let's get busy; we have a lot to do, and only a few hours to do it in. If we don't find the man from the park this morning, then we'll search again tomorrow and spend more time looking higher up the mountain."

We searched for hours, and then we had to give up for the simple reason it would be daylight soon, and we had to make it back to the safety of the family camp. The day wasn't a total loss though, because that evening I initiated Cristina and Jorge into The Knights of the Night. We even celebrated into the evening with a few beers and some music from Cristina's stereo.

I was sitting there relaxing, when Cristina's grandfather, Salvador, walked up to me and said in his broken English, "I would like to ask you something."

I replied, "Okay, what would you like to ask me, Salvador?"

"I am seventy-seven years old, and I'm the only man in our family camp. I would like to join The Knights of the Night because I need to protect this family every day."

"Let me see what I can do – can you get me a machete, and then call the family to come and watch, and I will make you a special Knight?"

He smiled as if I had made him the happiest man in the world, and he picked up his can of beer, tapped mine with it, and said, "Cheers!" He then headed for his room, and came back with a new shiny, decorative machete that had etching on the blade. Then he called everyone to where we were, and when they all arrived, I began.

I said, "Salvador, will you kneel before me please?"

After he had knelt, I said, "Salvador, I dub thee a special Knight with the task of protecting this family until the day you die." Then I tapped one of his shoulders with the machete and continued, "Salvador, I name thee Sir Salvador, and a true Knight; however, you must not use your new title until the world has been set free from the tyranny of the Illuminati that controls it at this time. Now, arise Sir Salvador, and assume your duties as the Family Knight."

I looked at the family who were applauding Salvador, and I saw more than one of the ladies crying with joy. Salvador had tears in his eyes as he gave me a hug, thanked me, and then he walked over to his wife Antonia and gave her a hug also. I couldn't help thinking that The Knights of the Night would never lose this war if we were having this same effect on thousands of people around the world.

We finished our celebration before nine in the evening, because we needed a little rest before going to the top of the mountain at midnight. We informed everyone if we weren't back in the morning, not to worry, as we might have to stay on the mountain overnight. Then we would continue working down the mountain tomorrow evening.

We left the family camp at midnight, and this time I was dressed like a Mexican wearing a straw hat and a Mexican work shirt. I put dark makeup on my face so my skin color was more appropriate in case we ran into someone who was curious as to why we were up there.

If we did run into someone, Jorge and Cristina would do the talking, and I would stay away from them as if I were looking for something. Our reason for leaving at midnight was because we didn't know how long it would take to get to the top of the mountain in the dark. Because it was a full moon, we anticipated it would make the hike easier, but we didn't really know for sure. Of course, we brought flashlights and headlamps with us also, but we didn't want to use them until we were further up the mountain. When you get halfway up the mountain you can use a headlamp pretty easily without sending a lot of light down the mountain for others to see.

It normally takes three hours to get to the top of the mountain during the day, but we were traveling at night while carrying backpacks with food and other gear, and consequently it could easily turn into a long and very tiring night.

This time we slipped right through town, went straight to the trailhead, and then started up the mountain. By the time it was five in the morning, we were roughly thirty feet from the top, and I was exhausted. I needed some rest and I needed it now, so I walked over to Jorge and Cristina and said, "Hey, I need some rest soon; I'm exhausted, and I have to admit I didn't think I was this weak and out of shape."

Cristina sighed, and said, "El Cabby, you aren't weak. Jorge and I are in good shape and we're exhausted, just like you are. Climbing this mountain is very hard no matter how old you are, or what shape you're in."

Jorge just looked at me, and nodded his head, as he said, "There's a deep cave not too far from here, and it's usually empty. We'll check it out, and if it's vacant, we'll spend the rest of the night and part of tomorrow resting there."

I looked at Jorge and Cristina who were less than half my age, and I could tell they were also tired, and I felt good about making the climb as well as I had. I said, "Okay, let's go, so this old man can get some rest."

It took us about fifteen minutes to get there, and I stayed away from the entrance to the cave while Jorge and Cristina checked it out. They returned, and Cristina said, "It looks okay, but the bats are going crazy around the entrance tonight, and I don't like the bats close to me. So I have an idea, El Cabby, you sleep away from the bats, and away from the entrance, and we will sleep about thirty feet in front of you. If someone does come looking around, they'll wake us up first, and you should be okay. Then when morning comes the bats will stop flying, and we can move into the cave after chasing them from the entrance. We should be able to sleep peacefully in there until we're rested, and then we can explore the rest of the mountain as we go down tomorrow night."

I said, "It sounds good to me."

A few minutes later we were resting, and I was sound asleep as soon as my head hit the pillow. I slept like a baby since I was completely exhausted from the climb. When I awoke, Cristina and Jorge were already up, and Jorge had gathered sticks and made a small fire to brew Mexican coffee. By the time we had our coffee and a little dry breakfast it was almost nine in the morning.

We decided to explore the cave before we moved in because we wanted to make sure it was free of animals and bats. Most of the bats were near the front of the cave, and we drove them out rather easily. The cave was quite large and had big caverns in it where you could live if you wanted to. We decided instead of sleeping there it would be easier to search for the man during daylight hours, so we started down the mountainside. We took our time as we went, and we didn't see anyone; it appeared as though the mountain was essentially deserted today, and it was very quiet. When we were a little more than halfway down the mountain we stopped to rest a few minutes near the ruins of a pyramid.

While we were sitting there, I had the urge to explore a little. So, while Cristina and Jorge checked out the pyramid ruins, I went to explore around the mountain instead. I heard an unusual sound and started to look for where it came from. I thought I saw a small animal up ahead and decided to check it out and it went around a corner about fifty feet from the pyramid ruins. I hurried up and looked around the corner to see if I could see it, but it was gone. There was a tree up against the mountain so I went to see if what I had seen had climbed the tree. The tree was growing straight up the mountain, and a rock from the mountain jutted out about halfway up the tree. I looked up the tree and saw a squirrel playing, and decided it was probably the animal I was chasing. It was then I realized there was a small opening just a few feet behind me, but it wasn't evident when you were standing up.

Then I brought Cristina and Jorge back to the cave, and asked them if they thought we should spend a few minutes exploring it. We crawled through the opening, which was about three-feet high and about three-feet wide, into a huge cavern, which wasn't very deep but was extremely well hidden. There were no signs of humans having been in the cave, although we did see signs of animals, perhaps even coyotes, but there weren't any here right now.

We made a drawing of how to find it from the ruins just in case we ever needed a place to hide. It was about four in the afternoon, and we decided to stay in the cave until nine at night when we would head home because we didn't want to get to the family camp until midnight at the earliest. We were also going to wait and see if any wildlife came into the cave after dark.

We left our new cave, which we named "Neddih" at nine, then headed down the mountain and towards home. We finally made it without incident, and we were exhausted by the time we arrived at the family camp.

We decided to forget about the man Martin had seen, as he had evidently moved on. It was after midnight, and Martin and Ivan hadn't made it back yet. I told Cristina and Jorge to get some sleep because Ivan and Martin may have had to wait an extra day for some of the equipment. Martin and Ivan finally arrived in the early afternoon the next day with the equipment in the truck hidden under some of Ivan's farming implements and burlap bags. Martin suggested we leave it in the truck, because there was a whole truck full of soldiers at the checkpoint. He said he was afraid they were getting ready to do a house-to-house search in Cañada de Caracheo.

Ivan said he was going to borrow a friend's car, go back to the checkpoint, and visit with a soldier named Pacho that he had befriended. We told him to be careful because they might become suspicious if he asked too many questions. Ivan returned a few hours later and said, "I hate to tell you this, but they're planning a big search of several of the pueblos in this area. Consequently, they are going to have a house-to-house search in three pueblos at the same time the day after tomorrow."

I said, "I believe we need to move me and everything in Ivan's truck to the cave we discovered, and we need to do it in the next two nights. We'll need to use as many people as we can in order to get everything moved without drawing a lot of attention. I will live in the cave until it's safe to return to the family camp. Does anyone have any idea how many people can help us tonight so we can move everything to the cave?"

Cristina replied, "We have six people in our camp who are capable of carrying some of the items to the cave. I'm pretty sure we can get Jorge to help, and with you, that's eight people who can go tonight."

Ivan spoke up and said, "My wife and I can help too, and with our help, it will make ten of us to help with the move."

I said, "Okay, this is what I would like to do tonight. Ivan, you and I will carry the communication equipment because it will be the heaviest items to carry. Jorge can carry all the guns as they have shoulder straps, and he can also carry a box of ammunition. Cristina, you and Ivan's wife can also carry some of the ammunition. We'll let Veronica bring the three machetes, a backpack with food, and water because she is a strong young lady. Enedina can carry the blankets and bedding for me to sleep on in the cave. Your sister Luz will bring a backpack with all my clothes and shoes. Cristina, your mother Luz can bring more food and water, and your sister Socorro is very small, but she can also carry some food and water. We will go up in two groups of five, with a five-minute interval between the first group and the second group. I will have to stay in the cave to set everything up and protect it so I won't return tonight. Tomorrow night, you can bring up the rest of the camping equipment like a few pots and pans, some water purification pills, a few plastic tarps, matches, flashlights, first aid kit, two gallons of gasoline, and five gallons of water, okay?"

Cristina asked, "Why do we need two gallons of gasoline?"

I replied, "It will be used to destroy the equipment and important information if the enemy finds us in the cave. If they capture me, they capture me, but they mustn't capture anything that will affect The Knights of the Night's operations around the world. If they gain access to our communication system, they could create problems for us worldwide."

Cristina looked at me with a serious expression on her face and said, "God help us if they ever capture you, or the equipment, El Cabby."

I said, "God help us in any situation!"

Cristina left to tell her family what we had planned, and she also told them to start getting everything ready for the move. Ivan left to get his wife after helping me unload all the equipment, weapons, and ammunition from the truck. When everything was ready to go, we all went to bed for a few hours' rest before we started up the mountain.

Then Cristina came into the room, and said, "El Cabby, I just had to come and tell you it's going to be difficult to be down here knowing you're up in the cave by yourself. You have become like family to all of us, and we love you."

I felt a tear forming in the corner of my eye as I listened to Cristina, and I choked up a little when I said, "I can appreciate your family too, because I love all of you as if you were my own family. I will worry about all of you when I'm up there safe and sound, and you're down here being inspected by the soldiers.

"Cristina, the day after the army comes to Cañada de Caracheo, I want you and Ivan to go to Guanajuato if he can make another trip. Go to our headquarters and let them know I've moved my location to a cave, and I could use two more people to help me keep the cave secure. While you're at it see if you can get a portable battery pack and generator to power the communications gear. Now, go get some rest, as we have a few tough days ahead of us." Then I stood up and gave her a kiss on the cheek.

The next two days were tough on all of us as we moved everything to my new home in the cave, and the following day the army did their inspection in all three pueblos, finding absolutely nothing.

Cristina and Ivan had gone to Guanajuato three days ago and hadn't returned yet. Every third night two people would bring me three days' worth of food and water, and I was really hoping tonight when they brought the supplies I would also hear news about Cristina and Ivan's safe return.

Chapter 8

May 4–7

I sat in the dark trying to stay alert as I listened for any sound from outside the cave, because it wasn't unusual to hear sounds at night as animals, or hikers, moved around outside. Since the cave was so close to the ruins it was one of our main concerns, because it actually increased the chance of being discovered if someone accidentally found it like I did.

So we made some camouflage to help hide the entrance and added some natural rock from the area to cover our tracks which were starting to wear a path to the entrance. Every night I would rake rocks around the entrance of the cave with a few branches to help cover the tracks we had made during the day. I felt very safe and secure, although I have to admit I got lonely at times, especially at night when there was no one to talk to.

The cave was about fifteen-feet deep by thirty-feet across without a square corner in it. The floor of the cave slanted slightly towards the entrance; therefore I hoped if it did rain, and some got inside, it would run right back out. One end of the cave was around five-feet wide and recessed about three feet deeper than the rest of the cave and it was like having a small built-in closet. I used it as a bathroom because I had an old portable plastic toilet which had been made for camper trailers, and I kept it in the closetlike space, and it was perfect there. If I had to use any toilet facilities during the day I would use the portable toilet; otherwise, I would go outside and walk down near the pyramid ruins just like other hikers did.

I had a small fireplace made of rock, and the only thing I had burned in it so far was a little charcoal to see how bad the smoke accumulated in the cave. The way the cave was shaped we had good ventilation and didn't have to worry about building up too much smoke. We could only burn the charcoal at night though, because the smoke would be very evident during the daylight hours.

At night, I used a small camping light which had a solar-powered battery and there was one place near the entrance where I could recharge it during the day. It would last about six hours on a full charge before the batteries ran out of power, and I would normally use it between dusk and midnight.

If I went outside, I always took my machete for protection, and never carried the Uzi, although the Uzi was loaded and ready to use if needed. If I ever fired the Uzi, everyone in a five-mile radius would know it because of the noise it made. Using it would almost certainly guarantee a visit from the Mexican Army.

Water was a problem because it had to be carried in, and it was a lot of work to carry enough water for drinking and personal hygiene. It was also important to be careful about how much water I drank so I would have enough left for personal hygiene. Every third day, I planned on going down to the family camp for a shower, shave, and good meal. In order to leave the cave, I needed someone to stay in it while I was gone for eight hours. I wouldn't have anyone to relieve me until Cristina or Ivan returned because Jorge had to work and help his father too much of the time. Everyone else in the Ortiz camp had to work at one thing or another to keep the family functioning.

It was one of those lonely nights around three in the morning, and no one had showed up with my water, food, or supplies, and I was starting to get worried. I knew that even if Cristina and Ivan hadn't made it back, the others should be here by now with my supplies, but they weren't. I couldn't help but wonder if something had happened in the family camp to make it impossible to come to the cave tonight. I decided to take a look outside and check if I could see anyone coming.

I moved the camouflage away from the entrance and then crawled through to the outside world. It was a cool night with a light breeze that felt refreshing as it passed over my face. The sky was overcast, and instead of seeing six million stars in the sky, you could only see one or two as the clouds parted overhead. It was then I realized why they were probably late with the food and supplies: it was very dark and overcast. I was sure that being so dark made it much more difficult to see the trail coming up the mountain. I decided to sit and relax outside for a few minutes in the cool breeze before going back inside. It was a beautiful view at night from just outside the cave as you could see the lights from Cañada de Caracheo, Huizzache, Valencia, then Cortazar, and finally Celaya. Depending on where you were at this elevation, you could see many different communities, because many small pueblos had been built around the base of the mountain.

I stood up and went back inside the cave closing the camouflage behind me, and then I sat down in the dark hoping my friends would soon be here. Before long I fell asleep, and all my cares and worries temporarily disappeared.

I woke up listening to the birds sing as I looked towards the entrance of the cave where the sunlight splashed and danced as the wind blew the camouflage around. There wasn't anyone here, but me, because no one had showed up during the night, and I was really concerned, because my friends and my supplies should have been here a long time ago.

I went towards the entrance as the sunlight on the ground disappeared as if a giant had just moved in and blocked the sun from hitting the mountainside. I moved cautiously, because I didn't know whether nature, or man, had blocked the sun. When I finally got closer to the camouflage, I noticed the wind outside was blowing a lot stronger than I had realized. The wind was whistling as it beat against the camouflaged entrance to the cave. Then a gust of wind hit without warning, and I felt a cold blast of air enter the cave. I shoved the camouflage back to look outside, and I looked towards the north and the sky was almost black. In the distance I could see lightning strikes, but they were so far away I couldn't hear the thunder. When I looked straight up in the sky, I could see where the light was separated from the darkness by the storm front as it moved in. Now I realized why I could see the light at the entrance a few minutes ago and why it was now gone. I stopped worrying about my friends, because I sensed my situation could be worse than theirs. They probably knew the storm was coming and decided to stay at the family camp last night for safety's sake. Now I knew I had to do things quickly in order to prepare for the ensuing storm before it arrived and I had a total catastrophe on my hands.

I rushed into the cave to study the situation and analyze quickly if there was anything I could do. If we had a hard rain from the north, the rain would hit on the side of the mountain and it could come down the mountainside like a raging torrent tearing soil, rock, and plants loose for hundreds of feet before it even reached the level of the cave. The cave I was in was more like a cavern than a cave, and if the rain came down the mountainside, it would follow the contour of the rock and actually flow from the center of the cave easily washing out through the entrance taking anything in its way with it. It might even remove the camouflage at the entrance along with the small trees and brush outside the entrance, revealing the cave and its contents, including me.

I started to pick up everything from the center of the cave to the entrance moving it back to where I thought it would be safe ground. Then I took a machete and cut a few stakes from the branches I had used to sweep the rocks in front of the entrance. I took the stakes and a big rock to the entrance and used the rock to pound the stakes through the camouflage and into the ground in an attempt to secure it. I didn't want the camouflage washing or blowing away in the storm. Then I started to secure everything in the back of the cave just in case the wind drove the rain through the entrance and back to the rear of the cave. If the wind and rain blew very strong, there could be catastrophic results doing more damage than just washing a few items away. In fact, if things turned bad, the cave may not be usable as my home anymore. Then I sat back and waited to see what would really transpire with the storm.

The wind was picking up and I could hear the bushes and trees being whipped around as the wind played with them like they were insignificant and unimportant. Then I started to hear the pitter-patter of the raindrops as they started to fall outside, and a few minutes later a flash of lightning beamed through the entrance so bright it illuminated the inside of the cave. The thunder that followed the lightning was worse than the lightning itself, as I felt everything shake on the mountain, including me. The thunder is always worse than the lightning I thought, as I braced myself, and tried to prepare emotionally for what was coming next.

The rain had started falling harder now, and the wind was blowing it far deeper into the cave. To make matters worse, the air was far cooler than I expected, and I was starting to chill. There was only a small entrance to the cave, but the wind was forcing the rain through the entrance to the point where some of the items I hadn't moved to the back of the cave were getting wet.

I moved as fast as I could and started moving everything further back into the cave and out of the rain. Just as I finished moving everything to safety again, I noticed something in my peripheral vision moving quickly across the floor of the cave and towards the entrance. It was my camping toilet and a few cans of my canned heat that had been stored in the little room at the end of the cave. I grabbed them from the stream of water that was running across that section and moved them to safety on a dry spot on the cave floor. Then I moved as fast as I could to the area from where they had been stored only to discover the roof over that section had been soft dirt and had now fallen to the floor of the cave. Water was gushing in that section of the cave like water pouring over a broken dam. Once again, I moved as fast as I could to get everything out of the way of the new stream of water and to a safe spot in the cave. I was winning the battle, but just barely, and the storm was still going full blast outside.

When I thought everything was safe and sound, I relaxed for a second and looked for a dry place to sit down. To my dismay there wasn't a dry spot in the cave which wasn't full of equipment, food, and clothing. So I took the plastic toilet, wiped it off, and sat on it as if I was going to the bathroom. *Oh well*, I thought to myself, *the storm can't possibly get any worse.*

Then another loud boom of thunder hit, and I jumped at least eighteen inches into the air. My heart was racing, and I don't think I have ever been so scared in my life. I sat down on the lid of the toilet again and started to laugh like a crazy man. I couldn't help but laugh, as I surveyed everything surrounding me: the solid flow of water washing through my home and the situation I was in. If anyone could have seen me now they would have thought I was insane, and perhaps I was.

The storm raged for thirty minutes as it slowly moved to the south, and then the thunder slowly diminished until it was just a soft boom in the distance, and finally I didn't hear it at all. I slowly moved towards the entrance of the cave, and removed the stakes from the camouflage and moved it to one side so I could look outside. "Thank God," I said to myself, "the bushes and trees are still here." I moved through the entrance and stood outside the cave surveying the damage realizing everything was okay.

Then I realized this was going to be a long day. I only had one small bottle of water left for drinking, and I still needed a shower. *How stupid,* I thought, *I could have taken a shower outside in the rain as the storm was moving away.* Some of my clothes had gotten soaked before I managed to move them further back in the cave, so I decided to put them to use. I stripped off the dirty clothes I had on and started using the wet clothes by squeezing the water out of them so it fell on my naked body as I washed. I was standing there wiping my nude body off as best I could, when I heard a familiar voice say, "Ha! It serves you right, El Cabby, for looking at our naked bodies." The statement was followed by a chorus of voices laughing, but one of those laughs couldn't be mistaken for anyone other than Berenice's infectious laugh I loved so well.

I turned around and saw four women laughing and pointing at my naked body: it was Berenice, Evangelina, Cristina, and Veronica. They were standing there soaked and looking like drowned rats themselves, but they had their clothes on, and I didn't. I started to go over and give them a hug even though I was naked, and they all headed for the door laughing and pointing at me. As they went outside Berenice said, "We prefer the storm, thank you; it's far more attractive than you are without clothes. Finish drying your body, and put your clothes on, then give us a hug, and we'll all be happy."

I replied, "Leave me alone, and when I get some clothes on, I'll call for you." They all left the cave to give me some privacy as I finished getting dressed, and a few minutes later I yelled, "Hey, you can come in now."

They came in and brought what supplies they had with them into the cave. Cristina said, "It looks like you had a lot more rain in the cave than I would have expected. But, it looks like you were able to save everything."

I looked at the girls and said, "You look like a bunch of drowned rats, and I suggest you get out of those wet clothes."

I said, "I'll go outside and see what's left of the terrain, and you can put on my dry clothes to wear while yours dry out. Then we can discuss what's happening."

Berenice said, "We'll yell at you when we're through changing our clothes."

I went outside to survey the damage from the storm just as I had before, but this time I looked down the mountain to Cañada de Caracheo and realized they might have received more damage from the storm than the mountain had. In a storm this big, a huge amount of water runs off the mountain and goes to, and through, many of the pueblos. There are a number of deep crevices on the mountainside that must generate raging rivers of water which eventually hit the pueblos and could cause flooding.

Then I walked over to the ruins of the pyramid to see how they had fared, and of course, they survived just fine. After all, the pyramids had survived through storms for hundreds of years, and one storm like we had today wasn't going to hurt them now. Then I headed back to the cave because Evangelina had yelled that it was okay to come back in.

I entered the cave and the girls had already cleaned up a few things, but it would take a few hours for all the water to evaporate off the floor of the cave. I walked over to Berenice and Evangelina, who were standing together, and gave them a big hug and a kiss on the cheek. Then I said, "I can't tell you how miserable I was when I was told the two of you died in the battle at Algodones. I didn't think I would ever get over it, because the two of you had become my family. Now I have both of you, plus I also have Cristina's family, so I am grateful and double blessed. You'll have to tell me everything about Algodones later, but first tell me, what are you doing here?"

Berenice said, "We're here, my dear friend, to help you defend the cave, as well as to protect you from yourself and the enemy." Then they all started laughing.

I turned around and said, "Okay girls, did you bring the generator for the communications equipment? I don't see the generator or battery supply, and I need them in order to stay in touch with the home office."

Cristina said, "Martin and Ivan will bring them up this evening along with some other information in a sealed packet for you from headquarters. They will be bringing up extra food and water too, because there's going to be three of you in the cave from now on."

"Forgive me," I said, "I hope that you mean Martin, Ivan, and I, because these are pretty tight quarters for two women and a man."

Evangelina and Berenice smiled at me with mischievous expressions on their faces, and then Cristina said, "I told you so."

After a few seconds of silence, Berenice spoke up, "El Cabby, who in the world did you hire to be your bodyguards and right-hand people?"

I looked at Berenice and grimaced as I said, "Oh geez! I didn't know we'd end up in a small cave on a mountainside, with no privacy whatsoever."

"Tough, isn't it?" Evangelina said. "Now you won't miss us. Meanwhile, we need to forget about the privacy issues which probably bother us more than they do you. For the last day and a half we had to get used to the idea of living with you in close quarters. Now it's your turn; the next time you hire bodyguards, and we'll pray you never have to, you need to hire men."

Cristina said, "Look, we have Martin and Ivan to help us for a few days, then Martin has to return to Guanajuato. So tonight they'll bring up the generator, extra food, water, battery for the communications gear, and a box of hand grenades. The next two nights they will bring up some heavy metal doors to make a hand grenade shield. We may have to jump behind it and pray, but it'll be a lot better than having nothing at all.

"We will also increase the number of supply deliveries to the cave, and we will bring supplies to you every other night instead of every three nights. We have Jorge and his family involved with the Knights, and they are going to assist with the extra trips. It's going to be difficult for us to do this over a long period of time without being discovered, so let's hope you don't have to stay here very long."

I said, "Well ladies, it seems like you have everything under control, and I appreciate it. Cristina, when you and Veronica get back to the family camp, will you ask Martin and Ivan to see if they can find a few tarps to create a divider? With the divider the girls and I can have our privacy. I could also use twelve bungee cords and twenty-five feet of regular clothesline rope."

Veronica smiled and said, "I've already asked them to go to the store and get you some tarps for room separators. They also found some lightweight aluminum poles to bring up and use to hold the tarps in place. There will be six people coming to the cave tonight in order to move everything as quickly as possible. You will have Martin, Ivan, my sisters Maria, Enedina, and Socorro, as well as Jorge. They are going to have a hard time with the doors because of their weight, so don't be shocked if they're a little late getting here. I will ask Ivan if he can go to the store and get some bungee cords and rope – is there anything else you need?"

I replied, "No, thanks Veronica; we will be ready for them whenever they arrive tonight."

Veronica said, "El Cabby, I want to become a Knight as soon as possible if it's okay with you. I'm only twenty-five years old, nonetheless I'm mature enough to handle whatever you or the Knights require of me, and I don't want to just bring you supplies. You see, I'd rather die in a gun battle, or from a hand grenade, than die being raped by the Illuminati. If I'm going to live, I want to have a life of free will, and liberty, so whenever you're ready to make me a member of the Knights, I'm ready to join."

I looked at Veronica and said, "You can join the Knights when I have a chance to talk to you and give you some information which will help you make an educated decision. If you prefer to have me personally bring you into the Knights, then come up tomorrow night and plan on staying overnight. Evangelina and Berenice can take you through the indoctrination, and I will swear you in when you're sure you want to join. Then you can get your Uzi and Blueberry the next time you go to Guanajuato. Tell me which you prefer, Veronica."

It was quiet for a few seconds, and then Veronica replied, "El Cabby, you're special to me and there isn't any other person in the world who I want to swear me in to The Knights of the Night. You can expect me tomorrow night, and I'll stay overnight, and then go home the following morning."

I answered, "Of course I will be honored to swear you in tomorrow night after the girls indoctrinate you." I hesitated for a second, and then I continued, "I have never witnessed so many women with courage as I've seen in Mexico."

Cristina said, "I told you my father works in the United States, and we see him every three years or so. In the meantime, there are nine of us in the family camp with my grandfather Salvador, and he's seventy-seven years old. We wouldn't survive very long if we couldn't handle every situation that happens. In our country, thousands of men have gone to the United States to work, and thousands of women have to be strong in order to survive here alone. You won't find too many weak women in Mexico; we can fight for what we believe in and we're willing to die for our men and our children."

I stood there thinking about what Cristina had said, and I realized the American people had no idea what their Southern neighbors really went through in order to survive and take care of their families. In many ways these wonderful people are an important part of the American strength.

I felt proud of my bodyguards, and the complete Ortiz family, including the father I had never met. It takes a lot of courage to leave your family and go to a foreign country in order to support them and see to their needs.

I turned to Cristina and Veronica as I said, "Well, the two of you had better head back to the family camp so you can get some rest and help Martin and Ivan get ready for their trip tonight." Then I walked over and gave them a hug and they left after saying goodbye.

Meanwhile, a Mexican soldier was looking through his binoculars and watching the trails on the side of Culiacan as he said, "Look, here comes some of the girls who were climbing Culiacan this morning and got soaked in the storm. Why in the world would they go through that storm just to return a few hours later? I wonder where they got the dry clothes they're wearing, and I also wonder what they did with all the things they were carrying up the mountain. Two of the other women aren't with them now, and I can't help wondering what happened to them."

The officer standing with him turned and said, "Be sure you record the information in the log book, because it sounds like we need to check out Culiacan. If you see anyone else going up the mountain who looks suspicious, watch to see where they go and enter it into the log also."

"Yes sir." The soldier replied, and he looked through the binoculars to see what else might be happening on the mountain. Then he asked the officer one more question,

"When are we getting our new night-vision equipment from the Americans?"

The officer replied, "We're supposed to have it already, but you know the Americans; they want our help, but they never want to help us unless it's going to benefit them. When they decide they really want to catch the people who fought against them on the border, we'll see our night-vision equipment. They're too busy licking their wounds because of all the trouble caused by the Knights. In some ways I'm proud of the Knights for standing up to the Americans. It took a lot of courage to do what they did, and the best part is most of the Knights involved were from South America and Mexico."

The soldier with the binoculars replied, "I know, and maybe someday the Americans will have more respect for us, and treat us better, because their actions are driving more and more Mexicans into joining the Knights. If it keeps going the way it is we could have an organization of South American Knights no one will be able to stop. Everyone thinks China will be the next great country in the world, but perhaps it will be a united Knights of the Night government in South America. The world could be facing a South American government so strong that it would exceed the influence, and strength of our Mayan ancestors."

The officer said, "Regardless of how we feel about what the Knights did at the border, they are evil and need to be stopped. The garbage about a South American conglomerate with power and influence is just a dream, and it's never going to happen. The only ones who live and die by a code in South America are those in the cartels, and they won't survive once everyone has the microchips installed."

The young soldier stood there in silence wondering if the officer was Illuminati, and the thought of it brought a chill of fear. He had read some of the fliers that were handed out throughout Mexico after the battle at Algodones. Now he was wondering if it was time for him to join The Knights of the Night. It would be better to give your life for a good cause such as freedom and free will, than giving it to something which would take them away.

Later that night, Martin, Ivan, Maria, Enedina, Socorro, and Jorge arrived carrying all the items they could, which included the twelve bungee cords and rope I had asked for. They came into the cave, and I said, "Well, I think we know how many people we can have in the cave at one time, and eight is too many. So I'm going to go outside, and I want Socorro, Enedina, and Maria to come with me. The rest of you can get everything put away and then set up the grenade shield at the very back of the cave and surrounding the small area where we have the toilet. We might as well let the mountain help protect us from any grenade that's thrown in here, and it will also give us more privacy when using the toilet."

The three girls and I went outside to let the others do their work, and I said to them, "I read the instructions from headquarters, and there were a few surprises I didn't expect. The good news is even though we didn't last as long as we wanted at Algodones, we did achieve the desired effect on many people around the world. Tens of thousands of people around the world are joining The Knights of the Night, and it's having an impact on every part of our organization. The bad news is we aren't capable of bringing in as many new members at one time. We don't have the weapons, or the supplies, and we're generally unprepared for what has happened. Many Knights around the world have been sworn in and then sent home until we can get what we need to equip them. These same people need to be educated about the enemies we are fighting, and they need to be educated now. After those new Knights of the Night have some training they will be better equipped to do battle with the enemy.

"Since I'm a past Grand Seneschal and understand the enemy better than ninety percent of the Knights in our organization, I have been asked to teach three hundred English-speaking Knights from around the world who will then return and teach others in their respective countries.

"This teaching will happen near here in a private school, and it will be done at night over the weekend of May twenty-seventh. The outside of the building will be blacked out and the school will close temporarily for repairs the week before we use it. We will bring in the students, thirty-five at a time over a six-hour period from midnight to six a.m. each night. We will have all the students by the end of the third night and start the training the next night from one in the morning until five in the morning for three nights.

"After the training is over the students will leave the same way we brought them in, and it will take another three days to move all of them out of the school and head them back home. I can't, and won't, tell you where this will happen, because there's no need for you to know.

"While I'm away teaching Evangelina and Berenice will be here in the cave, and I'll need everyone's help in bringing up supplies and seeing to their needs while I am gone."

Then Ivan came out of the cave and said, "We're finished with everything you asked us to do. Is there anything else you need us to do before we leave?"

"Yes there is," I replied. "Set up the hand generator to power the communications equipment, and I'll be there in a minute to see if it works properly."

Ivan replied, "We'll have it ready in a few minutes."

A few minutes later we went in and tested the equipment with Evangelina and Berenice taking turns winding the hand generator. It didn't take us long before we were talking to headquarters and I told them we were online for communications.

When the others left, the Mexican soldier was trying out his new night-vision equipment to no avail. "Damn it!" he said. "The Americans sent the equipment without the rechargeable batteries to make it work." He threw the equipment into a corner and went into the adjoining room where his commanding officer was having coffee with another soldier, and he said, "Sir, I have some bad news."

The officer looked up and said, "Well, what is it?"

The soldier said, "Sir, we have the night-vision equipment without the batteries to make it work."

The officer said, "Damn! I will get on our supply personnel as soon as they start work in the morning. Please remind me to call them before you leave your post tomorrow morning."

"Yes sir," the soldier replied.

Chapter 9

May 27

It was the first night of teaching, and the students would be mine for part of the first night. I had to present all my lectures in the first night, hoping this would motivate the students for the other two nights of training they'd receive. The idea was to scare the daylights out of them with my lectures the first night, so they would definitely pay attention the next two nights and learn as much as they could.

I thought we would start with the hardest subject first, and that meant teaching the class about the Illuminati, and what their part was in order to make a New World Order. I didn't really care how long it took to teach about the Illuminati, because of the two organizations they were the most dangerous. If we could defeat the Illuminati it was possible we would win the war. The Genebra Group has less than one hundred fifty members worldwide, and being extremely wealthy they don't have the courage to do the dirty work.

The challenging part in teaching the course would be getting the people to understand there is more involved than the Governments of their own countries and the Unions they were forming with other countries. Today these students would receive a new awakening which could change their lives and the lives of those they're going to teach when they get home.

Juan Pablo Jimenez, my friend from Northern Mexico, had been speaking to the students preparing them for an exciting time of learning tonight. Juan Pablo said, "Now I want you to meet someone who is called El Cabby by his friends. His Knights of the Night name is El Caballero Guerrero – The Warrior Knight, and he is a past Grand Seneschal of the Knights of the Night. He is living in a cave somewhere in Mexico while he recovers from wounds he received from a hand grenade at the battle near Algodones. It's with great joy that I introduce you to El Cabby, who is my friend and yours. Please come up here, El Cabby."

I headed for the podium as the people clapped their hands and cheered, then Juan Pablo met me with a handshake and a hug and I said, "Thanks Juan Pablo, I hope I can live up to the introduction and everyone's expectations."

I then proceeded to the podium where I took a drink of water and started my lecture. "Ladies and gentlemen, it's great to be here tonight to help you understand who you're actually fighting. Your enemies are far greater than your own governments. In order to win the war you will fight many enemies in order to keep your freedom and the ability to exercise your own free will. It's my task this evening to teach you about two of those enemies and the weapons they have and will ruthlessly use in order to try and defeat you."

I paused for a few seconds as I took another sip of water, then I said, "It might appear as though we're only fighting with our national governments who are uniting into Unions in order to form a New World Order. It's true the governments are pushing for the New World Order, but only because they believe it's the only way to end the global financial crisis we're in and bring some stability to the world again. Believe me, many government officials have no idea what's actually going on, especially those people at the lower levels of government."

I paused and took another drink of water. Pauses were important to allow the students to make mental notes of what was being said. Every student would receive electronic media of all the lectures after they returned to their countries of origin. Resuming the lecture I said, "About thirty years ago when we were approaching one million members in the United States and twelve million in the world, one of our Knights saved a man's life while he was being attacked by three men. The man our Knight saved explained that the three men trying to kill him were Illuminati, and they would continue trying to kill him until they succeeded. The young Knight didn't know what to do so he called his Seneschal and explained that the man he had helped was afraid for his life.

"Months later the man who had been saved from the Illuminati decided to become a Knight of the Night, and we gave him the new name of 'Nomolos T. Jones.' This was the beginning of our understanding of the truth about the organizations Nomolos had been affiliated with. We also realized we had to take action in order to counteract the plans of the Illuminati and someday in the future bring them to their demise. We also knew we weren't strong enough at the time to prevent them from developing the New World Order. But we hoped to become strong enough in order to stop the Illuminati by the time it was necessary for us to take action.

"When the financial crisis happened in the United States a few years ago, we knew everything that Nomolos had told us was correct. One of the things Nomolos had told us was that when the financial crisis occurred it would initiate the final steps of the Illuminati's takeover of the world. At the time the financial crisis actually hit the world, there was no doubt in our minds they had already started to implement their plans to set up the New World Order. It was at this time we informed all the Knights about what the Illuminati was doing and warned them it wouldn't take long for the Illuminati to put the countries of the world on their knees. Thanks to Nomolos, we had some idea of what to expect and look for as they implemented their plans.

"The plan of the Illuminati and the Genebra Group was to encourage and complete the formation of seven unions around the world, and it would facilitate the forming of the New World Order. After all, it's easier to get seven Unions to join forces and create a New World Order than it is to try and get more than 100 countries to agree on anything. They had already formed the European Union, the North American

Union, and the South American Union, before the global financial crisis had even started. Now they had to form the other Unions in the world, which would be the African Union, the Asian Union, the Russian Union, and finally the Island Union.

"When they began forming the other unions and started the injection of the microchips in the North American Union and the European Union, we knew we had to take immediate action to stop them, even though we weren't ready.

"So a plan was made for the Border Battle at Algodones although we knew we barely had a chance of lasting two days against the powerful American military machine. Nonetheless, our loyal Knights from all over South America went into an impossible battle in order to try and save the world by making the population of the world aware of what was really happening. We had posters made up for every country, in their own language, explaining what was going on and why we were fighting at Algodones, Mexico. The Knights of the Night distributed those posters at the same time the battle of Algodones was taking place. We hoped and prayed that people like you, and thousands of others, would join in the fight against the takeover of the world by the Illuminati.

"We thank God for all of you and the thousands of others from every country in the world whom you represent here tonight. Millions of people around the world have decided to join us in our fight for freedom and the prevention of worldwide slavery through mind control. I applaud you for your courage and determination to keep the people of the world free from domination by the Illuminati."

Then I began to applaud everyone who was present and motioned for them to stand up. Then I yelled, "Stand up and applaud yourself for your courage and willingness to give your life for a free world with liberty and justice regardless of race, color, or creed."

The applause lasted for at least five minutes as I stood there and watched, and then I raised my hands in a gesture for everyone to sit down. Slowly the noise subsided, and when everyone was seated I said, "We also knew the posters we handed out during the battle of Algodones only had the basic information about what was happening. During the next few nights you're going to receive all the information you need to take with you as you return home. You will share this information with The Knights of the Night in your countries in order to prepare them for the greatest battle in the history of mankind.

"We will take a fifteen-minute break in a few minutes, but before we do, I want to introduce a special guest and Knight of the Night who is with us here on this special occasion. He isn't going to speak at this time, but he is the reason we know what we know about the Illuminati and why we're all here tonight."

I looked to my left and said, "Would you please stand up, Nomolos, so these people can see a man of courage who was willing to risk his life for the sake of a free world."

Nomolos was just ten feet away from me on the stage and sitting with a few of the Seneschals. When he stood up the room went into another uproar of applause, and Nomolos waved to everyone as they cheered. Meanwhile, I went over to where he was and gave him a hug while I thanked him for what he had done for us, and for the world. Then I returned to the podium and said, "Folks, you can take a fifteen-minute break now to get something to drink and to use the bathroom. Please return on time because we have a lot of information to cover, and time is of the essence."

Fifteen minutes later I walked to the podium and stood there for a second as I took a sip of water from my glass. Then I shouted, "The Illuminati refers to us as sheep, so say, baaaa, baaaa, baaaa."

Everyone yelled back in unison, "Baaaa, baaaa, baaaa," and the auditorium vibrated with the sound of over three hundred people as they tried to imitate the sound of a huge flock of sheep.

I laughed as I raised my hand for silence, then I said, "Okay folks, you really do sound like a herd of sheep, and that's okay with me. Now I want you to know the Illuminati believe all the people who are not Illuminati, or the Genebra Group, are sheep because we follow others like sheep, and we aren't capable of leading ourselves.

"They also feel that the people in the United States are the easiest to fool, because they falsely believe their government cares for them. In reality, my friends, the government of the United States only cares for the wealthy, and the rest of the people who are the poor and the middle class are like sheep. The poor and the middle class are the ones who pay all the taxes supporting the wealthy and the United States Government. For instance with all the taxpayer money the government has given to the banks, including those who owe back taxes, every man, woman, and child will have to pay thousands of dollars in taxes in the future. Does anyone have any idea how much money the wealthiest people in the United States pay in taxes?"

You could hear someone in the crowd yell, "Nothing."

I said, "Someone yelled 'nothing,' and for the majority of the wealthy, it is the correct answer. Those who do end up paying a little tax, usually pay less than a few thousand dollars which is very little, considering what they earn."

One of the people in the audience yelled at me saying, "El Cabby, how in the world can you say that?"

I replied, "Well, for one thing I'm an American, and since I am an American, I have experienced some things myself that have alienated me towards the country I love. For instance, I am a veteran and as such I was supposed to receive medical care and medicine for life if I needed it. In the last ten years I've requested that the Veterans' Administration help me with the purchase of my medicine only. I didn't request medical treatment although it should have been available to me had I needed it. I had no reason to believe they would not assist me, because I had served twice as long as the average serviceman during the time that I was in the United States Navy. When I finally heard from the Veterans' Administration I was told that Congress had legislated away my benefits three years earlier. In fact they told me in the letter if I had requested the benefits three years earlier I would have received it. I was very disappointed in my government, and I had no choice but to continue paying for my own medicine. Eventually I resorted to buying the medicine here in Mexico, because it made them more affordable.

"There are thousands of people in the United States who have worked many years and paid Social Security, then had illness, or tragedies, that left them unable to work anymore. Social Security was supposed to give them disability payments to help them financially. Instead they deny many of their claims and never pay them for years, if at all. Some of those people have enough money to pay lawyers to fight the system and get their benefits. If the lawyers win the cases, then the lawyers get twenty-five percent of the money they collect. The government isn't taking care of its people when the people have to sue them for something they paid for over the years, and they have doctor's verification of their disability.

"To make matters worse, we've heard allegations saying claim handlers are given bonuses based on how many cases they can reject. The American public knows this goes on, as it's been reported on many television documentaries, and like sheep, they don't have the courage of their convictions. It's not just the American people who are like this; it's the middle class and the poor people from every country of the world.

"When a few thousand Knights from many South American countries, including Mexico, were willing to take a stand against the United States it showed the world what can be done with a little courage. Now those sheep are more and more willing to be counted, and they do have the courage of their convictions.

"The United States Government doesn't keep its word to its own citizens, or its military, or even other countries around the world. I'm an American citizen, and believe it or not, I still love my country with all my heart, and if the United States was being attacked by an enemy, I would willingly give my life to defend her. However, I will do everything in my power to keep the United States from becoming a part of a New World Order that removes our free will.

"Ten years ago you wouldn't have been able to convince me that ten percent of the families in the state of Florida would someday be on Food Stamps. You also wouldn't have been able to convince me that one out of every fifty children in the United States would be homeless. You would have never been able to convince me the people who are retired and struggling to get by on Social Security would have their cost of living increases taken away for two years. You would have never convinced me that the United States Government would turn its back on the servicemen who were more than willing to give their lives to fight her wars. These things have happened not only in the United States, but also similar things have happened in other countries like yours around the world.

"My friends, the saddest day of my life was when I realized many prominent people and politicians in the United States had joined together, because they were members of the Illuminati or the Genebra Group. They joined together for the purpose of destroying the free will of every man, woman, and child in the United States. But, this is also happening in countries around the world.

"Let me say, I personally believe that the President of the United States at this time is a good man who loves his country. He is being led astray by his own Economic, Treasury, and Federal Reserve cabinet members, who are also members of the Genebra Group. Just because the President is being led astray doesn't mean we should sit back and let the country die when we are capable of taking a stand ourselves. I hope that satisfies the question which was asked a few minutes ago. We all need to take stands in our own countries around the world. We need to reach within ourselves, find our faith in God, and the courage that comes with it. Then we need to take a stand for justice around the world, and if it costs us our lives, then so be it. I would rather die fighting slavery that's satanic than be a slave under that satanic system of government. For any person without the God-given gift of free will is a slave to those who make his decisions for him.

"Sitting in this crowd tonight are Knights from China, Japan, Morocco, South Africa, India, Germany, England, Scotland, Ireland, Czechoslovakia, Poland, Israel, Australia, Brazil, Ecuador, Mexico, Saudi Arabia, Russia, and many other countries. We have at least fifty countries or more represented here tonight, and every one of them is important. I'm speaking the most about the United States and its failures in recent years, because I'm an American. Your countries all have their own problems just like the United States does. We need to save every person in the world from having their free will removed through the use of mind control. So, let's get back to the Illuminati and look at some of its history and its founder.

"The Illuminati trace their history back to 1776 when Adam Weishaupt, a Bavarian Law Professor formed the group. The original goal of the Illuminati was to set the world free from being controlled by the church. Later in their history they decided to make a New World Order and control the world. For many years people believed the Illuminati had been disbanded in the year 1790, but they actually went underground, and we know they are still alive and well.

"The Illuminati is the largest secret organization in the world, and they get their name from the fact they are highly educated, and thus consider themselves to be illuminated. Since they're all highly educated and resolved to controlling the world around them by their standards they actually believe they'll make the world a better place to live. When you're brought up in an organization like this you're brainwashed into believing whatever the organization wants you to believe. This is what has happened to every member of the Illuminati when they are still children. They are highly educated people who won't stop at anything to have their New World Order.

"The Illuminati training involves many areas, such as sciences, finance, business, education, military, leadership, medical, and spiritual; these groups are broken down into several smaller groups for the benefit of the organization. For instance, the sciences break down into studies involving physics, chemistry, engineering, astronomy, nuclear, avionics, and so forth. The Illuminati works to have an organization with members who are involved in every facet of society, so they can have a global effect. Once the New World Order is in place they'll have achieved their goal to control the world, and its people.

"In the beginning the Illuminati knew they had to be patient, because it could take hundreds of years to infiltrate every government in the world in order to establish a New World Order. So every Illuminati had to understand what they were doing was important to the foundation of the New World Order. We truly believe in 1776 when they founded their organization, they were already planning the New World Order, and they knew it would take many generations of Illuminati families to achieve their goals.

"The Illuminati have very strict rules, and are very secretive about what they do, and except for the original members, the only new members are those who are born to Illuminati parents. It's important to note those members don't have a choice about being Illuminati, and when they are two years old their parents start taking them to training sessions.

"We have also been told by Nomolos there have been temporary members of the Illuminati who were not born Illuminati, and when that happens, the new people never really become members. These people are brought in to perform a specific purpose, and are considered expendable; the expendables are forced out after they have served their purpose, or they are eliminated. Even Illuminati who are born into the group are murdered if they decide to leave the organization, and this is what they tried to do to Nomolos.

"The Illuminati also have connections with other groups that have existed for many years; for instance, they are associated with the Vatican in Rome. We don't know how strong their relationship is with the Catholic Church, but we know there is a connection which has been there for many years. We also have knowledge of Illuminati who claim to have been participants in special Illuminati rituals which take place under the Vatican in secret chambers.

"It's possible many of your neighbors and friends are Illuminati, and you don't even know it. If you question how we know these things, then you need to know Nomolos has been teaching us all he's been cognizant of for years. We intend to share some of the information with you tonight, so please pay attention.

"The Illuminati have trainers who train the members at different levels; for instance, a child trainer might work with several children who are two or three years old. They would be teaching the children to be obedient, perseverant, patient, or even observant. For example, Nomolos tells us when he was a child he remembers being taken from his parents for a week or more at a time. During those times he would be placed in traumatic situations where his trainer would apply different stimuli to his body over and over, until he received the desired results. For instance, if you wanted a child to learn to control their emotions at the age of two years old you might shock them electrically. You would shock them over and over, until they learned not to cry when they were removed from their mother.

"Later when the child's mother came in she would also reward the child with hugs, kisses, and a lot of attention. With procedures like these two- or three-year-old children are broken, trained, and ready to pay attention and start learning by the time they are four years old.

"Before the children are four they are taught how to use firearms, and even shoot them on command, and if they are exceptional at this they may be trained as assassins. They may train children to kill when they hear a stimulus, like a buzzer ringing twice within a certain time frame, or the sound of a bell, or a particular voice command.

"When Nomolos was twelve years old he was flown to the Vatican, where he went through an induction ceremony which was traumatic and so terrifying that he still cries when he thinks about it. Because he showed himself to be weak, he was selected to be a male prostitute as a child for anyone who would pay for his services. When he was of age he became a male prostitute for the rest of his life. Being a prostitute in the Illuminati is as important a position as being a lawyer or doctor.

"If you are selected for male or female prostitution like Nomolos was, then you will go through certain training programs in order to be prepared for your task. The first thing you suffer is sexual trauma brought on by your trainer. By suffering trauma over and over, your mind dissociates itself from the conscious mind and tunes into the subconscious.

"The subconscious mind is far more powerful than the conscious mind, and with continual trauma, a child can be trained to utilize the subconscious mind for all sorts of special tasks. You can be trained to spy and steal intelligence or to just gather knowledge about different businesses and organizations. You can also be trained to have a photographic memory with which you can memorize thousands of pages of information for instant recall.

"The American CIA used similar techniques to train children for spy and assassin work using the CIA MK Ultra Project. If you Google CIA MK Ultra on your computers you will find all sorts of interesting information. There's even a video (on YouTube) of a congressional hearing with some of the children who had been traumatized in the MK Ultra Project, as they testified after they were grown.

"I read once that certain Government officials used a woman, who had been broken and trained by the CIA as a child, to be a spy and a human computer. She would memorize all the information her handler needed for a trip, and when the government official needed the information he would call on her to remember it word for word. In fact, the woman, whose name is Brice Taylor, has a lot of information and videos on the Internet about the work she did. She was in an auto accident and suffered trauma, and in recovering her memory she started remembering many things that had happened to her. Now she gives lectures around the country and has written a book called *Thanks for the Memories* about her experiences. You can Google her name on the Internet to find out more.

"The Illuminati support their organization financially in many different ways including prostitution, child prostitution, pornography, child pornography, gambling, money laundering, gunrunning, selling narcotics, and many other types of criminal activity. The Illuminati have such a huge organization imbedded in criminal activities around the world that the Mafia won't even cross them. They have no respect for human life, personal emotions, or the simple things of life. Compassion is something they cannot comprehend as part of the human consciousness. The Illuminati members put on a front during their day lives, and you will find them involved in churches, the PTA, Scouts, and many other honorable social things. Remember, they live two completely different lives, and during their evening lives they are Illuminati.

"Nomolos also taught us the Illuminati are trained in many different disciplines when they are children. When the Illuminati youth have finished their training they are considered to be 'Enlightened,' and being enlightened they are now Illuminati. It's important to note the Illuminati seek enlightenment all their lives and never stop learning.

"Everything the Illuminati are taught as children prepares them for their adult lives and for the establishment of the New World Order. The Illuminati are divided into several areas of learning in preparation for being adults, and these areas include Leadership, Sciences, Spiritual, Government, and Military. Yes, I said Military; there are Illuminati at every level of the armed services in every country of the world. All children are taught in every aspect of learning, but as they get older they branch off and specialize in designated areas. The hierarchy will decide who goes into what areas depending on their skills, or weaknesses, as they progress through their childhood training.

"Many Illuminati also work in daycare and churches, and it's not unusual for Illuminati to have higher positions on church councils and in private church schools. Even though some of them are encouraged to be part of Christian organizations, being a Christian is considered to be a weakness. The Illuminati are good mothers and fathers, and their children may not be close to others, or be friends with children who are not Illuminati. The Illuminati don't go to many social events, and seem to be withdrawn from making friends although they have many friends in Illuminati circles. If an Illuminati is your neighbor you may find they have regular scheduled times to visit their mothers, fathers, or grandparents. It won't be uncommon for them to visit others and stay overnight on a regular basis. These are the times when they're at their meetings, and these trips are nothing more than a way to hide what they are really doing.

"The hierarchy of the Illuminati is divided into different areas with the highest level being in Rome at the Vatican. The Illuminati consider Rome to be the center for spirituality in the world and it is important to note they have ties to the Vatican. They worship Satan, and depend on Satan for everything they do in life. It's important to remember there are many good Catholics in the world, and just because the Illuminati have ties with the Vatican, doesn't make everyone in the Catholic Church bad. I know we have many good Catholics who are members of The Knights of the Night, and they are good Christian people.

"It's also interesting to note a number of the world's greatest leaders have been Illuminati. You can tell when these Illuminati leaders are in office, because it's always during a period of great turmoil for the middle class and the poor. You see, they believe the poor and the middle class are considered to be the most inarticulate of the sheep. It's typical to take the poor and middle class's money through scams, lies, taxes, or whatever other means they can get away with. It's because the Illuminati believe we aren't intelligent enough to know what's happening to us. I hate to say it, but in many cases it appears that they are correct in their assumptions.

"For instance, during the Financial Crisis, those families whose homes were being foreclosed on by the banks were suddenly being hit by scams to take them for more money than they were already losing. You could read about these huge scams on the Internet, or in the papers, or watch shows about it on the TV news. The unusual thing is you never read about anyone being arrested for running those scams.

"If you have your identity stolen everyone blames you, even though you didn't have anything to do with it. If you need to have it cleaned up for the thousands of dollars that were charged to your name, you have to do it even though you didn't approve the purchases. The one who approved the purchases should have to clean it up. They made the mistake, you didn't, but the financial institutions don't ever clean up their mistakes, you do. Where's the justice in a system like this? There is no justice; there's no fairness, and it could be fixed so easily and cheaply. If you don't believe me then check your credit scores and find out in the process that for a low monthly fee you can have your identity protected. Ha! Guess who is running the business to protect your identity – the same financial institutions that won't protect you when they are approving purchases by an outsider from your bank account. It's a lucrative business, my friends; do you think those TV ads every night are free? Think again! It seems funny they never catch the identity thieves except on rare occasion and you don't hear about it when they do; you just hear the message, 'For a low monthly fee we can protect your identity.'

"It has been reported the FBI and the CIA have ties to the Illuminati and it makes you wonder how hard they are trying to catch the bad guys. You have to wonder who the bad guys are working with in order to have a list of everyone who is being foreclosed on in order to run their scams. It would be nice to see a list of all the criminals the authorities have arrested in the last ten years for pulling off those scams.

"On the other end of the spectrum are major corporations who just take your money in small amounts with, or without, you realizing you are being ripped off. For instance, many phone companies collect fees for smaller companies by adding the fees on to your phone bill without you even knowing it. The fees are listed at various places in your phone bill, and you pay them believing they are actual fees you owe. I know a lady with at least four of these fees added to her bill totaling around ten dollars a month. I was trying to help her clear them up, and when I talked to the operator at the telephone company she couldn't even tell me what they were for. She said they were fees people agreed to when they were on the Internet and filling out a form on a website, and the people didn't even know they were filling out something they would be charged for. Of course, the phone company is collecting this money for other companies; however, they are being paid for the service of collecting the money. Now take the poor lady's ten dollars a month and multiply it times ten thousand phone bills, or one million phone bills, and then multiply the number times twelve months a year. It's definitely worth the trouble of setting up phony companies like this when you're making millions of dollars a year. So be careful about what websites you visit, because you may have a few small increases on your phone bill which go to support your local Illuminati group.

"My friends, the world has become a very dangerous place to live in because groups like the Illuminati and the Genebra Group have made it very dangerous. Remember, just because they started this process and carried it out secretly doesn't mean they're not dangerous. They're like black widow spiders that come out of the woodpile at night. You may not see them during the day, but it doesn't mean they aren't there. When you get bit by a black widow spider you will never forget it. You will suffer, and you might even die. The Illuminati are trying to enslave the poor and middle class people of the world. So come on, my Knights, and let's inform the people of our countries to start checking every bill they pay. Tell them to ignore forms on the Internet without reading the total agreement, and if they don't fully understand everything it says, don't accept it.

"The Illuminati are associated with other major groups in the world and this is where they get a large part of their strength and influence. For instance, we are pretty sure the Illuminati may be affiliated with the Priory of Sion, The Opus Dei, and many other similar groups. It's believed the Illuminati have ties with the CIA, FBI, and the Bureau of Alcohol, Tobacco, and Firearms in the United States, as well as MI5 in England. Believe me, they have also infiltrated every major government in the world, including their intelligence service and military organizations.

"We have to ask ourselves how the Illuminati ever got this strong, or were able to accomplish all the things they have, and the answer is simple: We are the ones who allowed it to happen because we sat back over the years, and let them get away with it. We believed in our Governments and trusted their decisions were for the welfare of every man, woman, and child in their respective countries. The problem is the Illuminati influence on our governments was enough to control the political decisions which were made in favor of the Illuminati. We as citizens of our respective countries didn't pay attention, or take action, when things were going astray. Now we have to live with the results of our negligence and change the world back to what it should be. It is our task as Knights of the Night to take our freedom back before it's completely lost. It might seem impossible at this moment, but it isn't; anything is possible if you believe and have faith in God."

I yelled out the following words as loud as I could, "Believe and fight, my Knights!"

They responded by shouting, "Believe and fight, my Knights!"

I yelled it out again, and again, and when I did the people responded until the auditorium was vibrating with the sound of their voices.

I held up my hands for silence and I said, "One last thing, and we will take a break for forty-five minutes to have a light meal. It's important to note that you never leave the Illuminati and live; if you leave you may be found dead with a suicide note, and believe me it will look like a suicide. You may die in a traffic accident, a fishing accident, or a hunting accident, and I guarantee, they will look like accidents too. These are dangerous people who do not have a conscience and they will kill a baby, or a teenager, as easily as they'll kill you.

"There have been a few exceptions where people have escaped the Illuminati and lived, and we know of one whose name is Nomolos, our faithful Knight. There are also others, and some of them have lived for a number of years in hiding and told their stories like SVALI who you can find out about on the Internet."

I stopped for a few seconds and took a sip of water, then I said, "Okay folks, you can take a forty-five minute break now and eat your boxed meals. When you come back, we're going to talk about the Genebra Group."

Chapter 10

May 27

Everyone had a box meal with something to drink and a short time to relax before returning after a forty-five minute mid-evening break. They all needed time to relax and to absorb everything they had been taught in the first few hours. Nomolos and I ate our meals together, and visited at the same time.

I asked Nomolos, "What do you think, Nomolos, can we win this war, or are we just kidding ourselves?"

Nomolos replied, "I don't want to upset you, El Cabby, but the people we are going up against are dangerous, and they border on being lunatic, when they're upset. I don't know if we can get enough people disturbed enough to forget their ethics, and their Christianity, long enough to win this war. In other words it's hard to understand whether Christian people can become nasty enough to take on an enemy this horrible."

"Nomolos, the Bible has recorded many battles in which the followers of God took on enemies who were terrible people, and with God's help they managed to defeat them."

"El Cabby, I still have to give the Illuminati an edge in this war, because they are used to living in a cutthroat world, and they're heartless. If you can motivate The Knights of the Night enough, perhaps you can come close to winning this war, but I doubt it. Christianity is too soft, too full of forgiveness, and too weak to survive. Your Jesus said to forgive and forget, and when you forgive one Illuminati he will go back into the world, saying one thing with a smile on his face, and doing another behind your back. In a few years he will walk into your bedroom in the middle of the night and cut your throat while you're sleeping. Your warriors, El Cabby, have a heart, and they can't defeat the Illuminati if they have a heart. Now, this is my opinion, and I could be wrong, but you and I both know I was reared Illuminati. I lived as Illuminati, and when your Knight saved me I was still Illuminati, and the day I die I may still be part Illuminati. There are too many things planted in my subconscious which can't be removed and will go to the grave with me. Most Illuminati are near genius in a world of fools, because of being broken as children and learning how to utilize their subconscious minds. Perhaps, El Cabby, if God works with you in fighting the Illuminati you can win, but you had better be sure every single Illuminati dies, or in a few years you'll regret it.

"So you really need to motivate your people tonight, and get them excited, because whatever you do now may make the difference in the final battle for free will. Don't take me wrong, El Cabby, but you and I both know you're a great motivational speaker. It would be difficult to find one in ten thousand people who can stir anyone into action the way you can. We have less than four hundred people here tonight, and they are from different countries around the world. We will be lucky if one person in the whole group can motivate people like you do. The only thing we have going for us is the fact that we are recording you tonight, and a copy of the DVD will be sent to every person who is here. Perhaps your DVD can motivate as many as you do when you speak live, but I seriously doubt it. So let's pray God is with us, because if He isn't, then we don't have much of a chance on our own."

"Nomolos, just so there's no doubt, let me make this plain. I don't want anyone to forget their Christianity, or forget their ethics, or their morality, in order to win this war. I want them to keep their Christianity, and everything that goes with it, but I want them to do what they need to do so we can save the world. If the world doesn't survive as a Christian world, then it's nothing but a living hell for those who live on it. When it comes to being a motivational speaker then you also need to know that I feel God will open the ears of those who are listening. It won't matter whether they see it live, or on a DVD, they will hear what God wants them to hear."

"El Cabby, is life better than death?"

"Of course, I believe life is sacred, and so do you, and we both believe we were created by God and given life for a purpose."

"Well if that's true, and everyone here is going to die if we lose the war, is it worth the fight?"

"Of course it is, and I believe God would want us to be willing to give up our lives fighting for His gift of free will because it's sacred. God gave free will to all people, and I truly believe it's worth dying for. Remember, it's the one thing that separates mankind from the animals. The animals survive by their instinct, and we survive by choosing between right and wrong, and then acting on our decisions."

"Please don't take what I'm about to say as my position, because I am going to be the devil's advocate for a minute."

"Okay."

"The people of this world have asked for many of the evil things in their lives to happen because of their greed or their love of sensual joys. The people of the world didn't question anything happening around them, until they were aware of what they had lost, and the end of their time was near. The crimes were going on around them throughout their lives, and the Illuminati were at the center of most of it, yet no one stopped them, or even knew they existed. The Illuminati were selling porn around the world in videos, in pictures, and in real life they were prostituting men, women, and children. We believed our politicians and our governments when they told us they were fighting illicit pornography and prostitution, yet they allowed it to happen. Every now and then you saw a clip on the news about a person who had been arrested because of a pornographic picture on their computer, but you never saw the authorities bust anyone really big, because the big guys never get caught. The really big criminals are never arrested, and people never wondered why. Meanwhile, in our inactivity of protesting these crimes we strayed from God's will, and because we strayed, we actually helped the Illuminati accomplish their evil deeds.

"We also believed what we were told by our governments as the global crisis developed. They told us if we wanted to end this global financial crisis so everyone can have a place to live, and food to eat, then we needed to finish forming the Unions. The quicker we had these Unions formed, and their populations with microchips installed, the quicker we could start getting back to normal.

"Another thing we believed that our government told us was when everyone in the world had a microchip, we would go to a global currency, and everyone's credits would be electronically placed on their microchips. The Illuminati and Genebra Group said it would end ninety percent of the world's crime. We believed they were telling us the truth, because most crime is done for the sake of increasing someone's wealth. With the installation of the microchip the Illuminati could control the theft of money at least by those without an education in computer science. Even if someone stole material things for the sake of owning them, they were wasting their time. The new system the Illuminati developed would catch them and return the goods to the original owners. If someone stole your car and tried to sell it for financial gain, they would be wasting their time, because there is no money to be had outside the credits controlled by the Illuminati. With the new system, money is nothing more than numbers controlled by the financial system through satellite to every person's microchip. With the new system there won't be any banks as we know them today. But, there will be financial institutions that handle credits for making loans to buy homes, run businesses, and all the things we have always done to run our personal and government economies.

"Even if you stole your neighbor's television set because it's bigger and better than yours, its movement physically would be detected by a satellite, and the authorities would be notified. Everything of value will have a microchip in it and be tracked by satellite. Theft will become a thing of the past except for those at the top of the system. If those at the top are not honest then they will be able to steal from others by changing the electronic information systems and moving credits illegally.

"I don't know if you remember, but they started placing microchips in equipment and even some clothes in the 1980s and 1990s, and people didn't even know it. I remember when Hewlett-Packard started placing identification chips in all their printers, and I wondered why they would do that. When I inquired, I was told it helped Hewlett Packard know where the printers were being utilized and what for. Most of the people didn't even know, or care, whether Hewlett Packard traced their printers or not. Ninety percent of the people in the world don't know it ever happened, or is still happening. When the system is in place almost everything of value on the Earth will have a microchip for identification and control installed in it. It's true, life should be safer because of the microchip, and this global financial crisis will start to disappear as soon as the microchip is installed in every human being on this planet.

"We are also told there will be less people dying in the hospital emergency rooms, or in doctors' offices, because a person's complete health record will also be on their microchip. If you have a medical emergency the doctors will know everything about your health immediately by scanning your microchip. Medical response once the microchip is installed in your arm, or forehead, or both will be quicker and more accurate, so people should live longer, and have healthier lives.

"There won't be any missing persons anymore, because everyone will have the new version-two microchip installed in the forehead. The new version-two microchip will also have a global positioning system built into it and every person that has it can be located by satellite. The new satellite system when it is finished will be able to locate anyone on the globe in a short period of time as the sophistication of the system is improved. If your father or mother would happen to develop Alzheimer's disease and get lost in their confusion you will be able to locate them in minutes. If someone has a heart attack and dies, you will be able to locate their body wherever it happens to be. Even if the worst happens and someone raped your child, and buried them in the woods, you would be able to find the body through the global positioning system. In fact, it's possible they will be able to know when someone dies, because the microchip will inform them automatically. How in the world could this be worse than life has been since the beginning of time?

"Of course, if you want to eliminate someone for one reason or another, and you are Illuminati, or a member of the Genebra Group, you would just turn off their microchip, and kill them. Then reactivate the chip and report to the rest of the world they had a heart attack."

"Nomolos," I said, "you are the devil's advocate, because it sounds like you seriously believe everything you just told me."

Nomolos smiled and said, "El Cabby, I lived with these people all my life until I left because of the guilt I was feeling. Remember, we are born into the Illuminati; we are brainwashed by the time we are three years old, and the brainwashing continues for the rest of our lives. You grow up being distant from other kids at school, because you have the Illuminati kids for your friends. You also grow up living two lives, one as a normal kid during the day, and another as Illuminati during the night. You know all the other people in the world, who aren't Illuminati, are sheep, because they are people who need to be controlled, or they won't survive. You are taught the only people who should be free and make decisions are the Illuminati or the Genebra Group. You see, we're illuminated because of our knowledge, and we're very powerful. We know from the time we understand how to speak in simple sentences that we are the chosen ones. We are the Illuminati, and we know if the world isn't under our control by the time we die, then it will be Illuminati sometime in the future. We are patient; we are wealthy; we're going to have a New World Order because the human sheep of this world aren't intelligent enough or strong enough to stop us."

I sat there in a daze trying to assimilate everything Nomolos had just said, and because he had presented it so well, I thought he really believed it. Then I realized he shouldn't have joined The Knights of the Night if he actually believed what he had just said to me. I said, "Nomolos, what made you change your mind about what you were doing and decide to leave the Illuminati? The end result of leaving the Illuminati was losing your wealth, your family, your job, and all your friends, and it had to be very hard on you. When you left you must have known you would eventually be caught and murdered for leaving. You must have also known what the odds were of being able to survive on your own. So what was so terrible you would leave the Illuminati and risk losing your life?"

Nomolos had a serious expression on his face as he said, "El Cabby, I'm not sure what really happened, because it happened over a long period of time. The Illuminati had trained me as a boy to be a male prostitute, and in the Illuminati it's as honored a position as being a doctor, or a lawyer.

"Having and giving sexual pleasure as an occupation can actually give a person an enjoyable and fulfilling life if you keep yourself clean and take special measures to prevent disease after every customer. Besides keeping yourself clean, you're checked by Illuminati doctors on a regular basis. Unlike a common prostitute if you feel uncomfortable about having sex with a customer you can change your mind. It's not like working for a madam, or a pimp, where someone else makes decisions about who you have sex with. When you have sex, you make very good money, and you're not giving the lion's share to someone else other than the organization you love, which takes care of you.

"On a good night, you can actually earn more money than some lawyers and politicians make in the same amount of time. What makes it the most fun isn't the sexual climax you have from time to time, but it's in knowing you just ripped off another sheep. When the evening is over, you take the money back, and turn it in to your group, and they treat you with respect. I was pleased with what I did for the Illuminati, and I was probably happier than ninety percent of the other workers in this world.

"Then one night I had a date where I chaperoned a woman to the opera. It was quite common for us to chaperone women to different social functions so they didn't have to go alone. After the social function we would take them to a restaurant, or bar, and then back to their home. Many women in their late forties or fifties feel better when they have a young man as a date, because it gives them something to show off in their social circles. It also makes them feel better about themselves. After some of these affairs, the women will want sex, or they will want you to do special sexual acts for them, and if they do they will have to pay you a lot more for the evening. It's almost like a double reward for you when it happens, because you have more money to take back to the office, and it also gives you the satisfaction of enjoying sexual pleasures while you're earning it.

"Anyway, let's get back to my story. I had this date to go to the opera, and when I met the lady, whose name was Jennifer, I realized there was something special about her.

Jennifer was more relaxed with me than any of the women I had ever escorted, and she didn't treat me like someone less important than she is. She treated me like a special person, instead of a male chaperone, and I really enjoyed being with her. When the opera was over, we went back to her apartment, and she asked me to come in for a few minutes.

"Jennifer was very wealthy, and she had an apartment which was larger than any home I had ever been in. The apartment had to be at least four thousand square feet with four bedrooms, three baths, a sitting room, a living room, a library, and a separate den, as well as a kitchen and two dining areas. Outside the apartment, there was a small garden, a Jacuzzi, and a swimming pool with furniture around it and a small covered bar you could open up if you were entertaining guests. It's very luxurious, and even the foyer was bigger than my entire apartment, but being single I live very modestly. I was in complete awe of her, and what she owned, yet she treated me like I was a friend, and a decent human being.

"I didn't expect what happened after she had showed me her home. She asked me if I stayed for coffee and visited awhile if it would cost her more money, and I explained I could stay for the coffee at no extra cost as long as I wasn't there for several hours. I also explained it was normal most of the time when I escorted someone to take them for a meal afterwards, or at least a drink.

"Then I explained it wasn't unusual for someone to ask for sexual favors, and if they did, they would have to pay more of course. She seemed to be shocked women would ask for sex, and then she explained she had never had an escort before, so she didn't know what was normal. Jennifer asked me if everyone I escorted had sex, and I explained it might happen thirty percent of the time. She let out a sigh of relief, and then made us some coffee, and we enjoyed a few hours together with coffee, cake, and good conversation. It was a fantastic evening for me because Jennifer is a very nice and very sincere lady.

"We talked about everything under the sun, and I asked her how she had become so wealthy, and she explained to me her husband had been a CEO of one of the large investment banks. She also said it wasn't uncommon for him to make twenty million dollars a year in bonuses, along with his annual salary of one and a half million. Jennifer went on to say when they were first married they were very happy, but the longer he worked at his job the further they drifted apart.

"A few years before I chaperoned her for the first time she was going on a trip to Hawaii and then China with some of her friends on a four-week vacation. Her husband had been invited to come along with them, but he declined because of his work, and the fact there were important matters drawing near which he had to take care of. When Jennifer arrived at the airport on the day she was leaving she realized she had forgotten her passport. Since the plane was leaving in a few minutes she told her friends she would get the passport, and then catch the next plane to Hawaii in the morning.

"When she arrived at the apartment she went straight to her bedroom to get the passport, and she found her husband and another man sitting nude, and watching two women in the bed making love to each other. There was a camera filming everything the women were doing, and Jennifer was shocked, but she had the presence of mind to get her passport off the dresser. Then she went straight to the camera, and unplugged the hard drive which she put in her purse. She ran out of the bedroom and through the apartment while her husband was yelling for her to stop. Since he was nude, he couldn't follow her outside so she made a clean escape.

"Jennifer cancelled her trip, and spent the next few nights in a hotel because she didn't want to face her friends, or go home. All she wanted to do was see a lawyer and file for divorce as fast as she could. When she went to see her lawyer she took the hard drive she had unplugged from the camera and asked him to play it back to verify its contents. What he found on the hard drive was seven different sexual episodes between her husband and other women which were evidently taken at different times over several months. She had been considering whether there was anything they could do to rebuild the trust and renew their marriage before the lawyer told her what he had found on the hard drive. Once she viewed the video Jennifer knew there wasn't any hope for her marriage as far as she was concerned, so she sued her husband for twenty million dollars, and she got it. Of course her husband didn't want his career destroyed, and knew a good deal when he saw it, so he gave her everything she wanted."

"Nomolos," I said, "what does all this have to do with you leaving the Illuminati?"

"Well," he said, "we had coffee and cake, and several hours of conversation, and it was a great evening for both of us. When it was time for me to leave, Jennifer gave me extra money as a tip, and then I left. From that time on, whenever Jennifer needed an escort, she would ask for me, and we would always finish our evenings with coffee and dessert, and a lot of good conversation.

"After I had been Jennifer's escort eight or nine times I asked her about her social attitudes, and she explained she had grown up being the daughter of a minister. When she was in college she had gone her own way and deviated from her faith to the point of shattering the closeness she had with her family. Then, one day she found herself unwed and pregnant by the man she later married, and finally divorced. Ironically, their child died in childbirth, and Jennifer could never have children again for medical reasons.

"A few years later, her mother called because her father had surgery on one of his carotid arteries, and there were complications. Jennifer went to visit her father who was drifting in and out of consciousness because his brain was swelling. He told her he had forgiven her many years ago for leaving the church, but he also reminded her that according to the Bible the prince of the Earth is Satan. He told her if she really loved the world she would have to fight to change it because the world was satanic by nature. He made her promise to never forget there are two forces at play on the Earth: one is of God, and the other satanic. Jennifer told me the promise she made to her father was the most important thing in her life, other than the God she served. After telling me about her father, she told me she had also thanked God for meeting me, and having me as a friend.

"When I left her apartment I walked home even though it was twenty miles away. I cried most of the way because I realized for the first time in my life I was part of a terrible, evil organization. For the first time in my life I was ashamed of being Illuminati. My life had changed through hearing her story, and in realizing there was a God who loved all people including His enemies. I went home instead of returning to the office and turning in the money she had paid me. I tried to sleep, but I couldn't. I drank whiskey until I was inebriated, and I still couldn't sleep; finally as the first splashes of sunlight started to shine through the windows of my apartment I fell asleep in a drunken stupor. I have to say that night had been the best and the worst night of my life.

"The next morning I wrote Jennifer a note telling her I wouldn't be available as an escort anymore, because I was leaving the escort service. In my note I also recommended a different service and told her it would be better than the one I had worked for. The last thing I wanted was for her to be escorted by another Illuminati especially someone I knew wasn't reliable and trustworthy. I told her I was leaving the State of New York, and would never see her again, but I didn't leave the state. I had lived in New York City all my life, and I knew my way around the city, and thought I was more at risk living anywhere else.

"I tried to run and hide from the Illuminati, but I didn't have a clue what I needed to do. When you spend your lifetime being told everything you should and shouldn't do, you become like a child when you have to make your own decisions. I kept on the run for over a month trying to stay hidden by constantly staying in different motels every night. Deep down inside, I knew the Illuminati would catch up to me sooner or later, and it was just a matter of time.

"After a while, I started doing everything at night because I believed it would be more difficult to find me after dark. I even took a job at a corner convenience store working from eleven p.m. until seven-thirty in the morning. Then one night before I started work, three of the Illuminati spotted me and tried to throw me in their van, and I was fighting for my life when your Knight came to my rescue. While we were fighting, someone had come out of a local store and yelled they were calling the police, and then the Illuminati took off.

"I asked the young man for help, not knowing he was a member of the Knights of the Night, and years later I'm sitting here with El Cabby and ready to fight the Illuminati."

I asked Nomolos, "Have you ever told anyone else the complete story of how you decided to leave the Illuminati?"

"Of course," he replied. "I told your Seneschal, and the organization of Knights I joined, and they appreciated my story. I've been safe from the Illuminati ever since I became a Knight."

"Wow! What a story," I said. "Nomolos, I'm so glad I had time to talk to you tonight."

"Me too," Nomolos replied.

Then we heard a familiar voice over the loudspeaker saying," El Cabby, you're five minutes late in continuing your lecture."

I jumped up and said, "We'll talk more some other time." Then I ran to the auditorium as fast as I could.

When I arrived at the podium I said, "Okay folks, I'm sorry I'm late for this session, and I promise it won't happen again." Then I took a drink of water, and concentrated my thoughts for a few seconds, then said, "In the last session you heard about the Illuminati, but in this session, I am going to tell you about a very small group of people.

"The second group we are discussing tonight is the Genebra Group, and they are the youngest group of the two as they unofficially organized in 1954 at the Genebra Resort in the Netherlands.

"The Genebra Group meets secretly twice a year, and they are very open about wanting to establish a New World Order which they believe will make the world a better place. Some of the members and those who are invited to the biannual meeting of the Genebra Group serve in many government offices throughout the major countries of the world. There are also members and guests who attend the meetings from many professions and positions, including world bankers, financiers, businessmen, government officials, and royalty. The Genebra Group has a far-reaching effect on all of the countries of the world. It is said when the Genebra Group makes a decision concerning world change it will become a reality within the next five years. It's almost as if their influence and wealth controls what happens in the world and perhaps it does.

"The Genebra Group always rents a complete resort, and all of their services for their meetings, and they also bring their own security guards, sophisticated surveillance systems, and guard dogs. You are lucky if you can get within one hundred feet of the resort without a security guard getting between you and the resort.

"The Genebra Group always invites special guests to join in their meetings, and they have a propensity to invite the most prominent people they believe will be running for high government office. For instance, they have invited some of the United States Presidents before they were elected to office. Many people think it shows how much power they have when they invite presidential candidates to their meetings, and within a year some of them are elected President of the United States. It also happens with the Prime Minister of Great Britain, and again it seems that no one can explain how the Genebra Group makes these things happen.

"There is another unusual thing about the meetings of the Genebra Group, and it's they are seldom reported on the news even though they invite some of the higher-ranking members of the media to attend their meetings. If you check on the Internet you can find a few news services that have had short statements or comments at the time of the Genebra Group meetings, but no one reports on what actually happens at the meetings.

"Since the Genebra Group seems to have initiated the idea of the New World Order we are certain they're a major part of the problem. We believe the Genebra Group will control the financial end of the New World Order, and the Illuminati will rule and enforce it. The two organizations believe by controlling the poor and the middle class citizens they will make the world a much better place to live.

"Today, the Illuminati and the Genebra Group believe that the world is too complicated for the common layman to comprehend, and the people are too sheepish and uneducated to do anything, but have others leading them by the imaginary rings in their noses.

"With this final battle for freedom, liberty, and justice, we expect to show them we're not sheep but warriors who believe in what we're fighting for. With your help, courage, and convictions we will bring the world from this brink of disaster and return it to God's world once more.

"Okay, this will conclude the meetings for tonight, and it will also conclude my activities here as a speaker, so you won't see me the rest of the time you're here. I want you to know everything you learn during these three nights is important, and needs to be taught to our new members when you return home."

Then I shouted with a loud voice, "Train them well, pray hard, trust in God, and we cannot lose!"

They all yelled back in unison, "We cannot lose! We cannot lose!"

I left the podium with tears welling up in my eyes knowing that God was truly with us.

Chapter 11

May 27–28

Cristina and Socorro were waiting, and we left immediately in order to get back to Cañada de Caracheo to see how things were going at the cave.

Socorro spoke up, "El Cabby, do we really have a chance to win this war? Maybe I'm too young to understand everything, but it seems to me we may have lost the war already. Look at the odds: we're outnumbered twenty to one or more, the Illuminati will control all of the armies, navies, and air forces in the world. They have technology we don't even comprehend, or know how to use.

"We have a lot of courageous Knights with Uzis, and a few basic microwave guns, but we don't have heavy artillery, uniforms, aircraft or ships, and other materials that countries use in a war." Socorro was now crying and trying to speak with a choking voice as she added, "How in the world can we even survive a week, let alone win a war against the Illuminati?"

I replied, "I do believe we have an impossible fight on our hands, and I mean a fight impossible to win by any normal or natural means. I really and truly believe if we have faith, God can make the difference and help us win this war. Remember we didn't have a chance of winning the battle at Algodones, and we didn't expect to win it either. We only wanted to make the people of the world aware of what was happening in the New World Order. By the grace of God the outcome of the battle at Algodones has changed the whole world, and we now have thousands of people on our side who didn't even know The Knights of the Night existed before the battle. If we trust in God and have faith, then I believe we'll win the war against the Illuminati."

Socorro looked at me and said, "Thanks, El Cabby; it's important for me to know what you think, and I needed to hear the truth from your own lips. I also know you are a man of God, and I trust in God myself; therefore, I sincerely believe we will win this battle, but only by the grace of God."

The driver said, "El Cabby, someone's flagging us down, and I think you should get on the floor until we see what's going on."

It was dark and very hard to see the man who was standing alongside the road, waving a sweater in a big circle, trying to get our attention. I lay down on the floor in the front of the back seat trying to hide as we came to a stop, and the man approached. The driver put his window down, and placed his hand on an Uzi beside him in case he had to pick it up and use it.

"It's okay," Cristina said. "It's Ivan."

I sat up and said, "Ivan, what's going on?"

Ivan responded, "The soldiers at the checkpoint are stopping and detaining anyone who looks American because they believe someone in the area is a gringo and a Knight of the Night. My friend Jose told me what they were doing when I came through the checkpoint a while ago, and I wanted to let you know so you could take evasive action."

"Thanks Ivan. I was afraid this would happen sooner or later. What do you suggest we do tonight to get me back to the cave before morning?"

"Well, they have patrols out in Huizzache, Valencia, and Cañada de Caracheo. So, I suggest you stop at the Pemex station so the girls can go to the bathroom, and you can sneak out of the Hummer. I will park further down the road and meet you behind the station to help you sneak back to the cave. We'll have to hurry, because by the time you get to Cañada de Caracheo it won't be too long before daylight."

"It sounds like a good idea to me, so let's hope I can make it to the cave before morning."

"Well, you had better get moving, because we don't have much time."

"I'll see you behind the Pemex station in just a few minutes."

We headed down the road, and a few minutes later we were parked at the Pemex station, and I sneaked out of the Hummer and went behind the station. It was very dark, and when Ivan didn't show up after five minutes I was starting to get worried. If he didn't come soon I'd have no choice but to start the trip without him although I knew if Ivan was with me I would make the trip a lot quicker than I would by myself. A minute later I heard someone sneaking towards me from the field behind the station. I could hear him, but I couldn't see who it was in the dark. It was an uncomfortable feeling as I wondered if someone had caught Ivan and was now closing in on me. Then I heard Ivan's voice just a few feet away, and when I looked there he was.

"Hey, El Cabby," he whispered, "I'm here, but I've done a few things to hide myself as I walk in the dark, and I have a few things for you too. I have some camouflage paint and it will turn your pearly white skin a lot darker, and make you more difficult to see. I also have some black linen and large rubber bands we'll put on you once you've camouflaged your face and hands."

Ivan handed me the camouflage paint, and I started to spread it on my face and hands as he waited. While I was applying the paint, Ivan said, "This will also make you safer if we run into any stray dogs tonight."

I chuckled and said, "Ivan, how will this stuff keep me safer from the stray dogs?"

Ivan chuckled and said, "Everyone knows Mexican dogs love white meat, and with this paint the dog will think you're Mexican."

I held my hand over my face and subdued my laughter as I handed the camouflage paint back to Ivan who put it in his pocket. Then Ivan pulled some material from within his shirt that was about five-feet long by five-feet wide as he said, "Hold out your arms and spread your legs." When I did he fastened each corner of the black material to my wrists or my ankles. Now I had a black cape that covered my back, and if I placed my arms in a folded position over my chest, and bent my neck to place my head in a downward position, I was completely covered in black.

I said, "Ivan, this is really cool. I can't believe a piece of black material can be so easily used to create a cover for the entire body. You're really very intelligent, and I need to tap more of your knowledge, and put it to good use for The Knights of the Night."

Ivan chuckled and said, "No, I'm just a man who watched a kids' program on TV and saw some children do this in order to hide from an imaginary monster. It seemed like a good idea so I bought some material and some rubber bands just in case I had a chance to try it. It seems to work well, and we'll see what happens tonight."

I asked, "Ivan, how far is it to Cañada de Caracheo, and how long do you think it will take us to get there?"

Ivan replied, "It's about a mile to the checkpoint, and then a mile to Cañada de Caracheo. If we move quickly, you will arrive there in about an hour and a half, maybe a little less if we're lucky. It's now three in the morning, and we should be there about four-thirty. You should probably stay at one of the family camps, and then go to the cave tomorrow morning."

"I don't want to stay in a family camp tomorrow," I said. "I need to contact headquarters to see what's happening, and what they need me to do next. So, let's get going, and hope we get to Cañada de Caracheo without any problems."

We took off following the road to Cañada de Caracheo, and it wasn't long before we could see the checkpoint a few hundred yards away. Ivan said, "Look, El Cabby, I have a plan for getting around the checkpoint, but in order to make it work, I will have to stagger up to them like a drunk and distract them while you go around the checkpoint in the dark."

Before Ivan left me he removed his camouflage cape, and poured a two-ounce bottle of whiskey on his shirt so he reeked of liquor, then he removed the camouflage paint from his face and hands.

A few minutes later I sat there and watched as Ivan staggered up to the checkpoint. I heard the soldiers talking to him, "Ivan, man, you stink! What in the world have you been drinking? Where's your truck?"

Ivan replied, "Look, I hahad a few drinks of tequila anand then I had some whiskey that was in myyyy truckkk, booyyyee was that good! I couldn't see very wellel to drive because the road wasss moving left, and then riright, and then back leleleft again. Whee! I tell you it wasn't fun to watchhh, because it made drddriving very hard, so I parked me little trtrtruck near the Pemexs and dededecided to walk home. Iiiis that okay with you, Jose, my friend?"

I heard Ivan say, "Home," and I knew it was my key to get moving, so I started working my way around the checkpoint while trying to stay quiet.

Ivan continued speaking, "I kkkknow moving the rrrrroad back, and forth mmm must be some nnnnew army trick, so I wawawasn't gogogoing to mmmess with you guys." As he was talking, and staggering, he stumbled closer to the soldiers who had the guard dogs as if he didn't know what he was doing.

Jose said, "Hey, mi amigo, be careful you don't want to upset the dogs. They can get mean!"

Ivan said, "Hey, mymymy amigo, I brbrbrought my willlld dododog spray just in cacacase I ran into some wiwild dogs." Then he fell as if he was passing out, but he was holding his pepper spray with his right hand which was now spraying the dogs and their handlers. Ivan lay on the ground as if he had passed out from the booze, and meanwhile the dogs were yelping, and their handlers were madder than hell. Ivan just continued to lay there like a passed-out drunk.

I knew to start using my pepper spray if I needed to as I walked around the checkpoint just in case he had missed spraying a dog. In another twenty minutes I was in Cañada de Caracheo and sneaking towards the church. I only had another hundred yards to go until I was on the trail up Culiacan and to the cave. It had been a fast trip from the checkpoint, because I jogged most of the way.

Then I heard an army patrol coming down Culiacan, and they weren't very far away. They evidently spotted me in the shadows just as I saw them, and thank God, they didn't have any dogs. I saw someone point in my direction, and I sidestepped into the shadows hoping it would fool them into thinking they had just seen a bush moving in the wind. I thought it had worked, until I heard them running towards where I had been a few moments before. Now I had to run, and run fast, because they still didn't know whether I was an American, a Mexican, or a large animal, or perhaps a figment of their imagination.

"There he is," I heard a voice say as they started to chase me.

I moved as fast as I could go, because I was headed to the orchard inside the seven-foot cement wall. I intended to pull myself up over the wall as fast as I could and hide.

"He went that way!" One of the soldiers shouted.

I was running as fast as I could as I grabbed one of the trees beside the wall. Then I pulled with my arms, and swung my body up until it was even with the top of the wall, and gently slid down the other side to the ground where I lay silently.

I heard the soldiers on the other side of the wall looking for any indication of where I might have gone. One of them said, "Call the checkpoint and have them send two handlers, and their dogs, then we'll pick up the scent, and follow him wherever he went. Chances are he's still here, and if he is, we'll catch him."

I heard another voice say, "Checkpoint Iguana, this is gunny one, over. Do you read me?"

A second or two later, a voice came back, and it was so loud I could hear it, "Gunny one, this is Checkpoint Iguana, what do you need?"

The soldier on the other side of the wall said, "We need two handlers with their dogs, and we need them immediately."

The response made me feel good, "Sorry, my friends, a young farmer who was drunk and has a field near here walked up to the checkpoint a little while ago drunk out of his mind. He accidentally sprayed some pepper spray on our handlers and their dogs. The handlers are trying to clean the dogs up, but it's going to be at least two hours before the dogs can do anything."

I heard one of the soldiers say, "Let's split up, and two of us will take this street up the hill. Jose and Alejandro, you take those streets to the stream, and follow it to the edge of town. If he thought we had dogs he might have gotten into the stream to cover his scent. We'll meet here in ten minutes if we don't find anything, but if you do then fire your gun."

I lay there silently against the wall until it was safe, then I stood up, and moved through the orchard to the wall nearest the church. I pulled myself up a tree, and slid down the other side of the wall, and as my boots hit the ground someone said, "Put your hands up, and don't move!"

I slowly put my hands up and stood silently as I wondered why he didn't call the other soldiers. Then I realized he was by himself, and didn't have a radio. *But why doesn't he fire his gun*, I thought. *I know they agreed to do that if they saw me.* The man behind me said, "Keep your arms up, and place your hands on the wall, and don't make any false moves." I placed my hands on the wall, and I felt his hand patting me down as he checked for weapons. "Okay," he said, "keep your hands up, and turn around slowly." Keeping my hands up I turned around to look at a Mexican in civilian clothes holding a pistol pointed at me. "What's your name?" he said.

"I'm called El Cabby, and it's all you need to know."

"You're the American," he said as he lowered his pistol. "Put your hands down, El Cabby. I came here to find you. My name is Francisco, and I've been trying to find you for three weeks now."

I said, "Why did you want to find me?"

He responded, "I'm from Huizzache, and I heard rumors there was an American hiding near the mountain, and I assumed you must be a Knight of the Night, and if you were I wanted you to help me join your group."

"Well Francisco," I said, "we'll get you into the Knights very soon, but first, we have to get up Culiacan before the soldiers who are looking for me return. I have a hiding place part of the way up the mountain where we'll both be safe once we get there."

Francisco said, "I'll follow you."

I said, "We'll need to move fast because we have to be in the cave before the sun comes up."

About an hour later we entered the cave where two Uzis were pointing at us. Francisco said, "Oh ohhhh, hold it, girls! What kind of reception is this?"

I said, "We always like to give our visitors a warm greeting just in case they aren't friendly." I laughed, and then said, "It's okay, girls; he helped me escape from some Mexican soldiers at the bottom of the mountain."

Berenice said, "My name is Berenice, and she's Evangelina. We're El Cabby's bodyguards, and we'll die for El Cabby if we have to."

I interrupted the conversation and said, "You're going to have to tell us a little about yourself, Francisco, since you want to join the Knights, and we'll have to verify who you are before we can accept you as a member. So I'm going to ask Berenice to take you aside, and do the interview after she checks you for wires, and then we'll submit the information for approval."

Francisco responded, "I know several other Knights from Northern Mexico, and you can check with them about who I am."

I responded, "Since you know other Knights, it won't take long to verify who you are. Oh, and by the way, you will have to strip naked so we can check you for any wires, or tattoos, before we can start the interview process. You might as well get started by taking your clothes off now, and don't be bashful, because the girls had to strip when they joined, and they understand how embarrassing it can be."

Berenice laughed and said, "Hey El Cabby, do I get to inspect Francisco?"

"Berenice," I said, "we're in a cave remember; when he has removed all his clothes we will all still be here, so it may not be as much fun as you think."

After Francisco removed his clothes, and passed our inspection, Berenice and Evangelina took Francisco to one side of the cave to indoctrinate him. I was tired because I had been up all night, and I lay down to get some sleep. I knew the girls were familiar with the whole procedure and could handle everything. By the time I woke up, Francisco would either be a member of The Knights of the Night, or he'd be dead. A few minutes later I was sound asleep.

When I woke up there was light outside, and the girls and Francisco were sitting quietly and whispering. I sat up and said, "I'm awake now so you can talk out loud."

Berenice said, "Shhhh," as she put her fingers to her lips in a sign to keep quiet.

I immediately moved over to where they were, and whispered, "What's happening?"

Evangelina said, "There have been several soldiers outside for the last half hour. They keep moving around like they're looking for us, but we can't be sure what they're doing. We're trying to listen to what they say."

I kept quiet as they listened to the soldiers outside, and a few minutes later, Berenice whispered, "It sounds like they're looking for a place to set up an observation post, and I hope they don't choose this site or we'll be in trouble."

"It doesn't matter," I whispered. "If they set up an observation post on this side of the mountain, we're in trouble, and need to make plans to move out of here as soon as possible."

Luckily, the soldiers didn't find our cave, and they didn't stay outside much longer. Francisco was listening to them when they left, and he said, "Look, they're heading down the mountain now, but I heard them say they had three locations for an observation point. One is at the ruins; one is slightly to the right, almost directly in front of us, and I couldn't understand where the third location is. They evidently have to go and submit their recommendations, and I'm sure they'll return and set up their observation post as soon as a site is approved. So, I think you might have a few days to move at the best, but I imagine they could be here as early as tomorrow."

"Evangelina," I said, "I want you to call Cañada and see how many people you can get up here to move everything to the Ortiz camp as soon as it's dark. We'll need every available person to try and get it all moved tonight. We can disassemble the grenade shield and leave the pieces here if we have to, but everything else has to go. We'd like it to look as though some transients lived here and then moved on. Francisco, do you have a vehicle you drove to Cañada that we can use for transportation to Guanajuato tonight?"

Francisco replied, "Yes, I left my car parked at the Pemex station."

I replied, "Francisco, I'm going to have to get back to Guanajuato to the regional office. Since the army is setting up observation posts on Culiacan is a sign it's not safe for me to be here."

Francisco said, "I don't think it's going to work because the office has been moved. I tried to find it in order to locate you, but they don't have an office in the Mercado anymore."

"Francisco," I said, "there is an office, but they have gone underground, because things are getting more difficult there too. So, if any of you need to get to the office now, you go to the Mercado, and go in the main entrance and straight back to the stairs. Go to the second floor, turn to the left, then go to the last little store before the corner, and ask for Antonio. If he's there you'll see him, and if a lady's there ask for Antonio anyway, and she'll ask you what you want with him. Tell her you want to ask him if Malachi has been there lately. They'll call someone who will be there in a few minutes to take you to the office."

Francisco said, "So the office is there after all. I thought it had been moved, because everyone I talked to denied it was in the Mercado."

"Francisco," I said, "the office can change locations, and we will move to other cities if the Illuminati get too suspicious of our activities in Guanajuato."

Evangelina said, "I talked to Cristina on the phone, and there will be at least eleven people here by nine this evening to move everything to Ivan's house."

I replied, "Of course, I had forgotten, Ivan told me he had a place at his house where we can hide everything if we have to. Ivan has a big storage shed where he can put everything, and you can cover it up with some old tarps. Make sure you throw some dirt on the tarps so everything looks like it's been there for thirty years. I want you to come to Guanajuato the day after tomorrow and see Antonio, and he'll tell you where I am."

I said, "Francisco, as soon as they start moving everything down the mountain tonight we'll follow them, and then head for your car."

At nine o'clock everyone was there, and within fifteen minutes they were heading down the mountainside with their arms and backpacks full.

Chapter 12

May 28-29

Francisco and I followed the others down the mountainside, and then we departed for Guanajuato. Everything went well as we traveled by foot in silence, and before long we were in Francisco's car heading down the road to Guanajuato.

I said, "Francisco, many Mexicans are joining the Knights, and they are willing to give their lives in order to keep from being enslaved by the Illuminati. I'm proud of anyone who is willing to fight and die for justice, liberty, and the preservation of free will. Meanwhile, the Americans have militarized the border, claiming they want to stop the flow of drugs. What they really want is to make sure the good Mexicans don't get the weapons they need to defend themselves."

Francisco said, "El Cabby, why won't the Americans do anything like go after the people who are using the drugs? If there was no demand for the drugs, no one would be trying to take them across the border."

"Francisco, the Illuminati make a lot of money from illegal drugs, and they'll keep the drugs flowing to help finance what they're doing."

Just as I finished my statement, we went over the crest of a hill, and there was a dead donkey lying on the road. "Hang on!" Francisco yelled as his little red car flew into the air and bounced back to the pavement. The car slid at least three feet to the side of the road with the tires squealing. My head had hit the roof of the car when the car hit the pavement, and we were both shocked as we sat there for a few seconds, and gathered our thoughts.

Francisco asked, "Are you okay?"

"I think so," I replied. "But we had better check the car and get the dead donkey off the road before someone else hits it, and flies into us before we get out of here."

We got out of the car and dragged the donkey to the side of the road where no one could hit it. Then we checked the car which seemed okay, except for a loose front bumper, and a left front tire which was almost flat. I said, "I hope you have a good spare tire."

"I hope I do too," Francisco replied, as he took the key from the ignition, and opened the trunk to get the tire out. As we were removing the bad tire I noticed a silver button lying on the road near the rear bumper.

I said, "Francisco, what's this?" as I reached down to pick up the silver button. It was the size of a small watch battery, but it wasn't a battery, and it had a sticky substance on one side.

Francisco said, "I think it's a tracking button, and they probably placed it on my car while it was parked at the Pemex station. Someone may be following us or tracking us to see where we go. I have an idea about what to do with the tracking button if I can gather a few sticks while you finish changing the tire."

I hurried and changed the tire as Francisco gathered some sticks, and I drove as we headed down the road. Francisco cut the sticks into six-inch lengths, and then he taped them together making a little raft. Then he took the tracking button and taped it to the center. Meanwhile, I had turned off the road to Guanajuato onto a small road to La Sauceda, which is a small city about fifteen miles from Guanajuato. We came to a bridge and stopped just long enough to send the tracking button on the wooden raft down the stream. I said, "Francisco, let's hope this goes a long way before it gets hung up and stops."

Francisco said, "Let's get going, and I'll drive, although it would be fun to watch the soldiers make fools of themselves as they track their button." We got back into the car and headed down the road towards La Sauceda.

Meanwhile, a soldier watching the car's movement on his monitor called his officer to come and see what was happening. He said, "Sir, the car's not on the road anymore it looks like the vehicle is going cross country, on small lanes, or across fields. Is it possible their vehicle is a four-wheel drive?"

The officer walked over and studied the tracking button's erratic movements for a few minutes. Then he smiled and said, "Something's happened, and they found the tracking device, or they made a wrong turn down a country lane. They're moving much slower, and more erratically now. I think whoever is in the car needs to be stopped and brought in for questioning as soon as possible. The road they were driving on goes to La Sauceda, so dispatch a unit from Guanajuato to just outside La Sauceda, and set up a checkpoint. I want the people in the car apprehended and brought in to headquarters as quickly as possible."

The soldier replied, "Yes sir, I'll handle it immediately."

There was a group of soldiers on patrol outside the city of Guanajuato, and they were directed to set up a checkpoint on the other side of La Sauceda. They were told to stop the red car and bring the occupants into headquarters. Ten minutes later, the soldiers had set up the checkpoint and were ready for action. They had parked their Hummer just over a knoll where it wasn't obvious. The Hummer was sitting in the middle of the road with the machinegun ready to fire, and everyone was in their positions. The soldiers didn't know there was an eighteen-wheeler with a trailer full of stolen cattle coming right at them, and it would arrive five minutes before the red car would.

A few minutes later the truck was stopped at the checkpoint, and the soldier was talking to his officer at the command center. "Sir, I think this truck is loaded with stolen cattle, and there aren't any documents to prove otherwise."

"I'm in charge here!" the officer replied. "Take the driver's and the truck's information, and call me back. I'll have the Federales stop him down the road, and they can handle it any way they want to. You're there for a specific purpose which is far more important than those stolen cattle. So get him out of there before the red car arrives, and I mean immediately!"

"Yes sir!" The soldier responded, and then he yelled to the other soldiers, "Take his and the truck's information, and let him go, then call the information into the command center."

The soldier at the truck replied, "Yes sir!"

Francisco could see the red lights from the top of the truck trailer up ahead, and he could tell they weren't moving. He said, "Uh oh! I think something's going on up ahead," as he pulled off the side of the road, and we got out of the car to check. Francisco and I climbed the knoll of the hill in the dark, and we saw the Hummer pulled over to the side of the road as the eighteen-wheeler was slowly starting to pass them.

We got into the car as I said, "We need to pass them before the Hummer can block the road again, so keep your lights off, and go as fast as you can. As soon as the eighteen-wheeler's clear we need to fly by both of them. Francisco, I'm going to get in the back seat directly behind you, and attempt to shoot out the lights on the Hummer as we pass by. I'm also going to try to throw a hand grenade under it. Whatever you do, I don't want you to stop the car for anything. Now put the pedal to the metal, and let's go."

Francisco started the car and we were racing down the highway with our lights out. The soldiers hadn't noticed us, because they were too busy with what they were doing with the eighteen-wheeler. They couldn't even hear us because the deafening roar of the eighteen-wheeler was blocking out all the other noises around them. We had the element of surprise in our favor.

I was in the back seat with the window down, and my Uzi ready to fire, and I also had a hand grenade hanging on my shirt pocket, ready to throw when I needed it. When we were within fifty feet of the checkpoint one of the soldiers noticed us flying towards them at a hundred kilometers an hour. He jumped into the Hummer and was trying to get to the machinegun as I opened up with the Uzi, and took out both the Hummer's headlights. Then I grabbed the hand grenade, pulled the pin, and threw it under the Hummer as we drove by. The sound a few seconds later was horrific as the Hummer and the soldiers' bodies were meshed together for eternity by the heat of the explosion.

We just barely had enough clearance to get past the eighteen-wheeler when we saw six soldiers in front of us, with three on each side of the road aiming their rifles at us. I yelled, "Keep going, Francisco," as they opened fire, and a barrage of bullets flew through the car.

I took out three soldiers on my side of the road, and moved across the seat to try and take out the other three soldiers as we passed them. We were swerving back and forth now as Francisco tried to maintain control of the car. I suddenly felt a searing pain as something tore into my right calf. I cried out in pain as the car almost rolled over as it came to a screeching halt almost throwing me into the front seat.

I quickly moved out of the car and onto the roadway ignoring the pain from my leg, as I pulled the trigger of my Uzi and shot the last two soldiers knocking them off their feet. Everything was silent now except for the crackling of the fire where the Hummer had been sitting a few minutes earlier. The eighteen-wheeler was still in the center of the road where the engine had been turned off when the driver fled for his life.

I was standing there looking at my right leg, and it was bleeding profusely, and I knew I had to stop the bleeding or die. Without saying anything I unfastened my belt, and removed it from my waist, then wrapped it around my thigh pulling it tight, and slowing the blood flow to the wound.

Then I hobbled to the front of the car, and said, "Francisco, are you okay?"

I looked into the car, and saw Francisco was unconscious, but still breathing. He had several wounds that I could see, and he needed medical assistance soon or he would die from loss of blood. I went around to the passenger side of the car and got in. Then I put my arms under his, dragging him to the passenger side where I sat him up, and fastened the seat belt around him. Then I hobbled back around the car, and got into the driver's seat and took off down the road passing a dozen people who were running towards the fire from the Hummer.

I made it to La Sauceda, and turned onto the road towards Guanajuato, but I was starting to get dizzy from my own loss of blood. The car hit several speed bumps which knocked some sense back into my failing mind as I weaved back and forth barely keeping the car on the road. A few seconds later I was out of La Sauceda, and I knew I wasn't going to make it very far. I was driving off the side of the road, and down a hill when everything went black.

I slowly opened my eyes and tried to focus on anything that would tell me where I was, but the room was totally black. I heard voices outside the room, and I listened carefully. "You're sure you haven't seen or heard anything? These people are very bad, and they killed nine of our soldiers on the other side of La Sauceda, then they wrecked their car and fled somewhere. We know they're wounded, and they won't get far without help. We suspect one of them is an American, who could be a high-ranking member of The Knights of the Night."

"Damn!" a voice said. "If I see an American, I'll kill him myself, and then I'll call you. The Americans are the reason we're having this financial crisis around the world, and I hate them!"

"We all hate them," the soldier said. "But we're cooperating with the Americans in order to make the world a safer place to live, so don't kill every American you see. If you find and kill this wounded American it won't bother me though. But, if you turn him in alive, you'll probably receive a hundred thousand credits from the New World Order."

The other voice said, "Well maybe I won't kill him then, because I can use all the credits I can get."

The soldier said, "We're going to have to leave now, but we may come back to search your family camp later."

The voice said, "You can search here whenever you want, but they're not here. I hope you find them soon, and if you need any help just let us know."

The soldier said, "I wish everyone was as cooperative as you are, because it would make our work a lot easier. You have a good day, and if you see anything unusual call us immediately."

I heard the Hummer pull away, and head down the road as I lay there wondering who my benefactors were, and if the hundred-thousand credits would make them change their minds about helping us.

A few seconds later someone entered the room, and turned the overhead light on and said, "Who are you?"

I looked at him, ignoring his question, and asked, "Where's the other man who was with me in the car? Is he still alive, or is he here in your camp?"

The man said, "He's in another part of our family camp, and a doctor is looking after him as we speak; he may live, but if he does it's going to be awhile before he can do much. Who are you, and I want to know now. I'm risking the lives of my family in order to save yours."

"My name is El Cabby," I said. "I'm a member of The Knights of the Night, and I'm the man the soldiers would like to find."

The man said, "I knew it," then he ran back outside, while closing the door behind him.

A few minutes later, he came back and said, "We've notified the regional office you're wounded, and here with us. They told me someone would pick you up in the morning if they can get here. They asked us to try and stabilize your friend tonight, so it'll be safe to move him in the morning. My name is Don Pablo Gonzales, and this is my family camp in Rodeo which is a small pueblo near La Sauceda. My daughter Vero will be here in a few minutes to clean your wound, and then the doctor can check it when he's through working with your friend."

"Thank you," I said. "We are truly blessed we ended up in your family camp, because I thought I was dying when I passed out."

"I know who you are, El Cabby," Don Pablo said. "And I'm glad we could help you, and your friend. We're also Knights of the Night, and we're proud of it. We're under orders to stay quiet for now, but something big is going to happen very soon."

"I've been told the same thing," I said. "This is the second time I've been wounded this year, and I really want to fight again. Thanks to you, and your family, I may be capable of fighting again very soon." As I finished speaking the door opened, and a young woman walked in with a pan of water and some clean towels.

"This is my daughter Vero," Don Pablo said. "She is going to clean your wound and have it ready for Dr. Roche to look at when he's through with your friend. I'll return later, and see how you're doing," then he left the room.

Vero bent down and took a pair of scissors to cut a slit up my pant leg so she could get to the wound. Evidently the tourniquet I had made from my belt had been removed before I had regained consciousness. I said, "How are you?"

"Better than you are," she replied, as she pulled the pant leg away from the wound where it had stuck in the dried blood.

"Ouch!" I whined. "Can't you be a little gentler with an old man?"

She looked at me and smiled, "I'm sorry, I didn't mean to hurt you, but I thought a man who was able to kill nine soldiers in a few minutes would be able to take more pain."

"Vero," I said, "I hate pain and didn't want to be shot, so I had to kill those soldiers. Believe it, or not, I'd rather not kill anyone, and maybe someday this madness will all be over and I won't have to. I'm praying there will be peace in the world before I die."

Vero said, "Well, I'm not a doctor or a nurse, but I think you lucked out because this doesn't look like a bullet wound. It looks like a piece of shrapnel passed through the calf of your leg, and if I'm correct, you'll be sewn up and ready to go in a few minutes." Then as she was leaving the room she said, "The doctor should be here in a minute to look at your wound and stitch it up."

I replied, "Thanks Vero, I hope you're right, and it only takes a few stitches."

A few minutes later Dr. Roche came into the room carrying his medical kit, with Vero close behind him. He said, "Hello, my name is Dr. Roche, and I want you to know it looks like your friend may survive, but he's in serious condition. He has four bullet wounds: one in each arm, one in the chest, and one bullet grazed his neck. He's blessed I was able to get here as fast as I did. Vero thinks you were hit by shrapnel in the calf of your leg, so let me take a look, and see if she's right." He knelt down to work on my leg and after a few seconds he said, "You're right, Vero; it's from shrapnel. Give me a sterile cloth to finish cleaning it out, and then I'll sew it shut." A few minutes later he was through, and my leg was feeling better already. He said, "I can't be sure there isn't something else in your leg, but it looks like a clean wound. If it's still hurting in a few days or if it starts to look nasty we'll have to take an x-ray in Guanajuato to make sure I got everything out. Do you have any other pains I need to look at?"

"No, I think I'm okay," I said. "Would it be okay if I visited Francisco for a few minutes?"

"Perhaps tomorrow," Dr. Roche said. "I've given him something for pain, and I'm also giving him a pint of blood right now. He probably won't be conscious until tomorrow anyway, so it's better to let him rest tonight."

I smiled and said, "Dr. Roche and Vero, I appreciate all you've done for us, and I hope someday I'll be able to thank both of you more appropriately."

Dr. Roche said, "Vero, I will be sleeping in your camp tonight at Daniel's home, so I will only be a few feet away if you need me. If Francisco or El Cabby needs anything please let me know immediately. Francisco should be out for the night with all the morphine I gave him, but El Cabby could have some discomfort."

Vero said, "Thanks Dr. Roche. Hopefully, I won't need to bother you. Jose will be sleeping in the same room as Francisco, and I will sleep in the same room El Cabby's in. This way, we'll know immediately if they need anything. So goodnight Dr. Roche, I hope you sleep well, and I'll see you in the morning at breakfast."

A few minutes later, Vero came back into the room with a bedroll and a few pillows. She said, "I'll be sleeping in here tonight since it's my room." Then she made her bed on the floor and turned out the light.

A few minutes later I was sound asleep, but I kept drifting in and out of a nightmare all night long. I was being haunted by the ghost of a young soldier I had shot at the checkpoint. I will never forget the scene as he was falling to the ground he was crossing himself, as if he knew he was dying. He couldn't have been more than eighteen years old, and I hated watching him die for so many wrong reasons.

*   *   *

"Here we go, El Cabby," someone said as they came into the room carrying a stretcher. "We have to get going so we can get you to Guanajuato before the army finishes changing the guard this morning. Right now we have a fifteen-minute window, and after that, things can get more dangerous by the minute." A minute later I was on a stretcher and inside a panel truck beside my friend Francisco, who was still alive, but unconscious. We had two Knights in the back with us as we headed down the road on our way to Guanajuato and safety. I thought about the young soldier I had killed last night, and tears welled up in my eyes. *God, forgive us.*

Twenty-five minutes later we were in a special medical unit underneath the Mercado, and we were on stretchers when the doctor came in to check us. Francisco looked better, and he was receiving another pint of blood as the doctor looked at my leg. Dr. Roche said, "El Cabby, I think you're going to be fine, but I'm going to give you another shot of antibiotics just for safety's sake. If you want to start moving around, then use a cane until your legs are stronger.

"We still have two major problems though: the army is looking for you, and so are the people. The army has placed a one million-peso reward on your head, and it could easily change many families' lives, so some people would like to see you so they can claim the reward. Then there are many people who are talking and singing about you because you've become their national hero. The truth of the matter is, we don't want any of them to find you, because it could be dangerous to your health."

The doctor paused a few seconds, and he picked up a large bag full of dark powder which he handed to me as he said, "This is a powder called Burnt Sienna, and if you mix it with water, and rub it on your skin the color will change to a dark reddish brown. Then you'll have a skin color similar to many of the Mexican farmers who work in the sun all day. You only need to apply it to the parts of your body which are exposed, but use it sparingly, because this may have to last you a long time."

I said, "Thank you, Dr. Roche. I'll use it sparingly."

Then Dr. Roche turned his attention to Francisco, and started to check his vital signs as I lay there and watched. A few minutes later Evangelina and Berenice opened the door and came in, and I placed my fingers to my mouth as a gesture to stay quiet. Evangelina was carrying a cane and she handed it to me, and the three of us quietly left the room, and sat down in the reception area.

Berenice said, "El Cabby, you're a local hero with a reward on your head, and we can't wait to protect you someday if you ever give us a chance. After all, we're your bodyguards, and we're starting to feel guilty, because we're never there to protect you when you need us."

"A local hero," I said. "How in the world could I possibly be a hero? First, Dr. Roche tells me I'm a living legend for killing nine soldiers, and now you're telling me I'm a hero. All I did was what I had to do to stay alive, and I almost caused Francisco to lose his life."

"El Cabby," Berenice said, "war is hell! How old were you when you joined the Navy many years ago?"

"I was seventeen years old, and raring to go," I replied.

"You could have been killed when you were seventeen then," Berenice said. "Anyone who joins the military knows the risks involved, and is willing to take those risks for any number of reasons. So forget last night, and realize if we win this war thousands of people may get to live their lives in freedom. Tell me, were the soldiers you killed last night trying to kill you?"

"Of course they were," I replied. "They were obeying orders, and they didn't have a choice."

Evangelina chimed in, and said, "Well then, forget it, sit back, and enjoy the music because you're going to be hearing it for a long time."

Our friend Juan Jesus, who has a shop in the Mercado, came running up to where we were sitting and he said, "El Cabby, something serious has happened, and you're needed in the main conference room immediately. I'll show you where it is, if you will follow me."

With Juan Jesus leading, and the three of us following, we headed for the conference room, and a new revelation concerning The Knights of the Night.

Chapter 13

May 29

We entered the conference room where two Knights, Antonio and Alejandro, were sitting with grim expressions on their faces. Alejandro has a very important job with The Knights of the Night because he's a communication specialist for our region. He has the responsibility to make sure that all communications of a sensitive nature are maintained and kept secret. The fact that he was present in this meeting was an indication we were dealing with something extremely important and sensitive. Antonio is in charge of everything that happens in the Mercado and the home office, and is one of the nicest people I have ever known. The girls and I entered the room quietly, and went to the table where the others were sitting and sat down.

Antonio said, "El Cabby, I don't think the girls should stay in this meeting, because we're going to be discussing a matter that is extremely critical to The Knights of the Night. It's so serious I think we need to keep it on a 'Need to Know' basis until everything has been verified."

I replied, "Antonio, you've always been my friend, so I hope you don't take what I'm going to say in the wrong way. First, I outrank you and everyone else in Mexico. I am a past Grand Seneschal, and these young women are my bodyguards. I trust them; I have confidence in them, and I love them like family, so they're staying in the meeting."

Antonio's face turned crimson with embarrassment as he said, "El Cabby, I'm so sorry. I didn't mean to offend you, or the girls. I was caught up in the seriousness of the moment, and I wasn't sure anyone else should know what's happened, and I hope you, and your staff, will forgive me?"

I said, "Of course, we forgive you, Antonio. Now tell me, what's happened?"

Antonio replied, "It's my responsibility to report the Grand Seneschal may be either dead, captured, or missing in action. He was flying to Marseille, France, for a meeting with the French Knights of the Night, and his airplane's approach to the airport was over the Mediterranean Sea, but his plane never landed. The airplane was still thirty miles offshore at the time of the last radar contact, and there was a severe thunderstorm in the area. The airport reports the plane just disappeared from the radar screen, and didn't show up again. No one in or near Marseille has reported seeing the aircraft, or hearing a crash. Search aircraft have been launched, and no debris field has been seen on the water at this time.

"Everyone was, and is, treating this as a missing aircraft, but in thirty-two minutes it will be reclassified as a downed aircraft, because at that time all the fuel it had onboard would be gone. We're not admitting there were any Knights on the plane, and everyone thinks it was a flight of business people flying from Egypt to Marseille on a personal jet. We will need to fill the Grand Seneschal's position immediately, and we're in a situation globally that requires it is done quickly and efficiently.

"El Cabby, you know under the rules of our charter the Knight who takes temporary command has to be a past Grand Seneschal until a new meeting can be called. El Cabby, you're the only living past Grand Seneschal, and you are now in charge of The Knights of the Night worldwide."

I just sat there feeling numb contemplating what to do or say, finally I said, "How many people know about this?"

"Well as far as I'm aware The Knights of the Night in Marseille know, and we'll notify the other Seneschals around the world immediately after this meeting. We're requesting everyone to maintain silence about what has happened for the next twenty-four hours."

"Good, here's what I want you to do: send a message to those who know what has happened, telling them I have taken temporary charge of The Knights of the Night, and everything is under control. If we don't hear anything within twenty-four hours, I will assume permanent control of The Knights of the Night until the crisis is over. Also tell them I'll send a notice concerning my immediate agenda, and what we're planning in twenty-four hours."

"I'll send the message immediately. Is there anything else I can do?"

"Yes, see that Evangelina receives all the documentation and scheduled meetings the Grand Seneschal has made in the last three months. It's also necessary to furnish a copy of the minutes of every meeting the Grand Seneschal has attended in the last three months to Berenice.

"Evangelina and Berenice, you will go over all the information you are given and in twenty-two hours give me a written summation of everything you feel is important to the office of the Grand Seneschal. It's of the utmost importance to tell me anything you feel is of immediate concern; if you're not sure about something, tell me anyway."

"Antonio, do we have two offices we can give them to use here in the Mercado?"

"We don't have any extra space in the building."

"Okay, Antonio, get them a room with two beds at the Holiday Inn Express, and a car to take them there after they have everything they need. Girls, once you're in the Holiday Inn I don't want you to leave the room unless it's an emergency. It's imperative for you to utilize room services for all your needs including meals."

"Yes sir."

"I will come to your hotel room in twenty-two hours, or less, for a full briefing, and if there's anything of immediate concern then call me on my cell phone."

The girls left the room with Antonio and the others, and I stayed behind to contemplate what I would do next. I said a silent prayer to God seeking wisdom, strength, and courage to do whatever had to be done. It seemed impossible that this was happening to me at my age. I felt like I was too old for this. After all, I was almost seventy years old, and my sight was dwindling, my hearing was failing, and perhaps my judgment was failing too. I thought to myself, *How can any man my age be of any use in directing a global war against anyone as mean and vicious as the Illuminati? We need someone who is young, has a brilliant mind, and the strength of his youth to lead The Knights of the Night.*

Then I remembered something someone had told me many years ago when I was a young boy about ten or eleven years old. Sarah and I lived beside Raymond and his wife Betty, near Los Angeles, California. Raymond was an older man who loved to fix old cars. He would buy the cars cheap, fix them up, and then resell them for a huge profit. He was very kind to me, and so was his wife, and it wasn't uncommon for them to invite me over for a piece of cake or some other culinary treat. It's no wonder I loved to visit them and sit on their porch for hours at a time.

Then there were times when I didn't have anything to do. So I would meander over to Raymond's garage, and watch him work on one of his old cars. I would sit there for an hour or two mesmerized by his knowledge and his ability to work with his hands. One day he was working under the car, and he asked me for a 7/16-inch open-end wrench, and I went to his toolbox but couldn't find one.

I said, "Raymond, I don't see a 7/16-inch open-end wrench in here."

"Okay Tommy," he replied. "I must have used it and set it down somewhere, so go to my workbench, and open the middle drawer. Wrapped in a hand rag in the drawer you'll find a set of old open-end wrenches – please bring me the 7/16 wrench from the set."

"Raymond, why do you have those old wrenches wrapped up in the drawer, when you use new ones for working on the cars?"

"Tommy, what I am about to tell you is going to be our secret, so promise you won't mention what I tell you to Betty. If you will promise me you won't share our secret I'll tell you why those old wrenches are in the drawer just waiting for me to use them."

"I promise I'll never tell Betty."

"Well, I've had those old open-end wrenches for many years, and they have always worked just fine. Even though they were starting to look old, and worn, I knew they were good to work with for many more years.

"Then one Christmas about five years ago, Betty must have noticed the wrenches were looking old, and she bought me a new set of open-end wrenches. She bought them out of her love for me, and she knew I would use them for the rest of my life.

"I use them now because she bought them for me, not because the old ones aren't any good. You see, Tommy, I'm a master mechanic because of my knowledge, and skill, so it really doesn't matter whether I'm using a new tool or an old one. Either of these open-end wrenches in the master mechanic's hand will do the job."

I heard someone talking outside the door, and it brought me back to reality, and the fact I was saying a prayer. "Lord, as we face this impossible global situation, please utilize my abilities to accomplish your will. Let me be the old tool in my Master's hand, and with your will, knowledge, and strength, we will get this job done together. Amen." I sat there for a few minutes with my eyes closed as I felt the presence of God sink into my heart, mind, and soul. I had tears in my eyes as I contemplated what this old man would have to do to accomplish the task which was waiting for him, and as I finished my prayer, I nodded off.

A little while later, Antonio came into the room, and said, "El Cabby, the girls are on their way to the Holiday Inn with everything they need." Then he realized I was asleep, but it was too late because he had awakened me by speaking.

"Thanks Antonio. I fell asleep for a few minutes, but I think I need to get out of here for a while to get some fresh air, and clear my head. So, if you don't see me for several hours, don't worry about it, okay?"

"Of course it's okay; you don't think I would tell the Grand Seneschal what to do. If you're going to leave the Mercado please give me some idea where you'll be in case we have an emergency."

"I will do that for sure, Antonio, but I need you to do me a favor. Get me one of those straw hats like the farmers wear, and a Mexican-style shirt, size large, and bring them to the restroom please."

"I will have them there in a few minutes." A few minutes later Antonio entered the restroom and said, "Wow! El Cabby, you've certainly changed your looks, and you do look Mexican now."

"I can't afford to go in public looking like a gringo. I have applied burnt sienna mixed with water to my arms and face and now I look like a Mexican farmer. Let me have the shirt and hat, and then my disguise will be perfect as long as no one speaks to me." I put on the shirt and hat and looked in the mirror, and said, "Yes Antonio, I like it – do I look like a Mexican farmer?"

"Señor Gomez, did you leave your farm to come to Guanajuato for the holidays? With the outfit, and the burnt sienna on your arms and face, I can't tell you're not Mexican, and I know the difference."

"Good, I'm going to leave now, and if you need me, I'll be at La Pirinola Restaurant in San Fernando Plaza with my friends. I'll be having a beer and something to eat as I contemplate what lies ahead for The Knights of the Night. Oh yes, if you send someone for me, have them ask for Señor Gomez."

"Hopefully, I won't have to bother you, and I will expect you back by sundown unless you send word otherwise."

I picked up my crutches, put on my hat, and hobbled out of the shelter, and headed toward one of the entrances to the Mercado. Within ten minutes, I had managed to hobble to the San Fernando Plaza, and was looking for a table at my favorite restaurant.

La Pirinola Restaurant was full of people, with Martin, Alex, and Cuco running full blast to try and wait on everyone in a timely manner. Cesar was standing on the sidewalk at the back of the restaurant watching and waiting for a chance to help if he needed to. I hobbled up next to Cesar with my head down, and said in a very soft voice, "Sir, do you speak English?" When he didn't respond I asked, "Do you have a place where an old gringo can sit and rest?"

Cesar is a very nice and polite man, but he is also a businessman, and he replied, "Sir, if you look around you can see every table is full. Even though I can set up another table for customers, I will set it up for paying customers only. There are many benches around the plaza where you can sit, so please go, and sit on one of them. I only have room for customers who want to buy something to eat or drink."

"But sir," I said, "I'm an old customer and friend of the owner, and I'm sure he would find me a place to sit if he were here."

"My friend," Cesar replied, "I am the owner, and I assure you, I don't know who you are, so please leave me alone, and I mean now!"

I replied with my regular voice, "Cesar, I guess my disguise is working."

Cesar's voice changed as he replied in a whisper, "El Cabby, is this really my friend?"

I replied, "Yes," as I tipped my hat back slightly, so he could see my face.

"I'll be damned!" Cesar said. "You not only got yourself shot, but you must have received a transfusion with Mexican blood, because your skin color has changed."

"Yes it has, and if you can't find me a table, chair, beer, and fries in that order, you will be damned." I laughed, and then hobbled into the restaurant where I could speak freely.

I said, "Today I am Señor Gomez for the sake of my personal safety. Is it okay if I order a beer, and fries, and a place to sit down for a while? I promise I'll behave and be a good Mexican farmer."

"Of course you can," Cesar replied. "I'll tell Martin, Alex, and Cuco who you are, so they won't be shocked and give your identity away."

Within a few minutes they had set up a small table for me. I was enjoying my beer and the meal when Alex approached, and whispered to me, "There is a young lady who comes in every three days or so asking for Evangelina and Berenice. I know who she is, because she has been my neighbor for years, but I'm a Knight myself, and I don't want to say anything to her."

I said, "Alex, the girls will be eating here tomorrow night, and I will do my best to be sure they are here at seven. You just tell the lady her name tomorrow night is Chachis, and if she uses Chachis as her name, the girls will come and ask for her at seven tomorrow evening."

Alex went to the woman and said, "Tomorrow evening, I want you to use Chachis as your name, and the girls will be here at seven looking for a young lady named Chachis. Remember, if you want to see them and visit, you will have to use the name Chachis."

She said, "Thank you, Alex. Tomorrow night I will be here before seven, and my name will be Chachis."

Alex came back to the table and told me that tomorrow night she will be here and will be using the name Chachis.

I said, "Good, now this old man has to head back home as he's getting tired. So if you will excuse me, Alex, I'm going to sneak out of here, and go get some rest." A few minutes later I was in the Mercado to lie down for a good night's sleep.

Chapter 14

May 30–31

The next morning Evangelina called and told me that she and Berenice were ready to discuss the information I had asked them to go over for me. Within twenty minutes of the call I was on my way to the Holiday Inn Express, and our meeting.

I walked into the hotel room, and I said, "Okay girls, let's get down to business – what was the Grand Seneschal flying into Marseille for?"

Evangelina said, "He was flying into Marseille because they were having trouble with one of the Knights who decided to join the Templar Organization which is associated with the Veil Major. By joining the Templar Organization he was putting our whole operation at risk. He was a medium- to high-level member of the Knights, and he had too much knowledge which means he could have compromised our organization."

"Very good, Evangelina," I said. "Have you made any initial contacts to try and find out what has happened since the Grand Seneschal didn't show up for the meeting?"

Evangelina smiled and said, "I made an encrypted inquiry to the group in Marseille. They acknowledged they couldn't risk a chance on the Knight divulging any information, so they took him out the same night the Grand Seneschal disappeared."

I said, "Berenice, get a message to headquarters and make sure they've removed the Marseille's Knight's Blueberry address, password, and name from all communications. It should have already been done, but similar mistakes have happened in the past, and no one thought about it until it was too late."

Berenice said, "Okay, I will take care of it right now, and then I will give you a new set of the minutes. When I copied the minutes for you, I color coded each part of the minutes according to what they dealt with."

"Berenice, you're great!" I said. "I really appreciate how professional you and Evangelina are in your work. You girls need to keep in mind what you're learning now, as it may help qualify you for being a Seneschal some day."

"We'll never be eligible to be Seneschals; will we, El Cabby?" Evangelina replied.

I answered, "Well, if you're a Knight of the Night for five years, and your peers deem you the most worthy Knight for the position by electing you to the office of Seneschal, you certainly could."

The rest of the day was rather unusual because I was going over all the minutes from the Grand Seneschal's past meetings for the last six months. It was important, as well as interesting, to get caught up and find out what was happening in The Knights of the Night globally.

At five in the afternoon, I told the girls to go get cleaned up, because they were having dinner at La Pirinola Restaurant with a friend of mine named Chachis.

Berenice said, "Oh no! El Cabby, we have a friend we were going to call, because we always celebrate her birthday with her, and we're several weeks late now. Isn't it possible for someone else to entertain your friend tonight?"

"I'm sorry, Berenice," I said. "We've already scheduled the meeting, and you need to be there at seven, and it's a very special meeting which you can't miss whatever you do. It's also important that you remain low profile and not attract a lot of attention before you start the meeting.

"Be sure you're at La Pirinola Restaurant early because I think you're going to enjoy the dinner with Chachis even if it is business. Here's the key to my house in case you need to go somewhere secure to discuss anything such as sensitive business. I'll be spending the night here, and you can call me in case you need anything."

Evangelina replied with a sour-looking face, "Of course, can you tell us what this meeting's about, or do we have to wait until we're there to find out? It would be nice to have some idea what we're going to be doing."

I replied, "You will be meeting with a young lady named Chachis who wants to join the Knights. If you feel she is the right person, and she clears the security check from the home office, then you'll need to take her to my house and finish the indoctrination with her there."

"What the hell is going on, El Cabby?" Berenice said, with an irritated voice. "There are many other people at the Mercado who can handle this instead of us, and we deserve a night off, don't we?"

"I know you both deserve a night off, Berenice," I replied. "Tomorrow night you'll have a night off, and I'm sure you'll enjoy it. But tonight they're going to be transferring everything from the Mercado to a new location for the central office, and there won't be anyone to handle this meeting for us. If I could, I would arrange a night off for you. Since I am the Grand Seneschal I can order someone to take your place this evening, but then the two of you will have to help with the move. Which do you prefer – the dinner with a nice lady or helping with the move?"

"We prefer the indoctrination over the move, El Cabby," Berenice said.

I replied, "You girls go ahead and get out of here, and have fun tonight. Stay at my house all night, and you can get into the wine if you'd like to have a little party. Remember though, I will expect you both here at ten in the morning, and ready to go to work."

I was glad to have some peace and quiet for a change, because my brain had reached saturation because of everything I had to learn today. I called room service and had them deliver a bottle of Merlot, and I drank a few glasses while I watched a movie, and the wine put me to sleep. I woke up just in time for the news on TV. The reporter said, "We have startling news tonight that could prove interesting over the next few months. We may be having a visitor from outer space, and I'm not kidding. We're going to go to the New Astronomical Center at the Aerospace School of Astronomy."

Another reporter came online saying, "Last night, while making routine observations of the galaxy one of our students came across what we think is a new asteroid which hasn't been seen before. The school is calling the asteroid RAP-011112, with the RAP standing for the student's initials that discovered it. The asteroid appears to be in a flight path which could bring it close to the Earth; however, it's too early to say at this time. NASA is moving the Hubble Telescope so it can focus on it, and several astronomical centers are doing studies on its position and movement through the solar system. The lead astronomer at the site reports within the next ten days we will understand a lot more about the asteroid and where it's heading. This is Science Writer Richard Blonde reporting."

I sat up in my chair as they were still reporting, because I felt this could be significant news in relation to what we're preparing for in the future, but I didn't know why. A few hours later my cell phone rang, and I answered, "Hello, how can I help you?"

I recognized the voice on the other end of the line immediately. "El Cabby, something is going on, and it's really big!" Antonio said. "No one has figured out what's happening yet, but every phone tap we have on the Illuminati around the world is lighting up right now. We're monitoring everything we can while we're trying to figure it out."

"Antonio," I said, "it's good to hear from you, but I wish you'd wait until you know something for sure before you call me. One of the Illuminati leaders may have died, or they could be calling a meeting of their hierarchy to make new plans on how to eliminate us for all we know."

"El Cabby, we're almost through loading everything for the move to San Miguel, but we're getting calls from around the world to inform us in every country there are major communications going on between the Illuminati organizations. This may be the beginning of a move to shut us down, bringing an end to the Knights, and we felt you needed to know."

"Of course, you're right. I didn't realize whatever is going on is such a major event. While this situation is occurring, I'm going to ask you to do me a favor if you could. Please, put all The Knights of the Night organizations on level 'red' for the next 48 hours. If they're going to start something now we need to be prepared to go down fighting."

"Okay, El Cabby, we'll be on level red for the next 48 hours, and we'll monitor everything, and contact you if anything major changes. You have a good night, El Cabby, and we'll stay in touch and keep you up to date on everything."

"You have a good night too, Antonio."

Antonio hung up, and I started contemplating what we'd do if a worldwide attack on the Knights happened tomorrow. It would be tough, but we would have to do the best we could with what we had to fight with, and it wasn't much. I sat back to watch a John Wayne movie from many years ago where he was playing the part of a Navy pilot. He was flying in a U.S. Navy Corsair with the cockpit window open, his white scarf blowing in the wind. I thought to myself, *This is what the Knights need, a hero who never loses a battle.* Then

I realized, *We have the best hero in the world fighting on our side against the Illuminati. We have God!*

I'm a Christian, and we have God fighting on our side. There isn't any greater hero than our Father in Heaven, and we are going to win this war because of our faith in Him.

Then I had a thought: *What about The Knights of the Night in countries like Turkey, Greece, Saudi Arabia, Iraq, Iran and other Moslem countries: would God be on their side too? What about those countries where they practiced Buddhism, or other religions – would they lose their battles with the Illuminati because they weren't Christian? We had Knights of the Night in those countries too, so would they be abandoned if they were Moslem? Would God also fight on their side in this global conflict? I had no doubt in my mind God had created all the people of the world, and I'm sure He loves them all. Why couldn't all the people of the world believe in one God with many names, and wouldn't it be a better world if all the people realized one God can have many names?*

I was mulling this around in my mind as I fell asleep, and had a dream where God spoke to me and He said, "El Cabby, how many Gods are there in the world?"

I answered, "One, Lord. There is only one God."

Then God asked me, "How many different names do I have?"

I replied, "I don't know, Lord – only you know the answer to that question."

"You're right, my child," He replied.

Then He said, "There is only one God with many names and He does touch all parts of the world. There is also one evil entity, and he also touches all the parts of the world. Don't worry about who I will fight for, because I always fight for those who love me as they know me."

I suddenly awoke to the phone ringing, but I couldn't answer it because I was in another world, which was surreal. I wanted to stay where I was, because there was light, there was peace, and there was God. The only God and He loved all people, cared about all people, and cherished the lives of all people. He hadn't set down a few rules, in a few languages, for just a few people. He talked to and loved everyone regardless of their race, creed, or color. He talked to all people in their own languages, in their own countries, and in ways they could understand according to their culture. All I could do was to enjoy the light and the peace that emanated from God. If I never answered the phone, it wouldn't matter, because the phone was a worldly thing, and it had absolutely nothing to do with God.

The phone stopped ringing, and I mentally said, *Thank You, Lord.* I started to drift away to another world far away, but before I could get there, the phone started to ring again. It seemed so much louder this time and so much more urgent than before. I reached over and picked it up. "Hello."

"Hello," then a slight hesitation, and a voice said, "this is El Cabby, isn't it?"

"Yes, this is El Cabby, Antonio. I was asleep, and so I was slow to answer the phone, but I'm okay now, so what's up?"

"El Cabby, we had a call from one of our Knights who works for the Astronomical Department at one of the universities. He has explained as well as he can at this time the asteroid they discovered was seen a few days ago, but they didn't report it to the news. Preliminary calculations show it may pass closer than ten thousand miles to the Earth."

"Hey, that sounds like good news to me. Being so far away we don't have anything to worry about. Why did you call and wake me up to tell me something that isn't important?"

"El Cabby, an asteroid this size passing the Earth within ten thousand miles is considered dangerous to our solar system, but it's especially dangerous to Earth."

"Antonio, you're telling me we have something to worry about besides the Illuminati and their threat to the people of the world?"

"Yes, it's what I'm telling you, El Cabby; this is probably the reason for all the calls between the Illuminati organizations right now. It probably doesn't have anything to do with the war we are preparing for, because this situation deals more with the survival of the world. Our friend notified us that the scientists and the politicians aren't going to tell anyone what's happening at this time, because they don't want to create a global panic."

"I don't understand – if it's going to miss the Earth by ten thousand miles, why should I worry at all? Ten thousand miles is almost half the way around the Earth, isn't it?"

"You're right, El Cabby. I'm going to give you a quick lesson in astronomy, but keep in mind it'll be very basic. In our solar system, and in the galaxy, all the suns, planets, moons, and astronomical bodies are connected one way or the other by electromagnetic lines of force. Some planets are closer to Earth than others, and the difference is determined by many factors, including mass, speed, density, electromagnetic lines of force, as well as many other things. Any asteroid of size can interfere with those electromagnetic lines of force and cause catastrophic reactions on any or all of the planets. If the asteroid is large enough it may drive one of our solar system's planets out of its orbit, and take its place in our solar system. Many astronomers believe the planet Venus was an asteroid passing through our solar system, and was trapped by our magnetic lines of force, and stayed. If the asteroid did this to the Earth do you have any idea how many people would die? El Cabby, it would kill all life as we know it on the Earth; nothing would survive, plant or animal. Now, don't worry, El Cabby; this asteroid isn't large enough to displace any of our planets. I was just trying to give you an analogy of what could happen.

"The moon lies approximately two hundred and thirty-nine thousand miles away, and it affects many things on the Earth, including the oceans' tides. Now, imagine a huge asteroid coming to one-twentieth the distance from the moon to the Earth, and the effects it might have on all of us. First of all, depending on its mass and speed, it's possible that the Earth's gravitational force could draw it into the Earth, and I hate to tell you this, but that could also destroy all life on the Earth. The Earth has been struck several times by asteroids in our past, and every time it happened, with catastrophic results. Now I hate to tell you, but there are many scenarios which could take place with an asteroid of size capable of destroying all life on Earth."

I said, "Oh my God! Antonio, I had no idea any of those things could happen because an asteroid passed the Earth at a distance of ten thousand miles."

"El Cabby, listen carefully, please," Antonio said. "I'm not an astronomer or a scientist. We will have to wait and see what happens, but it looks like the astronomers, and the world governments, will not tell the public the truth until they absolutely have to. If they did tell the people the truth it could create a worldwide panic."

"Antonio, this is unbelievable! Can anything be done if they're correct about its size and path through the solar system?"

"I don't know. I suppose with our technology we could blow it to smaller pieces, if we could hit it soon enough with a nuclear warhead or two. Of course, it also means the Earth could be hit by hundreds of small asteroids, unless we had a way to blow them up before they hit us. It's also possible, I suppose, to place some rockets on the asteroid and gently push it enough to change its course away from the Earth. Let's face it, El Cabby: I just don't have enough education, or knowledge, to make good scientific guesses about what might happen."

"Antonio, is there anything beneficial that can come of all this?"

"They say there are always good things mixed with the bad. The good thing is they say it's going to be the eighteenth of June before the asteroid is here. If this is true, then we'll have longer to prepare for our war with the Illuminati. Meanwhile, the Illuminati will have their hands full trying to figure out what to do with the asteroid. If they want to control the Earth, and we continue to have faith in God, and the Earth is destroyed, we will be at peace with God and never have to live under the influence of the Illuminati. At that time we wouldn't be living on the Earth anymore, and neither would they."

"You're right, Antonio; we could reap many benefits from this so let's see what happens. I assume our friend at the Astronomical Observatory will keep us up to date on what's going on with this situation, am I correct?"

"El Cabby, he's a Knight of the Night. I'm sure he's going to keep us informed as best he can. Since he only works with the astronomical part of this problem, I'm not sure we will always be up to date with any plans they make on how to handle this asteroid problem. Remember also, we have Knights who work at different levels in the space program."

"Well Antonio, thanks for the update and the education in astronomical science. I will prepare a notice to be released tomorrow to all the Knights' organizations worldwide. We'll just give them the preliminaries at this point, and we'll keep them up to date as time goes by and we learn more ourselves.

"Regardless of everything else going on, I would like to have some reports on our weapons' procurement program if someone could get me some information on where we stand at this point. I'd also like to know how soon we are going to have all our Knights' organizations armed and ready for combat with a sustained amount of ammunition. According to our calculations a sustained amount of ammunition is the amount it takes to keep us fighting for over two months in every country. If you could get that information for me in the next few days, I'd really appreciate it. You have a good night's rest, and you can call me in the morning and give me an update on how the move to San Miguel is going, okay?"

"Of course, El Cabby. Right now it looks like we will be finished with the move by eight in the morning and ready to handle any situation by ten, but I'll see you're updated in the morning. You'll receive a message from one of my staff, because I'll still be catching up on my sleep in the morning."

"Okay Antonio, thanks for all the great work you and your people are doing."

"Good night, El Cabby."

*   *   *

Around ten a.m. the following morning the girls arrived as I was finishing my breakfast. They came into the room, and I heard an unfamiliar voice say, "Hey boss, how're you doing this morning? We brought you a piece of birthday cake from our party last night, and I'm now a member of the gang of four."

I stood up and walked over to Chachis and gave her a hug as I said, "We're glad to have you on board, Chachis. I assume the girls knew what they were doing when they approved you for this work. What in the world are you doing here this morning?"

"I'm here, boss, because a lot of people think you need more protection because you're constantly getting hurt," Chachis said. "I'll go to San Miguel tomorrow morning, and be gone for three days, and when I return I'll be following you like stink on a skunk."

"Well Chachis," I said, "I have no desire to die anytime soon, and I'm really getting tired of being shot every time I turn around."

Berenice spoke up, "Hey, just to set the record straight – if you weren't always sending us away to do other things you probably wouldn't have been shot."

"I know," I said. "Now just forget everything because we have a lot to talk about, and you won't believe what's happening now."

Chapter 15

May 31 – June 1

We had an unusual day as we talked about the asteroid, and the potential problems it posed for all of us, including the Illuminati. We were planning on taking advantage of the lull in activities by the Illuminati to help us prepare for the war. The Illuminati was more concerned with saving the Earth from the asteroid than we were, because we trusted in God for the world's safety. Besides, we didn't have the resources at our disposal to change anything concerning what the asteroid did anyway. The only thing we could do was to pray and hope the Illuminati was successful in their attempt to destroy the asteroid. We also had to use whatever extra time we had to try and prepare for what might happen if the debris landed near us and created a problem.

If the asteroid was going to strike the Earth, we couldn't change it. But, if we were able to reverse the evil that was now taking place on Earth, then we might generate a situation that would be more pleasing to God, and He might save the Earth.

Antonio had called in the morning and reported our weapons' procurement was on time, and we would have everything we needed for the Knights' organizations around the globe within the next month. He also reported we had a lot more money coming in, since our enrollment of new members joining The Knights of the Night around the world had more than doubled. So we ordered new computers, more microwave guns with portable generators, as well as setting aside a reserve fund in order to support The Knights of the Night after the war is over. There was no doubt in anyone's mind there were going to be thousands of Knights who would need help after the war was over, and we weren't going to abandon our brave Knights the way some Governments abandon their veterans by legislating their benefits away.

We also wrote a short release to be sent to all the Knights' organizations in the world about the asteroid and its possible effects.

Knights Official Notice

KON10087

We have learned that the asteroid RAP-011112 which was announced on the news this week may present a more serious problem than what the current world leaders would have you believe. We expect the Illuminati to be completely involved in attempting to solve the problem for the next few weeks, and this should relieve some of the pressure from all of our Knights' organizations, except in Mexico, where the Illuminati believes the Grand Seneschal is holding his office at this time. With this change in priorities from the Illuminati we will be accelerating our weapons' procurement program, and all our organizations should be fully armed within the next month.

We have information on the approaching asteroid including studies of velocity, mass, and chance of collision coming into our office on a regular basis, and we will keep you informed as we learn new information. The closer the asteroid gets to Earth, the more they'll be able to predict what the effect of its presence in our solar system will have on our operations and daily lives. We will do our best to keep you informed as we receive new information about what is happening concerning the asteroid's movement through the solar system.

We have also ordered one thousand new microwave guns, and they should be delivered within six weeks to many of the Knights' organizations throughout the world. These guns run off a portable generator, and are far more effective than the initial MWG-001 model was.

Please keep the home office informed of any unusual activities in your region which may affect our scheduled operations.

Thank you,

Grand Seneschal

GS – Release 090807678

After we sent the notice to all of our organizations we began a research project to try to ascertain where the most likely places an asteroid might hit the Earth. Since we weren't astronomical scientists or even astronomers ourselves, we needed to rely on information that we could extrapolate from the Internet. Chachis proved to be a great asset, because she had an extraordinary intelligence which was capable of analyzing and utilizing great amounts of information.

I was really glad to have her on our team, and by the end of the day I called Antonio in San Miguel to discuss her training and the issuing of her equipment. "Antonio," I said, "I have a slight problem, and I'm sure you can help me resolve it. The problem deals with my newest staff member's equipment and training. Do you have time to discuss it right now, or do I need to call back?"

"We can discuss it now as I'm taking a coffee break; what can I do to help, El Cabby?" Antonio replied.

I said, "Antonio, we brought Chachis into the organization last night, and she has been assigned to my staff. I was going to send her to you tomorrow for her equipment and to schedule her training. In utilizing her mental ability I discovered she has an exceptional mind that can be used to help us understand the current asteroid crisis. Would you like to help me keep her in my office as we work on this tremendous problem? If you would, then could you check out an Uzi and a Blueberry in her name as well as a laptop computer, and send them to us as soon as possible? If you could do it sometime today I would really appreciate it very much."

Antonio replied, "El Cabby, what about her training with the Uzi – you do want her to protect you, don't you? You realize without training she may very well shoot herself, or you, and your staff. Personally, El Cabby, I think you've been shot too many times already, and I would like to keep you alive long enough to get us through this crisis."

"Antonio," I said, "I told you she has an extraordinary mind, and from what I'm seeing she may also have a photographic memory. I believe if you send everything here, Berenice and Evangelina will be able to train her on the Uzi in a few hours. They can take her out to the old shooting range and fire a few rounds to verify her abilities and knowledge of the weapon. If there is any question in my mind, or hers, about her skills with the weapon we will schedule her into the training program immediately. As far as the Defensive Driver's Training Course goes I won't allow her to drive a car I am riding in unless it's an emergency. I believe she can already use a Blueberry, but if she doesn't, you and I both know the Blueberry is very easy to use right out of the box."

"I think you're the Grand Seneschal," Antonio said. "I would trust you with my life anytime, anywhere, and you know better than anyone else what Chachis is capable of accomplishing. So having the faith in you that I do, I think you should go with your gut feeling, El Cabby. If you are wrong about her abilities we can always bring her back here for her regular training. I do recommend you send her to the range so she can shoot a few bursts, and get a feel for firing the Uzi though."

"Okay, Antonio, I will look for the equipment to be delivered by a runner sometime today. Antonio, I want you to know I really appreciate your cooperation on this matter, and we'll talk later about this asteroid situation. For now, my friend, I hope you have a great day."

Antonio said, "You take care, and have a great day too, El Cabby."

"Okay girls," I said, "Chachis will be staying here with us tomorrow instead of going to San Miguel. Her Uzi, Blueberry, and computer will be delivered here sometime later today.

"Evangelina, I want you to teach her everything you know about the Uzi, and then take her to the shooting range we used in Guanajuato so she can get used to the Uzi when it's being fired.

"Berenice, you will teach her everything she needs to know about the Blueberry and its encrypted mode for transferring information to the home office.

"Chachis, you will have to stay away from driving any car I'm in until you have the Defensive Driver's Training Course at the home office, okay?"

Chachis replied, "Yes El Cabby, I won't drive you anywhere as long as someone is here to drive you where you need to go."

I looked at the girls, and they were all beaming at the thought of working together, and I was pleased too, because I felt like I was working with the best team I could possibly assemble. I was certain, if anyone could get The Knights of the Night through the crisis we're facing, then my team and I were up to the task.

"Okay girls," I said, "it's really critical we do our research on where an asteroid might land if it hits the Earth, and I'm sure somebody has already made some studies on this and placed the results on the Internet, so let's find them. We need to know now in order to plan appropriately and try to prevent any catastrophic surprises later."

After the girls had finished their research and preliminary analysis of the data, they sent the information to the astronomer who was keeping us informed about the asteroid's movement and size. His response was if their calculations in size, mass, and velocity were accurate, then the effects would be similar to what they had determined. Even though we didn't have enough information about the asteroid at this time we made a decision to go ahead and make contingency plans in case the asteroid did strike the Earth in one of the locations they had predicted.

When we were planning for survival we based our plans on the survival of The Knights of the Night in any of the twelve countries we had calculated would be most likely to be hit. We had access to thousands of pounds of military food rations sold at surplus stores around the world. We had never shipped food rations in quantity in the past, but we were going to ship them now. We wanted the rations to be strategically placed in all of the twelve countries we thought might be hit by the asteroid.

When it was time for supper we decided I would become Señor Gomez again, so we could eat at La Pirinola Restaurant. I prepared the burnt sienna and put it on my body, and then put on my Mexican clothes and hat, and we headed for the restaurant. It turned out to be a rather uneventful evening as we enjoyed ourselves, had a great meal, and made it back to our room safe and sound.

When it was a little after nine, all hell broke loose when the phone rang.

Evangelina picked up the phone, and said, "Evangelina here."

Then, all I heard was Evangelina asking a list of questions to someone on the other end of the phone: "When?" "Where?" "Who is being held?" "How many troops are there?" "Okay, here's El Cabby." She handed me the phone as she told Chachis and Berenice to get their Uzis and prepare to leave. The girls were scurrying around the room putting on their bulletproof vests and getting their Uzis, and I hadn't even been told yet what the crisis was.

I said, "This is El Cabby – what's happening now?"

"El Cabby, this is Antonio, and we just received a call from Ivan near Cañada de Caracheo. It seems that Cristina and her sister Maria have been detained by the army at the checkpoint outside Cañada de Caracheo on suspicion of aiding and abetting the enemy. It seems the army is serious about the charges, and we only have a short time to do anything about it. We suspect in a few hours they will take Cristina and Maria back to their base camp, and who knows what will happen then. You need to give us some advice about what we need to do, and we need your advice fast."

"Don't worry, Antonio; I have the only plan in mind which can possibly work in this situation, and keep Cristina and Maria's family safe and sound. We're going to handle it with my people, but you can get a contingent force of six Knights and send them to the school where we had the training. We will go by the code name of Clave Azul for communication purposes, and your force will use the code name Rojo Caballeros. We will either call them for help in an hour and a half or you can call them back to the home base at that time."

"Okay, you're code name Clave Azul," Antonio said. "We'll use the code name Rojo Caballeros. We'll talk later, El Cabby, good luck."

"Okay girls, you were correct in getting ready for this crisis, but I'm not going with you. If they knew I was there you might not be able to save Cristina and Maria as easily as you can without me. Here's what I want you to do: attack the checkpoint from the weak side with your Uzis after destroying their Hummer with a grenade, and the element of surprise will be on your side. After taking out their troops leave Cristina and Maria there, but give them a piece of paper saying you are members of The Knights of the Night, and you will strike again.

"By leaving a note with Cristina and Maria and everyone else dead, the army will know that Cristina and Maria are not Knights of the Night, or you would have taken them with you, and they should set them free. After everything is completed I want you to stay and hide fifty meters away from the checkpoint. Observe the relief soldiers when they arrive, and if they don't turn Cristina and Maria loose, then you call for the Rojo Caballeros to come in and assist you. When the Rojo Caballeros arrive I want you to take out the new contingent of troops, and take the girls with you to Cañada de Caracheo. I want you to get the rest of the Ortiz family out of there, and take them to my house in the Rosa Primera Colony.

"You need to get going now, because you don't have much time to complete your mission. Hopefully, I'll see all of you safe and sound with a victory under your belt in a couple of hours. Now get going and I want Evangelina to go over the operation of the Uzi with Chachis while you're on your way there. May God bless all of you." All three of the girls gave me a kiss on the cheek and headed out the door.

All I could do now was wait and see what happened. If three women can take out nine Mexican soldiers without any of the women getting hurt it will be a great victory for The Knights of the Night. I had tears in my eyes as I thought about the girls, and the price they might have to pay tonight.

It wasn't very long before the girls were pulling their car off the side of the road and getting ready to sneak around the Pemex station, and head towards the military checkpoint outside Cañada de Caracheo. Berenice said, "Chachis, when you put on the black camouflage cape let me help you so you get it on correctly."

Chachis replied, "I'm ready now, Berenice."

Berenice walked over to Chachis and showed her how to put her camouflage cape on, and a few minutes later she was ready to go. Berenice said, "Evangelina, are you ready?"

Evangelina replied, "I'm more than ready to do whatever it takes, but I'm not happy with the thought of killing someone."

Berenice said, "Neither am I, but remember, they won't hesitate to kill you, and believe me they will also take Cristina and Maria's life, if they think you're here to set them free."

"Chachis, here's the plan," Berenice said. "Your position will be at the right side, and behind the checkpoint, and you will only fire your Uzi if you absolutely have to. If you do shoot your Uzi, never fire towards where the girls are being held; we don't want to kill the ones we came to save."

Chachis replied, "Yes Berenice, I understand, but if the soldiers go after the girls I will shoot them."

"You do it, Chachis," Berenice said. "Make sure you always shoot towards the left, because if you shoot towards the central front, you may shoot me accidentally. Now Evangelina, I want you to shoot from the right, and the front only, and shooting to the left.

"I'll approach from the front where they usually have three soldiers with one of them manning the machine gun on the Hummer. No one will fire at anything, or anyone, until I use a grenade to destroy the Hummer. You girls stay fifteen meters to the right of the checkpoint, and when the Hummer blows up you attack. We should have nine soldiers to take out, three in the front, and one in the Hummer manning the machine gun, two on each side of the road to check the vehicles going both directions, and one on the radio, who is usually on the left-hand side of the road, and is in charge of communications with headquarters and usually wears a pistol.

"We need to kill them as quickly as we can because the longer it takes, the less chance we have of being successful. Chachis, you have the note saying we are members of The Knights of the Night, and you need to give it to Cristina as soon as we have control of the checkpoint. Do either one of you have any questions about how we are going to handle this?"

"I have one," Evangelina said. "What should we do if some of them surrender before we kill them?"

"I think that's a good question," Berenice said. "We brought three sets of handcuffs, and we brought pepper spray; if anyone surrenders we will handcuff them, spray them with pepper spray, and then knock them out. It's imperative they don't know what we tell Cristina and Maria or this plan isn't going to work."

Berenice asked, "Does anyone have anymore questions?"

They both said no, and Berenice said, "Okay, let's go."

Chachis and Evangelina followed Berenice as she headed off the road, and started slowly working towards the checkpoint where they all took their positions. Then Berenice stumbled to the road approaching the checkpoint staggering and stumbling as if she were drunk. She had her Uzi hanging on her back and hidden under her cape as she was mumbling and staggering closer and closer to the soldiers. You could see the soldiers smile as if Berenice was a pleasant gift from the gods, and it was obvious from their smiles they wanted some of whatever she had to offer.

"Caramba!" she screamed. "You are just what I need tonight – strong, muscular soldiers who are willing to help me find my way home." She smiled as two of the three soldiers in the front left their stations and headed towards her to give her a hand. They were too interested in her to notice the grenade in her right hand; when they were five yards away, she stumbled, threw the grenade, and tripped into the ditch beside the road. The grenade rolled under the Hummer, and with a fiery blast blew it to pieces making it completely useless. While she was rolling into the ditch she worked her Uzi to the front of her body and shot the other two soldiers who had come to help her. They were now screaming with the impact of the bullets from her Uzi penetrating their bodies.

Meanwhile, Evangelina and Chachis were attacking from the right, and Evangelina was using her Uzi effectively as she shot the four soldiers who were trying to recover from the explosion of the Hummer. It was at this point her gun jammed, and she couldn't shoot the soldier who was still sitting down trying to get his radio to function. Chachis hadn't noticed Evangelina's gun had jammed as she was busy giving the paper to Cristina, and telling them what to do and say after they left them at the checkpoint.

Meanwhile the radioman carried a forty-five caliber pistol, and he had taken it out to shoot Evangelina who was desperately trying to fix her Uzi.

Evangelina noticed the radioman lifting his gun to shoot her when she heard a strange sound. A man in black with a turban on his head rode his horse in from the left side and behind the radioman, cutting off his head with a swift swing of his sword. The radioman's head rolled onto the road as his body still gushing with blood from where his head had been fell to the ground.

Evangelina stood in shock not knowing what to think as the horseman shoved his sword back into its sheath, and rode towards her. He stopped his horse a few feet in front of her, and said in a deep mystical voice, "Fear not, for I'm on your side. Tell El Cabby that Emir has arrived, and soon there will be three other warriors to join in this fight for freedom and justice." Then Emir rode into the night and disappeared.

The girls stood there in disbelief at what just happened, and they said nothing, as Berenice motioned them to their new hiding place about thirty yards from the checkpoint. Within ten minutes a contingency of nine soldiers arrived and searched the checkpoint to make sure it was safe. Cristina and Maria played their parts well in explaining they had witnessed three women Knights of the Night, and the lone horseman, killing all nine of the soldiers at the checkpoint.

A few minutes later the soldiers called headquarters and told them what had happened, and the lead officer on the scene said, "Sir, the women being held for aiding and abetting The Knights of the Night are still here. It seems ridiculous to hold them any longer, because if they were

Knights of the Night, they would have been set free. The Knights let them live so they could be witnesses to the fact of what happened here tonight when three women Knights and one man on horseback killed everyone at the checkpoint and blew up one of our Hummers. Perhaps, we should kill the girls too, so we can make up our own story about what happened."

The officer at headquarters said, "Covering up the truth could backfire on us if someone actually saw the girls alive after the soldiers were killed, and there's no way to know whether that happened or not. Can you imagine how many more people would join The Knights of the Night if they thought we were killing their daughters in order to hide the truth? I want you to set the girls free, offer them a ride home, and apologize for everything.

"If they contact any of the news stations with this story we're going to look very bad for holding them in the first place. We won't look good anyway when they find out three women and one man can kill nine of our soldiers without any of them even getting hurt. I want you to keep your men at the checkpoint, and keep checking the local traffic. Meanwhile we're sending twenty extra troops and a couple of dog handlers to try and track the Knights who did this."

When Berenice and the others saw the girls set free and walking home on the road towards Cañada de Caracheo, they silently walked back to their car and drove to Guanajuato, and safety. Forty-five minutes later they were very excited but safe and sound in the hotel room with El Cabby.

Berenice said, "El Cabby, everything went perfect, except Evangelina's gun jammed. She would have been killed by the last soldier except for the fact she was saved by a man riding a white horse who cut the soldier's head off with a sword."

"Okay, okay," I said, "now tell me what really happened without any add-ons or games this time."

Evangelina spoke up this time. "It's true, El Cabby; we had killed all the soldiers but the radioman when my gun jammed. Berenice and Chachis didn't notice I was in trouble because it happened so fast, and they were busy accomplishing their own missions. I was trying to clear my Uzi when the radioman pulled his gun, and was getting ready to shoot me. Before he could fire his gun a man dressed in black with a turban on his head rode in on a white horse, and cut off the radioman's head with a sword. Then he rode up to me, and told me not to worry, because he was on our side. He also said to tell El Cabby there were three more warriors coming to help us."

"Okay Evangelina," I said, "I think your story is cute, but you girls don't really expect me to believe it, do you?"

"El Cabby, they're telling the truth," Chachis said. "But they forgot to mention he also said his name was Emir – how many Emirs do you know, El Cabby?"

I sat there stunned for a minute trying to regain my composure when I finally realized they were telling the truth. Then I said, "I don't know anyone named Emir. Did he look like he was from the Middle East or someplace else?"

"Well, it looked like he was wearing a black robe, or tunic, from a Middle Eastern country," Chachis said. "He had a black turban on his head, and he was very dark skinned. He was a lot darker than most Mexicans, and he had a black beard and mustache that was trimmed. He spoke with a strange accent which almost sounded French, but even after discussing it on the way here, none of us are sure what country the accent could be from. His horse was a perfect white horse without another mark on it that we could see. Remember, it was dark outside, and it all happened very quickly. It didn't sound like the horse had horseshoes on it either, because the sound is completely different than when you hear a horse with shoes on the pavement. One minute the horse and rider were there, and the next minute they were gone; it was all very haunting and unbelievable.

"Oh yes, there's one other thing we thought we wouldn't tell you, because it didn't make any sense, and it doesn't really change anything. Then just before we got back to the hotel, we decided it might be relevant, and we made a mutual decision to mention it to you. When Emir rode in on his horse we didn't hear anything before we actually saw him, and it wasn't surprising with everything going on around us. When he left we didn't even hear the horse's feet hit the ground after he was out of sight, and out of the light. It was as if Emir and his horse both vanished into thin air once they were in the dark."

I sat there for a minute trying to let everything the girls had just said sink into my brain. I didn't know what to think about Emir; was he a Knight of the Night who lives near Cañada de Caracheo? Was he a Knight of the Night who just happened to be riding a horse, and wearing his illegal sword, and was out looking for people who needed to be rescued? It certainly didn't make logical sense for anyone to do that either. Of course, riding a horse and carrying a sword in public is something we never do, because it's too obvious, and during these days wearing your sword was a sure way to get arrested for being a Knight of the Night. If you were seen wearing a sword by the soldiers you would probably be shot on the spot. Besides, The Knights of the Night's swords are more decorative than functional, and in Mexico a sword that is sharp is considered a weapon and could land you in jail.

I picked up the phone and called Antonio, and he answered on the second ring. "Hello, this is Antonio; what can I do for you?" he said.

"Antonio," I said, "do we have any Knights of the Night who live near Cañada de Caracheo, who wear black Middle Eastern-style clothes including a black turban and ride white horses?"

Antonio laughed, and said, "We've been listening on the news all night about the soldiers who were killed in an attack by three women with Uzis and a man dressed in black on a white horse. Is this a true story, or did they make it up, so they wouldn't look so stupid after our three lady Knights killed nine of their soldiers and blew up a Hummer?"

"Antonio," I said, "it really did happen, but we have no idea who the rider was. He told Evangelina that his name was Emir, and to tell me he had three other warriors who would be joining us soon. He did not mention The Knights of the Night, but he told Evangelina he was on our side which should have been obvious after he saved her life.

"Antonio, is it possible for you to check and see if we have any Knights who ride a white horse and live near the pueblo of Cañada de Caracheo?" I asked. "While you're at it, if you don't mind, also check to see how many Knights we have near Cañada de Caracheo who own horses. He said he had three other horsemen who were going to join us soon. This is all so unbelievable, but it's true, because I have five witnesses who will swear Emir saved Evangelina's life tonight by cutting off a soldier's head with a swift swing of his sword."

"El Cabby," Antonio replied, "I will check it out as soon as I can in the morning, and I'll get back to you as soon as I know anything. If you haven't heard something by noon you can assume we couldn't verify anything."

"Thanks Antonio," I said. "You get a good night's rest, and we'll talk to you in the morning."

I hung up the phone, and I said, "Well girls, we have no idea who Emir is, but it doesn't matter, because I am so thankful all of you came home in one piece. None of you can possibly realize how much I love you as family; you are like three daughters to me, and I intend to keep all of you as long as I can."

You could have cut the silence with a butter knife, because all of the girls were wiping away their tears. It was evident we had established a special bond which would last a lifetime. After a few seconds Chachis said, "I hope you don't mind if we order a couple bottles of wine from room service. We would like to celebrate our victory tonight, because none of us thought we would ever be able to kill one soldier, let alone nine. Now the memories of those soldiers dying are starting to haunt us, so it could be a long night before any of us will be able to get any sleep."

Evangelina chimed in, "Seeing the radioman's head rolling around on the road is something I will never forget. I may have to take therapy to recover my mentality after seeing it, even if I wasn't the one who cut it off."

"I know," I said, "war is hell! Memories of death and dying always haunt soldiers after their first kill. The only ones it doesn't bother are cold-blooded killers, and if I thought any of you enjoyed killing, I wouldn't want you on my team."

Berenice said, "Thanks for telling us, El Cabby, because none of us enjoyed what we had to do tonight. We all agreed it had to be done to save innocent lives in the long run, and it's what made us capable of killing. If we win this war we'll have actually saved millions of lives throughout the world who would have become slaves to be used, and abused. We know we did the right thing tonight, and it makes it worthwhile."

"I'm glad that you realized it was necessary to save other lives," I said. "I hope you will always remember it. Now call room service, and order four bottles of Merlot, and we'll have a party. I want to celebrate too if you don't mind, even if I wasn't there. You see, I'm very proud of all of you – it took courage to do what you did tonight."

We partied until the wine was gone, and then I fell asleep in one of the double beds while the girls slept in the other one. I woke up to the sound of the phone ringing, and as I reached for where I thought it was, I heard Evangelina saying, "Hello, this is Evangelina; what can I do for you?"

The voice on the other end said, "This is Antonio, and I'm calling to tell you we have a few Knights with horses near Cañada de Caracheo. None of them has a white horse, and none of them have black beards and mustaches, or wear Middle-Eastern clothing. So I don't know who came to your rescue last night, but it doesn't appear to have been one of our Knights, and I will get back to you if I hear anything else."

"Okay," Evangelina said. "You have a good day, Antonio."

"Don't hang up!" Antonio yelled. "We have more news coming this afternoon about the asteroid, so tell El Cabby we'll update him later today on what we know."

"Of course," Evangelina said. "Now can I say goodbye?"

"Goodbye, Evangelina," he said. "We'll call you later today."

Chapter 16

June 1

A little while later, we managed to get cleaned up, and we had breakfast delivered to the room, and we were eating while we watched one of the morning shows on the television. A news reporter said, "We have an unusual report this morning, and it comes from a small pueblo named Cañada de Caracheo that is near Celaya, Guanajuato. The army was holding two young ladies at a military checkpoint on suspicion of aiding The Knights of the Night. Before the two ladies could be transferred to army headquarters in the area, the checkpoint came under attack by three women Knights of the Night. After the women killed eight of the nine soldiers at the checkpoint, a man dressed in Middle Eastern clothing riding a white horse, rode in, and with a sword killed the last soldier by cutting off his head.

"We have been able to locate the two women who were being held, and we have them with us this morning for a short interview. This is Cristina and Maria Ortiz, who are sisters and live in Cañada de Caracheo, a pueblo a few miles from here. Good morning, ladies, I imagine you're glad to be alive this morning."

Cristina responded with a big smile on her face, "Yes, we're glad to be here this morning because last night it looked as though we would be harmed by the soldiers one minute, and then killed by The Knights of the Night the next. We were scared to death, and we're both still nervous after last night. The worst part is when you think about what the soldiers could have done to us, when we weren't even guilty of helping the Knights – it's very frightening."

The reporter asked, "Cristina, can you tell us why you and your sister were being held at the checkpoint last night?"

"I really don't understand myself," Cristina said. "We were returning home after visiting some friends, when the soldiers told us we were under arrest, for aiding and abetting The Knights of the Night. We objected, but they seized us, and said they were sending us to their headquarters for questioning. None of it made any sense, and we were fearful of what our own army might do to us."

"Do you have any associations with The Knights of the Night?" the reporter asked, and Maria answered with a serious expression on her face, "No! We don't have any associations with any of The Knights of the Night. They're a secret association, and they don't proclaim who they are in public, so in reality you could be a Knight of the Night, and I wouldn't even know it. So would you detain and question me for talking to you? I don't think so! I suppose as many Knights of the Night as there are in Mexico we could know several Knights of the Night and not even be aware of it."

The reporter turned to Cristina and asked, "Cristina, under the circumstances, weren't you frightened with the turn of events last night?"

Cristina smiled, and responded immediately, "Of course we were afraid! We were afraid for our lives with everything that was happening around us, especially when one of the women Knights approached us with a paper stating they were Knights of the Night. The woman told us to give the paper to the military reinforcements who would be showing up soon."

The interviewer asked, "Maria, can you fill us in on what you saw during the attack?"

Maria replied, "The first thing I remember is a drunken woman approaching the checkpoint, and teasing the soldiers, and in the next instant she tripped into the ditch beside the road, and a second later there was a loud explosion as the Hummer blew up and flew into the air. It was horrifying, and made us fear for our lives.

"After the explosion I closed my eyes for a few seconds, but I could hear the guns firing, and when I opened my eyes there were two women attacking the soldiers from the right side. One of them was shooting the soldiers while the other approached us, and to be honest I thought she was going to kill us too, but I was wrong.

"The woman who pretended to be drunk killed all the soldiers in the front of the checkpoint; the other woman killed all the other soldiers but one, and the third woman was approaching us. The one soldier who was still alive pulled his pistol to shoot one of the women who was having trouble with her gun, but before he could fire his gun a man dressed in black riding a white horse cut off his head." Maria started to cry and sob as she uttered, "I have never seen anything like it in my life, and I have never been so frightened!"

The reporter said, "Cristina, it had to be terrifying – can you tell us anything else?"

Cristina said, "Well, after the horseman cut off the soldier's head he then rode over to the woman whose life he had saved, and said something to her. Then he rode off into the darkness as fast as he had come in. I don't think the lady he had approached knew him, because she looked scared to death as he rode his horse over to where she was. It was as if she thought he was going to cut her head off next, and to be honest I believed he was going to kill her too. He looked like someone from the Middle East, and nothing at all like I would expect a Knight of the Night to look."

"One more question, Cristina, and then I'll let you and your sister go," the reporter said. "What do you think a Knight of the Night would look like if you ever saw one?"

"Is this a trick question?" Cristina said. "We did see three women Knights of the Night last night you know. They stood straight, walked with pride, and even though they didn't say anything out loud, their body language said a lot about how they felt. It said they were proud of what they were doing, and they would have no fear in doing it over and over again if they had to in order to keep their freedom."

The reporter said, "Cristina and Maria, thanks for coming down and filling us in on what must have been the scariest night of your lives. Okay folks, you've heard it live right here, and we'll keep you updated if anything else happens."

Evangelina grabbed the TV controller, and shut the television off, as she said, "Look, I hope nobody minds, but I don't want to listen to this all day. I'm still upset about having to kill those soldiers last night even if it was necessary to save our friends."

I looked at her, and said, "It's okay, Evangelina; we all understand how you feel, and it's better if you can stay busy so you don't have to think about it. I want you to take Chachis to the shooting range this morning, and let her fire her Uzi for a few minutes only. I probably shouldn't have sent her with you last night without some training on using her Uzi. Everything turned out okay, but I never want to put her in a situation like that again. Now, listen Evangelina, the range is abandoned, because we now have a new shooting range we're using near San Miguel. There isn't any way I want you on the range more than ten minutes after you fire the first burst of her weapon. It's very likely when you fire the Uzi someone's going to hear the noise, and report it to the army."

"Okay, El Cabby," Evangelina said. "We'll be back in an hour and a half or less. Is there anything else you want us to do while we're out?"

"No," I said, "we're going to receive more information on the asteroid sometime today, and when we do we may need your brilliant minds to help us understand what it means. In other words I need you here as soon as you're finished. If we finish our work early, I may treat everyone to another night at La Pirinola Restaurant, because it's evident you miss seeing Cesar, and his gang of waiters."

Chachis had already picked up her Uzi and placed it under her coat, and was ready to go to the range. Evangelina picked up the car keys, and they left the room leaving Berenice and I alone.

Then I picked up a manual, and started to read about HAARP, which is a United States program initiated a number of years ago for several purposes. HAARP is an acronym for High-Frequency Active Auroral Research Program and similar configurations, as well as HAARP are also known as ionosphere heaters. The information on HAARP proved to be very complicated, so I decided to look at a DVD that was sent with the literature.

When I opened the first video I saw a warning about children watching the video, and then I saw the logo for CBC News. I immediately stopped watching the video, and researched the acronym CBC, finding out it stands for Canadian Broadcasting Corporation.

CBC News was established in the 1930s, and it is the department responsible for gathering and producing the news on CBC television, radio, and online services. CBC News is the largest news broadcaster throughout Canada with local, regional, and national broadcasts and stations.

I decided to go ahead and watch the videos on the DVD that was delivered with the written material. I discovered the HAARP Project was designed after the inventions of Serbian-American scientist Nikola Tesla who had lived in the late eighteen and early nineteen hundreds. He was a genius who had many inventions, and one of them was the Tesla coil. A Tesla coil is a type of resonant transformer circuit invented around 1891. It is usually used to generate very high voltage, low current, and high frequency, alternating current electricity. He also had an invention which could theoretically pulse electricity from place to place without the utilization of electrical power lines. Nikola Tesla died without being able to implement or prove many of his inventions, but the patent rights have been sold to other parties to further develop.

A number of years later another inventor named Bernard Eastlund picked up on Tesla's inventions and ideas, and worked to perfect the theories and utilization of those inventions. Eastlund developed patents which were incorporated into the HAARP system. For instance, his inventions included the use of HAARP for weather control, the development of a missile shield, and the development of death ray particle beam weaponry to be used on the battlefield.

Bernard Eastlund's patents were sold to E-Systems, and then to Raytheon, who are huge United States contractors for the development of special weapons' systems. Finally, HAARP was recognized as a possible way of practicing mind control over large populations of people.

When I heard the last statement in the video I had to pause the video. *This is nothing but technogarbage.* I thought. After debating with myself for a few minutes about whether or not to continue watching the video I decided that since it was made by CBC News and presented during their regular programming hours it had to be fairly accurate, and therefore, I continued watching it.

The video continued to explain that in the 1960s the Russians bombarded the American Embassy in Moscow with microwave radiation in the hope of creating confusion in the minds of the American employees. I stopped the video again, because I remembered seeing it on the news many years ago, and I had a cold chill run down my spine because I realized this information was true. I thought to myself, *Could the Russians also have a system similar to HAARP?* I opened Internet Explorer again on my computer, and did some basic research to find out the Russians have their own ionosphere heater called "Sura" located in central Russia about ninety miles from the city of Nizhny Novgorod. I also found out there's a good possibility the Russians have also been experimenting with it in the use of population control. After all, if they were using microwave on the American Embassy in the sixties what could they possibly have learned and be using many years later.

I discovered there are several HAARP systems owned by several countries around the world. The United States has three HAARP systems set up in the world today: one is at Arecibo observatory in Puerto Rico; one is near Fairbanks, Alaska; and the other one is at Gakona, Alaska. The Russians have their own ionosphere heater called "Sura," located in central Russia. The European Incoherent Scatter Scientific Association (EISVAT) operates one near Tromsø in Norway which is capable of transmitting over one gigawatt of effective radiated power. The Canadian Government has one near Cape Race, Newfoundland, but this site evidently doesn't have the capability to transmit, and may be a passive post for listening to the transmissions which are emitted by other ionosphere heaters around the world. After reading about all these ionosphere heating sites I was definitely concerned, because the information I was learning was starting to upset me.

With all these sites heating the ionosphere for one purpose or another, at different times, and knowing they had the capability to affect the weather was very unnerving. Is it possible all these sites were adding to the problem of global warming? Was it possible all the tornados, terrible hurricanes, and unusual weather happenings around the world were being caused by these ionosphere heaters? I'm not a scientist, but I couldn't help but wonder how many catastrophes could have been prevented if there were no ionosphere heaters. Then you had to wonder if the inclement weather in the United States is being caused by the Russians. Or is the Russians' inclement weather being caused by the United States? If global warming was out of control around the world was it only being caused by greenhouse gases, or were the ionosphere heaters actually exacerbating the problem?

I was getting tired of trying to comprehend all this technogarbage which was more than I could handle, and my brain was shutting down, and within ten minutes my conscious brain had shut down, and I was asleep.

"Ouch!" I screamed as I woke up. "What in the world are you doing to me?"

Berenice said, "I'm sorry, but I remembered that we hadn't changed the dressing on your leg in two days. Since you're not getting much exercise, I know we have to keep it clean, or you could develop gangrene, and lose your leg. I thought I could change the dressing without waking you up. I should have known better. I'm very sorry, El Cabby!"

"Berenice," I said, "I appreciate what you're doing, but it really hurts now. So, let's get it done so I can continue studying this technogarbage."

"Look, El Cabby," Berenice said, "it really looks bad so I'm going to clean the wound with alcohol, and then hydrogen peroxide before I rewrap it. I also want you to take the last bottle of antibiotics the doctor gave you after I'm finished, okay?"

"It's okay, Berenice. I know the wound needs cleaned, and I'm sorry I said anything," I whined. "Let's just get it over, so I can get busy with what I have to do."

A few minutes later Berenice had finished, and I started taking the antibiotics. "Thanks Berenice," I said. "I really do appreciate you changing the dressing for me. I promise you if you have to do it again, I'll be a better patient than I was today."

The phone rang, and I picked it up, "Yes, it's me. What can I do for you?"

Antonio laughed, and said, "El Cabby, you never answer the phone that way – what in the world's going on over there?"

I said, "Well, I was tortured by Berenice a little while ago when she changed the dressing on my leg, and then Evangelina is out familiarizing Chachis with her Uzi so she knows how to use it. I have also tried reading a technogarbage report on HAARP, and Microwave Mind Control, which seems to put me asleep in seconds. Now what can I do for you, Antonio?"

"Well," Antonio said, "I wanted to update you on the latest information we have concerning the asteroid, if you have time."

"Of course it's okay," I said. "Tell me what's happening with our intergalactic visitor."

Antonio replied, "The latest word is it may pass closer to the Earth than we thought, but no one is absolutely sure yet. It looks like it's going to be a hazard any way you look at it. It appears that NASA is trying to decide how to break it up, and it looks like they will try to destroy it using fifteen Tomahawk cruise missiles each carrying a two point one megaton warhead. Of course this will depend on exploding the missiles at precise locations, at the right time in front of the asteroid, which is evidently thirty-two miles across and thirty-six miles long.

"The idea is to explode in front of the asteroid in an arc with the warheads approximately every two miles across the length of the asteroid which is moving at twenty-two thousand miles an hour. If they break it up they don't know if it will break into small pieces, or in big pieces, because there's no way to know at this time. If the asteroid breaks into small pieces some may still hit the Earth, and cause a lot of destruction wherever they land. If the asteroid breaks into big pieces and hits the Earth there's a chance of massive destruction wherever they land.

"The Tomahawk missiles will be launched in a sequence from three space shuttles which are being rejuvenated for this mission. The cargo bays are being modified at this time to hold the missile launchers, and the missile control equipment is being installed in each shuttle. The Tomahawk missiles will have to explode at approximately the same time, plus or minus a few milliseconds. Missile number one will hit within two miles of one end of the asteroid, and missile fifteen within two miles of the other end of the asteroid. All fifteen Tomahawk missiles will detonate within milliseconds of each other creating an arc and massive pressures which will hit along the entire length of the asteroid breaking its back in many places and, hopefully, destroying it completely.

"The other logistic which needs to be considered is the maximum range of the space shuttles, and that is six hundred miles, and the maximum range of the Tomahawk missiles is two thousand miles. The idea is to break up the asteroid as far from the Earth as possible so most of the debris will miss the Earth completely. The missiles will have to be launched at exactly the right time in order to hit the asteroid at a distance of at least two thousand five hundred miles from the Earth, and supposedly this can be done easily. Each of the missile launchers on the space shuttles will be able to launch a missile every ten seconds, but they all have to detonate in an arc in front of the target at basically the same time in order to be the most effective, and theoretically it can happen.

"Another problem they're not sure about is how much effect the radiation from the nuclear explosions might have on the Earth, and at this point they think it will be minimal and dependent on how much debris actually hits the Earth."

"How soon will they be making the attack to destroy the asteroid?" I said.

Antonio said, "El Cabby, it looks like it will be on the eighteenth of June when the asteroid is approximately two thousand five hundred miles from the Earth."

"Okay," I said, "but it's going to put the asteroid very close to the Earth if it fails."

"Yes, that's true," Antonio replied. "If this attempt fails, the asteroid, or parts of it, could hit the Earth within one hour of the failure."

"Okay Antonio," I said, "there's nothing we can do either way except to try and prepare for whatever's coming. Thanks for the update, Antonio; keep me posted, and I'll talk to you later."

I hung up the phone as Evangelina and Chachis walked back in. I said, "Hey, how did it go on the shooting range?"

"Everything went fine," Evangelina said. "Without any training she shoots better than I do."

Berenice said, "Do you think we'll have dinner at La Pirinola Restaurant this evening?"

"Yes," I said, "but I want you girls to dress down a little, and I will be Señor Gomez again, and we'll try to keep from attracting any attention. Berenice, try to control your laugh please, because half of the people in Guanajuato know the sound of your laugh."

"Okay," Berenice said, "I'll dress down, and I promise to control my laugh. I'll just sit there with a long face, and pretend I don't know you. Ha! Ha!"

I said, "Well girls, with all my study on HAARP this morning, I know the HAARP project may cause some warming of the ionosphere and might even affect global warming."

"Hold on," Evangelina said, "what in the world is HAARP?"

I said, "HAARP stands for 'High-frequency Active Auroral Research Program' – an experimental program for superheating the Earth's ionosphere. The HAARP phased-array transmitter radiates the Earth's ionosphere with high-frequency radio waves generating heat and making temporary distinct electromagnetic differences in the Earth's magnetic lines of force."

I had to stop and think for a minute about everything I had read earlier in the day. I said, "In an Arctic compound a couple hundred miles from Anchorage, Alaska, they have erected a powerful transmitter designed to beam more than a million watts of energy into the upper reaches of the ionosphere. The experiment involves a device designed to zap the skies many miles above the Earth with high-frequency radio waves. The United States Navy and Air Force who are co-sponsors of the project claim it is to develop new forms of communications and surveillance technologies. They claim it will enable the military to send signals to nuclear submarines, as well as to see deep underground. It can also be used to affect weather patterns, block enemy communications, destroy enemy missiles, and create atomic-type explosions without radiation. Then finally it supposedly is capable of affecting the way people think through the use of mind control."

I hesitated again to get my thoughts together, and then I continued, "My concern now is whether it's possible that HAARP is adding even more heat to the ionosphere, and when you consider Russia has also been using an ionosphere heater for many years, it's no wonder some of the past Presidents of the United States have denied mankind was creating global warming through greenhouse emissions. They also knew the United States, and a few other countries, might be the biggest cause of Global Warming. The United States has three HAARP systems set up in the world today: one is at Arecibo observatory in Puerto Rico; one is near Fairbanks, Alaska; and then HAARP is at Gakona, Alaska.

"I also found out there are several other ionosphere heating systems around the world. The Russians have their own ionosphere heater called 'Sura,' located in central Russia. The European Incoherent Scatter Scientific

Association (EISVAT) operates one in Norway, which is capable of transmitting over one gigawatt of effective radiated power."

Evangelina chimed in, "If the people of the world have their mindset changed electronically by HAARP, and perhaps Microwave Mind Control, then no one will even consider fighting the Illuminati. Everyone will just acquiesce and give in to whatever the Illuminati demands."

Chachis said, "Isn't there anything we can do to prevent this mind control by microwave, or HAARP?"

"I have been able to research two things which may work against microwave beam mind control, but I'm not sure how effective they are," I said. "In the sixties, when the microwave technology was first being tested it was used in Britain against a group of women who were protesting outside a military base. There wasn't any way but one for the women to realize they were being hit by a microwave beam, and it was through the utilization of a microwave leak detector.

"The women were having varying symptoms like:

1. Faintness;
2. Nausea;
3. Feminine problems;
4. Retinal burning; and
5. Tumors that grew rapidly.

"Remember, this was in the sixties when everything concerning microwave beams was in its infancy. It's reported that once they suspected what was happening to the women, they put sheets of aluminum foil inside the walls of the tents they were using, and the effects stopped.

"Later in the eighties when microwave mind control was more refined, it was possible to induce a lot of other effects. It's said they can even induce thoughts into your mind, and in some cases they can even induce words the victims can hear audibly, as if someone was standing near to them speaking.

"Many people claim they're being harassed by microwave beams by the Government today for one reason or another. Since this has become a weapon of choice for some government agencies, it has been reported the only thing you can use to eliminate the effect is to use grounded wire mesh in the walls of your home or in your clothes. We don't really know if these things work or not without testing it, and we are preparing some special uniforms now to see if they work the way we want them to.

"The scariest thing about all this is HAARP causes the same effect on large masses of people, but at the same time it heats up the ionosphere. No one is sure whether there is any protection against HAARP, and we don't even know how directional the HAARP waves really are. A number of years ago the people in Portland, Oregon, were having some strange experiences which many people believed were caused by HAARP. Also, the Russians in their application of HAARP technology were so effective the United States Government had to complain because they were affecting our maritime communications. The Russians didn't stop their use of HAARP though, but they did change the frequency slightly, and the effects which were happening to our maritime communications ceased.

"The United States Government claims they're no longer using HAARP in Alaska, but our Knights in Alaska say it's still being used occasionally. We don't know what they're doing, but they aren't even acknowledging they use the equipment.

"We have verification the Russians are still using their system, and we have no way of knowing how much this may also be affecting global warming."

"Wow," Berenice said, "this is really heavy-duty stuff for us to be fighting against, and if they utilize it when the real war starts we don't have a chance."

"I know," I said. "We're going to do some testing of our own with clothing and baseball caps with a very fine wire mesh sewed into them. If it works it may also present a defense we can use against their use of microwave mind control systems."

Evangelina said, "Hey, won't it also make you a great lightning rod?"

"Evangelina," I said, "I suppose it's possible it could have that effect, but in a lightning storm we'll just unfasten the ground clip from the shoes to the ground."

She said, "I hope it works."

"Ha! Ha! Ha!" Chachis laughed, and then she said, "I can see it now with us walking through a thunderstorm towards the enemy lines, and we're all lit up like Christmas trees."

"Okay, that's enough," I said. "We can joke all day about what's going on with our research, and with what might happen under certain conditions, but it won't change anything. So I'm going to get ready to become Señor Gomez. You girls can start getting dressed for dinner tonight while I get ready, and remember to dress down because we don't want to attract any extra attention while we're out."

"Yes boss," Berenice said. "I suppose we'll have to leave the Uzis at home, too."

"My Berenice," I said, "your laughter is like a breath of fresh air, and your Uzi also has a sting. Tonight you will leave them both at home, and we will all be safer because you do."

A half an hour later we left for the restaurant, and a great dinner.

Chapter 17

June 1–2

It was a great night at La Pirinola Restaurant with a good meal and dancing. On some evenings at the San Fernando Plaza, they play music for dancing, and dozens of people show up to dance the night away. The girls had a great time, and so did I even though we left while the party was still in full swing.

When we returned to our room I had a feeling something was wrong, but I didn't know what had changed. My life experience has taught me that when something feels wrong, there is almost always a problem somewhere, somehow, and you must find the problem and fix it if you can.

By using some very quick hand motions, I directed the girls back outside the room and into the hall where I whispered very softly, "Okay girls, I want you to pack everything up, and get ready to move now, and we'll leave in a half an hour or quicker if we can. You don't have to be neat about everything, just pack up your stuff, and stay quiet until we're out of here."

"What's wrong, El Cabby?" Berenice said in a soft, but concerned voice. "Why do we have to leave?"

"We may be bugged, so check everything with the electronic bug detector before you pack it, and pack everything as quietly as you can. I am going to say something out loud about staying through the night just in case anyone is listening, and then turn on the TV."

We walked back into the room, and then I said in my normal voice, "Okay girls, we're all tired so we'll spend another night here, and then we'll head for Aguascalientes in the morning. If we get an early start we'll be there in time for the opening of the art show." Then I turned the TV on to create some background noise while we packed to get out of there.

In a van in the parking lot, the Mexican Federale Police were listening to everything that we said. The officer in charge said, "Good, they're leaving for an art show in Aguascalientes in the morning. We will break down their door at three a.m. and catch them while they're sleeping."

Meanwhile, in the hotel room we were scurrying around quietly as we prepared to leave. As soon as something was ready to take to the car Berenice would take it to the door, and hand it to Evangelina who would take it to the car and load it. We were all very efficient and quiet as we worked diligently behind the background noise of the TV.

A half hour later we were in the car heading down the road for the Rosa Primera Colony, and my home. I had motioned for everyone to be silent as we got into the car. When we were halfway downtown I motioned for Evangelina to stop the car, and when she stopped I stepped outside the car and called Antonio on my cell phone.

Antonio answered the phone, "Hey! It's the middle of the night, El Cabby. What in the world's going on now? I need to sleep either during the day or at night so please make a decision, and let me know which it is, so I can get some rest."

"Antonio, I'm really sorry, but I'm not creating the problems. It's our enemy who's creating the problems, and I would rather be sleeping too."

"El Cabby, what's happened this time?"

"I don't want to tell you, Antonio; just have someone in San Miguel bring my staff and I new computers. Have them bring them to my home, and we'll give them the old computers when they arrive. I want you to be sure to destroy the old computers by fire so nothing can possibly survive."

"El Cabby, have you gone out of your mind? Those are pretty drastic measures to take. So, why don't you tell me what's going on that I don't know about."

"Okay Antonio, we went to La Pirinola Restaurant for dinner tonight, and when we returned to the room, I had a feeling something was wrong. So I ordered everyone to quietly pack up and make a quick departure.

"We are going to leave the car in the parking lot near La Dama's Bar. Then we'll take a taxi to my home in the Rosa Primera Colony where I plan on us staying a few days. If there was a bug in the hotel room we couldn't find it, but they may have placed the bug inside one of the computers. So if you turn the computers on it will give them your coordinates. We can't take a chance on that happening, so I want to be sure the computers are completely destroyed by fire."

"El Cabby, personally, I think you've lost your mind but you're the boss, as well as my friend, and you're always correct. So I'll do anything you ask me, and you'll have your new computers delivered in the morning, and your old computers will be destroyed exactly the way you've requested. Is there anything else you need me to do?"

"Well, there's one more thing. We need to change cars at the same time we change computers, and I want the car we are using now parked near La Sauceda. Tomorrow, I want it thoroughly checked for a tracking dot before it is moved to San Miguel."

"Okay boss, you will have your computers and a different car in the morning."

"Tomorrow morning will be fine. You could take care of the car tonight if you want to."

"El Cabby, it's after midnight, and I need another driver before they can return to San Miguel. I don't want to take a chance of them sitting in a car with a tracking dot if the enemy is trying to catch them."

"You're right, Antonio. I think my brain is starting to shut down with everything that's been going on this evening."

"My friend, you're carrying a heavy load so I will forgive you tonight, but if your suspicions are wrong, and all this is a waste of time and money I may think twice about your sanity next time. Oh there is one other thing, El Cabby, and it's about a gringo lady with bright red hair who has been in the office and wants to join the Knights. She's supposed to come back in the morning, and I don't know what to tell her – will you be coming over here anytime soon?"

"I'm not planning on coming over unless there's some kind of major problem I need to deal with in the office. I have my hands full with everything going on here. Is there anyone else in the office that can check her out, and bring her into the Knights?"

"We don't have anyone in the office because we are all busy finishing up the move. I am snowed under, and you're working me day and night. Besides everything else, El Cabby, I'm uncomfortable with this lady, because I see a sign of a bump on top of her right hand. She also has the signature mark above one eye, and a little bump there too, so I'm concerned she may have microchips installed in both locations."

"Look Antonio, now you have me worried; do you have a number to contact her?"

"Of course I do."

"Okay Antonio, here's what I want you to do when we hang up. Call her and tell her to be in the office at a quarter till seven in the morning. When she arrives in the office let one of the ladies strip-search her for wires, and if she's clean, check her purse, and perform a body scan with the microchip detector. If it comes up clean then I want you to send the car, computers, and her over here in the morning so they arrive at my house at eight. I don't want her to know what's going on, and I want you and the courier to stay quiet about what we are doing. Tell her she's going to meet El Cabby, and he will bring her into the Knights of the Night.

"Also call Dr. Aluri, and have him here at seven-thirty in the morning with all the tools he needs to remove both chips and warn him she may have a chip in her head above the eyebrow as well as in her hand."

"El Cabby, when in the world are you going to let me sleep? It's the middle of the night, and you just gave me two hours extra work to do before morning."

"Antonio, I can't get everything done without your help and there isn't anyone else I trust to help me in these situations."

"El Cabby," Antonio said, "don't soft soap me about my good work and dedication. Good work and dedication need a break and a time to rest."

"Okay, Antonio, let me put it this way. If our red-haired gringo lady is trying to infiltrate our organization, and was able to find you one day after you moved the operation to San Miguel, then the enemy is knocking on our door right now. If she is the enemy she has to be neutralized, or else the Illuminati will be knocking on our door tomorrow. It could be the only thing she needs is to find me, so she can tell them where I'm at."

"Yes, El Cabby, it makes a lot of sense, and I'm sorry I complained. Everything will be taken care of just the way you want it handled."

"My friend, we'll talk to you in the morning, and you try to get some rest, okay?"

I hung up the phone, and reentered the car, and we rode the rest of the way to La Dama's Bar in silence. Luckily a taxi had dropped off their customers, and we were able to take it to my house.

When we were in the house, I said, "Okay folks, you can talk now, but I prefer you don't. I want you to hit the sack, and we'll discuss what happened in the morning after we've had breakfast. Breakfast is at six if we have anything to eat in the house, and if we don't, someone will go see Luz and bring back gorditas for everyone. I'm going to be staying up a little longer so I can plan an early morning greeting for our new member, or non-member, of the Knights. Now get to bed, and get a good night's sleep, because tomorrow may be more interesting than any of us could ever imagine."

The girls looked at me with understanding, and headed for their bedroom. A half an hour later I went to bed after having a cup of Irish coffee. I woke up in the morning because the girls were shouting through the bedroom door at me, "Get up! Get up! Come and look at what's on TV!"

I replied, "What in the world is going on?"

"El Cabby, something happened at the Holiday Inn last night, and they're going to report it in a few minutes on the six o'clock news."

I put on my robe, and then went to the living room to watch the news with the girls. The reporter came on and said, "The Holiday Inn in Guanajuato reports at three a.m. in the morning five Federales broke down the door to one of the rooms and then riddled it with machinegun fire destroying the room completely. The room was unoccupied at the time, but had been rented to a Señor Gomez who evidently wasn't in the room. The Federales have acknowledged Señor Gomez is wanted for interrogation concerning The Knights of the Night and the incident which happened earlier this week near Cañada de Caracheo."

Berenice grabbed the controller and turned the television off as she said, "How in the world did you know something was wrong, or anything was going to happen, El Cabby?"

"I don't know, sometimes I have a prophetic dream which warns me something's going to happen in the future, and other times I just have a gut feeling. Things like this have happened many times in my life, and I have learned to pay attention to my intuitions. If the news this morning hadn't reported the shooting at the Holiday Inn last night you might have doubted whether I was sane or not."

"I doubt your sanity anyway. El Cabby, tell me how many fingers I'm holding behind my back?"

"Knock it off, Berenice; if it worked that way I would be one of the wealthiest men on the Earth.

"If I deliberately try to think about something in order to tell what is going to happen in one instance or another I'm always wrong. In fact, the more I think about something to try and figure it out, the farther off I'll be. I don't understand how it works, it's a gift, and I don't really care how it works as long as it works."

"I'm sorry I teased you about it, El Cabby."

"It's okay, now we have a lot to get done this morning to prepare for our visitor at eight. Has anyone checked yet to see if we have any food in the house?"

"Yes," Chachis said, "you have canned and boxed food on the shelf, but your fridge has been cleaned out except for what's in the freezer. Personally, I think you're wasting electricity cooling an empty refrigerator. I suggest you either turn it off, or get some food in it."

"Okay Chachis, I want you to go see Luz and buy enough gorditas for all of us, but I want mine with egg, potato, and hot sauce."

A few hours later everyone was ready when the courier and the red-headed gringo lady showed up at the door. I opened the door and said, "Good morning, we've been expecting you. Please come on in. Chachis, do you want to exchange the computers and check out the new car while we talk to our guest?"

As Chachis stepped outside with the courier I introduced Evangelina and Berenice to our visitor, and they stepped behind her silently as I said, "We have someone else for you to meet."

Dr. Aluri stepped into the room and walked toward our visitor as the girls grabbed her arms from behind. Dr. Aluri pulled out the hypodermic needle he was carrying, and gave her a shot in the arm and within seconds she was as limp as an old rag.

I said, "Okay girls, take her in, and put her on the bed, and handcuff her feet and her left hand to the bedposts."

Dr. Aluri followed them into the room and immediately took out his scalpel. Within a minute he had removed the microchip from her right hand, and dropped it into a dish of acid which immediately hissed and released fumes into the air. I picked it up, and took it to the backyard where I set it down in the rocks so the acid would continue to destroy the microchip, and we wouldn't have to smell the fumes inside.

When I returned to the room Dr. Aluri had his head magnifier and light on. He was bent over the lady with his head about eighteen inches away from her head studying the raised skin above her eyebrow as if he could see through it. After a few seconds he made a cut though the skin on one side of the lump, and a few seconds later he made another cut parallel to it which was a few millimeters away from the first. He took another tool, and somehow cut the piece of skin out altogether, then he picked it up and placed it on a piece of black plastic which was a matt black color and of very smooth composition. He took a bottle from the table and removed an eyedropper from it, and placed a few drops on the piece of skin, and immediately the room had a terrible stench from the dissolving flesh. I went over to pick it up and take it out back, but Dr. Aluri stopped me.

"Don't move it, El Cabby; this will be over in a few seconds and all we'll have left hopefully is some liquid and a microchip the size of a white human hair. If it's not there we have to repeat the process taking more flesh and hoping we get it the second time."

"You're the doctor." I stepped back.

A few seconds later Dr. Aluri picked up the microchip which looked like a stiff gray hair, and placed it in another dish with acid in it. As it hissed and smoked I took it outside, and placed it beside the other one which was now sitting there empty with a little liquid in it. The acid had apparently done its job on the first chip, and it was comforting because I didn't want the microchip in my backyard if it wasn't destroyed.

I went back into the bedroom just as Dr. Aluri was finishing with a few tape stitches to the gringo's arm and head. He looked at me and said, "I think that should do it; she will be out of it for another hour or so, and when she wakes up you can question her. I would leave her handcuffed to the bed until then, but someone should watch her to make sure she doesn't have an allergic reaction to the tranquilizer we gave her." Then he took another hypodermic, and put it in the drawer of the nightstand by the bed as he said, "This is truth serum, and if you have any doubts about whether she is telling you the truth when you talk to her, give her everything that's in the syringe. This stuff almost always works, depending on the constitution of the person you give it to. Now I have to head to my office, and get ready to take care of my patients at the hospital. Is there anything else you need, El Cabby?"

"Dr. Aluri, thanks for everything; the only thing you can do now is pray for us, because this little redhead is going to really be mad when she wakes up."

"She's not going to be wide awake immediately, and it might take her as long as a half hour or forty-five minutes to be normal again. So as soon as she starts waking up, if she's not belligerent, you might undo the handcuffs before she gets completely awake. Keep talking to her carefully as she comes out from under the anesthesia and let her know you care about her. If she's sincere about joining the Knights she'll be happy the microchips have been removed. I'm leaving now, and call me if you have any problems."

With that Dr. Aluri left as we stood there watching the gringo lady with the bright red hair. I had never seen hair this color on a person's head except once, and it was on a little carrot-topped child many years ago when I was a young man. I said, "Berenice, why don't you stay in here until she starts to wake up and then come and get us so we can talk to her."

Berenice, who had her new computer, nodded her head in consent, as she plugged it into an outlet and watched it boot. The rest of us walked to the living room so we could discuss what we wanted to do next.

"Okay girls," I said, "I hate to tell you this, but we need to continue our research into mind control. We have new computers so I think we had better get busy."

Berenice walked into the room, and said, "El Cabby, she's moving around already, but she's not completely awake yet."

I walked over to the side of the bed, and sat down on a chair beside where she was lying, and she was very quiet. I noticed her eyelids had a little movement, and her feet were moving just a little as if they sensed the handcuffs on them. I realized she was nearly out from under the medication, and in a few moments she would be totally conscious. Berenice was watching me, and I said, "Berenice, I don't want her to wake up and be cuffed because I'm afraid it will scare the daylights out of her."

Berenice replied as she walked to the side of the bed, "I have the key right here, El Cabby, and I'll unlock and remove the cuffs right now."

While she was taking off the cuffs I walked into the other room, and said, "Evangelina, you and Chachis come in here;

she's waking up, and I want her to see all of us, and maybe she'll realize it's impossible to try and escape."

A few minutes later as we sat around the bed our red-headed visitor awoke, and looked at us sitting there. She said, "What in the world happened?" She was touching the band-aid on her forehead with her fingers where the microchip had been removed, and then she touched the back of her right hand and felt the small band-aid there, too. She immediately smiled and said, "What happened to the microchips – did you remove them?"

I smiled, and said, "We gave you a shot to knock you out as you walked in, and the chips were removed and destroyed within a few minutes of your arrival. You are now microchip free, so how do you feel?"

She replied, "I think I'm okay, but I'm groggy, and feel like I've been drugged. How did you even know I had the microchips installed in my right hand and forehead? I didn't tell anyone I had microchips, and they weren't obvious, so how did you know?"

"They were very obvious to anyone with normal vision. When they first install the chips in a person they do a mental suggestion that they aren't obvious, through the microchip inserted near the brain. By doing this it gives the person getting the chips less turmoil with accepting them. Let's face it: the chips are usually very easy to miss after a few months, unless you know exactly where to look and what to look for. The microchip in your right hand is about the size of two pieces of rice, and makes a very small lump under the skin; however, it is thick enough to see if someone purposely looks for it.

"The one near your brain would be impossible to find or know where it is. When they insert, it generally leaves an air cavity the length of the microchip, and the small air pocket can separate the skin and leave a little bump which can be obvious. If they get a perfect injection of the chip then there won't be any way to find the microchip at all.

"The first microchips in the head were injected through the nasal cavity and were undetectable visually, but in many instances they were destroyed in the process of injecting them. So lately they started to use an injection system which puts them close to the surface of the skin, and they are inserted through the eyebrow and toward the top of the skull. They've found that ninety-nine point ninety-five percent of these were good insertions, except for the little bump which was sometimes made from air being trapped under the skin.

"Anyway, young lady, you just lie still and rest while we ask you a few questions we need to know the answers to; first question, what is your name?"

"My name is Danielle, and my friends used to call me Dani."

"Do you feel okay, Dani?"

"Yes, I'm okay; why are you asking?"

"Dani, you said your friends used to call you Dani. It doesn't make any sense, why wouldn't they still call you Dani?"

"My friends don't know where I am anymore, because I disappeared from Ohio where I lived, and I've been using the name Gabriella which means 'God is My Might.' I had read about all the women Knights in Mexico, and what you were doing here, and I decided to come and fight with you."

"I think that's nice, Gabriella. Is Gabriella the name you want us to call you by?"

"Please use Gabriella, because it's become a part of my life as I've searched for you. I could have joined with other leaders several times as I searched for you, but I wanted to become a member through El Cabby, and now I've found you, haven't I?"

"You're not a member yet; I need to know why you had the microchips and didn't tell anyone so they could be removed."

"I was afraid if anyone knew about the microchips I would never get near you or get to join the Knights. I was going to tell you as soon as I was a member so they could be removed."

"Gabriella, having these microchips in your body could have gotten you killed today. Do you realize we took a great risk in even allowing you to come here? The only reason I allowed it was because they scanned you and for some reason the scan showed your microchips weren't functional."

"No, they weren't turned off, but for some reason they never functioned. They told me it had something to do with the electrical system of my body and this happens in one out of every six million people or so. They had ordered me a pocket chip until they could figure out what to do with me. I guess you could say I'm one in six million they don't know what to do with. They didn't expect me to come to Mexico before I received the pocket chip, and there wasn't any way I was going to tell them."

"Wow! Gabriella, I didn't know they even had a problem like yours, so you knew all along your chips weren't working, and you still didn't tell us."

"No sir, I wasn't going to tell anyone until I was a member of The Knights of the Night, because I didn't want to risk becoming a Knight. Even if the chips weren't working I couldn't afford to take a chance on what someone might do."

"Well Gabriella, you've done quite well in answering your questions so far. Now, let's get to the important questions which will help you become a Knight of the Night.

"Your real name is Danielle something, so what is your last name?"

"Knight."

"No games, okay? Now what is your real last name?"

"Knight." She giggled. "I'm serious, my last name is Knight. It's the name I was born with, and it's the name I will be buried with someday, unless I decide to get married."

"Berenice," I said, "will you get Gabriella Knight some paper and a pencil so she can write down all the names of the people she has been close to in the last ten years."

Berenice returned a minute later with paper and pencil, and we let Gabriella sit at my desk to write all the names she could remember. Once we had the names we would search our database to see if they were already Knights. Normally, there are usually from three to seven people in one of these lists, and it was unlikely that we would be able to match any of the names someone gave us. If she lucked out it would make it much easier to bring her into the Knights with just one good match. Otherwise, it could take a week or so to verify her information, and make her a member. She would have to stay under guard for all those days, and since I was the temporary Grand Seneschal she couldn't stay with us, so we would send her back to Antonio. The only thing Antonio could do was lock her in a room for the duration and I didn't want to add anything to Antonio's duties if I could help it.

I asked Berenice and Evangelina to check Gabriella's information out and asked them to let me know if we hit a home run on the name search. Then I returned to the other room where I had a phone call, I picked up the phone and said, "So what's up now?"

Antonio's voice came across the phone loud and clear, "El Cabby, you were right about everything last night, and if you had stayed in the room you would be dead right now. The computers have been destroyed and the car definitely had a tracking dot; we blew up the car with an incendiary device we had planted in the gas tank last night. We kept the car under observation after we planted the device, and within a few hours the Federales were checking it out. We blew it up remotely when they opened the door to make it look like we had a tripwire on the door."

"Thanks Antonio, you were correct about Gabriella too; she did have two microchips in her body, but they had malfunctioned when they were installed, and they were going to replace them with a pocket chip like we carry. Dr. Aluri removed the microchips in less than fifteen minutes after she came into the house, and he's really a great guy."

"I know, he's a neurologist from India, and he joined The Knights of the Night to see what he can do to help us with the fight for freedom. He's not just a regular doctor either; he's a great person, a friend to everyone who knows him. He's always ready to help in any way he can, whether it's a medical situation or something else."

"He was certainly good this morning, and I would trust him with my life. Now, Antonio, I hate to tell you this, but we may have another problem for you to deal with."

"No! Absolutely not! I have my hands full as it is!"

"Antonio, listen to me; all you need to do is lock Gabriella up in a room with access to a toilet. Let her out for an hour or two a day, and see she gets three good meals to eat. You can have anyone who works with you handle it. It doesn't have to be you taking care of her."

"I don't have anyone to handle it, El Cabby."

"Antonio, what if I sent Chachis over to do all the extra things that need to be done for Gabriella? Antonio, you could lock them up in a room together at a local hotel, and they could order their meals from room service. You couldn't ask for a better deal, could you?"

"How long is this going to be for?"

"Just a few days, I hope. We have to verify her information before I can bring her into the Knights, and if we didn't have such an influx of new Knights joining around the world it would probably be done in one day. Now it could take a few weeks at the most, if we're lucky, and a month if we're not."

"Okay, here's what we'll do. You send them to the Granada Ranch Resort which is south of San Miguel, and tell Chachis to check in under her name. Everything will be ready when they arrive, and I won't even have to leave the office to handle this for you. El Cabby, I have to get busy, so send them over, and we'll have everything ready when they arrive."

"They'll be there in an hour or less; we'll talk later." I hung up the phone, and I told Chachis and Gabriella what was going to happen until Gabriella's clearance was complete, and within ten minutes they were on their way to San Miguel.

About two hours later the phone rang, and I picked it up. "Hello," I said.

"Damn it! El Cabby," Antonio said, "we have another problem."

"I don't believe this – what's happened now?"

"The army set up a roadblock near the Granada Ranch Resort, and I didn't know it. They stopped Chachis and Gabriella, and there was a fire fight."

"No! Don't tell me they're dead."

"No, they're both alive. Chachis has a flesh wound in her upper right arm, and Gabriella's fine, but the Mexican Army took another beating. The girls only had one Uzi with them, and that was Chachis' gun, but Chachis was wounded when the first volley was fired. Now, get this, there are nine soldiers against two women, and one of the women is wounded. Gabriella grabs the Uzi and opens the door and rolls out of the car while she throws a grenade that blows up the Hummer fifteen feet away, taking out four of the Mexican soldiers. Then with the Uzi she takes out the other five before they realize what's happening to them. She tells

Chachis to scoot over, and she starts driving while Chachis calls me to let me know what's happened. Gabriella is one hell of a fighter, and I will personally vouch for her after what happened today."

"Antonio, what are they doing now?"

"They're coming back to your house. I called Dr. Aluri and he will be there in an hour to fix Chachis' wound, and if you don't need her for a while I can use all the help I can get."

"Let's get her stitched up, and then I'll see if I can afford to let either one of them go."

"Okay boss, I'll talk to you later."

"Evangelina and Berenice," I said, "I want you to take a cab and go to the store. Bring back plenty of food and wine for a party tonight. Chachis has a flesh wound in the arm, and Gabriella took out nine soldiers by herself today in San Miguel. We'll bring her into The Knights of the Night tonight, and then we'll celebrate."

*   *   *

"We stopped at the checkpoint," Chachis said, "then the guards ordered us out of the car so they could search it. But, we had the Uzi and two hand grenades right on top of the seat. I knew if we got out of the car they'd see them, and we'd be captured, so I decided to try and run the checkpoint. I stepped on the accelerator, but before we had moved a foot one of the soldiers shot me in the arm I hold my gun with. A split second later Gabriella was rolling on the ground shooting soldiers with my Uzi, while I was ducking for cover because the Hummer was blowing up. She had thrown the hand grenade towards the Hummer as she rolled out of the car, and it blew up in the air right over the Hummer taking out four soldiers.

"After the explosion I sat up and saw all the soldiers were dead, and Gabriella was walking toward me as calmly as if nothing had happened. The only difference I saw in her was her green eyes had changed color, and they looked like cold steel. I swear to God they were the color of polished stainless steel, and she told me to move over so she could drive. By the time we had gone a block she looked at me, and her eyes were green again. She told me to call headquarters to tell them what had happened, and Antonio said to come back here, and we did. I have never seen anyone react like Gabriella did today, and the Mexican Army is going to have a hard time living this one down."

I looked at Gabriella as I said, "We're going to celebrate our new Knight tonight. While Gabriella and I talk, the rest of you get this place cleaned up, the food cooked, and the wine poured, because we're going to celebrate tonight."

*　　　　　*　　　　　*

Three hours later, the party was over, the guests were gone, and everyone was sleeping except me. I was mentally preparing for another day, and I prayed it would be more tranquil than this one had been. While I was sitting there I had a strange feeling come over me as I wrestled with my thoughts, because I felt there was some special connection between Gabriella and me.

Chapter 18

June 2–3

I was sitting in the family room with the TV turned down low, and sipping on my favorite drink, an Irish coffee. I was starting to relax, but something was haunting me about our new member Gabriella. I thought to myself, *Gabriella will make a good Knight because of the way she handled the crisis yesterday in which she destroyed the army checkpoint after Chachis was wounded. She was cool in combat, and had a determination which had brought her all the way across the United States, and halfway across Mexico to become a Knight of the Night. Why would anyone do that? I couldn't come up with a good reason for her tenacity other than to get to me. Then I realized some of the things I had been researching about the Illuminati might apply to Gabriella. Perhaps she was Illuminati, and had been brought up to be an assassin. It would be a great way to kill the Grand Seneschal at exactly the right time, creating chaos and confusion among the Knights as they were preparing for the final war for the freedom of mankind.*

The noise of the bathroom door closing broke my train of thought, and a minute or two later Gabriela said, "Hey, I thought you told everyone to go to bed and get some sleep, so why doesn't the Grand Seneschal need sleep too?"

I hesitated for a second, and then I said, "Gabriella, come on in and sit down if you want, but I won't be up much longer. I'm having my Irish coffee and relaxing before I go to bed, and a little Irish coffee always helps me sleep better."

"Oh my gosh!" Gabriella said. "I love Irish coffee! Many years ago when I was a child my mother and my father were killed in an auto accident in Ohio, and somehow I escaped with just a few bruises. My uncle George took me in the day after the accident, and then adopted me a few months later. George and his wife Blanche reared me along with their son Bobby until I was grown and left home at the age of eighteen to join the U.S. Navy. George was one of the nicest men in the world; he owned his own clothing store, was a devout Christian, and treated me as though I were his own daughter.

"I was only ten years old when all that happened, and I only remember two things about that night. During the accident I had the breath knocked out of me, and I was in the back seat of the car when a young man pulled me out of the wreckage and took me to the side of the road, and placed me in the grass. I was still struggling trying to get my breath when he bent over, and placed his mouth on mine, and then he breathed into my mouth forcing fresh air into my lungs. He only had to do it twice, and I was fine except for my fear of what was going on around me.

"I wanted to go over to my mother and father and see if they were okay, and I kept trying to get up to go to the car, but the young man wouldn't let me. He held on to my arm as I struggled to get away, but he wouldn't let go. I was crying and screaming for my mother and father who were still in the car, and not moving. I heard the ambulance coming closer and closer as I cried and sobbed for my mommy and daddy to wake up. When the ambulance pulled up with all its tires squealing the young man picked me up and carried me to the ambulance in his arms. He told the first attendant who had gotten out of the ambulance I had been hurt and needed sedation and the next thing I knew I had a shot in the arm. The last thing I remember was one of the paramedics looking at the other one and shaking his head at the car where my parents were. Then my world went black, because I knew what they were saying to each other, and I passed out."

I realized by what she had just said I had met Gabriella before today, but I didn't want to admit it, not yet anyway. "Gabriella, I'm so sorry you lost your family when you were so young. I know it had to be very hard on you. I really don't understand what it has to do with Irish coffee though, because it doesn't make any sense."

"I'm sorry, El Cabby. It had nothing to do with Irish coffee. I just got carried away."

"Okay, now tell me about the Irish coffee if you don't mind, because I've never met anyone in the world who drinks Irish coffee to relax like I do, so I'm really curious why you would."

"For weeks after I was living with George and Blanche I would cry after I had gone to bed, because it was the time when I missed my parents the most for some reason. When I first started crying George would come in, and read me a story, and while he was reading I was quiet. When he was through reading, and turned out the light, I would just lie there and sob until I went to sleep.

"Anyway, to make a long story short, after a few weeks of crying myself to sleep, George and Blanche would warm some decaf coffee, and put a little Disaronno Amaretto in it. I would drink it before they read me the story, and a few minutes after the story was over I was sound asleep. So, as a child a little Irish coffee was a miracle cure for my sadness and bedtime blues. Anytime during my childhood as I was growing up if something was bothering me and keeping me awake, I would ask if I could have a coffee before I went to bed. George told me once with my red hair and a million freckles it was the best drink for me because he said it was called Irish coffee. He said that if I ever had a chance to visit Ireland to do it, because there were a million young ladies there with freckles and red hair."

"Well, Gabriella, after telling me the story I will invite you to take my cup to the kitchen and make me another Irish coffee, and while you prepare mine, make yourself one."

"I was hoping you would invite me to join you. I never killed anyone before today, and remembering everything that happened was keeping me awake. Maybe an Irish coffee will help me relax just like when I was a little girl."

While I sat there waiting for Gabriella's return I couldn't help remembering that night, that cold September night, many years ago. I remembered, *I was only twenty-one years old when I witnessed that horrible accident on the highway. I was on a hill overlooking the highway when I saw the car go out of control, and smash into the tree. I saw two heads smash into the windshield instantly, and then I saw something moving in the back seat as I ran to the car. Once I realized it was a little girl I pulled her from the car, and took her to the side of the road where it was evident she was having trouble breathing, and I didn't know what to do. I panicked, and I placed my mouth over hers, and exhaled into her mouth hoping it would help, and after doing that twice she recovered. I didn't know if I should say anything to Gabriella or not, but it was apparently a good thing to do so we both understood the connection between us.*

Gabriella said, as she returned to the room, "I hope I didn't make this too strong for you because I always use a shot and a half of whiskey in my Irish coffee."

"Gabriella, you're a woman after my own heart because I do exactly the same thing."

"You know, El Cabby, I think I'm going to like being on your staff."

"Whoa, I haven't said you were going to be on my staff, now have I?"

"No, but I thought since I returned here I was becoming a member of your staff."

"Gabriella, perhaps I will keep you as a member of my staff, but I seriously doubt it. We have a lot of different areas in our organization that could use your help; you'll be here for the rest of the week and then we'll make a decision on where you go, and what you do."

"Well, I know you're the Grand Seneschal and you have the say, but I hope I get to return here and stay as part of your staff."

We sat there in silence for a few minutes sipping on our coffee and then I said, "I probably shouldn't tell you this, but I was the young man who pulled you from the car years ago and helped you breathe again until the ambulance came."

"Oh my God! You couldn't be the same person – you just couldn't be! I think it would be impossible for that to be true. Do you remember where it happened, and when?"

"Gabriella, it was me; it was just outside of Sandusky, Ohio, on a cold September night, and I was walking on a hill overlooking the highway, and I saw the accident. I was wearing a long-sleeve red-and-black plaid shirt, and I was scared to death, because I didn't know what to do when you couldn't breathe. So I did what I thought was the right thing to do, and I gave you my uneducated version of mouth-to-mouth resuscitation, and it worked."

Gabriella was running from the chair where she was sitting to the couch where I was, and she threw her arms around me as she gently sobbed, "Thank you, oh God thank you, El Cabby, for saving my life."

"You have to get under control, Gabriella; please quit hugging me and go back to your chair. If anyone came in, I wouldn't know how to explain what was going on even though it's innocent."

The clock started to chime behind me, and I looked to see what time it was, and as I turned my head it placed my lips close to Gabriella's and she gave me a soft kiss, and I panicked. "Now go back to your chair, please," I said with a stern voice.

Gabriella went back to her chair, and sat down, and quietly started to sip her Irish coffee. Then she said with a devilish smile, "I've wanted to do that for over forty years now."

"You wanted to do what?"

"The night you helped me breathe again was the first time I ever felt like someone kissed me other than family. For years I dreamed about you and giving you a kiss back, because I felt like your kiss saved my life even though deep down inside I knew it hadn't."

I smiled, and said, "Well, I guess you could say we're even now."

She looked at me with those beautiful green eyes that seemed to have flashes of light in them as she spoke, "Now what?"

"Now we finish our coffee, and go to bed, and tomorrow morning I will call Antonio and arrange for Chachis and your classes to start next Monday morning. Then at the end of next week, I'll decide where I'm going to assign you."

Gabriella whined, "Please keep me here with your staff, or as a cleaning lady. I don't care; please keep me with your staff."

"I'll think about it. Right now I don't know if I can control my emotions well enough to keep you around, Gabriella."

"You can call me anything you want as long as you keep me around."

I handed her my empty cup and asked, "Gabriella, would you take my cup to the kitchen when you take yours, and then turn the lights off when you go to bed?"

"Sure I will."

I went to bed, and even though I drank two Irish coffees I was going to have a difficult time going to sleep because my emotions had never been this scattered in my life. I knew it was going to be hard to make an objective decision concerning where Gabriella was sent at the end of next week. I knew one thing for sure and it was I wouldn't be able to keep her on my staff and be able to concentrate clearly. I thought, *Her red hair, freckles, and sparkling green eyes along with her personality would be too much of a distraction for me.*

The next morning I was slow in getting out of bed, and getting myself cleaned up, but I eventually made it to the kitchen and fixed a bowl of Cheerios. Good old heart-smart, good-tasting Cheerios have been the center of my breakfast for years. In my opinion breakfast is an important meal of the day, and I always enjoy breakfast one way or the other.

I walked into the family room where Evangelina and Berenice were sitting on the couch eating gorditas, and I sat down in my easy chair. The girls were watching the morning news as they ate, so I quietly sat down and joined them. A few minutes later Gabriella joined us and sat down.

I said, "How are you doing this morning, Gabriella?"

Gabriella smiled and said, "I'm fine, but a little sore where Doctor Aluri removed the microchip above my left eye. I remembered something last night from the Bible about the mark of the beast on every human being in the end times; does anyone else remember it, or am I confused?"

"You're correct; you'll find it in the Book of Revelations, and if you'll bring me my Bible from the stand by your chair, Chachis, I will read it to you, word for word, according to the NIV translation of the Bible."

Chachis got up from her chair, and brought me the Bible, and I immediately opened it, and started thumbing through to the Book of Revelations at the end of the New Testament. "Here it is," I said. "Revelation thirteenth chapter, and sixteenth verse where it says: 'He also forced everyone, small and great, rich and poor, free and slave, to receive a mark on his right hand or on his forehead, so that no one could buy or sell unless he had the mark, which is the name of the beast or the number of his name.' Now the verse in the Bible should have upset a lot of people long before the world ever got this deep into the mess we're in."

Gabriella turned around in her chair and said, "God, I'm really glad those microchips are gone now. When I was a child, I went to church every Sunday, and I don't ever remember hearing a single sermon pertaining to that verse."

Evangelina spoke up, "Well, I'm Catholic, and I don't ever remember hearing about it either. Berenice, Chachis, have you ever heard a sermon on the scripture El Cabby read?"

Berenice and Chachis both shook their heads to acknowledge they hadn't heard it either. I spoke up and said, "Listen to me, over the years, most of the ministers in this world stopped preaching the Bible because it was offending too many people, and it was driving them from their churches. By preaching what the people wanted to hear, they kept good numbers and a good income to pay their wages, and support their churches. In many churches today you hear the sermons about what's happening now, or what was in the paper yesterday. The officials of some denominations' hierarchy even support their ministers preaching whatever they need to preach in order to keep the numbers up and the income high."

Gabriella looked at me and said, "The Book of Revelation is about the end times, isn't it? Doesn't that mean the world is going to come to an end?"

"Not necessarily," I said. "In Matthew chapter twenty-four, verses twenty-four to thirty-six, Jesus says: 'No one knows about that day or hour, not even the angels in heaven, nor the Son, but only the Father. As it was in the days of Noah, so it will be at the coming of the Son of Man. For in the days before the flood, people were eating and drinking, marrying and giving in marriage, up to the day Noah entered the ark; and they knew nothing about what would happen until the flood came and took them all away. That is how it will be at the coming of the Son of Man. Two men will be in the field; one will be taken, and the other left. Two women will be grinding with a hand mill; one will be taken, and the other left. Therefore keep watch, because you do not know on what day your Lord will come.'"

Chachis said, "El Cabby, how do you know where to find all these things in the Bible?"

"Chachis, I've worked for different churches at different times in my life," I said. "Once as a missionary, and a couple of times as a local pastor. In both cases something happened to make me leave, and we won't get into that today. I will say I believe the end times are near, but I won't claim to understand when that will be. Throughout history since the crucifixion of Christ men have predicted they were living in the end times. The secret is to live every day as if the end times were going to happen in a few hours, or minutes, and if we did, the whole world would be a far better place to live in. Remember, once you die, how much can you go back and change? Nothing! We are each living in our end times if you want to look at it in this way. God has spoken to all peoples in his own way, and instead of picking out the differences in religions we should be looking for the common ground of all religions. If we did, it would make for a far better world to live in."

Gabriella spoke up, "Come on, El Cabby, I want to know more about what God says."

"Good for you, Gabriella," I said. "I will say this for all of you, and you can take my advice or ignore it. The Bible speaks to every person in a different way because we are all coming to His Word from different backgrounds, educations, and cultures. So God isn't going to speak to me exactly the same as He speaks to you. He may speak generally to both of us with the same message, but when it comes to both of us coming up with exactly the same meaning, that can't happen in my opinion. If you want to understand God's message for yourself then purchase yourself a good study Bible, and set it by your chair. Then read a little bit every night before you go to bed, or every morning before you go to work. Soon you will start to understand what God is saying to you. In the

Book of Matthew seventh chapter, seventh and eighth verses, it says: 'Ask, and it will be given to you, seek, and you will find; knock, and the door will be opened to you. For everyone who asks, receives; he who seeks, finds, and to him who knocks, the door will be opened.'

"I realize you can't find a good Bible in this part of the world very easily," I said. "So if you want to use mine at any time please feel free to take and read it. Please return it to the stand when you're through with it, and if you go to the bookcase in the living room, you'll also find several other versions of the Bible, and feel free to use any of those you are comfortable with, okay?"

"El Cabby," Gabriella said, "in the verse you read it said the mark of the beast would be either in the right hand, or the forehead. I had both, so does it mean it wasn't the mark of the beast? Why would the Illuminati put a microchip in both the right hand and the forehead?"

"Gabriella," I said, "I can't speak for the Illuminati because I don't know why they put microchips in both the right hand and the forehead. I will say this, and it's my opinion only, there is a whole lot of information on those two little microchips. Your credit information is on one of the microchips to be used for buying and selling. Your health records from the time you were a child until the day you die are on one of the chips. There's a built-in Global Positioning System so they can always know where you are. Then there's a possibility the one in your head is for communicating with your mind, and giving you directions, moods, thoughts, or orders depending on how you look at it. Now, I would really like to relax and enjoy not having to do anything today.

"Tomorrow is another intense workday for all of us. Evangelina and Berenice will be doing research with me again, and Chachis and Gabriella will be gone for the complete week. So, I suggest everyone just relax today, because it could be very intense around here before the week is over. I'm going to go to my room to watch my personal television, or read for a while, so don't bother me please. I may even take an afternoon nap for a few hours."

Chachis spoke up and said, "Before you go, boss, is it okay if we order three pizzas for dinner tonight? We can have a few glasses of wine with the pizza and relax while we watch a good movie."

"I don't care," I said. "Just make sure you call me before the pizza arrives so I get my share, okay?"

Chachis replied, "Okay boss, you have fun, and we'll call you later at pizza time."

I went to my room, turned on the TV, and stretched out on the bed as I flipped through the channels until I found a movie I wanted to watch. I had seen it many years before, and I lay back to enjoy it again. Within ten minutes I was sound asleep and oblivious to the world, and the movie.

I heard Gabriella knock on my door and say, "El Cabby, the news will be on in a few minutes, and the pizza should be here soon. So, if you want pizza you had better get moving."

A few minutes later we were watching the news and enjoying our pizza when the commentator announced, "We have some breaking news tonight: The United States, Russia, and India have all announced they will be signing a peace treaty with China in the next month."

I said, "Turn the TV off. We know what they're doing, and why they're doing it. They're just telling a lie to the people of the world, and they're going to do it over and over again as long as it takes until they get their New World Order. My guess is they're doing this because it's just another attempt to convince the people of the world that the New World Order will bring peace. But we know the truth, so shut it off, and we'll start the video for tonight, enjoy our pizza, sip wine, and thank God for each other's company."

A few hours later we all turned in for a good night's rest.

Chapter 19

June 3–4

The next day after breakfast we all had to go our separate ways, which meant Evangelina and Berenice were going to be with me doing research in the house, and Gabriella and Chachis would be attending classes in San Miguel. The three of us walked outside where Gabriella and Chachis were both being picked up to take them to San Miguel for their training. I walked over to them and said, "Study hard, learn a lot, and come home safely. When you are through with your training I'm going to put your new skills to work and we'll be a stronger organization."

I started walking to the front door and turned around to take another look just as Gabriella was getting into the car. Her beautiful green eyes caught mine, and everything froze in time for a split second, and I knew then I would never assign her anywhere else.

I turned to Berenice and Evangelina and said, "Okay girls, we have a lot to get done today, so we might as well get busy. I have two major questions I need answers to before the day is over: the first question is what happens if the cruise missiles fail to destroy the asteroid, and the Earth gets hit by a huge piece of the asteroid, say two miles square?

"I know you're not astronomers, or great mathematicians, but I do know you're great researchers. I want the two of you to work on this question until you have some answers or until I tell you to quit.

"The second question I will try to work on myself and it's to get a better understanding of microwave mind control as some governments are using it today. So, good luck girls, and let's get with it because time is of the essence."

"Yes sir, boss," they both replied in unison, and then they giggled as they went to their computers to get busy with their research.

I sat down to begin my own research while hoping I had enough knowledge in science, physics, and the function of the brain to comprehend it. Luckily, I could handpick what I wanted to read, because the home office had also sent me a list of relevant news articles with a brief description of their content. The articles covered everything from the basic research to the application of some of the research, and the final testing and utilization in particular areas of combat.

***Defense News,* January 11–17, 1993.**

"U.S. Explores Russian Mind-Control Technology," Author Barbara Opall.

This article covers the Russian development and utilization of Mind Control in the altering of the minds of soldiers on the battlefield.

***Time Magazine,* June 26, 1995.**

Report on Mike Koernke of the Michigan Militia who believes there are Americans being controlled by implanted microchips. The article also refers to the Southern California Law Review, February, 1974, Volume 47, Number 2, Michael Shapiro wrote the article, "Legislating the Control of Behavior Control." On page 239 he quotes P. London, Behavior Control 4–5, 1969: "Means are being found in all the crafts and sciences of man, society and life, that will soon make possible precise control over much of people's individual actions, thoughts, emotions, moods and wills..."

***Nexus,* October–November, 1994.**

"Directed-energy weapons currently being deployed include, for example, a microwave weapon manufactured by Lockheed-Sanders and used for a process known as 'Voice Synthesis' which is remote beaming of audio voices or other audible signals directly into the brain of any selected human target. This process is also known with the U.S. government as 'Synthetic Telepathy.' This psychotronic weapon was demonstrated by Dr. Dave Morgan at the November 1993 non-lethal weapons conference.

Scientific American, April 1994.

Scientific American reported that Janet E. Morris and her husband, Christopher C. Morris, "have been involved in promoting 'psycho-correction technology,' developed by a Russian scientist that is intended to influence people by means of subliminal messages embedded in sound or pictures."

David Brinkley, News Program Number 47592, July 16, 1981.

David Brinkley stated: "It is known that the Russians are working hard on controlling the Human Mind by remote electronic means." On the same show, he interviewed Dr. William Van Bise, a radio engineer, who investigated the Russian Woodpecker radio signal broadcast across the United States in the 1970s. Dr. Van Bise had evidence that the Russian radio signal was "at a frequency where the human body tends to operate. – 10 Hz is right in the range of biologic frequencies." In replying to a question, Bise stated that "the easiest way to disrupt the mental process would be with microwaves."

Microwave News, November–December 1993.

Microwave News reported, in November 1993, a three-day top-secret non-lethal weapons conference that took place in the Applied Physics Laboratory at John Hopkins University in Maryland. Four hundred scientists gathered at the University to discuss their work in developing non-lethal weapons' technologies, including radio-frequency radiation (RF), electromagnetic pulse (EMP) weapons, ELF, lasers and chemical weapons.

Among the subjects covered at the conference were "Radio-Frequency Weapons, High Powered Microwave

Technology, Acoustic Technology, Voice Synthesis and applications of extreme frequency Electromagnetic Fields to Non-Lethal Weapons."

Col. John B. Alexander, program manager for Non-Lethal Defense, Los Alamos National Laboratory, served as conference chairman.

The Mind Manipulators, The Paddington Press, Ltd 1984.

Alan W. Scheflin – Taught at Georgetown University

Edward M. Opton Jr. – Graduate of Yale & Duke

Ten thousand pages of formerly top secret U.S. Army and C.I.A. documents prove that for twenty-five years the United States government agencies undertook the most extensive mind-manipulation program in the history of the world. Every conceivable method for molding the mind was explored and refined; many of them were tested on unwitting American citizens.

Project L.U.C.I.D., Living Truth Publishers, 1996, pp 100–101, Texe Marrs.

G. Harry Stine foresaw a near future in which men could become like gods through the use of "intelligence amplifiers" implanted in the brains.

Stine wrote that, very soon, intelligence amplifiers – tiny microchip devices either implanted in humans or capable of being temporarily connected to the human brain and sensory channels – would actually allow others to get "inside a person's head." With such devices, we will possess the astonishing ability to hear the thoughts of others.

I couldn't believe everything that I was reading and then I came upon a ***U.S. News & World Report* from 7/07/97 called "Wonder Weapons.**" I found references that said you could liquefy someone's bowels, put your enemies to sleep on the battlefield, or cook them as if they were in a microwave oven. What more did the United States Government have in its arsenal that I didn't know about? I wondered how a small organization like The Knights of the Night could ever win a battle against these types of weapons.

I decided I couldn't comprehend everything concerning Mind Control technology and handle all the other things I had to do every day. So in order to even remotely start to understand it, I would have to put my complete staff on it as soon as possible, including Gabriella. I smiled to myself as I contemplated having her around and near me for every minute of every day. I relaxed at the thought and made a preliminary list for the girls to research.

The list for research included the following articles:

"Wonder Weapons" – *U.S. News & World Report*, 7 July, 1997 pp. 38–46.

"Non-lethal Weapons" by Larry Dodgen – *U.S. News & World Report*, 4 August, 1997 pg. 5.

Project Paperclip – CIA Project – Research on Internet.

Project Bluebird – CIA Project – Research on Internet.

Project Artichoke – CIA Project – Research on Internet.

Project MKULTRA files – thousands of Americans involved – presidential apology – Research on Internet.

The Zapping of America – Paul Brodeur New York:Norton, 1979.

Project Pandora file – CIA Project – Research on Internet.

Aviation Week and Space Technology, 8 November 1976, "Powerful Soviet Radio Signal Protested."

The Mind Manipulators by Alan Sheflin & Edward Opton Paddington Press 1978.

CIA Project Scanate File – Research on Internet.

New World Vistas: Air & Space Power for the 21st Century – Ancillary Volume; Scientific Advisory Board (Air

Force), Washington D.C.; Document #19960618040; 1996; pages 89–90.

Low-Intensity Conflict and Modern Technology, Lt Col. David J. Dean USAF, Editor, Air University Press, Center for Aerospace Doctrine, Research and Education, Maxwell Air Force Base, Alabama, June 1986.

The Wall Street Journal "Malaysia to Battle Smog with Cyclones"; by Chen May Yee; page A19, November 13, 1997.

Nazi Experiments – Resonance No 29 November 1995 – Published by the Bioelectromagnetic Special Interest Group of American Mensa Ltd., and drawn from a series of articles published by the Napa Sentinel, 1991 by Harry Martin and David Caul.

The Search for the Manchurian Candidate by John Marks Penguin Books, London 1979.

Operation Mind Control by Walter Bowart Fontana Books, London 1979.

Check out Delgado's "Physical Control of the Mind: Towards a Psychocivilised Society" Intracerebral Radio Stimulation in Completely Free Patients" in Schiwitgebel & Schwitzgebel (eds.). Speaking in 1966, Delgado asserted that his research concluded that "emotion and behavior can be directed by electrical forces and that humans can be controlled like robots by push buttons." Think 32 – July–August 1966.

Time magazine July 1, 1974.

"The Story of Mankind Research Unlimited, Inc." in the *Covert Action Quarterly* Issue 9, June 1980 by A.J. Weberman.

John B. Alexander's "The Warrior's Edge" published in *Military Review*. He is known to be involved in mind control and psychotronic projects.

Psychic Warfare and Non-Lethal Weapons by Armen Victorian.

Microwave Auditory Effects & Applications by Dr. James Lin in which he states, "The capability of communicating directly with humans by pulsed microwaves is obviously not limited to the field of therapeutic medicine."

Brian Freemantle's *The Octopus* published by Orion Books Ltd. 1995.

Walter Bowart's *Operation Mind Control – Stories Involving Vietnam Veterans.*

Texe Marrs' Project L.U.C.I.D. – The Universal Human Control System.

"Timeline of Important Dates in the History of Electromagnetic Technology and Mind Control" by Cheryl Welsh 1997. www.dcn.davis.ca.us/~welsh/timeline.htm

"Electromagnetic Weapons: As Powerful as the Atomic Bomb, President Citizens Against Human Rights Abuse," CAHRA Home Page: U.S. Human Rights Abuse Report by Cheryl Welsh 2001. www.dcn.davis.ca.us/~welsh/emr13.htm

Angels Don't Play This HAARP 1995 – *Advances in Tesla Technology*, Earthpulse Press. By Dr. N. Begich and J. Manning.

"The Soft Kill Fallacy," in the *Bulletin of the Atomic Scientists*, Sept/Oct 1994 by Steven Aftergood and Barbara Rosenberg.

Becker, Dr. Robert 1985. *The Body Electric: Electromagnetism and the Foundation of Life*, William Morrow, N.Y.

Babacek Mojmir: International Movement for the Ban of Manipulation of the Human Nervous System: http://mindcontrolforums.com/babacek.htm and go to Manipulation of Human Nervous System.

Nature Volume 391, January 22, 1998 p. 316 reference Jean-Pierre Changeaux – "Advances in Neuroscience May Threaten Human Rights"

Delgado, Jose M.R.: 1969. "Physical Control of the Mind: Towards a Psychocivilized Society," Vol. 41, *World Perspectives*, Harper Row, N.Y.

U.S. News & World Report: Lockheed Martin Aeronautics/ Dr. John Norseen; Report January 3/10 2000, pg. 67.

Marks, John: 1988: *The CIA and Mind Control – The Search for the Manchurian Candidate*, ISBN 0-440-20137-3.

Persinger, M.A. "On the Possibility of Directly Accessing Every Human Brain by Electromagnetic Induction of Fundamental Algorythms"; *Perception and Motor Skills*, June 1995, Vol. 80, pp. 791–799.

Rees, Martin, *Our Final Century*: 2003, Heinemann.

I closed the books and went in where the girls were working and said, "Okay ladies, I want you to stop everything you're doing. We're going to take a break, watch a little news, and then get back to work. When we go back to work, the first thing I want you to do is call San Miguel and have Chachis and Gabriella sent back here as soon as possible. We will train Gabriella the same way you trained Chachis, and it will have to do. There's just too much research which needs to be done for us to do it without their help."

"What's wrong, El Cabby?" Evangelina said. "Is there a problem we don't know about?"

I replied, "Evangelina and Berenice, you are both young intelligent women with good educations. I'm an old man with an education which was relevant fifty years ago. I'm not senile, and I'm not stupid, but to comprehend the technology in today's world is too difficult without a lot of research. I don't have the time to do the research I need to do, so all four of you are going to do research for me, and then you will need to fill me in on what the technology means in layman's terms. I intend to have all four of you researching as long as it takes to understand the information in layman's terms which will hopefully make sense to me.

"I'm going to start dealing with the tasks of the Grand Seneschal because I can do that just fine. The four of you will get me up to date on the technology in the evenings after supper so I can be more effective at what I'm doing. Now, let's have some coffee and donuts and rest a few minutes."

We sat down for coffee and donuts, and Berenice turned on the television to watch *News at Noon*. The commentator spoke up and said, "NASA announced today it has finished modifying three of the retired space shuttles so they can each carry five cruise missiles. The three shuttles will be launched in the next couple of weeks for a special test of their missile launchers and other updated equipment. This has happened with the cooperation of all the major countries in the world without protest and there will be Russian Cosmonauts along with American Astronauts onboard all three shuttles for the system tests. The space shuttles are being used for this test, because the new replacement for the shuttles may have this system installed next year as a preventative measure to help protect the Earth from asteroid collision. The new shuttles will be called 'SGEVs' which is an acronym for 'Space Guard and Exploration Vehicles.' The SGEVs will be owned and operated by the New World Order for the peaceful exploration of space."

Berenice said, "El Cabby, this is a big deal, and I can't believe the people around the world aren't upset and screaming for more information about what's going on. I know what's happening to a point, but I want to know more. Everyone should realize they wouldn't modify three shuttles with cruise missiles on such short notice just for the fun of it."

"I know, Berenice," I said. "It's one of those moments in time when everyone should be yelling for more information, but it seems as though they aren't even concerned. If you turn the television off, I'll explain a few things about what I want you to research, and how I think it's already being used."

Evangelina turned off the television, and both the girls sat back to listen to what I was about to tell them.

"Well girls," I began, "part of what's happening in the world right now in my opinion is a matter of Mind Control, and you'll be researching Mind Control for me later today. There are a number of ways to control what people think and feel in this day and age. One, you can implant a microchip near the brain, and communicate with it directly, so the information gets into the brain through the thought process. The person will actually believe he is thinking whatever thoughts you put into his brain."

Evangelina said, "Come on, El Cabby, you don't expect us to believe something like that, do you? Let's get serious! You have to be kidding."

"I'm not kidding, you can even use the same system so a person hears the words through the auditory canal just as if you were standing there talking to him. He just hears the words directly as if you were personally whispering into his ears."

Berenice and Evangelina were staring at me now as if I had lost my mind, and maybe I have because it even sounded like science fiction to me as I was saying it. "Remember, this is something you will be investigating this afternoon for me, and what I'm telling you now should help prepare you for the shock you might get from your research.

"You will also learn that you can affect people's thoughts and thinking processes through the use of microwave signals transmitted into the brain. This is why you see more microwave towers going up around the world than you have ever seen before. The new microwave technology utilized this way can generate feelings in people's minds concerning happiness, being content, sadness, depression, and many other aspects. This can be done easily through microwave beams transmitted from cell phone towers which are rapidly going up around Guanajuato and other cities in the world. The personal receivers for the microwave beams just happen to be in the new microchips that are being installed near the brain of every person on this planet. The people who are going to the concentration camps are the only ones who aren't getting the microchips. Who knows, they may get them installed while they're sleeping and never know it.

"Then, on a large scale involving mass populations, you can use ionosphere heaters like HAARP to transmit many suggestions, as well as feelings, to the mental processes of millions of people in large regions of the world. All three of these systems are probably being used right now to affect the feelings of populations in many countries around the world. They're probably sending or generating feelings of peace and contentment in some populations so they're not too upset over the financial crisis, and everything else that's happening to them. So now you know why some people around the world may not be too upset as they lose their homes, jobs, and personal belongings.

"This is a great test of the mind control systems to show the Illuminati just how many humans can be controlled and influenced at one time. I'm pretty sure this is going on in every country in the Northern Hemisphere. However, it's not nearly as effective in the Southern Hemisphere because all the ionosphere heaters are located in the Northern hemisphere but one, which is located in Arecibo in Puerto Rico. It has a low power output, if any, and may only be used as a receiving antenna for deep space signals. Personally, I believe they're using microwave towers in an attempt to control the people of the countries in the larger cities in the Southern Hemisphere.

"I hope what I just said will help you understand a little bit about what is going on, and I want you to know I believe it's been going on in most of the world for a number of years now. I also believe the ionosphere heaters have also accelerated the effects of global warming, and caused much of the severe weather affecting the world today.

"How do you think they can get away with taking the homes, cars, and financial stability of the people around the world without the people getting more upset than they do? They simply make the people complacent by using mind control systems to generate a secure, calm, and safe feeling in the people's minds regardless of what's happening around them. When many people lose their homes they shrug their shoulders, go purchase a tent, and camp out in tent cities on the outskirts of the cities in America. No one protests what is happening because those who still have something left don't have the willpower to stand up because the mind control systems have them under their control and keep them complacent. If the people of the world did a little research, they would find the rich are getting richer and the poor are getting poorer around the world and no one seems to care. If the people are upset, it's seldom evident on the news programs.

"When the TV news reporters question how the newly homeless are doing in their new situations, the responses from the people are statements like 'It's tough, but I'm really enjoying the reconnection with nature' or 'I think maybe I should've been living like this all along.' When they interview the kids, they get answers like 'I miss my friends a little, but I'm enjoying learning about the animals' or 'My dad and mom are my best friends now, and we go fishing three or four times a week' or 'Life was never this good when my parents had to work, and I had to go to school.'

"If we don't win this war for control of the Earth, we will soon be in the twilight zone like the rest of the people out there. The asteroid that's coming is what's saving us now, because it's keeping the Illuminati busy, and giving us more time to prepare for the war to control the Earth's population."

Berenice spoke up, "You mean to tell me the people of the whole Northern Hemisphere are being zapped with signals which make them complacent and content while they're being ripped off? They just smile, sit back, and relax while someone is taking advantage of them, and slowly steals everything they own?"

"You've got it, and it's not going to get any better either; it's only going to get worse. The latest figures we have show the number of people joining The Knights of the Night in the last three weeks has declined seventy percent in the Northern Hemisphere where we need the most Knights.

"We're taking action right now to try and shut down the ionosphere heaters. We have dispatched special teams who are wearing special protective clothing which we hope will protect them from the mind control signals. They're on their way to the four ionosphere heater locations in the world, and will be attempting to shut them down by using explosives which damage the antenna arrays. It's important to note though that even if we accomplish our goal of knocking the ionosphere heaters out, we're still in trouble with the masses in the Northern Hemisphere. The Northern Hemisphere has the greatest coverage by microwave towers, and we calculate over eighty-five percent of the people now have microchips installed in their hands. Our guess is that sixty-four percent of the people also have chips in their forehead.

"If we are successful, the ionosphere heaters will be out of commission within the next week, and then we will launch a plan to take down the microwave towers in all the major cities of the world. This feat is going to involve thousands of Knights in a coordinated attack around the globe. It also means that some towers will have to be destroyed during the daylight hours and that's not going to be easy."

Evangelina, who had a frown on her face, said, "It sounds like we have a plan. Whether or not we can destroy enough of the mind control equipment won't mean a thing though if we're not protected from the asteroid approaching the Earth at twenty-two thousand miles an hour. So we will save the world for a few weeks, until the asteroid destroys and wipes us all out. It doesn't make much sense to me!" Evangelina was almost in tears now as she continued, "Regardless of what happens we'll all be dead, won't we?"

"I know," I said. "Hang in there a little while longer, and we'll see what we can turn around in the next few weeks. We're a religious organization and we have faith in God, and I believe He will make a difference in the outcome of this war we are preparing to fight.

"Remember too, if our attacks on the microwave towers in the Southern Hemisphere are effective, we will have a better chance of winning the war. While millions of people in the Northern Hemisphere are complacent and content, millions of angry, ready to die Knights from the Southern Hemisphere will be streaming north to change things. We expect to destroy the remaining microwave towers in the Northern Hemisphere first if we can. If our new protective gear works for those attacking the ionosphere heaters, then we will outfit special teams in the same type of gear to attack those remaining microwave towers.

"It's possible with the ionosphere heaters knocked out millions of people in the Northern Hemisphere may come out of being under mind control, and realize they've been duped. This means that the tables could be turned on the Illuminati within a few days. Then with God's help in handling the asteroid, the world may still be saved, and people may still have their free will as God intended.

"Now, I want both of you to get busy on these references." Then I handed each of them a copy of all the information I needed to have researched. "Each of you split these into two groups, and when Chachis and Gabriella return, give them each one of the groups to research."

Berenice spoke up with a little bit of a whine, "El Cabby, there's enough here to keep all four of us busy for three months."

"I know," I said, "this is why I'm expecting everything within a week from tomorrow, and no earlier. If we don't understand everything by then the consequences could be very devastating, and we might as well surrender to the Illuminati. But I'm not ready to give up yet, are you?"

"We will get it done for you, El Cabby," Evangelina replied. "I'm glad I went ahead and called an hour ago to have Chachis and Gabriella return as soon as possible. They should be here before too long, and we can all work together far more effectively than just the two of us."

"Berenice," I said, "you've been doing research on mind control all day, and I know you've looked at the MK ULTRA CIA Project. People have been trained and programmed as spies for years by the CIA and the Illuminati. Our newest member Gabriella could be one of those people, and we just don't know it yet. Most of them don't even know they've been programmed; they just do what their handler tells them to do."

"You're absolutely correct, El Cabby," Berenice said. "Excuse me for not thinking about all the things I've been researching. Projects like the CIA MK Ultra Project seem so unreal when you're reading about it. It's like reading a science fiction novel. There was a movie made about it called *Conspiracy Theory* with Mel Gibson, and he plays as one of the victims. Millions of people watched the movie, and even with them mentioning the MK Ultra in the movie, I've never heard of anyone who became upset over it."

Two hours later, the girls still hadn't arrived, so I called Antonio in San Miguel. "Antonio," I said, "do you have any idea whether Chachis and Gabriella have left yet to return home?"

"They left over two hours ago and should be there by now," Antonio said. "Let me contact the garage, and see if anyone's called with a problem concerning the car they're using. I'm going to put you on hold, and I'll get back to you in a second, so please stay on the line." A minute later Antonio came back to the phone and said, "El Cabby, they apparently left a few hours ago and should be there by now. I have a courier waiting for something to do this afternoon, so I'm going to have him drive the route the girls would have taken to Guanajuato to see if he spots anything unusual. I'll have him call you if he finds out anything at all."

It was four o'clock in the afternoon, and we still didn't have any answers as to where Chachis and Gabriella were. Then at four-thirty I had a call from Antonio: "El Cabby, we found the car they were in about three miles south of Guanajuato pulled off the road far enough it was hard to see.

"The girls weren't in it, but they found the dead body of the courier who was driving. His name is Emmanuel, and he's a good friend of mine. They shot him at least twenty times, and three times in the head at close range. There doesn't appear to be any blood but his in the car, nor is there any blood outside. Whoever shot Emmanuel either took the girls and left, or the girls escaped before the bad guys made it to the car. We have six men and a dog ready to start searching for the girls, but at this stage we don't even know if it was the army or bandits who committed this crime. All we can do is sit tight and see what happens, and hopefully we'll know something by morning. If we don't hear anything by then we'll start an intensive search to find them. We have new people coming to help make up a search party in the morning."

"You're right, Antonio; you keep us informed and we will keep you informed if we hear anything here. Try to get a good night's rest and we'll talk to you in the morning."

"We'll talk to you in the morning, El Cabby; tell the girls we're doing everything possible to find Chachis and Gabriella."

With tears in my eyes I turned to Evangelina and Berenice who had been listening to me. I said, "They found the courier's body in the car all shot up, but there wasn't any sign of Gabriella or Chachis, and we have no idea whether someone has them or not. We need to stay here and stay calm until we hear something, but we need to be prepared in case the Illuminati figured out where we are.

"Just to be safe we're turning this house into a fortress right now and we're the warriors who will defend it if we have to. I want all blinds and curtains closed as if we left for a day, or two, and I want a light in the family room and kitchen turned on. I want Berenice in the computer room watching the back of the house, and Evangelina on the second floor watching the front of the house after dark. When it's dark enough to go to the roof without being noticed I will go there and protect against a roof entry. It's the easiest access to many of the homes since they're all attached. We have two hours until dark, so get something to eat, and try to rest until nightfall, because this may be an all-night affair. Keep your Uzi loaded and by your side at all times. Also have plenty of loaded ammunition clips in your pockets."

*   *   *

It was beautiful outside when I was sitting on the roof, the sky was clear, and there were a million stars twinkling overhead in the night sky. There was a slight breeze, and everything was quiet except for the sound of music as a Mexican ballad wafted through the night air along with the smell of bougainvillea from the neighbor's flowers next door. It was going to be a long night, and I knew it, but I had to stay vigilant in order to keep us safe.

It was just a little after four in the morning when I heard someone coming across the roof very quietly. I thought to myself, *Here we go, they're going to go down the ladder, and through the sliding door into the master bedroom.* I stayed crouched where I was hiding, and I very slowly and quietly released the safety on my Uzi.

I was straining my eyes to see how many of them were coming, and I knew they were either Federales or Army because they were using hand signals. The first one approached the ladder and signaled the other one to guard him as he started down. I stayed where I was, realizing that the first person wouldn't break through the sliding door until they were both on the landing outside the bedroom.

A few seconds later, I heard a chirp like a bird in the distance and the second person started down the ladder. Now we had the moment of truth, because I didn't want to shoot if I didn't have to. Too much noise would bring even more soldiers or police, and I didn't want that to happen.

I ran to the ladder and pointed my Uzi directly at both of the intruders standing on the landing. I said in a very calm voice, "Okay, if you want to live, lay your weapons down on the landing, slide the door open, and quietly step inside with your hands up." I whistled, so Evangelina would be ready for them when they came through the door and into the bedroom.

A few seconds later, I had two new Uzis in my hands as I came into the bedroom. To my surprise waiting for me in the bedroom with big smiles on their faces were Gabriella and Chachis.

Chapter 20

June 5

Chachis made it to me first as she crossed the room and threw her arms around my neck, and gave me a kiss on the cheek. Chachis said, "El Cabby, I'm so glad to be home; I really believed we were going to die out there. If it wouldn't have been for Emir and Zheng, I'm sure we would have been killed."

I smiled and said, "I know who Emir is, but who in the world is Zheng?"

Chachis said, "He is a new rider with Emir, and there's a third one on her way to join them. We will fill you in on everything when we have the debriefing."

Then Gabriella threw her arms around my neck, and gave me a kiss on the cheek, and said in a very soft voice, "El Cabby, when I thought we might be killed this afternoon all I wanted to do was to see you one more time before I died. You're the person who kept us going, and the only reason we're still alive, other than Emir and Zheng."

"Okay ladies," I said, "we've all had a long day, and an even longer night. It's four-thirty in the morning, and we need our rest. I'm going to send Antonio an email telling him you made it back safely, and then I'm going to bed. I want you to secure the house and then go to bed, and set your alarms for ten-thirty in the morning, and it will almost give you five hours' sleep. We will start work by noon after I debrief the girls on what happened today. So let's close the house up and hit the sack now, and that's an order."

We were all tired, but the look on the girls' faces told me they would continue to talk for a while after they were in bed. *It doesn't matter*, I thought, *I suppose if I were a woman, I would probably want to talk too, but I'm a man and I need my rest.*

In less than five minutes, the house was quiet except for the noise of water running in the showers as Chachis and Gabriella cleaned up after a long, hard day. I sneaked into the kitchen and made an Irish coffee, and quietly returned to my room. It took me about ten minutes to drink my Irish coffee, and then I fell asleep thinking about Gabriella.

The alarm on my clock was too noisy in the morning, and I wanted to flee from its high-pitched ringing sound. I quickly reached over and shut it off, putting it out of its misery. In the process I pulled the sheet away from my eyes letting a streaming ray of sunlight hit my eyes. Immediately, the neurons in my brain started to fly around the cerebrum, flowing through the synapses and reminding me I had to get up.

*   *   *

A few minutes later we were all seated in the room, listening to Chachis recount what had happened the day before in San Miguel. Evangelina and Berenice were both taking notes so we could have a good comprehensive report of everything they experienced.

Chachis said, "We were just a few miles from San Miguel when Emmanuel noticed that we were being followed. He put the pedal to the metal as fast as he could on those curvy roads, and actually put some distance between us and the other car. It didn't last for long though because we came around one of the sharp curves in the road and there was a car parked across the road facing a huge drop-off near the mountain. Emmanuel was quick and actually went around the back of that car by driving on the side of the mountain to get around them. When the car chasing us came around the corner it swerved to miss the car sitting sideways, and it flew off the road and down the mountainside. We actually thought we had made a good escape when the car which had been sitting sideways started to catch up to us.

"Emmanuel said we were only a few minutes from Guanajuato, and he was going to turn down a little country road after we passed a dangerous curve. He told us he would stop the car, and we needed to get out, and run straight ahead following the road to its end on a hill. Then we were to go down the hill to the stream at the bottom, and follow the stream to the Rosa Primera Colony. Then all we had to do was to follow the main street to El Cabby's home.

"He was sure the car following us would be going too fast to make the maneuver he was going to make, and it would fly by giving us some time to escape. He said it would also give him just enough time to maneuver the car to block theirs. Then with his Uzi he would attempt to take them out when they did show up.

"Anyway, we swung around the curve and we got out and ran to the top of the hill. We hid behind some trees as we watched Emmanuel pull out his Uzi and prepare to take out the guys in the car. When they drove in they had their guns firing. We could see Emmanuel was struggling with his gun which had evidently jammed after the first round had been fired. All three of the bad guys opened fire and we could see Emmanuel slumped over in the car having been shot almost instantly. It didn't matter though, because they kept on shooting his dead body. We were crying, because it was horrible to watch as Emmanuel was murdered in cold blood, and we couldn't do anything about it.

"We turned to flee down the hillside towards the stream, but before we had even made it to the bottom of the hill they were shooting at us. I thought for sure we would end up dead, because there wasn't much cover. Two of the bad guys were coming down the hill after us, and one was staying on top to give them directions. We found a small crevice in the rocks above the stream where one of us could hide. Gabriella said she would hide there, and I should cross the stream to the other side. When the two guys showed up I was to hold up my hands to surrender. Gabriella would be close enough to take them out if they kept their attention on me.

"I did what Gabriella said and crossed the stream to wait until the two were close. I couldn't hear the man on top of the hill anymore though, and when I looked up, there was a man on a black stallion holding the man's head in the air. He thrust his sword skyward as if to say 'we're here for you,' then they started down the hill towards us on horseback."

I said, "Hold it a second, you said there was more than one horse rider on the top of the hill, Chachis?"

"Yes. The man on the black horse was there with another rider on a white horse. The man on the black horse looked like he was wearing some kind of leather armor that overlapped itself. He looked bald, but I could see he had a pigtail hanging from the back of his head. He was portly, but not fat, and he wasn't very tall sitting on his horse. The other man was dressed in black and had a turban on his head, and I knew it was Emir, who also had his sword pulled as if he were ready to kill.

"Anyway, they were working their way down the hill, as the two bad guys arrived across the stream from me, and I stood up to surrender. They stopped dead in their tracks facing me, as if they were surprised I was surrendering. Meanwhile, Gabriella said, 'Okay idiots, it's your turn to die.' She shot both of them after they turned to shoot her and we thought they were both dead. I turned around to pick up the weapon I had placed on the ground behind me and one of them reached for his gun to shoot me. Gabriella ran across the short distance between her and them, and kicked the gun out of his hand and shot him in the head.

"A minute later Emir and Zheng showed up on horseback."

"Hold it a second, who is Zheng?"

Gabriella said, "Zheng is a Chinese man who was riding with Emir, and we only know his name because he said his name was Zheng. He was wearing leather armor with Chinese designs carved into it, and his horse was a black stallion which also had leather armor. Zheng said we needed to ride on the horses behind them, and they would take us to safety. We galloped on down the stream following it to Rosa Primera Colony, and we were within a hundred feet of a dirt road. They told us to follow the dirt road after dark to the Rosa Primera Colony and work our way to your house.

"We made it to the top of the first house by climbing the tree beside it, and then jumped across the rooftops until we were here safe and sound with you.

"Zheng told us that although there were two riders now, there was a third rider on her way, and she would be riding a red stallion. Then later there would be a fourth rider joining them. When I asked him if there were only going to be four riders, he just smiled, and then he and Emir rode off into the darkness. It was very scary because as soon as they were out of sight we couldn't hear their horses anymore, and they were galloping in the stream without making noise.

"Anyway, El Cabby, we're here safe and sound, and thanks to Emir and Zheng, we'll be able to keep fighting. Oh, and Emir has a leather case attached to his saddle with a bow and arrows in it. We didn't see him use it today, but the bow and arrows must be there for a purpose."

I replied, "Well, considering I've never seen Emir or Zheng, it's going to be difficult to issue them weapons. If you think about it, we don't even know if they are members of The Knights of the Night. All I know is that I appreciate their assistance, because this is the second time they have come to our rescue.

"Now tell me, do either of you have any idea who the men were who were trying to capture or kill you?"

Gabriella said, "They weren't soldiers for sure, and they weren't some kind of trained undercover men either. They were wearing suits and ties and it looked like all of them were wearing black suits, but I'm not sure. I'd say they were cold-blooded killers, because of the way they killed Emmanuel. I don't think they had feelings of their own, because they acted more like trained zombies than human beings. What do you think, Chachis?"

"I think you're right, Gabriella," Chachis said. "When I stood up to surrender and looked at them it was like looking at two dead men. If you hadn't said something when you did, and taken them out, I think they would have shot me the same way they did Emmanuel."

"Can either one of you remember anything unusual about where they showed up or what they were doing in order to find you in the beginning?"

Gabriella spoke up, "Well, the fact is one car started to follow us within a few minutes after leaving San Miguel and that tells me they may have already known we were there. Then for the other car to get ahead of us means it was already out there and knew when we were going to arrive. You don't just block off the road between here and San Miguel right after a sharp curve, unless you know the car you want is the next car to be there. So, I think that maybe our car was being tracked by a GPS system and so was the car that was after us. They had to know exactly where we were in order to know when to block the road."

Chachis spoke up, "The more I think about it, they had to realize we were in San Miguel somewhere, and were following us, and knew every move we made. It's also evident they know our office is in San Miguel and where our car is serviced in order to plant a tracking button on it. El Cabby, I think we need to warn Antonio, and move out of our office in San Miguel immediately."

"I think you're right," I said. "I'll get in touch with Antonio, and see if we can move the site to Celaya. After all, ninety percent of the major decisions are made right here, and as long as we're a long way from our headquarters, we're relatively safe. They evidently believe we're in San Miguel right now, and we'll send them on a wild goose chase in Cortazar."

"You mean Celaya, don't you, El Cabby?" Berenice said.

"Yes and no," I replied. "We have a courier who will be here at two this afternoon with some information about the asteroid. We'll send a message back with him telling Antonio that we need to move the office to Celaya within the next two days. We will also tell him to use the code word 'Cortazar' as the city name for Celaya. This should throw a confusion factor into everything and it may confuse them enough so we can find the mole who is giving our secrets away. Meanwhile, they'll be looking for us in Cortazar and perhaps it will keep them busy for a week or so.

"Today is the fifth of June, and in thirteen more days they will have destroyed the asteroid or it will be destroying us. Either way, they have their hands full with everything going on around the world right now. Let's keep them confused looking for us in Cortazar, as long as we can, and we'll continue to make plans for what we can do to stop them after the asteroid crisis is over.

"Okay, I want you girls to get busy on the research I need you to finish on mind control and microwave weapons. It's critical to my understanding for you to get through the information as soon as possible, and be prepared to brief me about what you learn. Now get busy, I'm going to my bedroom to call Antonio, and you can contact me there if you need me for something."

The girls went to work, and I went to call Antonio. I dialed his number and a few seconds later he answered, "Hello, this is Antonio."

I said, "Antonio, I hope you got the message saying the girls are okay, and they made it back around four in the morning. They had help from Emir again, and from another horse rider named Zheng, and they believe he's from China."

"You have to be kidding me. I guess it explains the six heads and bodies they found, doesn't it?"

"There were only three bad guys, Antonio. The girls told me how many there were when we debriefed them. The girls killed two, and the third lost his head to Zheng's sword, according to Chachis. So I don't know how you came up with three more headless bodies."

"All I know is they reported on the news that there were six bodies with their heads cut off and two others were shot. So they must have called for help and they sent five more bad guys out to get the girls.

"Antonio, I don't understand where Emir and Zheng came from, but I'm not going to complain. I could use thousands more like them on horseback, and fighting for our side. Ironically, Zheng told the girls there is another rider on the way, and she's a woman on a red stallion. But, before we talk too long, I need to ask you if you had to move the office again, would it be easier than the last time?"

"Well El Cabby, we learned a lot from the last move and it should be much easier the next time, but I'm in no hurry to move again."

"I'm sorry, Antonio, we'll be moving the office one more time and you might as well start getting everything ready. We believe the Illuminati know where the office is in San Miguel because of what happened with the girls. I'll send you the information from the debriefing, and you'll understand why we think there's a problem in the office. We aren't going to discuss the next move on the phone though.

"When the courier arrives today with the information on the asteroid, I will send a packet back with him telling you what we're going to do and when. We believe we have a mole in your organization in San Miguel. I want you to pick the most likely person in the organization who you believe might be a mole and give them the information we send you. If the enemy responds to the information we'll know it, and take them out. If you don't select the right person as the mole, the enemy won't respond, and we can try someone else. So, study your people well today and decide who you think it might be.

"Now Antonio, do you still have a friend in San Nicholas who has a hot air balloon?"

"Yes, Jose's still there, although I haven't seen him in a while. I can give him a call if you need a favor."

"Tomorrow morning I'm going to send Chachis, Berenice, and Evangelina to Cortazar in a car. I want someone to pick them up behind the main church, and drive them to San Nicholas, where I would like them to get on the hot air balloon and be flown back to Guanajuato. Do you think we can arrange a ride for the girls in the hot air balloon?"

"Well, first of all, I'm not sure the weather will be good for getting the balloon off the ground tomorrow morning. If the wind is blowing over ten miles an hour, they can't launch the hot air balloon. I'm going to put you on hold, El Cabby, while I call him on another line, and I'll be right back."

A few minutes later, Antonio came back and said, "Okay El Cabby, here is what Jose says, 'If the wind is less than ten miles an hour, they'll be prepared to load the girls in the gondola on the hot air balloon at noon. If the wind is greater than ten miles an hour, they will wait until it's less than ten miles an hour, and then launch so it could be an overnight trip for the girls.'"

"Let's hope they can launch tomorrow, because we need to catch the mole as soon as possible."

"Have you told the girls what you're going to have them do? They may be afraid of flying in a hot air balloon."

"We'll just have to see what happens. You have a great day, Antonio, and look for the packet of information I'm sending this afternoon."

"I'll be watching for it, El Cabby."

I hung up the phone, and went to the room where the girls were working and said, "Okay girls, we have a change in plans for tomorrow. Chachis, Evangelina, and Berenice will drive to Cortazar and to a location behind the main church. Someone will pick you up there and drive you to San Nicholas where you'll get on a hot air balloon and fly back to Guanajuato. Of course in Guanajuato you'll bring a taxi back to this house. If the wind's too strong, they can't launch the balloon and they'll fly you back the next day."

Berenice spoke up, "Why isn't Gabriella coming with us?"

I smiled as I said, "Berenice, there's only one reason why Gabriella is staying behind. Take a look at Gabriella, and tell me what stands out most about her appearance?"

Berenice smiled and said, "Gotcha, El Cabby, she's too obvious with all those freckles and bright red hair."

"You got it," I said. "We can't afford to have a red-haired woman returning on the hot air balloon. One thing people in this country love to do when they see a hot air balloon is to watch it. I can see the little children chasing the balloon as it comes down to drop you off. It wouldn't surprise me if someone takes a picture for the paper, and you three ladies look like typical Mexican women, but Gabriella doesn't. She looks like a sweet Irish lady who is a long way from home, but the Illuminati will associate her red hair with the woman who took out their roadblock in San Miguel. I want to keep us all safe and sound, and putting Gabriella in the hot air balloon may jeopardize all of us."

I said, "Now let's get busy because we have a lot to do."

The rest of the day was pretty quiet as the girls dug through tons of research information, and I know they were frustrated by all the technology they didn't understand. I said, "You girls need to understand right now I don't want the technogarbage that comes with all of these things you're researching. What I need are simple answers to questions like: one, what effect does it have and on how many people in any given area? Two, does it arm, disarm, control large groups of people? Three, what is the weapon's range and effectiveness in that range? Four, is there any way we can stop this weapon or disarm it easily?

"I realize you don't understand the answers to all these questions either, but give it your best shot, because this is all I'm asking of you. I think you've all done a wonderful job so far and just keep up the good work. It took years for someone to design and make these new weapons with state-of-the-art technology and you're not going to understand these weapons completely in a few hours."

Later I said, "Now, order some pizza, turn on the television, and relax awhile. Then when you're ready, go to bed and get some rest because you've all earned it. Tomorrow morning at eight, everyone but Gabriella and I will be leaving for Cortazar, and I want you to have a fun trip. So get some rest, and be fresh as possible in the morning, because as simple as this trip sounds, you need to be rested and alert before you leave."

Meanwhile, I went to my room to kick up my feet and relax while I thought about what was coming. I had the file on the asteroid that had arrived earlier in the day to scan as I rested. I took off my shirt and lay back on the bed with two pillows behind my back and started to read the information on the asteroid. The plans were basically the same as they were before only now they planned to detonate the warheads eighteen to thirty miles in front of the asteroid, so as to create an airburst effect and possibly disintegrate the asteroid as well as slow down whatever was left of it. They were going to create the largest man-made nuclear explosion in space in the history of mankind. The asteroid would be screaming at twenty-two thousand miles an hour at a nuclear blast the equivalent of thirty point one five megatons of dynamite.

The only other thing that had changed was that the Russians and the Chinese were launching six newly designed spaceships they had designed in Russia and put together using technology and scientists from both nations. They were originally called "Low Orbit Space Cleaners and Offensive Weapon Spaceships." Their new name was an acronym of those words and the spaceships would be referred to as "LOSCOWS." The LOSCOWS carried a long range, high powered laser capable of firing thirty times a minute with enough power to take down a piece of the asteroid as large as six hundred meters across. They were self-contained, robotic ships controlled from a remote location, but capable of doing their task without any remote inputs by being placed in automatic mode. They could automatically measure the trajectory and size of the asteroid pieces, and make decisions as to which were the most dangerous and hopefully destroy them before they hit the Earth. The LOSCOWS maneuvering power came from solar engines which also furnished power for the lasers. The LOSCOWS were very small and didn't need much maneuverability because of the range and power of their lasers. They also had a system to tell them if they were in danger of being hit by space debris, and those targets would be taken out first.

El Cabby was just about to fall asleep when Gabriella came to the door and knocked. "What is it?" El Cabby said.

"It's Gabriella," the voice replied. "There is some news concerning all the ionosphere heaters and we thought you might want to know they damaged or destroyed the four major heaters in the world."

"Good, thanks for letting me know, Gabriella." I lay back against the pillow and was sound asleep in a few minutes.

Chapter 21

June 6–15

It was eight in the morning, and the girls were getting ready to leave for Cortazar. Gabriella and I were standing out front with them and I said, "Okay girls, I want you to be careful, and don't take any chances, stay alert all the time, paying attention to any cars which may be following you.

"Remember, you will use the Uzis which came with the car if you need them. So, when you change cars in Cortazar you're to leave the Uzis in this car. You can't land in the hot air balloon in Guanajuato with Uzis in your hands so a reporter can take your picture. To say the least I want you to hurry home as soon as possible after you land here."

Berenice said, "Why in the world are we doing this? It doesn't make any sense at all."

"Berenice, we're moving our home office, and if the enemy is watching us here then we want them to think you girls are moving to the new office. Hopefully, they will follow you to see where you go if they see you leaving here, and if they don't know you're here you will be safe all the way to Cortazar. There is only one person other than Antonio who knows you are flying back in the hot air balloon. They think you're going to make a landing at La Sauceda, and we expect them to attempt something when you do. Ironically, you're not going to land at all, but we will have a reception committee to take them out, or capture them. We will also know who the mole is in Antonio's office.

"Think about it, every time you've been on the road lately we've had encounters with the Illuminati, and somehow they knew about every movement we were making. They knew when we were in the Holiday Inn Express, and when Chachis and Gabriella were going to the hotel in San Miguel, and they set up a roadblock just before they arrived. They knew when you left San Miguel to come home, and it could have cost you your lives. I would say it's more than coincidence it's got to be a spy who informs the Illuminati about everything we're doing. Now you girls get out of here and stay safe, but keep your Uzis close and ready to use for God's sake."

The girls got into the car and drove off as I waved to them and said a silent prayer for their safety, then Gabriella and I went back into the house to start our own work. "Gabriella, you keep working on the research about microwave mind control using microwave signals from the towers around the world. We also need to know how the new implant placed near the brain fits into the scheme of things with microwave communication to the masses. Around four this afternoon before the girls get home you and I will get together and discuss what you've learned today. I hope you understand I really appreciate what you're doing to help with this research."

By four in the afternoon Gabriella had researched enough to basically understand what was happening in the utilization of mind control applications using microwave signals. She briefed me with what she had learned, and then I said, "Well, it sounds like the ionosphere heaters are very effective on large masses of people, and the microwave tower function is just as powerful only for shorter distances. Since we took out the ionosphere heaters yesterday in the Northern Hemisphere, we may have a chance of freeing millions more people by going ahead and attacking the microwave towers in both hemispheres as soon as we can. Thanks, Gabriella, for your hard work; now you take a break and the girls should return before too long."

Two hours later Berenice, Chachis, and Evangelina returned from their trip to Cortazar. I met them at the door, because I heard the taxi pull up. "Hey, it's good to have you back. How did everything go?"

Evangelina responded, "We had a great time and everything was fine. In fact we didn't have one hard bounce in the gondola when we landed an hour ago. We flew over La Sauceda where evidently someone thought we were going to land, and instead of surprising us, they had a surprise waiting for them. I'd say the whole operation and flight was a success."

I said, "That's great news! I should be hearing from Antonio soon because it was part of our plan to catch the mole, and evidently we were successful and things should be a lot safer now."

Berenice spoke up, "We're all going to be happy if they caught the mole. Let's face it, we could use some peace and quiet for the next few days. How did you and Gabriella do today – did you get a lot accomplished?"

"We did fine," Gabriella said. "We did a lot of research on mind control through the use of microwave towers, and I feel like we completed a good day's work."

The phone rang and I answered, "Hello, can I help you?"

Antonio responded, "El Cabby, we've caught our mole, and I hate to tell you it was my secretary Esperanza. I hate to admit it, because she had access to too many things which were going on in The Knights of the Night around the world. We're sure she was giving information to the Illuminati, and getting paid very well for it. The good thing is, we're also pretty sure she wasn't working with anyone else in our office, although there's no way to be absolutely certain. She's been locked up, and is being held until after the war is over, and then we will try her for treason."

"Good," I said, "I also heard on the news we were successful in taking out the ionosphere heaters, so I assume our protective uniforms worked at eliminating the microwave signals?"

"Apparently it works, although the message I received said they would have to modify the boot clip in order to make it function better. I'm not sure what that means, but it's certainly to our advantage to have some great engineers working on our side."

"I think it's great news, Antonio. We originally planned on waiting ten days after taking out the ionosphere heaters to start destroying the microwave towers. I want you to check and see if it's possible to start the operation three days from now in the Northern Hemisphere. If we can free the people from the mind control influences at this time it would be better than trying to do it later. I'm sure we'll pick up more recruits once they're gone, and we'll have a better chance of winning the war if we can shut their mind control system down. So, Antonio, why don't you contact the Seneschals in charge of the Northern Hemisphere, and start a coordinated attack at midnight the night of the ninth if they think it's possible to do it that soon? You can let me know their response in the morning when you have their inputs.

"We need to produce as many of the protective uniforms as quickly as we can, because it evidently makes a big difference in getting through the microwave mind control areas. I want the Illuminati's mind control system destroyed before the asteroid comes even close. If the asteroid is going to destroy the world, so be it, but I want this Earth to go out as a place where the people have free will as God intended. So it's critical we produce as many of the protective uniforms as possible, and get them to the field."

"I sure can. I like the idea of destroying their mind control equipment as soon as possible. It will be a lot easier to do it now then it will be after the asteroid is destroyed or hits the Earth. I'm not sure they can destroy the asteroid and save the Earth anyway. So, if we're going to go down fighting I think we should get this war in gear while they have their pants down, so to speak."

"Okay Antonio, let me know what the Seneschals say. If we get a positive response then we'll start attacking the microwave towers in the Northern Hemisphere at midnight, the ninth of June. Then, we'll start wiping them out in the Southern Hemisphere at midnight on the fourteenth of June. By the time the asteroid is here on the eighteenth hopefully most of the people here on Earth will have free will and be able to think for themselves once again."

"I like it, El Cabby; let's hit them where it hurts!"

"Starting this war before they're ready may be the best thing we can do. You have a good night, Antonio, and I will add a job well done, my friend." I hung up the phone and walked back into the room with the girls and said, "We caught the mole – it was Esperanza, Antonio's secretary. She is being held until the war is over, and then she'll be tried for treason.

"We will now plan and start our attacks on the microwave towers around the globe starting on the ninth of June in the North, and the fourteenth of June in the South.

"When all the people on the Earth have the ability to think clearly again, without outside influence, we'll have a new advantage in this war which we don't have now. Hopefully, we will be in that situation before the asteroid arrives on the eighteenth of June and hopefully the Illuminati will be successful in destroying the asteroid without significant damage to the Earth."

Chachis said, "Does this mean we won't have to do any more research? I'm really getting sick of all this research."

"Okay," I said, "we'll see if we can cut back on some of the research and try to live normal lives for a few days. So you girls just handle all the things you need to handle right now for my office and in doing normal communications. For the next few days we'll try to concentrate on our normal workload here."

Three days later at midnight on the ninth of June, The Knights of the Night had a coordinated attack on the microwave towers in the Northern Hemisphere. We made the decision to attack the microwave towers in the highly populated areas first, making sure we had freed as many people as possible from the mind control network which had been built. We had no way of knowing how long it would take to knock down all the microwave towers in some of the countries, but we were hoping we could take out a substantial number of them in a few days. We hoped every time we knocked a tower down we would free a thousand or more individuals from being under the Illuminati's mind control system.

We were the most successful on the first night when we took out over four thousand microwave towers in the United States alone. With three Knights per team we utilized six thousand of our Knights that first night. Every night after the first one became more difficult, but by the end of the third night we had taken out approximately nine thousand of the microwave towers in the United States. We had also printed up new fliers that were being delivered during the night to homes in the areas where we had taken down towers. The headline on the fliers said, "Welcome back to God's World." The flier went on to explain how the Illuminati had been using microwave technology to control their minds. We urged them to remove their microchips if they could, and explained how they could help The Knights of the Night in the battle for a free world.

On the night of the thirteenth we were sitting in the house and waiting for the latest report on how many towers we had taken out, and how many people had decided to help us in this battle. The phone rang and I answered it and said, "Hello."

Antonio was on the line and he said, "El Cabby, we have some really good news because our Knights took out another thirteen hundred towers last night. And we have some military militias in the United States who have decided to help us destroy the microwave towers. The militias in several states took out at least seven hundred more towers in rural areas. We have inquiries from some of them asking about joining us in order to fight the Illuminati. We're telling them to fight like Knights and we'll get together after the war is over. Things are really looking up for us and we have word the militias are going to join in the destruction of more towers tomorrow night.

"In Europe we have militias or their equivalent fighting for us in England, Scotland, and Ireland, taking out hundreds of towers in the last twenty-four hours. In many countries throughout Europe, as the towers controlling them are destroyed, the people coming out from under mind control are upset. They are cognizant of the difference in their thoughts and personalities and after reading our fliers they are very upset and helping us in one way or another. It appears that around the world significant things may be happening in our favor."

"Wow! Antonio, that's great news and tomorrow night we'll start the battle against the towers in the Southern Hemisphere. If we're this successful in the Southern Hemisphere, then we're going to face the battle of our lives with a chance of winning."

"The military troops under the control of the Illuminati are setting up protective forces around the remaining microwave towers. We have lost over three hundred fifty Knights globally in the process of destroying microwave towers so far. In large suburban areas where many of the towers are located on the top of skyscrapers it's making it easier for the enemy to protect the towers, and consequently making it more difficult for us to destroy them. All in all though, there is a lot of good news coming in and we are freeing more and more people from being influenced by mind control."

"I think that's great, Antonio. Is there any other good news?"

"I'm sorry, El Cabby, but there isn't any other good news right now, but you have to admit things are looking better than they have in a long time."

"Antonio, remember, keep up the good work, keep the faith, and trust in God and we'll be fine."

     *   *   *

On June fourteenth things really started to get busy on the news and in the countries around the world; with all the happenings that were now taking place, things started getting hot really fast. We were watching the news as it started and the commentator began speaking, "Good evening folks, we have some special news this evening that is being transmitted around the world at this very time.

"It seems that the asteroid we've been tracking for weeks is on a course that could very well strike the Earth in four days. The asteroid is traveling at approximately twenty-two thousand miles an hour and is large enough at this time to destroy all life on Earth on the eighteenth of this month. Now listen carefully to what I'm about to say, and you might want to write down a list of items you should pick up in the next few days. I'd suggest you get a pen and paper and listen to what I have to say as you write down this information.

"Tonight the Russians and the Chinese will launch six LOSCOWS into a low orbit around the Earth. The LOSCOWS will be placed at exactly the right locations so that the six of them can protect the Earth. LOSCOWS stands for Low Orbit Space Cleaners and Offensive Weapons Space Ships. The LOSCOWS have been designed in the last five years by a combined team of Russian and Chinese scientists. They are unmanned automatic low orbit spaceships designed to remove space litter floating in space as well as large meteors and asteroids which could enter the Earth's atmosphere.

"They are self-contained laser-firing spaceships that are unmanned, but able of detecting space debris automatically and disintegrating it with lasers. The LOSCOWS have power to manipulate themselves, long-range lasers, and a computer and radar system to detect and destroy the most dangerous debris first and the less dangerous debris last. The LOSCOWS receive their power from a new type of solar engine. The LOSCOWS get all of their power from the sun's rays and use nuclear batteries as well as power from the sun for powering the long-range lasers. The LOSCOWS will make up our second layer of defense against the asteroid approaching Earth.

"Our first layer of defense will be three retired space shuttles that have been refitted and brought back into service. Tomorrow night two of the space shuttles will be launched, and then a third one will be launched on Saturday night. The three space shuttles are each carrying five cruise missiles with a two point one megaton nuclear warhead. The space shuttles will maneuver to a distance six hundred miles from the Earth in the direction from where the asteroid is coming. On Monday, June the eighteenth, at exactly the correct time to hit the asteroid at its peak distance from the Earth, the space shuttles will launch a coordinated firing of all of their cruise missiles.

"The fifteen cruise missiles will all detonate in a specific pattern that should form an arc in space approximately eighteen to thirty miles in front of the approaching asteroid. This means that the asteroid will be hit with the equivalent of thirty point one five megatons of dynamite that will explode seconds before the asteroid arrives. If everything happens as planned the asteroid will break up into small pieces that will be streaming away from the Earth. The explosive arc made by the fifteen cruise missiles is designed to cause the debris to be projected at an angle that will keep most of the debris from hitting the Earth. It's not likely that all the debris will miss the Earth though, and hopefully the LOSCOWS will automatically take these out with their lasers.

"As a safety measure authorities are asking that everyone store enough drinking water as possible in their basements or shelters to last for two to three weeks. For a family of five it would be a minimum of twenty to twenty-five gallons for drinking and cooking and another twenty to twenty-five gallons for personal hygiene.

"We recommend using baby wipes or similar products along with antibacterial products for sanitation purposes. Also, store as much food as possible that doesn't need refrigerated in the same location.

"You will also need flashlights, cooking tools, and dishes, as well as plenty of blankets and clothing to keep you warm. You have four days to get prepared for any event that might happen so we recommend you get started now. There will be a large amount of radiation released into deep space that shouldn't hurt us, but we will monitor it and ask that regardless of what happens, you stay in your shelters, at least until the morning of the twenty-second of June.

"We cannot promise that buildings, cities, islands, or even countries will not be destroyed by debris from the asteroid, but we have planned as best we can in the time we had to get ready. Hopefully our work and planning will not have been in vain. We are asking you to stay calm and plan appropriately as best you can. We will do what we can from our control center and there's nothing more that can be done.

"Now we present other breaking news from around the world. The New World Order announced today the loss of thousands more microwave towers from around the world. They are being destroyed by The Knights of the Night, as well as by some militias or other organized fighting groups in many countries around the world. The destruction of these towers will handicap our communications equipment and make it more difficult to keep you informed of what's happening after the asteroid hits. Please keep an eye open for anyone who looks suspicious and is approaching a communications tower with a bag or any other object. Call our new emergency number of 777-7777 anywhere around the world and the New World Order will send out law enforcement personnel immediately. Remember, we will need these communication towers after the asteroid hits to communicate with you so please help us keep them safe."

"Turn that off," I said. "You might know they'd try to scare the people into stopping and reporting our troops as we take out the microwave towers. Gabriella, call Antonio and tell him we need to get everything moved to the shelter under the Mercado. Also tell him we will be moving my office there in the next two days."

Gabriella said, "Consider it done."

The next day was tough as we tried to organize, pack, and move the equipment we would need to take to the Mercado in order to set up a command center. It was a tough day, and when it was all over, we returned home so we could sleep one more night in our nice soft beds and have a private shower. These were things which weren't going to be available once we moved into the Mercado. We would be sleeping on cots, sharing showers, and having a lot less privacy.

The girls prepared homemade pizza and beer for our dinner at the house. All the restaurants and stores were closed because they had been cleaned out by people getting ready for the asteroid. People were fighting in the streets over food, water, and many other supplies. As night settled in, things were even crazier than we had anticipated with mob rule starting to take effect through many parts of the city. We lived about two blocks from a local police substation, but it had also been abandoned. The local police weren't paid enough to abandon their families during this time of crisis.

It seems the only people still working hard on catching their prey were the local Illuminati who had received information we might be holed up in a house in the Rosa Primera Colony. We never thought that anyone was looking for us as we ate pizza and watched a movie called *Million Dollar Baby* starring Clint Eastwood. The movie had just ended, and the girls were still in tears when we heard gunfire out front, and down the street.

I said, "Okay everyone, turn out the lights, and get your Uzis. I'm going up on the roof and check things out. The rest of you stay down, and don't return fire unless they're actually coming into the house. They don't know if anyone's here or not so stay quiet. I'll see if I can figure out who it is from the roof, and when I know who it is I will give my bird whistle. When you hear the whistle I want Gabriella to come up and I'll tell her what I want you to do. Now do what I said and stay down; remember, don't fire unless they're actually coming into the house."

I snuck up the stairs in the dark and made my way through the master bedroom and climbed the ladder to the roof. Once I made it to the roof I crawled over to the front of the house staying down. I had already cocked and loaded my Uzi in case I needed it. I quietly made it to a position where I could look down to the street below and see what was happening.

I saw five men in black suits and knew instantly they were Illuminati as they moved down the street towards our house. They had evidently checked out the first three houses on the street, and were now at my house. This would not be an easy house to get into, because we had an eight-foot metal gate and a ten-foot wall in front of the house. We could take them out as they came over the wall or gate.

I crawled back across the roof and went down the ladder and made my birdcall, and within a few seconds Gabriella was there. I said in a whisper, "There are five Illuminati out front, and they have two on the right and two on the left and one hiding behind the center of the metal gate. I'm sure they're planning to do something pretty quick, and here's what I want everyone to do. Go back and place Evangelina at the kitchen window, then put Berenice at the living room window. Tell them anyone coming over the wall is to be taken out immediately. Then you and Chachis come back up here and bring a couple of hand grenades with you. I will want you watching the roof to the left of the house, and Chachis watching the roof to the right of the house. I will take the center and I will have the grenades. Make sure that no one does anything unless someone actually comes over the wall or gate, do you understand?"

Gabriella nodded her head in an affirmative motion then she went back inside to tell the others what I wanted them to do. Within a few minutes the girls were in position on the roof, and we were waiting to see what the Illuminati would do next, but they had stayed in the same locations as if they were waiting for someone.

A few seconds later someone came around the corner carrying a satchel charge to blow the gate out. Then at the same time, Chachis, who was watching the right side of the roof, raised her hand and made a low birdcall as she saw someone working their way toward her. Almost immediately Gabriella did the same. There were eight of them, and five of us. They had a satchel charge, and we had a few hand grenades. We didn't have reinforcements, but they probably did. Once the fighting started, their reinforcements could join the fight and be all over us.

I grabbed one of the hand grenades since I was going to have to stop the one with the satchel charge, and hope the blast would take out a few others at the same time. Before I could pull the pin, three horsemen came around the corner with swords drawn. They cut off the heads of the three Illuminati on the street. The other two took off running down the street, but before they got twenty yards, they were also headless.

I jumped from where I was and with my knife out I went after the man on the roof to the right. I told Chachis to help Gabriella take out the other guy without firing a shot if they could. In less than a minute I had taken out my man by cutting his throat, and I was on my way back to help the girls. Gabriella was lying on the roof and holding her side with one hand and the Illuminati's gun in the other. Evidently she had taken his gun away before he stabbed her. Chachis was fighting him, but it looked like he was winning the battle. I grabbed him from behind, and a few seconds later he went down with blood pumping out a hole I had stabbed in his jugular vein.

I told Chachis, "Get the girls and go to the ladder, so you can help us get Gabriella down off this roof. As soon as we get her into the house, Chachis, call Antonio and have him send a Hummer for us. We're getting out of here as soon as the Hummer arrives. In fact, Chachis, tell Antonio to send three Hummers, two of them with Knights to guard us. Also, tell him Gabriella has been stabbed, and we need a doctor to sew her up as soon as we get back!"

Gabriella looked at me and said, "Look, I'm not hurt that bad." She tried to stand up, but gave a loud moan as she fell back to the roof.

I said, "Gabriella, I think you've lost more blood than you realize. I'm going to carry you to the ladder, and we're going to get you into the house where you'll be safe until the Hummers arrive."

A few minutes later we had her in the house on the bed. Berenice was nervously working on her as she said, "All I have to do is keep pressure on the wound until we get her to the doctor."

I said, "You're right, Berenice; just keep pressure on the wound. Now will someone tell me who those three horsemen were?"

Evangelina looked at me and said, "There weren't three horsemen out front; there were two horsemen and one woman on a horse. The woman who was riding the red horse had three ancient-looking scrolls tied right behind her saddle and she told us that her name was Magda. She told us there would be another horseman coming, but he had a more important task to do when he showed up. Magda also told us help was coming in three Hummers even before we had called and they would clear the way for our return to the Mercado. Then she said, 'Blessed are those who're willing to fight and die for their country and world in God's name.'"

A few minutes later the Hummers were there, and we were heading back to the Mercado while I asked one of the drivers, "Did you have any problem getting here?"

He glanced at me and then he said, "No problem at all; we passed a lot of headless bodies on the way though, and it's very unnerving. If you look, you'll see the bodies and the heads lying in the street."

I smiled and said, "Don't think of it as unnerving, but instead think of it as being blessed."

He replied, "You must be crazy. I told you there are bodies with their heads cut off along the way."

I said, "Listen, we were told by three people riding horses and carrying swords they would clear the way for you."

"God damn!" he said.

I looked at him and said, "I don't think this is a good time to take the Lord's name in vain if you understand what I'm saying."

"Yes sir," he replied with a sick expression on his face.

Five minutes later we were in the Mercado, and the doctor was sewing up Gabriella while a nurse was giving her a transfusion. The doctor said, "She'll be all right by morning, but she will need to rest a few days in order to regain her strength."

I looked up and said, "Thank You, Lord!"

Chapter 22

June 16

The next morning we were all sitting and having coffee and donuts in the conference room in the command center under the Mercado as we watched the morning news at nine a.m.

The commentator said, "Last night we had the successful launch of two of the three space shuttles that will attack the asteroid in two days. This morning we're going to take you live to watch NASA launch the third space shuttle, Horus."

The scene shifted from the newsroom to one of the launch pads at Cape Canaveral with the space shuttle sitting on it. Within seconds of changing the picture the engines fired up and the shuttle started to rise from the launch pad. The ascent of the shuttle was so slow; it looked like it was never going to free itself from mother Earth. I held my breath because for a second I thought it was going to topple backwards and explode. A few seconds later it started to rise substantially and the commentator said, "The weight of the newly installed missile launcher and the five cruise missiles add a substantial weight to the space shuttle. Now shuttle number three, renamed Horus, after one of the Ancient Egyptian gods is going to join Aker and Osiris, which were also renamed after Egyptian gods. The crews of the shuttles had the honor of renaming their shuttles.

"The shuttles will stay on location in space for approximately one hour after firing their Tomahawk missiles. The explosion of the cruise missiles will take place approximately two thousand five hundred miles from the Earth. With the speed of the asteroid being twenty-two thousand miles an hour, after one hour has passed, the shuttles will be safe to return to Earth.

"There is also a possibility the shuttles will orbit in space for three days depending on the outcome of the asteroid attack by the fifteen cruise missiles. If they stay for three days, they will each go to new positions in space, placing them at equal distances around the Earth. Then for the remainder of the time the shuttles will watch and monitor the Earth looking for any damage the asteroid may have caused.

"The worst scenario would be if any of the fifteen cruise missiles don't explode, and it leaves a window in the protective arc for the shuttles and the Earth to be hit by asteroid debris.

"We all need to hope the fifteen cruise missiles work as planned, and if they don't, then let's pray the LOSCOWS take the big pieces of the asteroid out before they hit the Earth. Also we forgot to mention the LOSCOWS have an IFF identifier on them. IFF stands for 'Identification Friend or Foe' and it will identify the shuttles as Friends, and not mistakenly laser them.

"The shuttles will spend tomorrow getting into position and practicing countdown procedures for launching their cruise missiles in the coordinated attack on the asteroid.

"Now we return you to our normal broadcast of the *Today's Every Day Morning Show*."

Before anyone could say anything, Chachis came in and said, "El Cabby, I think we have a major problem we need to resolve, like right now – immediately!"

I said, "What's wrong, Chachis?"

Chachis responded with a serious look on her face, "The other night when we were leaving the house I helped carry Gabriella to the Hummer, and in the process I left something very important behind. I left my computer under the couch in the living room where I put it when we thought the Illuminati might be attacking the house. In my computer I have many of the strategic plans we've made in case we needed to defend certain locations like the Mercado. It also has the complete layout of this underground installation and how we would defend it. If the Illuminati search the house and find it, we'll be in a lot of trouble. El Cabby, I have to get it – if it's not too late already."

"Chachis, I asked everyone if they had all their gear before we left the house, and no one, including you, said a word. So, how in the world did this happen?"

Chachis frowned as she spoke, "El Cabby, I had asked Gabriella to get my computer if anything happened to me, and I would get hers if anything happened to her. It seemed like a failsafe way to do things; when Gabriella got hurt and I was helping her to the Hummer, she reminded me to grab her computer. When you asked us if we had everything, I looked at the computer under my arm and forgot it wasn't mine. It was a stupid mistake, but it wasn't deliberate. I hate to say it, but we have to go get the computer if it's still there."

I said, "You're right, Chachis; we do have to do something." I turned to Antonio and said, "Antonio, do we still have a helicopter to use, and how long would it take to get it here?"

Antonio was on the phone and talking to the pilot. "We can still use the helicopter for two hours, and then they're taking it back to Mexico City. It's on its way as soon as they can refuel it. It can carry twelve people, and it will land in San Fernando Plaza in approximately twenty minutes."

I said, "Okay, I want Chachis, Evangelina, Berenice, Francisco, and Nomolos to fly in the helicopter to my house. I want the pilot to let them out on the roof, and they can go down the ladder through the master bedroom. Chachis, it's your computer, and you know where it should be, so I want you to go and get it as quickly as you can and get out of there.

"Nomolos, I want you watching the roof to the right in case someone attacks from that direction. Francisco, I want you to watch the other side of the roof. Evangelina, you watch the street in front of the house, and Berenice, you go with Chachis, but stay on the second floor and watch the back of the house.

"The helicopter is going to be very visible and every Illuminati in the Rosa Primera Colony is going to know you're there, so be as fast as you can. Get going and good luck. I want to see you back here in less than an hour!" It only took ten minutes for everyone to be on the roof of the house, and the helicopter returned to San Fernando Plaza where it landed and waited for the message to return. While they were there they picked up two more Knights with Uzis in case they needed extra firepower when they returned.

Chachis made her way down the stairs, and when she didn't see anyone she slowly walked over to the couch. She reached underneath the couch and grabbed the computer in her right hand, just as a hand covered her mouth and something hit her on the head. Then four hands grabbed her unconscious body; two held her feet, and two hands held her under her arms. They went through the front door and out into the street with her computer lying on her stomach as they carried her.

Evangelina stood up and said, "Okay guys, just set her down in the street gently, or I'm going to kill you right where you stand."

One of the Illuminati turned around and said, "Go ahead and shoot. We know you won't hit us without killing her, and we don't think any of you wimps are going to chance that, are you?" Then they started on down the street carrying Chachis toward the corner. All of a sudden someone on horseback came around the corner on a very pale white-colored horse. He was riding at a full gallop with a sword raised over his head. The two Illuminati instantly dropped Chachis in the street and reached for their weapons, but it was too late. With one long and perfect sweep of his sword he took off both their heads at the same time.

He looked up at Evangelina and said, "You can tell El Cabby all four horse riders are here and ready to fight! My name is 'La Mort,' and like the others, I cannot lose a battle because we were sent by God. Each of us has a specific purpose in this war against evil for the planet of Free Will." He looked at the corner where the other three riders were sitting on their horses. Then La Mort turned his stallion and rode back to them while he held his sword in the air over his head. A few seconds later all four horses stood on their hind legs for a second, and then the four riders turned and rode back around the corner. Immediately after turning the corner the sound of the horses' hoofs hitting the cobblestone disappeared.

Nomolos yelled, "Call the helicopter and get it here as fast as possible, and meanwhile Berenice and I will get Chachis and bring her up to the roof."

Chachis was sitting in the street below as she said, "I'm okay. I can make it on my own." She ran slowly into the house with her computer under her arm. A few minutes later they were disembarking from the helicopter, and heading back to the Mercado with Chachis' computer.

Chapter 23

June 17

June 17th was here and tomorrow might be the last day for life on Earth if the plan to destroy the asteroid didn't work. I made the decision to give as many of my people who had family within a hundred miles a chance to visit at home for a few days. They could return after the all clear was given over their local TV because after the asteroid had passed some areas might be safer than others.

I had two Hummers fueled and ready to take them anywhere they wanted to go within a one hundred-mile radius. Berenice, Chachis, and Evangelina all had families within a hundred miles so they went home with my blessing.

I didn't know what to do with Gabriella because she didn't have any more family than I did, and we had become like two peas in a pod together. She was sharp, funny, loving, and carefree, all at the same time. Her freckles and red hair gave her that sweet Irish look and temperament that lit up the whole world around her. She was as lost as I was at this time in our lives because neither one of us had any family. I told her if she needed company today and tonight, then I was available. I did not want her lying in a bed by herself on the last night of her life if the world was really going to end tomorrow. She was thrilled at the chance of being with me, even though I said no messing around.

Antonio has a big family that lives near the Mercado and they all have small booths, or stores, in the Mercado where they sell their various items. Antonio is a very special man; he doesn't like war, and he loves God. He is devoted to our cause, but if someone had come in with a gun to shoot him, he wouldn't have defended himself. He would have given his life being true to the faith that makes up the strength of his life. Antonio had worked in the United States for a number of years doing landscaping, and his English was impeccable. I gave Antonio a special deal for the next four days and said that his family could stay with us in the shelter where it's safer than any other place in Guanajuato. They would have to help with the chores, such as fixing meals, emptying trash, and sweeping up the shelter daily. His family was comprised of the eighteen nicest people who graced the face of the Earth by living on it. They all have the same faith Antonio has, and they walked with God as they knew Him. We were blessed they were going to stay with us in the shelter.

We had Nomolos also staying with us, and being ex-Illuminati, he didn't have any family either, except for other Knights of the Night. Nomolos was a special person who was hard to relate to at times because he was born into the Illuminati. They trained him to be a boy prostitute as a child, and a male prostitute as an adult. Without Nomolos, The Knights of the Night would have lost this battle with the Illuminati a long time ago, and we would all be walking zombies at this time. Because Nomolos shared his knowledge of the Illuminati we could better comprehend how the Illuminati thought and felt. We could guess how they would fight, and what they might do when they were cornered. Nomolos was our Illuminati brain that kept us ever alert to what the Illuminati were thinking and doing.

Martin from La Pirinola Restaurant along with his wife and three children were also staying with us. He was going to be our official waiter for the next four days, and his wife was going to help with watching her children.

Francisco, who had been shot several times when he was with me in one of the first confrontations of the war, was also with us. Francisco had the task of taking care of the inventory of weapons and ammunition as well as the hand grenades. We are blessed to have him working with us and handling our inventory of arms and ammunition.

To top it off, we had all ten people from the Ortiz family who lived in Cañada de Caracheo staying with us in the Mercado. Not only were the older girls well-trained fighters with the ability to handle an Uzi, but they could also shoot with deadly accuracy. The younger girls and their mother were going to be doing whatever we needed. Grandfather Salvador was still the family Knight of the Night, and his wife was going to be helping with the cleanup after meals.

To finish off our group we had one doctor and one nurse, who were actually husband and wife. Their job, of course, was to handle any medical emergency that might happen during the next four days.

There were going to be forty people living together in peace in the Mercado for the next four days. Nevertheless, it was going to be quite an endeavor with all of us striving to get along with each other in peace and harmony. We had planned and organized everything for the last day. In the afternoon we even had a video and entertainment for the children.

Then at five-thirty in the afternoon, everyone who wanted to watch the news was welcome to watch the last fifteen-minute news that would be broadcast. The news wasn't that informative other than letting us know that the LOSCOWS were ready and had been test fired. The three space shuttles were on location six hundred miles from Earth, and they would fire their cruise missiles at approximately ten-forty-seven a.m. EST the next morning. Then sometime about ten minutes later, the debris would start hitting the Earth's atmosphere, and hopefully burn up before it ever hit the Earth. If nothing happened within twenty minutes we would probably be safe.

After the news was over the television went silent, and all of us sat there silently for a few minutes until we heard music in the hall. Antonio had arranged for three hours of music from around the world played throughout the shelter in the halls. It was good music and all the people enjoyed it.

People were dancing, singing, and having a great time. It had the effect of helping you forget what might be coming tomorrow and that is just the effect we wanted it to have.

After the children were put to bed at nine p.m., all the adults gathered in the conference room where we had Antonio lead us in prayer for our safety and well-being according to God's will.

Then after the prayer we had an open session where we all shared meaningful episodes that had happened in our lives, or confessed things we had never shared with anyone before. Most of us shared at least five minutes or longer, and there was not a dry eye in the room when we were finished. I have to say it was the most healing experience I had ever had in my life. The neatest part of all this was it was Gabriella's idea. After we had shared our prayers and confessions we said another prayer to God for guidance and strength, and then we all went to bed.

I went to my room first and put on my pajamas, and then Gabriella came in, carrying her nightgown. I had to crawl into bed, and put my head under the covers while she changed. I felt pretty childish doing that since I was seventy years old, but Gabriella demanded it was the way it had to be.

"El Cabby," Gabriella said, "I can be your family any time you want, regardless of how you feel. I know that I love you. Not because you saved my life as a little girl, and gave me my first kiss, but I love you, because you are you."

My face was about eight inches away from Gabriella's, and I took the back of my hand and caressed her cheek as I gave her the softest kiss I had ever given anyone. Then I said, "Gabriella, if we can survive through everything coming in the weeks ahead, we can survive anything. I will get to know you better, and maybe we'll get really serious someday soon. Now we have to get some sleep so we're rested and prepared for whatever happens tomorrow."

"I know," she said. "Just stay right where you're at, okay?" Then Gabriella rolled over on her other side and reached her arm around, gently taking my hand and pulling it forward so that my arm was around her body. She then gently nudged herself back towards my body until her backside was against me, then she said, "Now that's cozy, isn't it?"

I smiled and said, "If it were any cozier I would call it messing around, but I like it, so go to sleep now, and we'll sleep like babies all night long."

Gabriella muttered in a very low voice, "I love you," and then she fell asleep.

I had tears in my eyes because I never thought I would tell anyone what I was about to say as I said, "I believe I love you too, Gabriella."

Gabriella was sound asleep, yet somehow what I had said registered in her subconscious mind as her mouth formed the cutest little smile she had ever had in her life.

Chapter 24

June 18–19

The next day started early with wake-up music at six a.m. in the morning. By six-thirty a.m., most of us were eating breakfast, drinking coffee, and chatting about what might happen today. The remarkable thing was I didn't hear a single negative remark from anyone while we ate breakfast, and I didn't see one tear or one sad face on any of these courageous, wonderful friends. We all had a positive attitude and everyone felt we'd be here at the end of the day smiling and happy enjoying life together. I was sitting at the table with Gabriella sitting beside me. I had asked her to stay close every minute of the day, because we could strengthen each other. I was falling more in love with her with each day.

We had a meeting an hour after breakfast in the conference room. I said, "Okay ladies and gentlemen, we have a lot to do and a few hours to do it in. The first thing on our agenda today is to look at the papers in front of you. Find your name and designated safe areas. If you hear the message to go to your designated areas, then head there and seek shelter in your space. At one minute before the time any debris might fall from the sky, we will say 'prepare for falling debris.' All that means is to be in your designated areas and under the steel tables set up in your area. These are special stainless steel tables that are very strong and reinforced. If any debris would manage to break through the roof and the eight-inch solid concrete roof over our heads these tables may be our saving grace today.

"Now Antonio, Nomolos, Francisco, Gabriella, and I will be in the conference room all morning and we will be monitoring all the communications between the space shuttles and the Illuminati's communication center. We will react based on what we hear them say verbally to each other, but we will not be able to see what they are seeing. Therefore, if they say debris falling toward Central Mexico, we are going to say 'prepare for falling debris' over the PA system. The debris might disintegrate in the atmosphere or crash a thousand miles from here, and we may not hear a thing. In the same token, if debris does fall on Guanajuato we will be prepared. You will stay under those steel tables until you hear an all clear over the PA system or one of us comes into your area and says 'all clear.'

"We will have dinner today at ten-thirty a.m. this morning, and I know that sounds ridiculous to eat so early, but we need to have full stomachs going into the debris shower. If we are hit with some of the debris in Guanajuato, it could be hours or days before we could get another hot meal, so let's have something in our stomachs just in case that happens. If everything goes well, and we survive the debris shower, then we will have another light dinner around three p.m. this afternoon.

"Does anyone have any questions? Okay, since there aren't any questions take as many copies of the paperwork in front of you as you need and good luck to all of you."

I said, "Come on, Gabriella, let's listen to the space shuttle communications. Antonio, let's turn on the communications equipment and relax, as we listen for a while to see what they're doing. It has to be getting interesting in the shuttles right about now."

The voices came through the speakers loud and clear as we listened attentively: "Command center to all shuttles, Aker, Horus, and Osiris, we want you to start spinning up the gyros on your cruise missiles and give us a go when they're aligned and showing a stable light on your panel."

We listened and after about ten minutes we heard, "This is Horus, all missiles gyros are red light and stable."

About ten seconds later we heard, "This is Osiris, all missiles gyros are red light and stable."

Another twenty seconds went by and then we heard, "This is Aker and we have a problem on missiles one and three; they aren't giving us any indication of being stable. However, missiles two, four, and five gyros are red light and stable. What do we need to do to get this problem fixed quickly as you know we need to launch all these birds before long?"

"Aker, this is mission control; please follow this sequence of events on your missile control panel. Switch to shut down, and wait until the Shutting Down indicator shows on your screen. When the Shutting Down indicator comes on, switch to Gimbal Lock and PIGAs off. Tell us when you have switched to Gimbal Lock and PIGAs off."

"Mission Control, this is Aker, and we have switched to Gimbal Lock and PIGAs off."

"Aker, on command in ten seconds from the word mark I want you to switch to Spin up Gyros on cruise missiles…Mark…ten…nine…eight…seven…six…five…four…three…two…one. Spin up Gyros on cruise missiles is on."

"Thank you, Aker. Tell us when you have an all missiles gyros are red light and stable."

Eleven minutes and then twelve minutes went by without any word, and then we heard Aker say, "We have all missiles are red light and stable on our panel. What's the scoop, Mission Control, why did it take so long to get the red light and stable?"

"Aker, this is mission control, and we can't tell from here, but it may be that your Gyro Power Supply is not producing the full ten volts AC that it needs to get the gyros up to speed and spinning fast enough. We will have you check it now. Go to the control panel for all missile systems, and set the Power Supply rotary switch to position number three, and tell us what it reads."

"Mission Control this is Aker; we have an eight and a half volt reading on this power supply."

"Okay Aker, do the following: at the bottom of the panel you will see several marked adjustment screws for the Power Supplies. Go to the adjustment screw for number three, and adjust it counterclockwise until your Power Supply indicator reads ten volts."

"Mission Control, this is Aker, and the highest voltage we can adjust it to is nine point one volts; is there anything else we can do?"

"Aker, I'm afraid we can't do anything, but here's what's possibly going to happen. When you launch the missiles today, the gyros on all five missiles are not going to be spinning as fast as we would like. Because of that, your gyros and PIGAs are going to be slightly off, affecting their locations in the arc unless we can reset their target parameters. We need an almost perfect arc in order to disintegrate the asteroid effectively. We believe the slight difference in voltage is not going to create any major problem, but we won't know that until everything's over and done with. With our schedule to Fire missiles coming up soon we won't be able to make your system any better than it is now."

"Okay Aker, Horus, and Osiris, we are coming up on launch minus thirty minutes. Mark launch minus thirty minutes and watch for a full sequence of lights on your panels, and Aker, yours might be just a few seconds slower than they are supposed to be. When we reach launch minus fifteen minutes, all shuttles switch on the Nuclear Armed switch to arm all missile warheads. Give me a go as soon as you have a Missile Armed Light on all your missiles."

A few minutes later we heard, "Horus, we have a Missile Armed Light on all missiles."

A few seconds after that we heard, "Aker, we have a Missile Armed Light on all missiles."

Another second went by and we heard, "Osiris, we have a Missile Armed Light on all missiles."

"This is Mission Control, when we get to Launch minus five minutes, I want you to switch to Remote Launch Sequence, and then tell me when all your lights indicate Remote Launch Sequence Activated."

A few minutes later we heard, "This is Mission Control. When I say Mark switch to Remote Launch Sequence, and within a few seconds, you should see a light indicating Remote Launch Sequence.

"Countdown from ten…nine…eight…seven…six…five …four…three…two…one …Mark."

Aker has light. Osiris has light. Horus has light.

"Okay guys, in two more minutes we're going to launch all your missiles in ten-second intervals. After fifty seconds they will be on their way, and we will have control of them. If you observe any problems with the launch sequence we need you to tell us immediately."

"Launch missiles starting now, tell us if you see any problems with the launch of any missile."

Fifty seconds later, we heard:

"Aker, all missiles are launched."

"Horus, all missiles are launched."

"Osiris, all missiles are launched."

"This is Mission Control and all fifteen missiles are on their way, and looking good at this point. They are starting to form the arc as programmed, and it looks like blast time is maybe another four and a half minutes away."

One minute and a half later we heard, "Arc is forming, and shape still holding good, three minutes or less to blast time."

Another two and a half minutes later we heard, "Arc is almost perfect except on the right side of the arc, and three of Aker's missiles are slightly back at this point, blast time now about thirty seconds away."

Thirty seconds later we hear, "Blast on all fifteen missiles, asteroid size is diminishing, and it's moving to the right and the left of the arc as planned. Several large pieces are streaking through and on trajectory which might hit the Earth."

"Mission Control calling LOSCOWS Control Center."

"LOSCOWS Control Center here, what do you need Mission Control?"

"LOSCOWS Control Center, it looks like we have at least three huge parts of the asteroid streaking toward the Earth. It may take several laser blasts to destroy them, and there is also a debris field from the blast, but it looks relatively small and may dissipate in the atmosphere. Are you picking up any of the large pieces on the radar yet?"

"Mission Control Center, leave us alone! Our LOSCOWS are automatic and will do their work faster than we can tell you about it. Here come the huge pieces of the asteroid now and it looks like they are all larger than five hundred meters across. LOSCOWS one and three are firing on one piece and it is not on the screen anymore. It's dust!"

"LOSCOWS two and four are firing on the second huge piece and meanwhile one and three are picking up the third piece that's approximately four hundred and twenty meters across. Both huge pieces are now dust, and the LOSCOWS are automatically selecting and destroying the most dangerous large pieces of the debris as they show up."

"Mission Control, this is LOSCOWS control, and it looks like our little babies have cleaned up everything of size from the debris field. This is a new level of expertise for the Chinese, Russian Technological team, and Mission Control, we are thrilled with our performance even if you're not going to acknowledge it."

"Okay, LOSCOWS control, we acknowledge the significance of your performance. If you hadn't performed as well as you did today the Earth may not be here – job well done!"

"Mission Control calling Aker, Horus, and Osiris, how are you guys holding up; were any of you hit by debris?"

"Mission Control, Aker okay."

"Mission Control, Horus okay."

"Mission Control, Osiris okay."

"Mission Control, should we separate and get into formation to head for the ranch as a three unit, twenty minutes of separation landing at the Cape or not?"

"All space shuttles set your distance and line up for landing approach, but let's make a forty-minute separation landing; there's no sense taking any chances now. You did a job well done; tell us only if you're reading a high radiation level on any of your gear. Also monitor radiation levels extensively and inform us appropriately if you find any high levels of radiation in your descent."

"Okay Mission Control, this is LOSCOWS control, and we're going to set the LOSCOWS on Automatic Target Acquisition, and they will disintegrate anything approaching the Earth except the shuttles because they have their IFF turned on, I hope."

I sat there absorbing everything I heard from the Illuminati Communications Center. Then I sent a message over the PA system, "We have good news everybody: it appears at this time the asteroid has been destroyed, and there is a minimum debris field that should burn up in the Earth's atmosphere. We will still be in the shelter for a minimum of three days, but doing that is going to be a piece of cake compared to what might have happened. Tomorrow we will have a meeting of all the adults in order to plan a defense of the Mercado. In another hour, or whenever the food is ready, you can serve the second dinner for today. But, before we do anything else let's take one full minute of silence to give thanks to God for a safe delivery from the asteroid."

A minute later I looked at Gabriella and said, "I think it's good news for us, sweetheart, as long as there's no messing around, and remember that's the rule."

I told Antonio, "Antonio, will you see a message gets out immediately to all the organizations we have an all clear for asteroid debris?"

"Yes sir!" Antonio said, while trying to keep a straight face.

Meanwhile the Mexican Army was working with the Illuminati, making plans to try to find us. They were certain we were located in or around Guanajuato somewhere. The Commanding Officer Colonel Juan Jose was speaking: "Listen, I understand the importance of the Illuminati in everything we do these days, but it's not our fault your entire company has been decimated by four horsemen with swords. Let's face it, your men are looking pretty inept, Señor Johnson. I can't believe with all the firepower, skills, and training your Illuminati have at their disposal they can't take out four riders on horseback who are carrying swords and little else."

Señor Johnson spoke up, "They're not all carrying swords; one of them is also carrying a bow and arrows, and he has managed to pick a number of my men off because his bow doesn't make any noise when he shoots it. Now Colonel, I'm demanding you assign me one hundred troops to assist in the operation we're getting ready to launch tomorrow morning."

"You can't demand anything from me! Who in the world do you think you are?" Colonel Juan Jose said. "We are on a three-day alert to stay in the shelters, and those orders came from your offices at the New World Order. Is it possible that you now have more authority than your superiors, Señor Johnson?"

Señor Johnson said, "Look, we're taking advantage of this situation to attack The Knights of the Night while they're down. If we can take out El Cabby and his staff tomorrow when they think we're not allowed out, we will have control of all The Knights of the Night globally, and this battle will be over within a few days. So I need those one hundred troops, and I need them in the morning!"

"No!" Colonel Juan Jose said. "I may give you twenty troops because that's all I can afford to give up at this time, and I will command them to not leave their shelter until we have an order from your superiors proclaiming it's safe to go out.

"Remember, the New World Order is not in control of Mexico until we give you control, and we haven't done that yet. I will make a report to General Gonzales about this meeting and your ridiculous request to put my troops at risk because of your stupidity. You can have your twenty troops as a courtesy when the all clear goes out for our region, and not one minute before. Good day!" Colonel Juan Jose walked over to his radio control officer and said, "Get General Gonzales' office on the phone and see if I can talk to him for a minute."

"Yes sir," the radio control officer said, "I will call you when he's available, Colonel."

Colonel Juan Jose walked over to where Señor Johnson was standing and talking to one of his men, and the Colonel said, "Señor Johnson, you can have your men when the ban is lifted, and we get an all clear from your superior's offices so get out of my office now! Don't bother coming back until the all clear has been proclaimed on the local TV!"

Señor Johnson walked to the door of the office, and just before he reached it he turned around and said, "Colonel

Juan Jose, before this is over you will be a trooper scrubbing floors, and I can guarantee that!"

Colonel Juan Jose turned around and yelled, "Out! Get out of my office now!"

Señor Johnson pulled out his Glock nine millimeter pistol and pointed it at the Colonel, and said, "I have half a mind to…" and then he stopped as four Mexican soldiers pointed their rifles at him. Then a few seconds later he put his pistol back into the holster as he glared at the Colonel.

Colonel Juan Jose yelled again, "Out now, or die!"

Señor Johnson turned and walked out the door slamming it behind him.

The Colonel said to the Radio Control Officer, "If you get General Gonzales on the phone, I'll be in my office."

The Radio Control Officer replied, "Yes sir, it seems General Gonzales will not be available until later this afternoon, sir. They just informed me he is in a serious meeting concerning what actions he will take after the all clear signal is given."

Colonel Juan Jose said, "It's okay; whenever you get him, I'll be in my office." Then Colonel Juan Jose walked into his office and over to his desk. He sat down, reached into his shirt pocket, and pulled out his private cell phone to call a number. After a few seconds he said, "Hello Antonio, this is your friend Juan Jose. I have a special message for you so listen carefully as it may very well be one of the last messages I can send you. The Illuminati are putting a lot of pressure on us for more support, and a Señor Johnson who is in charge of the local Illuminati was just here. He said they needed one hundred of my troops for a special operation in the morning to destroy The Knights of the Night Control Center. I refused and said they could have twenty troops, but only after the 'all clear' signal for our region is issued from his home office. Now I'm pretty sure that my superiors will rescind my order before the day is over.

"I believe you need to tell the Knights of the Night organizations around the world the Illuminati will attack in the morning. I know what they are planning to do here, and as far as I know it may be a global plan. It certainly won't hurt to be prepared if it's a global attack. This phone call will probably be the last act I ever do as a Colonel in the Mexican Army, but as soon as I get a chance I plan to join The Knights of the Night. So Antonio, good luck with whatever is coming your way, get prepared, and plan your defense well, my friend."

Antonio replied, "Colonel, I can't thank you enough for the warning, and we will notify everyone of what you said. We'll get prepared to defend ourselves as best we can, and as far as I am concerned you're a Knight of the Night through your actions, words, and deeds. I will always count you as a special friend, Colonel. If you want to come to the Mercado in two hours with any of your troops who would like to join us I will meet you at the south entrance. We can use all the help we can get in the coming days, and you are more than welcome. I will look for you at 11:00 a.m. at the south entrance just in case you decide to be there; how's that for an invitation?"

Colonel Juan Jose replied, "I doubt if I can pull it off, but I'll see what I can do. Goodbye and good luck, Antonio."

"Goodbye Colonel," Antonio said as he hung up the telephone, then he turned to El Cabby who was sitting and sipping coffee with Gabriella and said, "We'll probably be attacked by the Illuminati in the morning along with a hundred Mexican troops. Our friend Colonel Juan Jose just warned us and I'm going to look for him at the south entrance in two hours. If he comes he may have some of his men with him who want to join the Knights and help us with the fight tomorrow."

I said, "Okay Antonio, thanks for the warning, and thank you to Colonel Juan Jose for possibly saving our lives. Antonio, the first thing I want you to do is to call our people who are on leave, and tell them we need them to return immediately if at all possible. Get the Hummers ready to pick them up even if we are violating the New World Order's all clear rule. Make sure they understand we're being attacked tomorrow morning by a force of Illuminati and soldiers and we need all the help we can get. When you're finished with that prepare an encoded message and send it to all our organizations globally, and tell them to prepare for an early morning attack. Also explain we can't verify this is a global thing, but it's happening here, and they should be prepared just in case. You know, Antonio, this may all work out to our benefit because they will attack in the morning thinking we're not prepared, and we may have a few surprises in store for them."

Antonio replied, "I'll get right on it, and when I'm through we'll set some charges and prepare a grand entrance for our guests who are coming tomorrow morning."

I looked at Antonio, and said with a smile, "Antonio, I thought you and your family would not kill anyone regardless of what they would do to you."

Antonio replied with a smile, "I don't mind telling you where to plant some charges so they will have the most effect tomorrow morning, and it won't bother me as long as I don't have to blow them up myself. Now please leave me alone, El Cabby. It looks like I have a lot of work to do."

Two hours later Antonio and I went to the south entrance of the Mercado to look outside. We didn't see anyone so I slowly opened the door and stepped outside to look around. The streets were vacant and there wasn't a soul to be seen anywhere; of course, there shouldn't have been anyone, because the all clear signal hadn't been given yet. I stepped back inside the door and locked it, and then I said, "Antonio, there isn't a soul moving out there, so I think the Colonel isn't going to make it."

Antonio smiled, and said, "El Cabby, your hearing has been bad ever since the grenade caught you a few months ago. I hear something and it sounds like a lot of trucks coming down the road, but it's probably too much noise for just the Colonel and a few of his men."

Now the trucks were out front and they stopped as we watched them through a window in the door. I said, "Well Antonio, I see the Colonel and he's standing by himself, but I also see four Mexican Army trucks in front of the building and another one further up the street. I don't know whether to open the door or not, but I guess I have to, because I trust the Colonel. I hope he hasn't turned back to the other side and brought us a surprise of his own. Look, I am going outside and I want you to lock the door behind me. If I'm not back in five minutes call Gabriella and tell her to get some men up here with Uzis just in case something's wrong." I opened the door and stepped outside as I listened to Antonio close it and then lock it behind me.

Colonel Juan Jose smiled and said, "Ah, my friend El Cabby, I always hoped I could see you under better conditions than these."

I said, "Colonel, you haven't turned on me, have you? Why do you have five army trucks out here and what in the world is in them?"

The Colonel smiled, and said, "No, I didn't turn on you, El Cabby, but I did bring some help if you can use a few more soldiers in the fight tomorrow."

I said with a grin on my face, "It smells like a trap to me. How many men do you have with you, Colonel?"

The Colonel looked at me and smiled as he said, "I was afraid this was going to happen and I'm glad you have your Uzi with you, El Cabby. I am going to line up twenty of my unarmed men in front of you, and if you don't want them fighting with you shoot them with your Uzi. When you're through with them then you can shoot me." He yelled out a command in Spanish and twenty men with their weapons jumped out of the first truck and fell into formation with their weapons in their hands. Then the Colonel yelled another command and all the soldiers laid their weapons on the ground and stood there waiting for whatever was going to happen next.

I said, "Tell them to pick up their weapons, Colonel. We can certainly use another twenty soldiers in the battle we're facing tomorrow morning."

"You don't count very well, El Cabby, because I make twenty-one soldiers."

"You got me that time, Colonel." Then I started to walk toward him as he yelled another command, and immediately the other trucks started to empty. Then he said, "How about eighty-four more soldiers, El Cabby – can you use eighty-four more troops tomorrow morning?"

Then after a second the Colonel said, "Oh, and I brought a truck full of supplies just in case you could use them too. I thought maybe you weren't set up to feed and house all my troops, and we brought some extra ammunition and heavy weapons – is that okay, El Cabby?"

"You betcha," I said. I had a tear running down one of my cheeks, and I quickly wiped it away with the back of my hand as I yelled, "Antonio, open the door, and get ready for a little company."

Antonio opened the door and came outside and said, "Yes sir." He then walked over to Colonel Juan Jose and gave him a hug as he said, "This is the most welcome thing I've seen in my lifetime, Colonel."

I said, "Colonel, I'm going inside. Antonio will bring you down to our shelter as soon as you get everything organized up on this floor with your men and supplies. We will make our stand there from the second floor because it gives us the benefit of elevation with our target entering on the main floor. We will need all your men to fight without their jackets, and I would like them to take them off as soon as they are in the building. We don't want to be shooting any of them by mistake today or tomorrow morning. If your men could post guards at the entrances and someone tell them we called back some of our Knights today. The password is Monatika."

Chapter 25

June 20

The next morning started with a loud excruciating bang as we blew up the army trucks they had brought the troops and supplies in. We blew three of them up in front of the Mercado where one truck was destroyed and on fire halfway up the street towards the top of the hill in front of the Mercado. We also blew up one truck in each direction and about one hundred feet down the street that runs in front of the Mercado. Our reason for blocking the street was because we expected the Illuminati and the Mexican Army to bring in their tanks to wipe us out quickly.

The Mercado is full of many small stores which sell clothing and everything else you can think of. In fact our Mexican soldiers are now wearing typical Mexican clothing and sombreros instead of their uniforms. We stationed twenty-one troops outside the building and one hundred yards up the hill behind us. They are to work in groups of seven, and each group had a rocket-propelled grenade launcher and several satchel charges. The rockets had the capability to take out a tank tread if they had a direct hit. The twenty-one Knights sole purpose in life this morning was to destroy any tanks that might show up at the Mercado.

On the second floor of the Mercado we had six fifty-caliber machine guns aimed at the three different entrances, and anyone coming in any of the entrances would be entering a crossfire of fifty-caliber rounds. We had also placed shaped charges around the entrances with their sole purpose to bring part of the building down on the troops after enough soldiers had entered the building. Then after the entrance was blown and enough of their troops were inside, we planned to blow charges in the stores surrounding the entrances. These were enormous charges, and we hoped they would bring down part of the roof blocking the front entrance making it a miserable and dangerous way to enter the building. In addition, on the second floor besides having four fifty-caliber machine guns we also had four more men with rocket-propelled grenades.

Three blocks away at the San Fernando Plaza, we had another forty Knights in Mexican clothing hidden in three of the restaurants, and when they heard the charges blow at the Mercado, they were to come running and charge the attackers from the rear.

We were heavily outnumbered, but we were going to do everything we could to win this fight for survival. All of our regular Knights were still down in the shelter ready to die for what they believed in. I was there with my staff and people while I had communications with Colonel Juan Jose, one of the newest members of The Knights of the Night. All of his soldiers were now Knights of the Night also, and we were proud to have them fighting with us.

The trucks were still burning when we heard the rumble of small tanks approaching about a quarter of a mile away. They could only use small or medium tanks in Guanajuato because the streets are very narrow. Underneath the city streets are fourteen tunnels that carry most of the traffic to the various colonies and to the downtown area. Driving those tanks created a very precarious situation, because I'm not sure how strong the roads are made when underneath some of them you have tunnels. It was possible a tank firing its cannon might fall right through one of the streets and into a road in the tunnel underneath it.

It was evident from the noise of the tank engine one of those tanks was coming up a tunnel that runs a few feet from the Mercado. One of the soldiers took a satchel charge, and threw it down the entrance to the tunnel, and when it blew up, part of the tunnel around the entrance collapsed, blocking out the tank. Our twenty-one soldiers with rocket-propelled grenade launchers were dispersing in groups of seven and going after different tanks. They managed to knock the treads off two other tanks at a distance where the tanks couldn't even see the Mercado, let alone use their cannons on it.

The fight had just begun, and we were feeling very good about everything because we had such strong success at taking out their tanks. There weren't any Mexican troops or Illuminati trying to attack yet, and it looked like we may have won the battle already. Nothing, absolutely nothing, was going on outside the Mercado and we didn't know what to think; however, we knew one thing for certain: they hadn't given up yet either.

I left the shelter and went up to check things out, and I wanted to ask Colonel Juan Jose what his thoughts were concerning their next move. Colonel Juan Jose replied, "I don't know, El Cabby, but all this silence is a bad omen. They have some kind of plan and they're waiting for something, or someone, to arrive in order to make it happen."

I said, "If they're bringing in reinforcements, how long will it take them to get here?"

"El Cabby," the Colonel said, "they have lots of options available. They can easily bring in some heavy mortars then place them in the street behind the museum and blow us out of here. They can bring in ten thousand troops if they want, making it impossible for us to defeat them. They could use long-range artillery as well, and take this building out with a few barrages. They have a lot of options, but we only have two."

"It's pretty evident, Colonel," I said, "we can fight, or we can surrender, and that's it. Right now, I don't even know what the odds of us winning are." Suddenly, gunfire started peppering the Mercado from several directions, and as we took cover I said, "I guess they decided to do something, Colonel, because this isn't friendly fire, is it?"

The Colonel motioned for one of his radiomen to come over so he could take the phone and talk to one of his spotters. He also talked to one of the men with the anti-tank forces outside, then he looked at me, and said, "The fire is coming from some fifty-caliber machine guns they have set up in adjoining buildings. Our anti-tank guys have some rocket-propelled grenades left, and they are going to take them out if they can. Meanwhile there are a couple hundred soldiers and Illuminati troops approaching on foot from the east. We will have their machine guns shut down before the troops get here. I've told the troops at the restaurant to attack in ten minutes. So, I suggest you get down in your control area and secure the hatch, or prepare for a heavy firefight."

I took out my phone and called Antonio. "Close the hatch and secure it because I'm staying here to fight."

Antonio said, "Are you crazy? We need you here and alive, more than we need you out there and dead."

I replied, "Just do as I say, Antonio, and do it now!"

"Yes sir," Antonio said.

I looked at the Colonel, and said, "We will die together if we have to, then we'll be Knights of the Night forever."

The Colonel laughed and said, "Has anyone ever told you you're crazy, El Cabby?"

"Of course," I said. "Now let's get a few of these bad guys as they come through the entrance."

All hell broke loose as the enemy started coming through the entrances with our fifty-caliber machine guns taking them out right and left as the bodies piled up in the entrances. There were so many dead bodies it was blocking their new troops from coming in. It was carnage, as we simply massacred their offensive. Every now and then someone would get past the entrance and it was starting to look as though we didn't have a chance of winning. We had lost maybe twenty men inside the Mercado, and they had lost eighty or more when they stopped the assault. A few seconds later the only gunfire you could hear was outside the Mercado as they fought our forces that had attacked from the rear. It sounded like our troops were giving them a pretty good fight, and while they were distracted we ordered thirty of our Mexican soldiers to check the perimeters on the first floor, and take out anyone who might be hiding.

Meanwhile, one of the Colonel's men came to tell him something, and he said, "El Cabby, you're wanted over by the steps."

I replied, "Okay Colonel. How many men have you lost so far?"

The Colonel replied, "With all the men we lost outside, and in here, I've lost over sixty men. It won't take long to finish the rest of us off, if they're lucky."

I said, "Well, let me see what I'm needed for, and I'll get back to you so we can plan our final stand together, Knights of the Night, to the end together!" I got up and ran toward the steps where I found Gabriella, Evangelina, Chachis, and Berenice sitting with their Uzis. I said, "What the hell are you ladies doing up here? This isn't a good place for you to be, so get into the shelter now, and that's an order!"

"What the hell are you talking about, El Cabby?" Evangelina said, "There's a time to live, and a time to die, and we're ready for whatever happens. All three of us were hired to be your staff, and your bodyguards, and we're not afraid to be your bodyguards. So we're not going back into the shelter as long as it looks like you need us here. The Ortiz girls are all set up around the fifty caliber machine gun on the south entrance, and we're staying with you to the end." An instant later the shooting began again.

The Colonel motioned as he sent one of his men to me, who was shot just as he arrived; he stuttered as he died,

"We're blowing the entrances in ten seconds." I yelled to the girls, "The entrances are blowing in a few seconds so keep your heads down." A few seconds later, the entrances blew with a horrific sound. I looked to the south entrance where the Ortiz girls were fighting, and saw Cristina hanging by one arm where part of the floor had collapsed. As I watched her fall to the first floor, it looked as though she was still alive and okay.

I opened up on the entrance in front of us where there were a dozen soldiers shooting at us. All of a sudden a hand grenade landed a few feet away, and Evangelina yelled, "It's okay, I've got it!" She threw her body over the hand grenade as it blew up, saving our lives. Berenice screamed as she saw her friend die in front of her. She ran to the steps, and as she descended she killed at least a dozen soldiers in her wild frenzied attack. She was out of her mind and undergoing battle shock as she ran out of ammunition. An enemy soldier about twenty feet away was ready to kill her when Cristina, who was still alive, took him out. Cristina ran to Berenice and knocked her out with the butt of her Uzi, and then half-carried, half-dragged her up the steps to safety.

All of a sudden everything became very still again as the enemy ceased their attack. I crawled down to where the Colonel was, and Gabriella came with me. The little Irish lady with the red hair and freckles, who I had fallen in love with, wasn't going to turn me loose, and if I was going to die, she was going with me.

One of the Colonel's men walked over to him and said something. Then the Colonel turned to me displaying a serious frown on his forehead and said, "El Cabby, it's my turn to tell you what we're going to do. I hope you don't mind listening for a minute." He was bleeding from the scalp line where some shrapnel had evidently hit him, and I could tell by the bleeding from his left shoulder he was seriously injured.

"Okay Colonel, I'm listening, and I just hope this makes good sense."

"It not only makes sense, El Cabby, but also I have enough men under my command to make it happen whether you like it or not."

"No, Colonel. This isn't part of a trap, is it? You're not going to turn us in, are you?"

"I hadn't given it a thought, El Cabby. When I think about the hundred million pesos' reward, it's appealing though. Did you know they're willing to take you dead or alive?"

"Colonel, what are you planning to do?"

"Okay, listen carefully: if they capture or kill you today, The Knights of the Night are through around the world. You and your team are the brains and the inspiration for all the other Knights on this Earth, as well as my own men who are ready to die for you. I want you and your team to survive regardless of what happens to my troops and me. We are good Mexican soldiers, but there are only fifteen of us left, and we're ready to die to save you and your team. Whatever this lull in the fighting is for, it's bad for all of us, because I know they're going to do something terrible to end this thing once and for all.

"Since you have an outside air intake for your command center up the hill behind the Mercado, here is what I think needs to happen. I want you to go back down the only entrance in or out of your command center. When you're in there we're going to cover the entrance with a lot of potting soil we found here in the Mercado. Then we're going to pile the excess bags of potting soil in the room and make it look like it's what was kept in there. My men and I will fight to the death regardless of what happens, and when it's over, you and your team will still be safe. In the middle of the night, you can come out and escape to fight another day – what do you think?"

"Let's face it, Colonel, we both know it might work, but my people are all Mexican except for Gabriella and me. There isn't a person on my team who wants to sit downstairs, knowing you're being killed one at a time up here."

"Okay El Cabby, you can have your people come up to fight now. There's nothing better for the Illuminati to do than to take pictures of the body of the last Grand Seneschal and the end of The Knights of the Night. They will even have your remains to show on the news around the world as they announce their victory over you, and God. The Knights of the Night will no longer exist tomorrow morning, and the Illuminati will have control of the world. Is this what you want your friends and Knights of the Night to hear around the world tomorrow?"

"Okay, okay, okay! I'm going back into the shelter on one condition only, and if you won't meet that condition, we'll all die here today."

"What's your condition?"

"Colonel, you and your men will put your uniforms back on, and you will fight and die wearing them. If they make a video of the slaughter, let the Mexican people know they were killing their own Mexican soldiers. Make a banner with your troops' company name on it, and fly it in the Mercado. If you and your troops are dying for Mexico, then let the Mexican people see it on their news tonight. If you're going to die, then die like the heroes you are, because Mexico needs some real heroes like yourselves right now. Colonel, if you aren't willing to do that, then we're all going to die here today."

"El Cabby, you will get your wish, and we will die in our uniforms, so we can be the martyrs our people will never forget. Now you and the rest of your people get in the shelter so we can finish hiding the entrance, and maybe something good is going to come out of this carnage."

I told Gabriella to get everyone into the shelter and into the conference room for a meeting. When everyone was there, I explained what was going to happen to our Mexican friends. We were all upset, and most of us cried, knowing they were willing to die in order to keep The Knights of the Night alive.

Two hours later without anything happening, I called the Colonel and asked him what was going on up there.

He replied, as he saw two old fighter planes carrying napalm bombs approaching the Mercado, "They're burning us out with napalm." Then he hung up the phone, and in the conference room we could hear the sound of the napalm bombs, as they hit the Mercado spreading death to our friends above us. Because of the air ventilators carrying sound from the hill behind us, we could hear our brave Mexican soldiers screaming as they burned in a horrible death. We were unable to do anything, so we just sat there and cried as the bravest Mexican soldiers I have ever known, burned to death for their country, and for the freedom of all mankind.

In the middle of the night, the Mercado was still burning in small fires here and there, but basically the whole building had been destroyed. We finally made our way out of the shelter very quietly. When we were all assembled on the cement floor the floodlights came on, and we saw a hundred armed Illuminati and Mexican soldiers surrounding us.

General Gonzales said, "Ah at last, El Cabby, we thought we might have to come in and get you. I am General Gonzales, and we figured out what was going on a few hours ago. Then it was just a matter of waiting for you and your people to come out. We thought we'd give you a chance to save these good Mexican people who are on your team, as well as thousands of others around the world."

Francisco yelled, "If you're going to kill him, then you can kill me too, because he's as Mexican as I am."

The General smiled, and said, "You will have your chance to die a lot quicker than you think, my crazy Mexican, so don't push your luck."

I said, "What do you have in mind, General?"

"El Cabby," the General said, "tell The Knights of the Night around the world to lay down their arms and surrender, and we'll let you and your friends live."

"I can't do that, and I wouldn't, even if it means losing my life."

"I'll give you and your people two minutes to be certain you want to die for a lost cause, and then we're going to kill you."

Antonio walked to the front where I was standing and said, "We won't die here today, because God sent His Angels to rescue us."

The General was laughing now. "Have you all lost your minds – where are the angels, you idiot?"

"Here," Magda said, as she rode her red stallion to where there was light.

"Here," Zheng said, as he rode his black stallion to where there was light.

"Here," Emir said, as he rode his white stallion to where there was light.

"Here," La Mort said, as he rode his pale white stallion to where there was light.

The General laughed. "The four of you armed with swords think you can stop my men with their automatic weapons?"

Magda walked her horse a few feet ahead and then she said, "We are Angels of the Lord, and we cannot be killed. We were sent here to see God's gift of Free Will remains on this planet for many more years. Now I'm going to lift my sword over my head for one minute, and if you haven't surrendered by then, we will attack. You and your troops will be dead in a few seconds; therefore, you need to surrender now or die! At least we're giving you the free will to choose whether you want to live or die." She became silent, lifted her sword over her head, and held it there.

The General said, "You couldn't possibly believe we're that stupid; we weren't born yesterday."

Magda gave out a shrieking scream like no man on Earth has ever heard before, as she and the other riders attacked the frightened soldiers and killed them all in less than a minute. The horses were galloping a few feet off the ground, and I swear to God that not one hoof made a sound as they rode on their killing spree.

When the slaughter was over the riders all stopped in front of the ruins of the building where Magda pulled out a scroll and began to read. She raised her voice so that everyone could hear, "The Book of Revelations, chapter six, verse one," she said. "I watched as the Lamb opened the first of the seven seals. Then I heard one of the four living creatures say in a voice like thunder. 'Come!' I looked, and there before me was a white horse! Its rider held a bow, and he was given a crown, and the rider rode out as a conqueror bent on conquest.

"When the lamb opened the second seal, I heard the second living creature say, 'Come!' Then another horse came out, a fiery red one. Its rider was given power to take peace from the Earth and to make men slay each other. To the rider was given a large sword.

"When the lamb opened the third seal, I heard the third living creature say, 'Come!' I looked, and there before me was a black horse! Its rider was holding a pair of scales in his hand. Then I heard what sounded like a voice among the four living creatures, saying, 'A quart of wheat for a day's wages, and three quarts of barley for a day's wages, and do not damage the oil, and the wine!'

"When the lamb opened the fourth seal, I heard the voice of the fourth living creature say, 'Come!' I looked, and there before me was a pale horse, its rider was named death, and Hades was following close behind him. They were given power over a fourth of the Earth to kill by sword, famine, and plague, by the wild beasts of the Earth.

"May the Lord bless the reading of this His holy word," she said.

Then Magda rode over in front of me and said, "You must leave as quickly as possible and take as many weapons and ammunition as you can. Go to the cave on Culiacan, and prepare to fight your last battle this morning. Meanwhile the Ortiz family must stay in their family camp. You, Berenice, and Gabriella along with Antonio must be at the cave. Antonio must have a Holy Bible with him, and from the beginning to the end of today's fight he must read the Book of Revelations out loud concerning the seven churches and more. He must read from the first verse of the second chapter to the end of the fourth chapter over and over until the fight is over. Now go, and we will clear the route for you!" They turned their horses away from us and rode off into the night sky without making another sound.

We all heard what Magda had said, and we headed back into the shelter to get as many weapons and as much ammunition as we could carry. Then we hauled it back to the trucks the three drivers had gone to get. Fifteen minutes later we were on our way to Cañada de Caracheo. When we arrived there were a hundred people waiting to help carry the guns and ammunition, along with our supplies to the cave.

Then just before sunrise we arrived at the cave, and we were tired and exhausted. There was a guard post which had been set up with a fifty caliber machine gun right outside the entrance to the cave. We dragged the dead soldiers' bodies away and decided to use this weapon as our first line of defense. We also found thirty gallons of gasoline to run an emergency generator they had put in the cave. We took the gasoline, and dug trenches fifty yards away on each side of us going around the mountain and filled them with gasoline. We planned to spray those holes with bullets to ignite huge fires if anyone tried sneaking up behind us. It would make a nice temporary firewall and would protect us for a while anyway. Then when we had everything ready we sat back to see what would happen next.

A mile away the Mexican Army and the Illuminati were gathering and getting ready to make their attack up the mountain. They knew exactly where we were because the trail of death led from the Mercado in Guanajuato to the cave on Culiacan. They had a thousand soldiers against two women, a man reading a Bible, and an old man. They had also set up six artillery pieces about a mile from the base of the mountain, and they were all aimed at the cave. We knew that our chances weren't very good, but we also knew that God was on our side, and we were doing exactly what we had been told to do. There's something to be said about listening to God and doing exactly what He asks of you.

Precisely at eight-thirty that morning it all began with the approach of two Mexican fighter aircraft carrying napalm bombs to burn us off the mountain. I crossed myself as if I were Catholic, then I started firing my machine gun, and within seconds one of the planes blew up in a ball of fire as one of the bullets hit a napalm bomb. The second plane started to swerve and shake as the bullets hit the cockpit and evidently killed the pilot. Then the plane went out of control and made a steep turn and dive and then straightened up and flew away from the mountain. It flew towards the artillery a mile away, and when it crashed its napalm ignited and took out all the artillery. A few seconds later the mountain shook as the ammunition for the artillery exploded in one huge fireball.

I looked down the mountain and I could see the soldiers had formed an arc around the base of the mountain and were starting up using the worst possible tactics they could use. They were attempting to climb straight up the steep mountainside. They could only take about ten steps, and then they would have to stop and rest their legs. It would take them a long time to get where we were, and they'd be exhausted and useless for a fight before they made it. I decided not to shoot and waste the ammunition until they were close enough to be sure targets and easy to hit.

I sat back and said, "Now look girls, if anyone attacks from either side you need to shoot at the gasoline trenches to set the gasoline on fire. Then, using your Uzis, take out anyone you see trying to come around or through the fire. The gasoline trenches will only burn so long, and then they will burn out, so be prepared to kill a lot of soldiers when that happens. I will use the fifty caliber machine gun on the soldiers coming up the mountain, but I can't take them all out. Even as slow as they are moving, sooner or later we will have to retreat to the cave. Then we'll have to fight with our hand grenades and pray for God's help." Then I said, "Berenice, I want you to know I love your laugh, and I'm hoping to hear it for many more years to come. So keep that in mind as we fight this morning. It may seem impossible to win right now, but remember God is on our side."

Berenice had tears in her eyes as she said, "Thanks for reminding me, El Cabby. I will do my best to kill every one of those satanic Illuminati that gets in my sight."

I replied, "Berenice, revenge belongs to the Lord. Just do what you have to do, and keep a clear head, and we'll be fine."

She wiped the tears away from her eyes and said, "I know you're right, El Cabby. I need to keep a clear mind and a level head. After all, I am your bodyguard."

I replied, "You betcha, Berenice," then I turned my head to Gabriella who was watching me and I said, "Gabriella, can I call you Gabby?"

Gabriella smiled and said, "I don't care what you call me as long as it's in a nice way, and you're smiling when you do it. Gabby is a nice name, and it does sound as if you like me, so go ahead and call me Gabby if you want."

I looked down the hill as the troops were getting closer, and I said, "Well, if we get out of this alive today, Gabby, I'll call you 'My Wife' within a year." Then I started shooting at the approaching troops, and they were falling like flies, but at the same time some of them were shooting back making it hard for me to concentrate. A few minutes later, I was nicked in the left shoulder as someone hit their mark.

Gabriella shouted as she threw a hand grenade setting off one of the gasoline trenches, "Leave my man alone!" A few seconds later Berenice threw a grenade which started her trench fire also. They were both shooting intermittently as soldiers showed up on either side to attack us. Then the unexpected happened as the machine gun jammed, and I said, "Okay girls, into the cave, and start praying."

We all leaped from where we were, and ran into the cave where Antonio was reading the Bible out loud as fast as he could. We didn't know what to do so I gave each girl a hand grenade, and said, "Listen to me. If worse comes to worse, you can pull the pin and hold for one second. Then gently roll the grenade through the opening at an angle so it blows up to the side of the entrance. But, don't do it unless I tell you to, because God's riders saved us last night, and I think that God will also save us again today."

A few seconds later, we saw our angels on their horses right outside the cave entrance. Once again Magda was the spokesperson as she rode to the front. She gave them one minute to surrender, and for a second, I thought they had because it was so quiet. At the end of the minute she screamed at the top of her lungs, "So be it, you've made your choice." Then she rode back to the other riders and turned her horse around. They all faced away from the mountainside, and then they just sat there in silence as the soldiers started firing at them again.

All of a sudden there was a bright light outside the cave so intense it lit the whole inside of the cave and the countryside for miles around. When the light dimmed, we could see a rider dressed in white on a brilliant white stallion, and the rider had a two-edged sword in his mouth. We could see Him take the sword from His mouth, and with His right hand He swept the sword through the air from left to right, and we could hear the screams of all those who died. He then placed the sword back in His mouth and rode away as the light became brilliant again until He was out of sight.

Magda cried and let out a great wail of sadness, and she said, "God doesn't take great joy in the death of the wicked. He only takes great joy when the wicked repent."

Then she rode her stallion over in front of the cave we were in and called for us to come out. The four of us came out together, holding hands, as she said, "It is the wish of God, the Father, Son, and Holy Ghost, that the world repents and comes back to the way He would have it be. You have Knights of the Night in every country around the world, and they have also won great battles today with the help of God. But, there are still wicked people in the world, and you and your Knights of the Night have to weed them out. Get them to change their lives through seeking forgiveness, and if they won't, then they must be killed. It's a matter of free will. El Cabby, you and your Knights will weed them out, or they will slowly drag the world back into sin again.

"If the people of the world do not heed this message in a timely manner, then the world will not survive much longer.

"In order to prove to the world that God and His Angels are real and speak the truth, the Lord, God, says that the Son of God will ride a white stallion in the sky tomorrow morning, and as He circles the Earth, everyone will be able to see Him, even if they are blind – for God's light is brighter than the lack of vision. The Son of God will ride the circumference of the Earth to prove your covenant with God. The Holy Spirit will also touch all the people of the world while the Son of God rides tomorrow. This way the people will know what they see and feel is from God the Father. From that moment the world will have another chance to redeem itself once again. This will be the last chance for the people of the Earth to unite and destroy evil as they seek God's Will for their lives.

"Your people will have free will once again, and if they choose to throw it away to sin, they will die a terrible death in the fire. The rest of you will join us for eternity." Magda pointed her hand down toward the ground and her sword. The sword arose from where she had put it and placed itself in her hand. Then she raised her sword toward heaven, and the four riders rode their stallions into the sky towards the morning sun.

The people who were there wept with joy, and all the people around the world wept because they had also heard what Magda had said.

El Cabby looked at Gabriella and said, "Let's find a good seat in the morning because I would never miss seeing Jesus Christ ride by in all His Glory." They started walking back to the cave where they would rest until the next morning.

The next morning while they were sitting there, Gabriella smiled as she turned and looked into El Cabby's blue eyes and said, "Hey, I think we ought to get married before the year's over – what do you think?"

"I think it's a good idea," I said, and then they both looked up, as they saw Jesus Christ riding by with the double-edged sword in His mouth. Then, a few seconds later with Magda leading, Emir, Zheng, and La Mort rode by with their swords drawn.

Addendum

In this addendum you will find references to information I read which stirred my imagination and led to my writing this wonderful story. I read or watched many of the items in this addendum, but that doesn't make them actual or true in any way, shape, or form. This story is fiction, and is designed, hopefully, to make you think about your world today, and what may very well be happening around you.

It is important to note that having listed the items below as references does not mean that the author agrees with what they say or imply.

Mind Control References...

Cannon, Martin, *The Controllers,* 1980.

Opall, Barbara, "U.S. Explores Russian Mind-Control Technology," *Defense News*, January 11–17, 1993.

Bones, James, "Stick'em Up," *The Times*, September 21, 1996.

McRae, Ron, *Mind Wars,* St Martins Press, 1984.

The New Mental Battlefield: "Beam Me Up, Spock," *Military Review*, December 1980.

David Brinkley New Program No. 47592, July 16, 1981, Interview Dr. William Van Bise who investigated Russian Woodpecker Signal.

Baker, C.B., *Electronic Mind Control*, 1984.

"Mind-Altering Microwaves: Soviets Studying Invisible Ray," *Los Angeles Herald Examiner*, Section A, November 22, 1976.

New World Vistas, United States Air Force Scientific Advisory Board, Ancillary Volume, 1996 pp. 89–90.

Learning Channel, "Weapons of War," September 21, 1997.

Scheflin, Alan W., Opton Jr, Edward M., *The Mind Manipulators*, Paddington Press Ltd. 1978.

Dettmer, Jamie, "It's War, Jim, But Not As We Know It," Scotsman Publications Ltd., Scotland on Sunday, Lexis-Nexis, August 3, 1997, p. 5.

Marrs, Texe, *Project L.U.C.I.D.*, Living Truth Publishers, 1996, pp. 100–101.

Cambell, Christy, "Microwave Bomb That Does Not Kill," *Sunday Telegraph*, September 27, 1992.

Walker, Sam, "An Array of 'Less Than Lethal' Weapons," *Christian Science Monitor*, September 5, 1994.

Prepared Testimony by Lieutenant General Robert L. Schweitzer, U.S. Army (Retired) before the Joint Economic Committee, Federal News Service, Lexis-Nexis, June 17, 1997.

Possony, Stefan, "Scientific Advances Hold Dynamic Prospects for Psy-Strat.," *Defense & Foreign Affairs*, July 1983, p. 34.

(Dr. Possony is the founder of International Strategic Studies Association, a former member of Mankind Research Unlimited, and a former psychological warfare expert with the Office of Naval Research.)

Volkrodt, Dr. W., "Can Human Beings be Manipulated by ELF Waves?," *Raum & Zeit*, June–July 1989 (A West German Publication).

Tennenbaum, Jonathan, "Some ABCs of Electromagnetic Anti-Personnel Weapons," *Executive Intelligence Review Special Report*, 317 Pennsylvania Ave. S.E., 2nd Floor, Washington, DC 20003, (202) 544-7010, February 1988, pg. 9.

U.S. News & World Report, December 26, 1983, pg. 89.

Thomas, Timothy, L., "The Mind Has No Firewall," *Parameters*, Spring 1998, pp. 84–92.

Pasternak, Douglas, "Wonder Weapons," *U.S. News & World Report*, 7 July 1997, pp. 38–46.

Dodgen, Larry, "Nonlethal Weapons," *U.S. News and World Report*, 4 August, 1997.

Snezhnyy, Denis, "Cybernetic Battlefield & National Security," *Nezavisimoye Voyennoye Obozreniye*, No. 10, 15–21 March 1997, pg. 2.

"Mind Bending Disclosures," Time/CNN, Monday August 15, 1977.

Begich Dr. N. and Manning, J., *Angels Don't Play This H.A.A.R.P., Advances in Tesla Technology,* 1995, Earthpulse Press.

Aftergood, Steven and Rosenberg, Barbara, "The Soft Kill Fallacy," *The Bulletin of the Atomic Scientists*, Sept/Oct 1994.

Becker, Dr. Robert, *The Body Electric: Electromagnetism and the Foundation of Life,* William Morrow, NY, 1985.

Delgado, Jose M.R., "Physical Control of the Mind: Towards a Psychocivilized Society," Vol. 41 *World Perspectives*, Harper Row, NY 1969.

Marks, John, *The CIA and Mind Control ~ The Search for the Manchurian Candidate,* 1988, ISBN 0-440-20137-3.

Persinger, M.A. "On the Possibility of Directly Accessing Every Human Brain by Electromagnetic Induction of Fundamental Algorithms," *Perception and Motor Skills*, June, 1995, Volume 80, pp. 791–799.

Tyler, J. "Electromagnetic Spectrum in Low Intensity Conflict" in *Low Intensity Conflict and Modern Technology*, ed. Lt. Col. David J. Dean, USAF, Air University

Press, Center for Aerospace Doctrine, Research and Education, Maxwell Air Force Base, Alabama, June 1986.

Rees, Martin, *Our Final Century,* 2003 Heinemann.

Collins, *In the Sleep Room,* Key Porter Books, 1998 pp. 94, 101–104.

Lifton, R.J., *The Nazi Doctors: Medical Killing and the Psychology of Genocide,* Basic Books, 1986, pp. 289–290.

Hunt, L., *Secret Agenda: The United States Government, Nazi Scientists, and Project Paperclip,* 1945–1990, St Martin's Press, 1991.

Russel, D., *The Man Who Knew Too Much,* Carroll & Graf., 1992, pp. 673–674.

C.I.A. Documents Concerning "1954 Project to Create Involuntary Assassins," *New York Times,* February 9, 1978, pg. 17.

Sea, G., "The Radiation Story No One Would Touch," *Columbia Journalism Review,* March/April 1994.

Pasternak, Douglas, "John Norseen, Reading Your Mind – and interjecting smart thoughts." *U.S. News & World Report,* January 3/10, 2000, pp. 67–68.

Elliot, Dorinda, "A Subliminal Dr. Strangelove," *Newsweek,* 9/22/94, pg. 57.

Justenson, Don R., "Microwaves and Behavior," *American Psychologist,* 3/75, pg. 396.

Lin, James C. PhD., *Microwave Auditory Effects and Applications,* Thomas Books, 1978, pg. 190.

Brodeur, Paul, *The Zapping of America,* WW Norton & Company, 1977, pg. 85.

New World Vistas: *Air and Space Power for the 21st Century* – Ancillary Volume; Scientific Advisory Board

(Air Force), Washington D.C.; Document 19960618040; 1996; pp. 89–90.

Adams, Ronald, I and Williams, R.A., *Biological Effects of Electromagnetic Radiation (Radiowaves and Microwaves) Eurasian Communist Countries,* Defense Intelligence Agency, March 1976.

Adey, W. Ross, "Neurophysiologic Effects of Radiofrequency and Microwave Radiation." *Bulletin of the New York Academy of Medicine.* V55. #11 December 1979.

Project Mkultra: The CIAs Program of Research in Behavioral Modification, Joint Hearing before the Select Committee on Health and Scientific Research of the Committee on Human Resources, United States Senate, Washington: Government Printing Office, 1974.

Frey, Allen, "Human Auditory System Response in Modulated Electromagnetic Energy," *Journal of Applied Physiology,* V17, #4, 1962.

Lawrence, L. George, "Electronics and Brain Control," *Popular Electronics,* July 1973.

"Matador with a radio stops wild bull," *New York Times,* May 17, 1965.

Bowart, Walter, *Operation Mind Control,* Dell, 1978.

Mind Control Videos...

HAARP – YouTube Video

HAARP CBC Broadcast Weather Control Part 1 – YouTube Video

HAARP CBC Broadcast Weather Control Part 2 – YouTube Video

Cointelpro #24 – YouTube Video

Cointelpro #25 – YouTube Video

Brice Taylor – MK Ultra Victim 1 of 3 – YouTube Video

Brice Taylor – MK Ultra Victim 2 of 3 – YouTube Video

Brice Taylor – MK Ultra Victim 3 of 3 – YouTube Video

CIA Monarch and MK Ultra Mind Control Videos 1 – 15 YouTube Video

CIA Monarch and MK Ultra Mind Control Videos 2 – 15 YouTube Video

CIA Monarch and MK Ultra Mind Control Videos 3 – 15 YouTube Video

CIA Monarch and MK Ultra Mind Control Videos 4 – 15 YouTube Video

CIA Monarch and MK Ultra Mind Control Videos 5 – 15 YouTube Video

CIA Monarch and MK Ultra Mind Control Videos 6 – 15 YouTube Video

CIA Monarch and MK Ultra Mind Control Videos 7 – 15 YouTube Video

CIA Monarch and MK Ultra Mind Control Videos 8 – 15 YouTube Video

CIA Monarch and MK Ultra Mind Control Videos 9 – 15 YouTube Video

CIA Monarch and MK Ultra Mind Control Videos 10 – 15 YouTube Video

CIA Monarch and MK Ultra Mind Control Videos 11 – 15 YouTube Video

CIA Monarch and MK Ultra Mind Control Videos 12 – 15 YouTube Video

CIA Monarch and MK Ultra Mind Control Videos 13 – 15 YouTube Video - No Longer Available

CIA Monarch and MK Ultra Mind Control Videos 14 – 15 YouTube Video

CIA Monarch and MK Ultra Mind Control Videos 15 – 15 YouTube Video

MK Ultra Scientists – The CIA Public Enemy #1 – YouTube Video

MK Ultra Victim Testimony A – YouTube Video

MK Ultra Victim Testimony B – YouTube Video

MK Ultra Victim Testimony C – YouTube Video

Code Name Artichoke CIA Project 5 Videos – YouTube Video

Illuminati...

"SVALI Is Alive" – Text on ex-Illuminati Trainer. http://svalispeaks.wordpress.com/2008/10/11/svali-is-alive-update-on-her-whereabouts/

"SVALI" – Text on ex-Illuminati Trainer. http://www.projectcamelot.org/svali.html

"The Illuminati in America" – Text on ex-Illuminati Trainer. http://educate-yoursef.org/mc/mcsvaliinterviewpy1.shtml

"SVALI Speaks" – Text on ex-Illuminati Trainer. http://www.mindcontrolforums.com/svali_speaks.htm

The Illuminati, Larry Burkett, 2004.

Illuminati: The Cult that Hijacked the World, Mark Dice, 2009.

Founding Fathers, Secret Societies: Freemasons, Illuminati, Rosicrucians, and the Decoding of the Great Seal, Robert Hieronimus, 2006.

Illuminati 2012: The Book the World Does Not Want You to Read, Nishan Kumaraperu, 2008.

Terrorism and Illuminati: A Three Thousand Year History, David Livingstone, 2007.

Masks of the Illuminati, Robert A. Wilson, 1990.

SVALI & Illuminati Videos:

Interview with SVALI – Illuminati Defector 9 Videos – YouTube Videos.

The Illuminati I – Videos 11 Videos – YouTube Videos.

American Freedom to Fascism by Aaron Russo – YouTube Video.

Illuminati Freemason New World Order – 7 Videos – YouTube Videos.

North American Union RFID Chip – YouTube Video.

Rockefeller Reveals 911 Fraud – YouTube Video.

Also Google "The Bilderberg Group" for more research!

Made in the USA
Monee, IL
14 September 2022

13946829R00213